PATRICK DUNNE

D1392197

A CAROL
FOR THE DEAD

TiVOLi

Tivoli
an imprint of Gill & Macmillan Ltd
Hume Avenue
Park West
Dublin 12
with associated companies throughout the world

www.gillmacmillan.ie

© Patrick Dunne 2005
0 7171 3804 6

Print origination by TypeIT, Dublin
Printed and bound by Nørhaven Paperback A/S, Denmark

*The paper used in this book is made from the wood pulp of
managed forests. For every tree felled, at least one is planted,
thereby renewing natural resources.*

1 3 5 4 2

In memory of my mother and father
and of Mary and Liam;
and for Rowan

A sad tale's best for winter.
I have one of sprites and goblins.
Shakespeare, *The Winter's Tale*

December 16th

Chapter One

Her body looked like metal that had been charred and twisted in a fire. But when I reached out and took her hand, the skin was like moist leather, the way my gloves became when I'd been throwing snowballs as a child. And just then snow as fine as flour began sifting down, speckling the black earth and the woman compressed within it.

Seamus Crean, the digger operator who had found her, was sitting above me in the cab of his JCB, having angled the bucket so I could better observe the body lying lengthways inside it. An hour earlier, Crean had been widening a drain along the side of a marshy field

3

when he scooped up what he thought at first was a gnarled bough of bog oak wedged in the peat. He climbed down to investigate and was horrified to see that he had unearthed the remains of a woman. That the corpse was female, he had had no doubt; and now I could see why. Although from feet to skull she was smeared thin as sandwich filling between two layers of damp peat, her right arm and shoulder emerged from the muck full and perfect in every detail – from the whorls of her outstretched fingertips to the fine hairs on her skin, from the cords of muscle and sinew in her forearm to the pressed-out pillow of her breast.

The field in which the preserved remains had been unearthed lay across the Boyne river from Newgrange, one of several passage tombs in the five-thousand-year-old ceremonial necropolis of Brú na Bóinne, a World Heritage site. Small fragments of bone are all that has ever been found of the Neolithic people who built the Boyne tombs, so I was excited by the – admittedly slim – possibility that the bog body might be from that distant period. If so, it could shed some much-needed light not only on who the tomb-builders were, but on what exactly they were *at*.

Yet, as soon as I began to examine the body trapped in its clammy sarcophagus, my inclination to regard it purely as an object was overwhelmed by sympathy for the woman and her unkind fate: not only immersed – possibly drowned – in a watery grave, but then, over time, transformed into a leather fossil that would soon be put on display for utter strangers to gape at. And so I wanted to approach her with some decorum, and I thought that touching her hand – even squeezing it gently – was a beginning. My fellow archaeologists would not have approved. Shaking hands with mummies isn't strictly professional.

My next concern was with something apparently buried with the woman. According to Crean, it had been under the exposed hand of the corpse, partially hidden in a chunk of peat that had been split from the main slab by the bucket's teeth. He described it as being like a wooden carving or a doll, and said that it had fallen into the drain below when he tried to retrieve it.

I signalled to Crean, who cut the engine of the JCB and climbed laboriously down from the cab. By the time he alighted, his already florid cheeks matched the red in his heavy plaid jacket.

The wheeled digger was perched on a raised causeway that ran along the drain to the river's edge and separated the marsh from a neighbouring pasture, in the centre of which some Friesian cattle, enveloped in a cloud of their own mingled breath, were huddled under a leafless tree. The snow was falling more heavily and the mid-afternoon light was quickly fading. It was time to get the body under cover. I could rely on the Garda Forensics team to do that, and they were due any minute.

Crean had started his work that morning by

clearing away an elder hedgerow so that he could reach across to the far bank of the drain. Where the bushes had been uprooted there was now an uneven ledge, a metre or so below ground level and about the same distance above the bottom of the drain. As Crean approached, I slid down onto the ledge, and from there into water that came halfway up my rubber boots. 'Where exactly did it fall, Seamus – the thing you said she was holding?' I was facing the far bank, out of which he had dredged the body, and from this vantage I noted how much material had been excavated – far more than required to widen a drain, I thought. But I was starting to fret about preserving the site.

'I don't know if she was holding it or not, Missus,' he said as I turned around again. 'It was more like she was reaching out for it.' He was standing on the causeway above me, nervously lighting a cigarette with a cupped match. I realised that, while I had been using his first name freely from the time I arrived, he had no idea who I was.

'Sorry, Seamus, I should have introduced myself. I'm Illaun Bowe.'

He looked at me blankly.

'I'm an archaeologist. After you contacted the Visitor Centre, I was called in to assess the find.'

'How do you do, Missus Bowe?'

Missus? Crean's form of address implied that I was a good deal older than him, despite my estimation that he, like me, was in his mid-thirties. Overweight and slow-moving, he gave the impression of being a slow thinker as well; but I was impressed by the fact that, on discovering the body, he had stopped work, called the Newgrange Visitor Centre on his mobile phone and sent away the dump truck he had been loading since early morning.

'I'm fine, Seamus. Now, where did it land?'

'There,' he said, hunkering down and gesturing with his cigarette. I couldn't see anything apart from the side of the drain and the black ooze that was stealthily rising higher up my boots. *Dammit, why doesn't he just come down here and show me?*

Crean pushed away a coil of hair flopping onto his forehead from a mop of greasy curls that put me in mind of wet seaweed. 'It's just there, beside you … halfway down.' He seemed determined not to come any closer. Only then did I realise he was scared.

I bent to inspect a fractured lump of soil clinging to the ledge carved out by the digger. Inside it I could make out something that resembled a curved leather pouch. I thought of a swollen wineskin: it bulged at one end and was puckered along the top, where it would have been sewn up. Like the corpse, it had absorbed the tannin in the peat, but it was less tarry in appearance. *How could Crean have mistaken this for a doll?*

I glanced up – I wanted Crean to hand me down one of the red-and-white ranging rods I had brought with me, so I could mark the spot and take a photograph –

but he had moved out of sight. The side of the bucket was jutting out overhead, and I noticed the woman's hand extending over it, silhouetted against the ashen sky and pointing down to where I was standing. I blinked for a moment as snowflakes caught in my lashes. Then I turned my attention back to the bag-like object.

I leaned in closer to examine it, and something – a faint odour of decay, I think – made me realise I was looking at the body of an animal. And yet not quite an animal, not fully formed – unless … I quickly stepped back, my eyes forcing me to reach an absurd conclusion: this was a curled-up cocoon, and the corrugations I had attributed to stitching were its multiple pupa-limbs.

The notion that a huge grub in a leathery case had been incubating for years in the bog was ridiculous, and yet I was overcome with revulsion. *So what must it have fed on?*

I didn't get time to think the unthinkable: as I recoiled the bank must have quaked, enough to free the sac from the earth adhering to it and to send it rolling into the drain. Instinctively I raised my foot to prevent it hitting the water.

I thought it would burst open on impact, but it thumped solidly against the inside of my boot as I wedged it against the bank. I could see a deep gash on the side that had been hidden from view before. It had obviously been inflicted by a steel tooth on the bucket,

8

and it exposed a substance the colour and consistency of smoked cheese.

Then, to my horror, I detected movement along my leg. I watched helplessly as the bulbous end of the creature sagged back and I found myself staring down at what might have been a shrivelled human face, except for the fleshy horn sprouting from the middle of its forehead and, below that, under a gelatinous plug of matter, two eyes gazing out from a single socket.

I looked up to see where Crean had gone, but all I could see were the hydraulic arms of the yellow digger and, behind them, the snow-covered branches of trees spread out against a pewter cloud like bronchi in a chest X-ray.

From the side pocket of my parka I pulled out a latex glove, which I had removed before touching the dead woman's hand. 'Seamus!' I shouted, pulling on the glove with some difficulty; my fingers were stiffening with the cold. 'I need you down here.' I would have to lift the creature up onto the bank before it slid down my boot and into the water.

A cough made me look up again, and there was Crean, standing above my head with a square-bladed shovel in his hands. 'I had it lashed to the bike,' he said, crouching down and pointing it towards me. 'Never know when you'll need a shovel.'

Taking a deep breath, I seized the thing and laid it on the shovel. It felt firm between my hands, and I estimated it weighed about two kilos.

Crean lifted the shovel with a grunt, holding it as far from himself as he could manage. 'What will I do with it?'

'Put it beside the body, near the ranging rod, so I can take a photograph.' I began to haul myself up from the drain.

'What do you think it is?'

'You said it fell out from under her?'

'Yeah. But what the hell is it?'

You have a wonderful imagination, Illaun. But keep it in check. That mantra had followed me from playschool to PhD.

'I don't know … a cat or a dog, maybe.' I didn't want to scare him even more. And, to prevent my wonderful imagination running riot, I had settled on the opinion that it had to be some kind of animal.

Crean deftly shucked it onto the slab of peat, beside the striped metal pole that I had placed roughly parallel to the woman's body. I took out my Fuji digital and flashed off a couple of shots; and then, as if I had set off a chain reaction, another light came slicing through the falling snow, its rapid revolutions strobing the flakes into swirling blue sparks.

A Garda squad car pulled up at the gate behind my lavender Honda Jazz. Then came a black Range Rover, in tandem with a white van bearing the words 'TECHNICAL BUREAU'. Two yellow-jacketed Gardaí started down the path, followed by a tall man in a green duffel coat and a tweed fisherman's hat –

Malcolm Sherry, State pathologist. Although only in his early forties, Sherry liked to affect the airs and appearance of a country doctor from a bygone era. The irony was that his boyish good looks – wicked smile, impish blue eyes and, beneath his grown-up hat, feathery blond hair like a baby's – were sometimes a disadvantage when it came to convincing others that he could reliably interpret the dead. But as far as I was concerned Sherry was a welcome sight; from previous dealings with him following the discovery of ancient skeletal remains, I knew he appreciated their importance to archaeologists.

I went up the path to greet him. At the back of the van I could see three other individuals, two men and a woman, pulling on white coveralls.

'Ah, Illaun, is it yourself?' Was there some condescension in Sherry's voice? Probably not. His rustic manner of speech went with his image. 'What do you think we have here – one of our venerable ancestors?'

'Think so. Unfortunately, she's not *in situ*, but I estimate she was under about two metres of bog. That indicates a fair old stretch of time. She's not alone, either.'

'Oh? I wasn't told to expect two.'

'I'm not sure what the other is. Some kind of animal, looks like.'

Sherry arched an eyebrow. 'Woman trying to rescue her pet pooch falls into boghole?'

'A six-legged dog? I don't think so.'

Sherry raised the other eyebrow.

As we approached the JCB, I described what had just happened in the drain. Then I introduced Crean as the man who had discovered the body.

Sherry clapped him on the back. 'You did the right thing, Seamus; well done. Now let's take a look. In here, is it?' He peered into the backhoe, over the split stump of an elder bush stuck in its teeth.

'No. It's in this one.' Crean led him around to the wider bucket at the front of the machine.

Sherry glanced up at the sky. 'It's very gloomy, Seamus. And it will take a while for Forensics to rig up their lighting. Could you turn those on for me, like a good man?' He pointed to the lights on the roof of the cab.

Crean climbed up wheezily into the driver's seat, but before he could switch on the lights, a screech of tyres out on the road made us all turn in that direction. A silver S-class Mercedes had turned in through the gate and was bearing down on us.

Crean shouted a warning. 'It's Mr Traynor; you'd better –'

He was drowned out by the car skidding to a halt, spitting gravel. Out of it leaped a balding, dark-haired man in a heavy blue overcoat, purple shirt and silver tie. His plump, black-stubbled face was marbled with capillaries. 'You people are trespassing on my property,' he barked at me. 'I want you out of here –

now!' The shape of the final word allowed him to bunch his mouth tight in fury.

One of the Gardaí, wearing sergeant's stripes, stepped forward. 'Take it easy, Frank. We're investigating the finding of a body.'

'Only ancient remains, I believe. I want them removed for examination elsewhere. I'm sure you'll oblige me, Sergeant?'

'Of course, Frank. We just have to go through the motions, then we'll be out of your way – isn't that so, Dr Sherry?' The sergeant was being far too conciliatory for my liking.

Sherry, who had been taking a look in the bucket, joined the circle. 'You were saying, Sergeant?'

'I was just telling Frank here –'

Traynor stepped up to Sherry. 'That you're all getting off my property, pronto.'

The three men were in a tight circle around me. Not for the first time in my life, I was in the midst of people taller than me addressing one another over my head – literally. I became aware of the strong scent of Polo aftershave.

'Hold it!' I said, loud enough for them to pay attention. 'Dr Sherry and I have been appointed by the State to carry out certain procedures here, free of interference – that's the law.' I wasn't so sure that it was, but I thought it might do the trick for now. I nodded to the pathologist to pick up the baton. He had more authority in this situation.

'Dr Bowe is quite correct, Mr ... ah ... ?'

'Traynor. Frank Traynor.' He looked Sherry up and down with obvious contempt. 'The fishing season hasn't started, has it?'

I saw a smirk on the sergeant's face.

'I'm Malcolm Sherry, State pathologist. And you're the owner of this field, I understand?'

'You understand correctly.' Traynor was on the verge of mimicking him. I noticed that his shirt, his face and my car out on the road were all a similar shade.

'Well, understand this correctly. We know nothing yet about the body that's been found here, nor about whether or not a crime has been committed.' He looked gravely at Traynor, as if to hint that any objections might cast suspicion of some kind on him. 'Until I say so, this field is out of bounds to everyone – including you.' He looked up towards the Technical Bureau's van and raised his voice. 'Let's get some crash barriers down here. I want this area secured.'

Traynor was about to object but hesitated; then, as bullies often do when faced down, he switched to ingratiation. 'Of course you have to do your work, Dr Sherry; I understand that perfectly. Any idea when you'll be able to remove the body?'

Sherry and I exchanged glances. He knew I would want the area cordoned off for a thorough examination even if he decided it wasn't a crime scene. While he was deliberating, the white-clad Forensic team, ably assisted by Seamus Crean, arrived with a couple of tubular crash barriers and a roll of blue-and-white tape.

'Irrespective of when we move the body, this area will be declared a crime scene and sealed off ...' Sherry looked at me again.

I raised an index finger and mouthed a 'W'.

' ... for some days, possibly a week.' He was buying me time and saving me having to cross swords with Traynor.

But Traynor noticed the signals passing between us. 'It's you, isn't it?' he said, rounding on me. Some stray molecules of Polo went up my nose and made it twitch. 'You have "archaeologist" written all over you.' He ran his eyes down me as if checking off all the items he needed for verification – green Gore-Tex waterproof parka, ski sweater, jeans, rubber boots, multicoloured woolly hat. He was probably disappointed I wasn't carrying a trowel. 'Always trying to stop progress, you lot,' he growled.

I remained calm. Traynor had perhaps revealed more than he intended. 'What do you mean, progress?' I said. 'What's so progressive about widening a drain?'

'Not that it's any of your business, but I'm not widening a drain; I'm stripping out the entire bog.'

That could only be for one reason. But surely it couldn't be happening. We were less than a kilometre across the river from a World Heritage site, in a part of the valley off limits for development.

Traynor walked back to his car looking self-satisfied. His scent still hung in the air. The snow had stopped falling and the ominous cloud had fragmented, allowing a cuticle of moon to float into view like a stray snowflake. Darkness was closing in and, with clear skies, the promise of a sub-zero night. And that could pose a problem.

Two of the Forensics clanked past me with lighting and photographic equipment and an inflatable tent, which would provide the team with shelter and the site with some protection from the elements.

As Traynor reversed back up the causeway, I stripped off my latex gloves and fished out my mobile phone from an inside pocket. My priorities now were to get a legal injunction against any further destruction of the site, and to prevent the bog mummy's tissues from deteriorating through drying out or, as seemed more likely tonight, through frost damage. I called Terence Ivers at the Dublin office of the Wetland Exploration Team, the organisation charged with recording and preserving archaeological material found in Irish bogs. It was he who, after being notified by the Visitor Centre at Newgrange, had asked me to go to the site on their behalf. I left a message, noticing as I did that Traynor had halted near the gate and was talking out his window to Seamus Crean, who was helping the third member of the Forensic team to unload another crash barrier.

My phone chirruped as Crean, carrying one end of

the barrier, passed me by. 'Terence, thanks for getting back ... Excuse me a second.' Crean was walking with his head bowed, blushing. 'What did Traynor say to you, Seamus?'

'He fired me, Missus. Said he wanted this place dug by Christmas and I'm after costing him thousands of euros.'

I was stung by the unfairness of it. 'I'm sorry,' I said. Crean walked on. Traynor's spiteful action only reinforced my determination to get the better of him. But Ivers needed to act fast.

'Terence, I have good news and bad news. First, the find looks old, possibly Neolithic. That's the good news.' I knew I was sticking my neck out by suggesting that the remains were from the Stone Age, but it might add urgency to the case. 'Second, if the find-spot is to be surveyed we need to get a court injunction, fast.'

'Damn. What's the story?' I could imagine Ivers at his desk, taking off his glasses, cradling the phone between jaw and shoulder and polishing the lenses nervously with the end of his tie as he listened. There were probably beads of perspiration already appearing on his temples.

I looked at my watch. It was coming up to four. Ivers had only a very short time in which to get to a court that was in session and lay the facts before a judge. I filled him in briefly, and then together we summarised the main points that we hoped would get us the injunction: find possibly of major historic importance; destruction of site imminent, with loss of further material that would assist archaeological inquiry; permission for development in land zoned as a Heritage Park highly unlikely to have been granted in the first place.

'I'll liaise with Malcolm Sherry on what to do with the body in the short term, if that's OK with you.'

'You do that,' he said. A droplet or two of sweat had probably run down his jowls by now, and, judging his tie unequal to the task, he was dragging a drab-looking handkerchief from his pocket.

'And I take it you've notified Muriel Blunden at the National Museum, as well.'

Ivers grunted confirmation. Because of their overlapping responsibilities, there was a degree of friction between WET and the Museum, frequently made worse by Muriel Blunden's abrasive personality and her readiness to assert the Museum's statutory authority over the junior organisation.

'Then we'd better keep her informed of what we're doing now,' I said.

'Why don't you do that, Illaun? I've got to get going on this injunction.' Ivers put down the phone.

I gritted my teeth and rang Muriel Blunden's mobile number. Powered off or out of reach. I rang the Museum and got a secretary, with whom I left a brief message for the Excavations Director. It was a relief not to have to talk to Muriel.

Then I introduced myself to the Garda sergeant who

18

had spoken to Traynor. 'And I'm letting you know, Sergeant ... ?'

'O'Hagan's the name. Brendan O'Hagan.'

'You should be aware, Sergeant O'Hagan, that we're seeking an injunction to stop any further work on the site here.' I handed him one of my business cards.

Without looking at it, he slipped it into his breast pocket. 'You'll have a fight on your hands going up against Frank Traynor.'

'You know him well, then?'

'Ah, he'd be a well-known businessman in this part of County Meath. Tough customer when it suits him. All above board, of course.'

'What's his line of work?'

'Frank Traynor?' He winked at the Garda officer accompanying him, then sighed loudly, as if underlining for the other man the kind of patience you had to display when dealing with strangers. 'Frank's a property developer – hotels, mainly.'

I gasped. I had imagined a house, a private dwelling with maybe, at most, a craft shop selling coffee and souvenirs to tourists. Even that would have contravened the ban on development. But a hotel? Not here. Not along this flat expanse of river meadows, whose only contours were unexplored grassy mounds in which were stored secrets as old as time.

Chapter Two

/

Angels we have heard on high
Sweetly singing o'er the plains,
And the mountains in reply
Echoing their joyous strains:
Glo-o-o-o-o–

'Hold it – hold it, please … Hello?'

Gillian Delahunty, our musical director, had ceased playing the organ and was trying to call a halt to the runaway choir. A few harmonised voices carried on regardless, until Gillian clapped her hands loudly and they sheepishly petered out.

'I said *legato*, not *staccato*! It should flow ... like so ...' She made a wave-like motion with her hand. 'All in one breath ...'

It was first-night enthusiasm: carol practice in the church, instead of the parochial hall, which was our usual venue for rehearsals. And I would normally have been full of the good feeling carol-singing creates, but I wasn't.

From the time I'd left the site, something had clung to me like a bad odour. Not the whiff of decay – this wasn't physical. I would have described it as a feeling of melancholy. But why? Let's face it: archaeologists like nothing more than finding preserved human beings, be they desiccated in desert sand, cured in salt mines, deep-frozen on mountaintops or pickled in bogs. Mummies are time machines, allowing us to travel back and tick off what was on the menu for a peasant's last meal, or tell if a monk's joints grated from arthritis, or trace the tracks of the parasites that gnawed a pharaoh's liver.

I'd taken a long shower when I got home, for therapy as much as hygiene. And then, still trying to lift my mood, I'd decided to dress up a bit, choosing a seasonal theme for the night that was in it: a dark-green velvet sleeveless dress over a red T-shirt, plus a pair of vintage silver Docs I could never bring myself to throw out, all topped off by silver bell-shaped earrings and a red beret to keep some control over my unruly curls. But despite these efforts – and a brief flicker of amusement when one of our elderly male choristers flirtatiously called me 'a little Christmas cracker' – I couldn't shake off the feeling. My mind was still elsewhere.

I was looking down on a frozen field that for perhaps thousands of years had held the bog woman in its chemical embrace, slowly dissolving her bones, gradually rendering her skin to leather. But how did she get there? And was she as old as I hoped she was?

At least there was a chance we would find out more about the circumstances of her burial. As I drove home to Castleboyne, Terence Ivers had called me to say we had won a temporary injunction from a District Court judge. The likelihood was that the National Museum would license us to carry out a full excavation before any further work on the site was allowed. Ironic, I thought, that what we would be doing as archaeologists was not that far removed from what Traynor had wanted to do in the first place. Archaeological excavation equals destruction, as it says in all the textbooks.

Traynor would have been notified of the injunction, so I had impressed upon Ivers that he should warn the local Gardaí of the court's ruling about the field, which I now knew was called Monashee. Seamus Crean had told me its name before I left the site, as the snow began to twinkle with points of frost in the lights of the JCB. I thought of the Gaelic word and what it meant. 'That means "the fairy bog", I think?'

'"The Bog of Ghosts" is what we called it as kids,' Crean said dourly.

'Spooky, eh?' I said.

He didn't smile.

Monashee. Remembering that bodies from the distant past are sometimes called after where they've been found, I thought: *Monashee … Mona-shee*. Here was a ready-made woman's name.

'Let's call her Mona, then,' I said to Crean. 'Makes her seem more of a person, don't you think?'

He didn't answer.

Accompanying me to my car, he mentioned that people in the area believed Monashee was haunted. 'It never gets the sun during the day, and they say you should never set foot in it at night.' I could tell he believed that the remains he had uprooted were proof of the place's sinister reputation.

But from now on maybe Monashee would not be haunted. The field I could see in my mind's eye no longer had its tenant. Tonight Mona was in the old morgue at Drogheda Hospital.

I had shared my worries with Malcolm Sherry, about preserving the body as best we could before a decision was reached about its future. It had been in the anaerobic environment of the bog, where there was little bacterial activity; now it would begin to deteriorate, like any organic matter exposed to the air. And this process would be accelerated if it was allowed to freeze and thaw again. Much would depend on how

23

thoroughly altered – in a word, tanned – her flesh was, and this would only be revealed by examining her skin in cross-section.

After a quick examination of what he could see of the woman's remains, Sherry agreed that the body had been underground for a long time – just how long would require a battery of tests to confirm. In the meantime, he thought it best to proceed as he usually would on discovery of a possible crime victim. 'Though it will be difficult to work on her here, because she's wedged in the peat. The question is how we can get her to a morgue.'

'It would suit my purposes if she could be moved with the slab of peat remaining intact,' I said. 'I'll want every scrap of the matrix examined. So here's my suggestion. Drogheda Hospital is only a few kilometres away. Why not leave things as they are in the JCB, pack polythene sheeting around the slab and ask the Gardaí to escort Seamus Crean to the hospital? I'll make sure he gets paid for doing the job. When he gets there, he can lower the load onto the polythene so it can be hauled inside somewhere out of the weather.'

'Excellent idea. And I'll leave Forensics here to poke around for a few hours.'

There was something else on my mind. 'I don't trust Traynor to stay away from here for long, so if your guys put up scene-of-crime tape and leave the tent overnight with a Garda on duty, it will help to deter him and protect the find-spot until we get the go-ahead to dig.' I was thinking of other arrivals, as well as Traynor – some just curious sightseers trampling the site; others, far more destructive, armed with metal detectors and shovels.

Sherry told the Gardaí and the Forensic team what we had decided, and I asked Crean if he would transport the body to Drogheda.

'I would, Missus, but it's not my digger. Mr Traynor hired it and I'm meant to leave it here. That's why I have the bike for getting home. It would really annoy him if he found out.'

'I think Mr Traynor will be quite happy to see it being used if it means getting the body off his land.'

'I'd prefer if it was going to annoy him. But I'll give it a go.'

I smiled at Crean's show of spirit and gave Sherry a thumbs-up.

'I'm going to take a quick look at the other speci-men,' he called over to me. 'Then we'll pack them up.'

I rang my secretary, Peggy Montague, filled her in on what I was doing and asked her to contact Keelan O'Rourke and Gayle Fowler, my two full-time staff. They were out at the proposed site of a new interchange on the M1 near Drogheda, where we were just completing some test-trenching for an environmental impact assessment, an EIA. I told Peggy they would be needed at the hospital early the next morning, to excavate the block of peat in which the body had been lodged – something which would require bagging and tagging a substantial amount of soil.

'Illaun … Illaun …' Someone urgently whispering. I felt a sharp sensation in my ribs and snapped back to the present.

'Would you like to join in with us, Illaun?' Gillian Delahunty's eyes were boring into me.

My friend Fran, beside me, sniggered under her breath. It was she who had elbowed me.

'Sorry, Gillian,' I said. 'I was daydreaming.'

Gillian frowned disapprovingly before addressing the choir. 'Take it from the first "King of Kings" – sopranos, let's hear you. Ready, please!'

Somehow we had got through 'Angels We Have Heard on High' and well into the 'Hallelujah Chorus' from *Messiah* without my being aware of it. Had I been singing at all? I had no recollection. But my less-than-full commitment had obviously been noticed in the ascending 'King of Kings and Lord of Lords' section, a challenge for the sopranos.

As we sang, I watched Gillian's feet dancing on the organ pedals and noticed she was wearing green ankle-boots. I wondered if Mona had worn leather footwear and, if so, whether it might have survived. I wouldn't know that – or even if her lower limbs were intact – until after Sherry had completed his autopsy, something he preferred to perform with only members of the Forensic team present. But, from previous experience, I knew I could rely on him to draw anything he thought relevant in archaeological terms to my attention.

Before leaving the site, I had climbed up into the driver's cab to take a photograph of the find-spot, which I'd staked out with ranging rods. Below me Sherry's team were starting to pack polythene sheeting around the peat, while he examined the other occupant of the bucket. Less than a hundred metres away I could see the Boyne sliding like black oil past snow-clad banks; on the far side, crowning the summit of a hill above the river, the low dome of Newgrange with its quartz façade glowed in the dusk, only a shade less white than the snow around it.

I climbed down again, and Sherry came around the side of the digger. He leaned close to my ear and said in a low voice, 'I think that creature may be your bog lady's offspring.'

After the Handel piece, our last Christmas carol of the night was 'In the Bleak Midwinter', one that seemed to be imbued with the same mood that had enveloped me all evening. Through Christina Rossetti's words my feelings at last found a voice.

In the bleak midwinter
Frosty wind made moan,
Earth stood hard as iron,
Water like a stone;
Snow had fallen, snow on snow,

Snow on snow,
In the bleak midwinter
Long ago …

Frances McKeever had been my friend since playschool. The only physical resemblance between us was our pale skin, but she had freckles on hers. She was also red-haired, green-eyed, long-limbed. I was none of these things.

Fran was also a full-time geriatric nurse with two teenage children to rear by herself. She had rung me the day before, to arrange to meet for lunch or dinner before Christmas, and I had promised to get back to her; but it had slipped my mind.

'It's always the same at Christmas,' she said. 'We see less of each other than we do the rest of the year.'

We were walking down the bare wooden stairs from the choir loft, Fran one step ahead so that our faces were more or less level.

'Are you on days or nights?' It wasn't always so easy to rendezvous with Fran, who worked a lot of unsocial hours.

'I'm on nights this weekend, Friday to Sunday, then off for the week. Back on duty Christmas night. Not a bad deal, eh?'

'You'll miss the practice this Saturday, then?'

'Yes. But I'm sure you'll all manage.'

'OK, let me think …'

'Hey, how about a drink while you're doing that? Just a quickie on the way home.'

'Sorry, Fran. There's been a bog body found near Newgrange …'

'I heard about it on the news. You involved?'

'Yes. And it's going to keep me busy tonight. Starting with a visit to Finian to get his opinion.'

Fran made a snorting noise. 'Bah, that guy … he should either piss or get off the pot.' Fran took a dim view of Finian Shaw. He and I had been close for fifteen years and though of late he seemed to be acknowledging that we were more than just friends, as far as Fran was concerned, he was not only playing with my emotions but also stymieing my chances of getting another man, as she put it.

'Charming turn of phrase, as always.'

'OK. Let's do lunch on Monday at Walter's. Twelve-thirty, OK?'

'Deal.'

Fran's irreverence was a welcome relief from the gloom that seemed to have settled into my heart as stealthily as the snow in the poem.

Chapter Three

'That field is an anomaly,' said Finian, his steel-grey eyes afire with enthusiasm for his discovery. 'A rectangle of bog sitting there on its own, surrounded by fertile meadows. From the air it must look like a stain on a patchwork quilt.'

Finian Shaw was a history teacher and folklorist who had abandoned teaching for his primary passion – gardening. But his was not a hobby that involved pottering around a few raised beds. At Brookfield, the family farm on which he had been reared, he had created a garden that drew visitors from all over the world.

Finian's hair and close-cropped beard were black

shot through with silver, just as they'd been when he was teaching me in secondary school. Tonight he was wearing a black polo-neck and grey chinos. Except for his work clothes, he rarely strayed from black and grey, a complete contrast to the breathtaking displays of colour he made bloom at Brookfield. But this was the fallow time of the year, and Finian was at a loose end. I had phoned him on my way home, given him brief details of the find and said I'd call to the farm after choir practice. I could use his knowledge of the county and its history.

He had spread out an Ordnance Survey map of the Boyne Valley between two piles of books on a low table, in a room that was part study, part drawing room, and was kneeling on the thin carpet to examine it. Arranged in a crooked circle around him was a battered leather suite, two armchairs and two sofas, each scattered with unmatched cushions. Surrounding this inner ring of furniture were various objects and features set against the walls: a PC on a desk, side-by-side with an eighteenth-century glass-fronted writing bureau; two alcoves filled with bookshelves, flanking a large marble fireplace; a pair of tall windows draped with green damask curtains, an upright piano in the bay between them. Most of the spaces between these items were occupied by lamps, on stands or on cloth-covered occasional tables, and on the walls were numerous prints and framed photographs, lit by candle-shaped sconces. Finian called the look 'Farmhouse Fusion'.

On the armchair closest to the glowing fire, his father Arthur lay back snoring. Opposite him their elderly golden Labrador, Bess, snoring in a different key, took up most of one of the sofas.

'Look here,' said Finian, tracing the U-bend of the Boyne around Newgrange with the forefinger of one hand while lifting one of his books with the other and quoting: '"The fertile floodplain of the Boyne from Slane to Donore overlies carboniferous shales and ice-age gravels ... "' He raised his head from the book. 'So how can there possibly be a bog there?' He frowned at me like an inquisitor sniffing out heresy.

A floorboard under the carpet creaked as I knelt down opposite him and laid my PowerBook and sketchpad on the table. I pointed to an elevated bean-shaped feature on the map, south-east of the river: *Redmountain – 120 metres.* The ridge formed the local horizon, above which the sun would climb on the shortest day of the year to illuminate the opposite hill. Between it and the Boyne lay Monashee.

'It's not as anomalous as you think. There are wetland areas here ...' I pointed to a feature called Crewbane Marsh, on the left leg of the U; then I traced my finger along the river, almost to the top of the right leg. '... and here – Dowth Wetland.' Monashee lay between the two areas. 'I suspect that water draining down from the ridge above got trapped, forming a fen to start with.'

An extra-loud snore came from the armchair.

Arthur, now in his late eighties, had nodded off a short time earlier, after chatting to us for a while about catching salmon in the Boyne as a lad. He had little interest in the discovery at Newgrange. The mention of the river was just another excuse for him to indulge his recollections.

'Hmm ...' Finian tapped the map with his finger. 'Now that I think of it, wasn't there a rare species of fen grass – a rush of some kind – discovered in a field along the riverbank there, only a few years ago?'

I sat back into one of the armchairs. 'You mean *Juncus compressus*?'

'Spot on. Round-fruited rush. I'd forgotten you were so well up on our wild flora.'

'Not me, Finian; my dad. Other kids might have been brought to the zoo on a Sunday; P.V. Bowe brought his on field trips searching for wildflowers. Some of it sank in, I guess.' As had the Latin lessons, and the lines from plays that he used to learn off by reciting them aloud to us in the car.

Finian folded up the map. 'It occurs to me that, if there are only one or two small areas of bog in the vicinity, it points towards your lady being a sacrificial victim, doesn't it?'

'Or volunteer.' Reassessment of the practice of human sacrifice in pre-history has suggested that some 'victims' were willing participants in their own executions. But Finian had a good point. She would hardly have strayed by accident into the boggy field. And it nudged the argument further in favour of her being prehistoric: human sacrifice and bog burials had died out even before Christianity came to Ireland.

'Well, I don't know if there's any evidence of violence,' I said. 'We'll have to wait until the autopsy tomorrow morning.'

On my way to Brookfield, Malcolm Sherry had rung to say that – after considerable time and effort – they had extracted Mona from the block of peat, and that he was postponing any further examination of the body for another twelve hours. He had been allocated the old morgue, housed in a separate building on the hospital grounds, which suited both our purposes. Our examination of Mona would not take place in a facility under siege from the recently deceased.

Finian sat in the other armchair and started to flip through my sketches, while I found the digital photos I'd loaded into the laptop.

'So you found yourself at Newgrange earlier than expected. Didn't you tell me you were going there for the solstice?'

'Yes. The second part of an interview for *Dig*. It's an American archaeology magazine that's doing a feature on Irish women in the profession, and they've asked us to assemble there at sunrise on the day. For photos, mainly.'

'Will you be going inside?'

'No. Apart from a couple of VIPs, it's limited to twenty people drawn by lottery. And we've all seen it before, as far as I know. It wouldn't be fair.'

'Bet you there'll be a politician or two there.'

'The Minister for Tourism and Heritage is scheduled to put in an appearance, I believe.'

'Told you. And that reminds me: I have an invitation for two to a pre-Christmas soirée at Jocelyn Carew's house in Dublin. I'd love you to come.'

'When is it?'

'Em ... soon.' He went to the mantelpiece and picked up a plain white card printed in black. 'Jocelyn and Edith Carew – At Home,' he intoned. 'Drinks seven to ten pm, December twenty-first.'

'That's next Monday night!' Same day I was having lunch with Fran.

'Yes, I'm sorry. I'd intended asking you long before now.'

I closed my eyes and tried to think what other engagements I had, if any. That close to Christmas, probably only social ones, or perhaps the choir, but my mind had drawn a blank. Unless something was unavoidable, I would skip it or move it. Professor Jocelyn Carew was an Independent member of the Dáil, as well as being a medical doctor, drama critic and conservationist; I was certainly curious to meet him and his wife 'At Home'. And to be there with Finian would add to the enjoyment.

'Love to,' I said. 'I'll let you know for sure tomorrow, if that's all right.'

'Whenever. I've said yes already. It's just that I really don't want to go on my own.'

That was infuriatingly typical of Finian – to offer

me an invitation, then make it appear like an afterthought. I let it pass. He knelt back down at the table and peered at a photo I was displaying on the PowerBook screen, something in it making him frown.

'If the intention was to clear the bog, why was Crean using a JCB? Far too heavy to work on soft soil.'

'He must have intended to dig down to the rock or gravel below; then he'd have a solid base on which to drive in and dig out the rest of the topsoil.'

'Hmm … you said the body was originally lying about a metre and a half beneath the surface. That's not very far down if you're hoping for a prehistoric date.' Finian was thinking of the rate of growth of the bog. 'For your theory to be right, Monashee has to have been growing for over five thousand years. Surely it should be much deeper.'

'It might have been, at one time. But it was probably dug away for fuel – who knows? Drainage would also lower the overall level. And there's something else that gives me cause for optimism. Any archaeologist will tell you that Ireland boasts one of the oldest bog bodies in Europe – well, a skeleton, actually. The remains of a man found in Stoneyisland Bog in Galway clocked in at about six thousand years old – that's Early Neolithic.'

'Fair enough. But what are the chances, Illaun? Let's do a rough calculation.' He sat back into his armchair and held up the little finger of one hand between the thumb and forefinger of the other – a gesture he always made when summarising information. 'How many bog bodies have been discovered in Ireland in total?'

'About eighty.'

'How old were they, on average?'

'The majority … probably medieval.'

'Five hundred to a thousand years old, let's say. And across the rest of Europe?'

'Iron Age, mostly.'

He calculated for a moment. 'Two to two and a half thousand years old?'

I nodded. 'On average.'

'So the likelihood, Illaun, is that this lady ain't a Stone-Ager.' He grinned like a boy, proud of his little pun. 'And your best hope is that she's a Celt.'

'But, my learned friend, she was buried in the vicinity of Newgrange in circumstances that we both agree were unlikely to have been an accident – meaning the location was significant to whoever put her there – whereas, by the time the Celts arrived, the meaning of Brú na Bóinne was already long lost. So if her burial had a purpose, then it has to be Neolithic. I rest my case.'

The phone rang out in the hall. Finian excused himself and left the room.

The activity interrupted Arthur's sleep, and he woke up in mid-snore. '… Boyne Drainage Scheme … stupid bastards … destroyed best salmon river …' He had sat up and was resuming his input into the conversation at the same point where he had nodded off. A mild stroke had affected his speech so that he slurred some of his words, but it was easy to get the gist of what he was saying, because it was his favourite hobby-horse. 'See … on wall …' He was gesturing behind him. I followed his thumb to a framed photograph of a woman standing beside a fish that was hung up by the tail. It was nearly as tall as her and swelled to about the width of her shoulders. 'See! Big salmon at Newgrange … and female anglers … even then.'

I walked over and read the inscription:

Mrs Myrtle Hastings with a 60lb. salmon caught on the Boyne below Newgrange in 1926. Length 4ft. 6in. Girth 2ft. 9in.

'So many salmon … trout … Could walk across river stepping on their backs …' Arthur cackled. 'And not just game fish – pike, eels, perch …'

'Mmm …' I had no wish to offend him, but my interest in the topic was waning. He must have sensed this, because he halted his inventory and said, 'Father once told me a black body … found floating in Boyne … Newgrange … a hundred years ago or more. A man – a Nubian, they said … built pym … pymr …'

'Pyramids,' I said, sitting down in the armchair Finian had vacated. Arthur must have heard snatches of our conversation as he drifted in and out of his doze. He had my full attention now, and he knew it. His eyes were twinkling mischievously. 'So they thought there was some connection between the body and the construction of Newgrange?'

The old man nodded. I knew he had a reputation for telling tall tales, but this didn't sound like one.

Finian came back into the room at that point.

'I'm off to bed. Good night,' said Arthur.

Finian handed him his walking-stick and helped him to his feet. Bess climbed down from the sofa and followed Arthur out of the room.

'Your father's just told me something that could be very significant as far as our bog body is concerned,' I said, as Finian closed the door after them.

He gave me a sceptical glance. 'What's he on about now?'

'There may have been another one found in that area.' I repeated his father's story. '... So, if that was another bog body – but mistaken at the time for a black person – it would strengthen the case for securing the whole field for a proper excavation. We may have stumbled across a sacrificial burial site. God knows how many bodies have been preserved there.'

'You'll need more than one of my father's yarns.'

'The *Meath Chronicle* archives?'

'But you haven't got a date. It'll be like looking for a needle in a haystack ...' Finian noticed I was looking at him intently. 'You expect *me* to do it?'

I gave him a big smile.

'Oh, all right, then,' he said, sitting on the sofa in front of the laptop and peering at the photo of the foetus or whatever it was in the digger beside Mona. 'Sherry thinks she may have given birth to this?'

'Or it was still in her womb.' I hadn't asked the pathologist to clarify his use of the term 'offspring', and the gash on its side might be an indication that it had been ripped from Mona's body by the digger.

Finian looked aghast. 'It's not human, surely?'

'I'm afraid it is. And I think I've seen something like it before. Recently, too.'

Finian looked at me over his glasses.

'Not in reality. A representation. On a church or a grave-slab – something like that.'

'A painting? Something nightmarish by Hieronymous Bosch, maybe?'

'No. Definitely a stone carving.'

'Did this guy Traynor know it had been found along with the woman?'

'I don't think so. Why do you ask?'

'Just trying to figure out why he doesn't want you near the place.'

'Yeah. It's funny how he wants to tear up the field, but he objects to us doing practically the same thing.'

'Who do you reckon alerted him to the find?'

'Sergeant O'Hagan, I'd say. He and Traynor seem pretty close.'

'Speaking of which,' said Finian, patting the seat beside him, 'couldn't we sit a little closer?'

I joined him on the sofa.

'That's better,' he said, closing the laptop and putting his arm around me.

I leaned my head on his shoulder. 'You do want me to go to Jocelyn Carew's party with you, don't you?'

'Of course I do,' he said, drawing me closer. 'I'm sorry I made it sound so offhand. I was just embarrassed at having forgotten to ask you until now.'

'That's OK,' I said, snuggling against him. 'You're forgiven.'

I got home just before midnight. Turning on the kitchen light, I noticed a yellow Post-It note on the door of the fridge. My mother had inadvertently picked up my father's habit of leaving notes like this around the house, and it reminded me painfully of him every time. I peeled the note off the door. 'BOTH FED. BOO WITH ME.'

My mother and I lived separately in what had been the family home, a 1930s bay-windowed bungalow on the outskirts of Castleboyne. The arrangement meant that I could keep an eye on my mother as she coped with a condition even lonelier than widowhood. And the house also served as the business address of Illaun Bowe, archaeological consultant, giving me a base in the area from which most of my work came.

The fact that County Meath was daily being absorbed into greater Dublin meant that the archaeological landscape was under constant threat, which was good for my business – a paradox that had not escaped my notice. With a staff of four, including myself, it was nevertheless a modest enterprise. When expertise beyond my own was needed, I had a panel of specialists to call on and a site team – often made up of students and graduates – that I could assemble at short notice.

I was about to turn off the kitchen light when my stomach told me with sudden urgency that I hadn't eaten since breakfast. It was too late to make anything, so I searched the fridge and found a limp slice of pizza. Biting off a piece, I chewed it hungrily, but even with my sharpened appetite I could detect little flavour in it; I put the remainder of the slice in the microwave and set the dial.

A single deep-throated bark came from the extension where my mother was sleeping. Horatio was asking me to acknowledge his presence and no doubt to rid him of Boo, who was probably lying on his doggy cushion. If I didn't go now, he would wait politely – and infuriatingly – until I had just settled into bed before barking again. I opened a door leading into the shared utility room, which contained a washing machine, a dryer, my bicycle, umbrellas, garden implements, mud-caked rubber boots and the pets' food bowls, and which also acted as a sort of buffer between my mother's part of the house and mine. Horatio was scratching the far door; another sound, a soft thud, indicated that Boo was throwing himself at it, something he preferred to do rather than mew, for some inscrutable cat reason. When I opened the door, what looked like a wisp of smoke streamed past my leg while two large paws landed on my shoulders. I lifted my chin to avoid full contact with Horatio's dripping muzzle and got licked on the throat instead.

'Yes, boy – good boy. Down!' The fawn-coloured Great Dane was really my father's dog, but now he provided company for my mother as well as affording a sense of protection – although the truth was that any intruder would probably have been greeted by little more than a slobbery lick on the face. 'Night, Horatio,' I whispered, and closed the door.

The microwave pinged as I went back into the kitchen; I took out the pizza and slapped it on a plate, poured some milk into a tumbler and went through to the living room to watch the news. Boo, my grey Maine coon cat, had just stretched out on the same sofa where I had been thinking of sitting. Rather than struggle to lift him off while he attached himself to various cushions, I decided it was best to go to bed. I was tired, and Friday was likely to be a long day.

After munching the pizza and finishing the glass of milk while I sat on the bed, I climbed in, turned off the light and tried to bring to mind as much as I could about bog bodies. That was a mistake: I kept seeing myself in the drain at Monashee, holding the creature as it uncurled. Having tossed and turned for long enough to know that sleep wasn't coming, I put on a dressing-gown and slippers and shuffled off to the office.

There was nothing much of relevance on the shelves, so I tried the internet. There were numerous sites

43

devoted to mummies, the Egyptian variety leading the field as always. In the bog-body category there were some statistics – two thousand known finds across northern Europe, about a hundred radiocarbon-dated, et cetera, et cetera – and popularity lists, the top attractions in a sort of Euro Bog-Body Contest. *'Let's hear it for our contestants, ladies and gentlemen. First on stage is that handsome, red-stubbled Dane – yes, it's Tollund Man. And representing Germany, with her half-shaved head, it's the trendy teenager, Windeby Girl. Next we go to Holland, and with typical Dutch quirkiness they've entered a headless male couple – the Weerdinge Duo. And finally, for the UK – he may have two identities, but he only owns one item of clothing – yes, it's Lindow Man, a.k.a. Pete Marsh, sporting his sexy fox-fur armband …'* I wondered if Mona would eventually join this bizarre parade on the mummy websites of the world.

Many of the bog people were thought to have been midwinter sacrifices. The stomach contents of Lindow Man even included the pollen of mistletoe, something we associate with a seasonal kiss but which the Celts saw as a sacred plant belonging to neither earth, sky nor water. What would they make of my stomach contents if I were to be found two thousand years in the future? Flour, cheese, olives, tomato, artichokes and anchovies – that would keep them scratching their heads for a while.

My flippant mood faded as the grim realisation

dawned that every one of the people I'd been reading about had suffered at the hands of other human beings even before being immersed in dark bog-holes; some of them had been strangled, some clubbed to death, others butchered, and at least one subjected to all three atrocities. And, while a few were reckoned to be the victims of capital punishment rather than ritual sacrifice, either way they bore mute testimony to a harsh life on the edges of the mires of northern Europe, a life that that must have seemed all the bleaker during the long winters.

What, precisely, had I been I looking for on the Web anyway? I yawned and stretched and thought about it for a few moments. The desultory search I had been conducting was in the realm of popular science, when I ought to have been consulting some of the academic sites to which I subscribed. I started again.

Horatio barked in the other part of the house. I listened to him growl for a few seconds; then he was still. Probably responding to a dog in the distance, inaudible to me – just as Horatio was inaudible to my mother, who slept with wax plugs in her ears.

Without much difficulty I reached a promising destination – a list of grave goods that included human and animal remains buried with Neolithic and Iron Age bodies across northern Europe. I scrolled down through the various finds: pots, axes, leather capes, amber beads, cattle bones and horns; here and there a poignant reminder that concern about our appearance is a characteristic human trait – a woollen hairband, a net bonnet, a comb. And then I saw a bizarre item among the rest. A young woman in Østrup in Denmark had been found interred with the skeleton of a swan, a creature the Celts believed could traverse the worlds of both the living and the dead – perhaps because, like other waterfowl, it occupied a liminal zone between earth and water, as did the bog itself.

Horatio barked again. He was uneasy for some reason, and it was unsettling me in turn. A dog's bark late at night seems to register with us differently than it does in the daytime – possibly a throwback to when we first shared our caves with them in exchange for their guardianship.

I rubbed my eyes and yawned again. I needed sleep. Blearily I refined my search to focus on infant remains only. This yielded a woman from Borremose bog in Jutland found with her newborn baby, the remains dated to the early centuries AD. Next came something closer to home – an early Iron Age female skeleton from County Roscommon accompanied by an infant's skull. Then there was a find of similar age from Yorkshire: a man and a pregnant woman found buried alive, pinned together by a wooden stake, the foetal remains between the woman's legs suggesting she had miscarried as she died.

But there were no similar finds from the Neolithic period. Children and adults turned up together, here and there, but not newborn infants with their mothers.

As I had known deep down, my hopes that Mona was as old as Newgrange were finding no support in the archaeological record.

Something started vibrating under my left hand, and I jumped. Without realising it, I'd been idly caressing my silenced mobile phone as I trawled the Web. Now it was buzzing like an upturned beetle trying to right itself. Wondering who could be ringing me at this late hour, I flipped up the silver carapace and answered the call.

'I'll say this only once. Leave Monashee alone.'

My heart missed a beat. 'Excuse me?'

'The body's been taken care of … so back off.'

Then I realised the voice was familiar, though thickened by alcohol. 'Is this your way of doing things, Mr Traynor? Intimidating people in the middle of the night? I'm not very impressed.'

'Don't give a fuck. Monashee is mine. You've no idea what you're messing with.'

I could almost smell the drink on his breath and, mingled with it, the too-sweet scent of his aftershave. 'Yes, I do. A drunken bully.'

'None of your business. I'm warning you …' He muttered something unintelligible as he tried to find the End button on his keypad. 'I'm warning you,' he repeated, and hung up.

December 17th

Chapter Four

'There are two of them, Missus. One is a tracked machine and it's travelling along the cutting made by the JCB, chewing up the rest of it as it goes along. There's not going to be much left of the field by the end of the day, at this rate.'

I was pulling on jeans, mobile phone cradled on my shoulder as I listened to Seamus Crean. He was talking from his house in Donore village, about three kilometres from Monashee. Anger and bewilderment made my movements awkward, and I hit the phone a glancing blow so that it fell and skittered across the polished wooden floor of the bedroom. I saw the time again on my clock radio as I bent down to pick up the phone: 6.30 a.m. Still pitch-dark outside.

Half an hour earlier, my phone had fooled me for a few seconds into thinking I was hearing the dawn chorus instead of being dragged out of sleep into another dreary December morning. It was a small price to pay for making birdsong my choice of ring-tone. I fumbled with the keypad, hit the right one eventually, heard Crean's voice on the other end and sat bolt upright in bed.

'I'm sorry, Missus, for waking you up …' He paused, breathing heavily.

'Is that you, Seamus? What's the matter?' I had given him my card the previous day, so he could ring me with a fee for his services.

'I think Traynor is up to something …'

I thought of his threatening words only a few hours earlier. This was scary. 'Go on.'

'Fella just came banging on the door, looking for the keys of the JCB that I parked back at the field last night. I didn't thank him for waking up the whole house at this hour of the morning, I can tell you.'

'Did you know him?'

'No. Never set eyes on him. Foreign, I think. Dropped off by a big transporter that went on in the direction of Monashee.'

'Do you have a car, Seamus?'

'I have the bike.'

'OK, listen carefully. Cycle past Monashee and take

a look. If there *is* something going on, don't get involved and don't hang around. Just come back to the house and report it to me.'

'Right, Missus. Will do.'

I went into the bathroom, ran the shower till it steamed, threw off my pyjamas and stepped into the geyser-hot cascade.

Traynor was up to something, all right. 'The body's been taken care of,' he had said; what had he meant?

I washed my hair and let the shower play on my face as I sluiced the shampoo away. Had Traynor been duly notified of the injunction? And when was it technically due to come into effect? I leaned out of the shower, took a heated towel from a rail and dried myself. Surely the judge had grasped the seriousness of the threat to the site and made his order effective immediately.

My skin still tingling, I tied a smaller towel into a turban, wrapped myself in a heavy bathrobe and went into the kitchen, where I filled a bowl with strawberry crunch and milk. As I turned on the kettle, I felt Boo's plume of a tail whisking against my bare calf. He wanted out.

I padded down the hall and opened the door into the chilly utility room for him. Instead of exiting through the cat-flap onto the patio, he mewed at me to open the back door; when there were humans around, he liked to avail of their services. 'All right, Boo, let's go look at the morning.'

An icy gust of wind greeted us as I opened the door, and a bright quarter-moon bathed the snowy ground in a blue glow and threw deep shadows under the shrubs and trees in the garden beyond the patio. Boo slid out past me, the breeze parting the thick hair of his ruff. Then he heard something, flattened himself in a second against the ground and melted into the shadows in pursuit. He could alter his shape at will. And, despite his occasional effete ways, his ancestry in the backwoods of Maine made him indifferent to cold weather, most of the time.

A sudden shiver made me close the door. And then it occurred to me that I had never introduced myself to Traynor. I had given my business card to O'Hagan, who must have passed my number on to him. The two were even closer than I had thought.

I had gone back into the bedroom to get dressed when Crean rang back. Now I was on my hands and knees, stretching under the bed for the phone. I could still hear him talking as I retrieved it, at the same time picking up a Post-It note, which I crumpled and placed on my locker.

'What did you say, Seamus?' I held the phone firmly to my ear.

'They're skirting around the area that was cordoned off. The tent is gone, but the barriers are still there.'

It was small consolation. And it gave me a clue to what Traynor was playing at. It looked as if he had, in fact, heard about the court order. And I was sure

Terence Ivers had notified the Gardaí that the injunction would need enforcing. 'The uniformed Gardaí who were at the site yesterday. What station are they from?'

'Donore.'

'Hmm ... I have an idea. But it involves you doing me another favour.'

'No problem, Missus. And be careful on the road if you're driving.'

I thanked him, explained what I wanted done and arranged to meet him later in Drogheda.

I finished dressing – jeans and jumper, for a day that would include time spent in a chilly abandoned building and an informal bite of lunch. No need for make-up, apart from mascara and lipstick, which I would apply in the car later on. I returned to the kitchen, made some tea and filled an insulated beaker to drink from in the car. In the utility room I laced up a pair of waterproof hiking boots, which I reckoned would adapt to most of the circumstances in which I was likely to find myself. I would put my rubber boots in the Jazz as back-up. Lastly I grabbed my parka, checked that my hat and gloves were in the pockets, and slung it over my arm.

As I opened the front door, Boo, tail upright and symmetrical as a fake Christmas tree, whizzed past my leg and disappeared into the warm recesses of the house. For a moment or two I considered doing the same.

Even though the snow was barely dusted onto the

road surface, the overnight frost had made it treacherous. And, since most of my journey was along twisting country back-roads, a drive that would usually take me thirty minutes was going to take twice that long. At least Mona was out of the weather. I hoped Sherry would begin work early so I could get to see her by midday at the latest.

I turned on the radio to catch the seven o'clock news and weather. Nothing in the headlines caught my attention, so I lowered the volume and waited until the forecast came on to turn it up again. It seemed a thaw was on the way, with no snow threatened except on higher ground. I left the radio on while a woman did a roundup of the morning papers, a digest of headlines and offbeat stories. I was about to change the station to get some music when I heard her say, 'And lastly, a mummified body found by the River Boyne may hold up plans to build a new hotel. Could this be a case of "Mummy, I shrank the business?"'

Mona seemed to be getting the quirky treatment in the news. But, to my surprise, the programme presenter then announced there would be more on the Newgrange find in the next hour.

I quickly switched over to Valley FM, a local radio station. A pre-recorded piece on the Newgrange find had just ended, and the studio presenter was going to a live phone interview. 'And with me on the line is local businessman Frank Traynor, on whose property the body was found ...'

I could hardy believe my ears. 'What?' I shouted at the radio. I turned it up higher, afraid I'd miss something Traynor said.

He purred his way through the interview, apparently unaffected by his drinking the night before. Yes, indeed, it was a fascinating find. Gardaí were relieved it wasn't a murder case. The body had been taken away. It might end up on display in the Boyne Valley Visitor Centre eventually.

'Or even in your new hotel, Frank,' the interviewer rejoined.

Traynor chuckled. 'You know, that's not a bad idea.'

'Opening by the end of next year, I believe.'

'Provided we don't get held up at this stage. And, as you know, it's much needed in the area.'

'Indeed it is. But you'll have some who'll object, of course – it being near a World Heritage site and all that.'

'Oh, yes – the do-gooders who put obstacles in the way of development at every opportunity. Well, I can guarantee to anyone listening who may be worried that this hotel will not intrude on the landscape. No more than the Visitor Centre down the road does.'

'Well, that's reassuring. Frank Traynor, thank you and good morning.'

The nauseating interview was over. I noticed my knuckles were white on the steering-wheel even though I was warm as toast.

In hopes of a more balanced approach, I switched

back to the national radio service for their report. But even my much-vaunted imagination couldn't prepare me for what I heard next.

'And Muriel Blunden of the National Museum is with us in studio to talk about this latest discovery ...'

I had missed the introduction to the interview, so hearing Muriel's name straight off was like a bolt out of the blue. I felt my face colouring. Why had she agreed to an interview? In controversies over development she usually stayed well below the radar, which made her unpopular with people working in heritage. Was she about to redeem herself?

'Before I ask you how significant it is,' continued the male interviewer, chiselling each word with his well-honed voice, 'perhaps you could tell us a little about these so-called "bog bodies" – how frequently they're found and where they come from.'

Blunden trotted out the standard information, mentioning in passing some of the exhibits on display in the Museum, from Gallagh Man, found in 1821, to the headless male torso dug out of Croghan Hill bog in 2003.

'And will you be preserving this one?'

'That depends on the condition of the body and its historical relevance, which will in turn be determined by its age.'

This was an odd response from a professional archaeologist. Bog bodies are so rare that even partially intact ones are preserved.

'And how old do you think it is?'

'At this early stage we can't say. But it's unlikely to be of great antiquity, given how close to the surface it was discovered.' Why was she playing it down so much? What was going on?

'Will you be requesting that work on the site be suspended, in the event that there are more bodies buried there?'

'No. These tend to be single, one-off inhumations. The body has already been removed; we'll complete an examination of the find-spot over the next couple of days, and then the developer can continue with his plans for the site.'

And that was that. The Director of Excavations at the National Museum had spoken. It was unbelievable. A couple of *days*? It would be difficult to complete a detailed drawing of the site, never mind an excavation, in such a limited time. I imagined archaeologists all over the country choking on their breakfasts. She was openly siding with the developer.

Slightly dazed, I pulled into a gateway at the side of the road, killed the radio and tried to think. It was as if there had been an overnight coup in the country and a new regime installed in place of the legitimate authorities.

The engine was still running and the heat in the car suddenly became too much, so I powered down my window. As the cold air swept in, my breath rose in a plume and counter-flowed out into the pre-dawn darkness. Why was Muriel Blunden against a proper survey and excavation of the site?

Ivers. Surely he had been told about the Museum's decision and the reason behind it – or had he, like me, just heard about it for the first time, heard Blunden checkmate him on the airwaves before he had an opportunity to argue the case with her? It was possible.

Through the bars of the gate I could see the indigo cloak of the eastern sky turning bitter orange at the hem. I pressed the button to raise the window, looked in my side mirror, slipped into first gear and began to indicate as I moved out on the road. With my mind thus engaged in several actions at once, I was slow to react to the unexpected churr of my phone, which wasn't in its cradle – I had left it lying on the passenger seat, a habit I found hard to kick. I stabbed one foot on the clutch and the other on the brake and snatched up the phone before my voicemail came on.

'Illaun, it's me, Terence. Have you been listening to –'

'Muriel Blunden on the radio? Yeah, I heard her. What a way for me to find out, Terence.'

'I'm sorry, Illaun. I was only told late last night and I didn't want to disturb you. Left a voice message on your mobile this morning at about six-thirty. Did you not get it?'

That was when I had been talking to Crean. I

remembered the phone falling under the bed; I hadn't looked at the screen since.

'I didn't check for voice messages, Terence, but thanks for trying.' I guessed he didn't use text messaging. 'So why has Muriel pulled rank on you?'

'Politics.'

'Small "p" or big "P"?'

'What do you mean?'

'Organisational infighting or government interference?'

'A bit of both.'

'Who's behind it?'

'Ultimately, this guy Traynor.'

'So he can build his hotel? But I doubt if he even has planning permission – not for a building opposite Newgrange. It would never be allowed.'

Ivers laughed cynically. 'You don't think so? With this present government, anything is possible.'

'But what's the rush? Why all the pressure? I even got a phone call from Traynor last night telling me to back off.'

'I don't know why it's so damn urgent. I only know the guy has contacts and he's using them.'

'So who's the politician?'

'Look, we're both on mobile phones. I'm not going to risk saying anything else for the moment.'

Even for Ivers, this was a bit paranoid. 'Oh, come on, Terence.'

'Suffice to say it's at ministerial level.'

'Did Muriel tell you that?'

'No way. I just … know it.'

'Which minister?'

'I'm saying no more.'

I knew he wouldn't budge. He was probably sweating profusely already.

'What about my role in this? I can't just walk away from it. Especially when someone's trying to bully me.'

'I told Blunden you were on the case. She made no comment one way or the other. I'd say keep going as if nothing's happened. I'm not walking away from this either.'

'Her definition of the find-spot sounds very narrow. Did the injunction not make it clear it was the whole field?'

'No. It was left open to interpretation by the experts, which allowed Ms Blunden to step in and opt for the narrowest one possible – the immediate area of the find only. But we're going to go back to the judge and insist that we want access to the entire site.'

'Well. You'd better move fast or there's going to be no site at all.' I told him what Seamus Crean had reported to me.

'Bloody hell. The Gardaí in Donore were meant to keep an eye on it.'

'I think the sergeant there is in Traynor's pocket. That's why I asked Crean to call Slane Garda station and tell them that a crime scene was being interfered with. That may have helped disrupt things for a while.'

Under the roof of an old bicycle shed near the disused morgue, my two employees were burrowing into the shell of peat from which Mona had been extracted. Gayle Fowler and Keelan O'Rourke were both in their twenties, just setting out on their careers as archaeologists.

The original block of soil was much reduced in size, while just beside it stood a mound of clear polythene sacks, numbered in sequence to indicate where each chunk of peat had been relative to the others. Next to this was a collection of smaller Ziploc bags containing various loose items they had collected.

'Hi, guys. How's it going?'

'It's bloody cold,' said Gayle. She had a trowel in one grimy, cotton-gloved hand and was using the back of the other to wipe away a drop at the end of her nose. Gayle was wearing a llama-wool hat with earflaps, a souvenir of her backpacking trip to Peru the previous year; a yellow reflective jacket with silver Dayglo stripes, and fleece-lined waterproof over-trousers, added considerably to her already well-padded physique. Keelan, on his knees leaning a striped ruler against a section of soil, ignored me for the moment.

'Have you had breakfast?'

Gayle sniffed. 'We bought a couple of doughnuts and coffee on the way this morning.'

'Well, then I suggest you guys go and have something to eat. I've opened a tab for you for in the hospital café. You can use it any time today. Anything turn up?'

Gayle pointed to the stack of bags with her trowel. 'A palynologist's paradise, I'd say. Enough pollen to make your rhinitis run rampant.' Palynologists study pollen, and pollen analysis would not only yield information on the plants that had gone into the making of the bog – sedges, rushes, mosses, grasses – but would also allow us to check the wind-borne pollen of other species that had rained down on it against the well-documented pollen record of Ireland since the last ice age, and so give us a time zone for the formation of this layer of Monashee.

'Any signs of human interference – old cuts into the peat, that kind of thing?'

'Nah,' said Keelan dismissively, finally standing up. Skinny and pale with a scraggy black beard, he was clad in a long grey Russian Army greatcoat that was at odds with the brightly coloured Andean hat – a gift from Gayle – he too was wearing. 'A lot of the matrix had crumbled or collapsed, what with the digger and the extraction of the body ...' He aimed a Polaroid camera at the place where he had positioned the ruler. 'There were also some round black pellets of something, which we found lying together. In the area near where her head was.'

'Animal, vegetable or mineral?'

As the Polaroid rolled out, Keelan picked out a labelled Ziploc and held it up for me to observe. 'Organic, I'd say, but hard as ball-bearings – see? Seven in all.' Gathered in a corner of the bag were what looked like so many dried peppercorns. He rotated the bag so I could look at them from various angles.

'Hmm … seeds, possibly?' I said.

My mobile phone rang. It was Malcolm Sherry. He had completed his autopsies on both sets of remains and was waiting for me.

I collected a file of notes, Polaroids and drawings relating to the motorway survey from Gayle and headed towards the old morgue.

Chapter Five

Two autopsy tables stood parallel to each other, their rusting legs bolted to the white-tiled floor, from which numerous tiles were missing, giving it a checkerboard appearance. The remains on each table were covered in a green sheet; above them were a pair of chipped and dusty white lampshades, one of them missing a bulb. The old morgue, with its peeling whitewashed walls and broken windows, had no hospital atmosphere left – it seemed to have vanished along with the smell of disinfectant, which had been overwhelmed by a musty odour tinged with the whiff of sour milk.

Malcolm Sherry's green scrubs, plastic apron and

tweed hat were hanging up on the only coat-hook still projecting from the door. He was standing between the two tables, wearing his duffel coat; seeing me hesitate, he said, 'This is one occasion when body fluids aren't a hazard, I'm glad to say. Besides which, it's cold enough in here to freeze the balls off a brass monkey.' His breath condensed as he spoke. I needed no more persuasion to leave on my warm parka.

Sherry moved to the back of the better-illuminated table, where the bulkier of the two green-swathed objects lay. Then, with a latex-gloved finger, he beckoned me forward for my first encounter with Mona in her entirety.

When Sherry pulled aside the sheet, my first reaction was one of awe mixed with a niggling sense of shame. Mona was lying on her back, her outstretched arm now pointing to a patch of flaking plaster on the wall behind her. The previously invisible left arm was flexed along her side, and her fist was clenched and resting on her left breast. The right breast was visible, full if a little flattened, and still bearing a stippled areola surrounding a distinct but compressed nipple. Some coin-sized spots of skin on the breast had been abraded, revealing a substance that seemed to be the colour and consistency of the plaster on the wall.

But, as my eyes sought first her face and then the rest of her, I felt growing disappointment: much of the body was missing. The remains were more like a cast, an exoskeleton left behind by some creature that had burst out of its own skin. The top of Mona's head, still bearing some strands of hair dyed red by the bog chemicals, had retained its shape; but from the forehead down, the face was like a collapsed rubber mask with holes left for the eyes and mouth and, oddly, the ears. There was hardly any flesh left on the lower part of the skeleton. A charred-looking length of spine snaked out from under the sunken ribcage and down to the pelvis. Glued to the sacrum was what looked like a thick puddle of tar, which I assumed was the residue of her internal organs. In terms of archaeological classification Mona qualified as an 'extended inhumation', because her lower limbs weren't flexed but stretched straight out. However, the bones of one leg ended at the knee, the other's above the ankle.

Sherry was looking at me, saying nothing as I took in the full picture. I smiled bravely. At least she was more than a mere skeleton or a collection of leathery rags. But Mona would not win any bog-body beauty contests – wouldn't even be entered in one.

'Well,' I said, 'looks like she's been through a lot.'

'More than you think,' said Sherry. 'But first things first ...'

As if presenting a lecture, he swept his hand out in a gesture that took in the entire body. 'We have here the remains of a female aged between fifteen and thirty-five and approximately 1.47 mètres in height. Prolonged immersion in the acidic, anaerobic conditions of the soil in which she was discovered brought about the two most notable features of the body's condition: number one, the preservation of a substantial area of skin and fatty tissue in the torso, face and upper limbs; and, number two, the total tanning of the flesh. However –'

'Total?' I interjected. My hopes of an early date for Mona perked up again. And the more leathery she was, the slower her rate of decomposition would be.

Sherry adopted a less formal tone. 'Her epidermis has sloughed off, but I'm fairly certain the dermis has been completely transformed to leather. I sent a section for microscopic analysis earlier this morning. Should have the results soon.'

The loss of the skin's outer layer is a frequent occurrence with bog bodies, and the pristine fingertip ridges of the dermis beneath have misled researchers in the past into thinking these individuals have done no manual labour and must be of noble birth. 'Great, Malcolm. Sorry to interrupt you.'

He shrugged to indicate it was of no consequence. 'Interrupt away. I was about to say that the remains must have been lying close to flowing water, which accelerated the demineralisation of some parts of the skeleton.'

'Probably where it was seeping from the bog into the drain,' I suggested.

'That could account for it. Anyway, the bones of the skull, front and back, were completely eroded. The ribcage, the vertebrae and the remaining bones of the lower limbs are intact but decalcified and pliable, more like cartilage. The preservation of the outer torso is fair to good, but the upper limbs are remarkable – entirely mummified: skin, bone, muscles, ligaments, fingernails, even the hairs on her arms.'

He was making Mona sound like a fine specimen despite her deficiencies.

'But no remnants of clothing or textiles that would help us gauge her age?'

'Not a single thread. We'll have to wait for the boffins to carbon-date her.'

'Which can be quite a challenge where bog bodies are concerned,' I said, then added, 'as you know, of course.'

'Yes, I'm aware of the way the body can absorb the age of the bog around it.'

Sherry knew his stuff. There had been wide discrepancies in the dating of Britain's Lindow Man, and they were explained away at one point by this phenomenon. Of course, if Mona was the same age as the part of the bog where she had been found, that was no problem; but if she had been buried by people who cut a grave for her into older layers of peat, then that could skew the reading. And it would be at least a month, probably more, before we got the preliminary results of the carbon-dating.

'But,' he added on reflection, 'with the body of a recent murder victim, you'd be likely to find some fragments of fabric. The complete absence of clothing in this case – not a single fibre – could be indicative of considerable age.'

'Because the material was destroyed by the bog acids over a long period of time?'

'Either that or she was buried naked to start with.'

Of course. 'And that would only be likely in a ritual of some kind. Which definitely brings us back in time.' My hopes had risen again.

'Let's wait and see. One thing's sure: we won't be pursuing her murderer. Not until time travel becomes available, at any rate.'

It was the second time he had referred to murder. I wondered what was coming.

'As a matter of interest, Malcolm, have you told the Gardaí you've officially ruled her out as a recent homicide?'

'Yes.'

'When exactly?'

'Only about an hour ago.'

'Hmm … that's odd. Traynor seemed to be in no doubt about it on the radio earlier this morning.'

Sherry sighed. 'I said it to Sergeant O'Hagan yesterday, for his own information.' There was little doubt left in my mind that O'Hagan was Traynor's man.

'Traynor's also started bulldozing away the bog,' I said. 'He seems to have the approval of the National Museum. Hard to believe, but true.'

'He's a big shot in this area.'

'You know him?'

'No. But I stayed in Drogheda last night – met a local GP for dinner, guy I went to college with. Traynor has bought other property in the Boyne Valley area as well. From some religious order, apparently.'

'And he plans to build a hotel at Monashee, right?'

'So it seems.'

'But he could never have been granted planning permission for a hotel there. It's a World Heritage site.'

'Stranger things have happened,' Sherry said dryly. 'You say you heard him on the radio this morning. A local station, I'll bet?'

'Yes, Valley FM.'

'He owns it.'

'*What*?' This man Traynor was shrinking my vocabulary.

'Well, as good as. He's the majority shareholder.'

I was starting to understand Traynor's arrogance, and I was irked that he was getting away with it. But right now I wanted to know more about Mona and her fate.

I pointed to the area of her pelvis that contained the viscous stain. 'Remains of her internal organs, I assume?'

'Ah, yes – interesting,' said Sherry, warming to his subject. 'Although the chest cavity is intact, there are no preserved organs contained therein, nor any brain matter in the cranium – or, should I say, calvarium.' He passed his fingers across his scalp to demonstrate.

I nodded. At least we were even, each guilty of underestimating the other's knowledge. The calvarium is a technical term for the dome of the skull – the only unflattened portion of Mona's crumpled face, which for some minutes now I had been avoiding.

Sherry walked halfway along the table. 'But, by some twist of fate, the parts of her body connected with childbirth have been preserved' – he inclined one hand towards her chest, the other to her pelvic area – 'the mammary glands, and the organ of generation itself.'

'That's her uterus?' I leant down, fascinated, to examine it further. I could see where he had made an incision in the pancake-sized lump of organic matter. 'It's bigger than I thought.'

'Of course it is. Because it's not involuted. She had given birth only a short time before she died.'

'It's not just a twist of fate, though, is it?'

'What?'

'That those parts survived.'

'No, there are good reasons. In women the uterus is frequently the last organ to decay. And sometimes in wet conditions fatty tissue turns to adipocere, which is what happened to her breasts.'

'Adipocere … grave-wax?'

'Correct. We refer to the process as saponification – turning to soap. I'll get back to that shortly. But let's talk about the birth. There are parturition scars on the pubic bone, which, if they don't exactly confirm it, at

73

least add weight to the argument that she had been delivered of a baby. I therefore assumed she had died in childbirth or soon after. I speculated that this was her first pregnancy, that perhaps she had conceived out of wedlock and when her time came she deliberately hid in the marsh to escape detection; then they both died there of exposure – and, in her case, exhaustion, given the kind of birth she must have had.'

'It's a nice theory, but I'm getting the impression you don't buy it.'

'Because it doesn't quite match the facts.'

'Which are?'

'Fact one, her body' – he swept his hand out over it – 'wasn't left above ground for any length of time after death. There are no signs of insect infestation, no scavenger marks on either flesh or bone.'

'So she was buried either alive or immediately after death.'

'Correct. Fact number two: she was murdered ...' Sherry paused and swallowed hard. His emotions were surfacing. 'Murdered and mutilated. Her lips and ears were sliced off. And they cut out her eyes.'

I began to connect with Sherry's feelings. No wonder I had been finding it hard to look at Mona. It was as if her ruined face had been willing me not to stare at it.

'See here –' Sherry outlined the openings in the sides of her head, the lipless, gurning mouth, the gaping eyeholes. 'Come a bit closer, if you don't mind.'

I moved along the table, forcing myself to examine the blackened *Scream* mask with its pathetic clump of ginger hair.

'I assumed at first the eyelids and lips had been lost before preservation set in – something quite common in natural mummification. But cartilage would be slower to decay; in fact, it survives well in boggy conditions. So the missing ears were a mystery. And you'll notice the tragus on each side is intact – that's the little lobe in front of the auditory canal. That made me even more suspicious. Why had those bits of cartilage not shrivelled away as well? On closer inspection, I could see the wound margins where the auricle – the main part of the ear – had been severed from the face by a sharp instrument. Same with the lips, as you can see.'

There was no doubt that all the edges had an unnatural, carved appearance. I tried to catch the effect in a quick sketch.

Sherry ran his finger inside the rim of one of the eyeholes, which I noticed had a more ragged look. 'But the wounds here are not as neat; there was some digging and gouging with the point of the blade before they succeeded in their objective. That's how I realised they had gone for the eyeballs, not just the lids.'

'Jesus, Malcolm ... she had a horrific death.'

'Yes, she died savagely – but not from any of those wounds.' Sherry moved back to his position behind her head and lifted her chin to show me. Her throat had been slashed, practically separating her head from the rest of her body. 'And she was strangled into the bargain. See here ...' He pointed out a groove in the skin just under the incision, below where her earlobe should have been. 'This was made by some kind of ligature.'

I looked at him expectantly.

'No, it's not there any more. One thing's sure: cutting her throat while she was being strangled would have been a bloody business.'

Oh, God. Why did it have to be such a fate? And what had she done to deserve it? What law had she broken, what taboo had she infringed? Mona's end was looking more like punishment than sacrifice. So there was a real possibility – it made me grimace to think of it – that she been mutilated before being put to death, not after. It was all pointing towards the likelihood that she was from the Iron Age.

'You're probably wondering what anyone could have done to deserve to die like that.' Sherry tilted his head in the direction of the other autopsy table. 'I think the reason is over there.'

A chill not connected with the temperature in the morgue crept over my skin.

'So let's take a look, shall we?' he said, drawing the sheet over Mona and moving to the other table. I placed my sketch-pad and pencil on the edge of Mona's table and joined him.

He was about to remove the second sheet when

there was a knock on the door. 'Blast,' he said under his breath; then, brightly, 'Come in.'

A white-coated woman opened the door halfway and proffered a yellow envelope. 'Dr Sherry, I have those results for you.'

'Thank you,' he said, looking at his watch. I checked the time on my mobile phone. It was 12.40. I had been meant to meet Seamus Crean ten minutes ago.

Sherry started to unroll his gloves. 'Look, Illaun, if you don't mind, we'll leave this till later. I've arranged to meet someone for lunch.'

'Me too. And I'm late.'

He smiled. 'Same here. I also have to go to Drogheda Garda station to file an official report that will release them from having to carry out any further investigation, so see you back here at – what? four?' He dropped the gloves into a plastic waste-disposal bin and took the key of the morgue from his pocket. 'Or I could leave this with you in case you get back earlier and want to do some drawing?'

I took the key from him, but then I hit on a better idea. 'Tell you what – I'll leave the key with one of my team, and then whichever one of us is back first can collect it.'

'Fine with me.'

As we left the morgue, my feelings about Traynor came to the surface again. But there was no point in getting angry at him – better to mount an effective legal challenge to his plans. The one I should really be outraged at was Muriel Blunden, a public servant who, instead of defending the people's heritage, was facilitating a threat to it. But why had she taken such a perverse stance on the issue?

Chapter Six

Seamus Crean had suggested we meet at St Peter's Church in the main street. Drogheda was not a town with which I was well acquainted, and the church was a highly visible landmark.

There was a sleety drizzle falling, and I wandered up the steps and into the porch to see if he was sheltering from the weather. Not seeing him there, I pushed through the brass-handled swing doors and found myself in a vaguely familiar interior. It was a good example of Gothic Revival, and it had been recently restored, which perhaps was why I wasn't sure whether I had been there before. To satisfy my curiosity I walked down a side aisle; approaching the altar, I saw that my memory was accurate. Inside a glass reliquary surmounted by a gilt latticework cone was a man's head, his roasted skin like blotched yellow-brown suede, his closed eyelids giving him a serene appearance that belied his violent end.

This was the preserved head of the martyr St Oliver Plunkett, which I had not seen since childhood when we were taken to see it as part of a school excursion. The tour had also included a visit to Newgrange, and I wondered if our teachers had ever noticed the odd parallel between the church that housed a charred skull, and the tomb that had once contained a collection of cremated bones.

To the left of the saint's shrine, an area of the church had been devoted to him; it featured another reliquary containing parts of his skeleton, the door of his prison cell, various plaques and paintings and a selection of booklets, one of which I picked up and began browsing through. I soon came across the chilling words of his death sentence for treason:

> And from Newgate prison you shall be drawn by sledge through the City of London to Tyburn; there you shall be hanged by the neck but cut down before you are dead, your bowels taken out and burnt before your face, your head shall be cut off, and your body divided into four quarters to be disposed of as his Majesty pleases. And I pray God to have mercy on your soul.

Overkill. Just like Mona. Had she too been the victim of religious persecution?

I was standing a few metres from a row of red-cushioned pews set in front of the main shrine. On the far side of the seats was an offering stand with rows of smoking prayer-candles, and silhouetted in the glow was a figure. There was a man kneeling in the pew nearest the shrine, shoulders hunched, head bent. I had been unaware there was anyone else in the church.

The man lifted his head, blessed himself and rose to leave, but only after he had genuflected and turned around did I see it was Seamus Crean. I followed him out and caught up with him in the porch.

'Seamus, I thought I'd missed you.'

'Sorry about that, Missus; I was just lighting a candle. My mother has great faith in St Oliver.'

'I see.'

'He might help me get another job before Christmas, she said.'

We walked down the steps. I noticed Crean had washed his hair; it was lighter by several shades, and most of it stood above his head in a frizzy column.

'Have you had any lunch?' I asked him.

'Well, no …'

'Let's go somewhere and have a bite to eat, then. And it's on me.'

He hesitated for a moment when we reached the street.

'Is there a problem?'

'Nothing fancy, if that's all right with you.'

I smiled. 'No problem. You pick a place. Whatever suits you suits me.'

We crossed the street in a grey drizzle, beneath cheerful Christmas lights; they were doing little to lift the spirits of sullen-faced drivers caught up in barely moving traffic, no doubt exacerbated by the weather and the onset of the seasonal shopping rush. Crean brought me to a spacious pub where the lunch was buffet-style, served onto trays from brightly lit hot plates and *bains-marie* offering roast beef, fried fish, boiled ham, cabbage and potatoes. It was just what was required on a miserable December day, and we both tucked into beef smothered with gravy, our plates piled high with vegetables. I was drinking water, he had a pint glass of milk.

'So what happened this morning?' I asked, after we had eaten a forkful or two each.

'It was a bit of crack, to be honest, Missus. I got off the bike down the road a bit, saw the squad car arriving at the field and the boys in blue getting out. A minute or so later, the lads working the diggers is standing talking to the Gardaí on the side of the road. The work had stopped at this stage, so I cycled up to the squad car. "What's the matter, lads?" says I to the workmen. "Do you want Mr Traynor to come and sort this out?" One of them says, "Yeah, but we can't get him on the phone." Then one of the Gardaí asked me if I knew where Mr Traynor was. "I do," says I, getting back up on the bike, "and there's no chance of getting him down here. He's gone to Dublin for the day.""

I laughed at Crean's audacity, something I hadn't thought was in him. 'And what's happening there now, do you know?'

'Some people came to survey the place just as the work was starting up again – said they had to measure it or something, waved some kind of legal papers at the digger lads. They said work would have to stop until they were finished.'

This was good news. Ivers must have persuaded the judge to give WET access to the whole site. Traynor wasn't having it all his own way, despite having Muriel Blunden on his side. But why was he so anxious to have the place torn up immediately? Had it something to do with avoiding the planning process?

'What's the opinion locally about this hotel of Traynor's? How did he get planning permission?'

Crean checked to see who was sitting near us. Satisfied we could not be overheard, he nevertheless leaned towards me and lowered his voice conspiratorially. 'Seems he bought different plots of land from Grange Abbey.'

'So?'

'Well, they're a nursing order of nuns that's been in the area from way back. Came in with the Normans, they say. All their land has ancient rights attached to it.'

'What kind of rights?

'Rights to do anything with the property, build or whatever. That's why Traynor thinks the planning laws don't apply to him.'

'But those rights wouldn't hold up in law today.'

Crean leaned closer. 'No matter. Traynor has the County Council and the Minister for Tourism and Heritage behind him.'

'Derek Ward?'

Crean nodded.

Of course. Minister Ward was a Dáil member for the constituency, and the party he served had a history of riding roughshod over environmental planning laws. That was where Traynor evidently got his political clout.

'There's also a rumour,' Crean whispered, 'that the deal with the nuns will give the order a share in the profits from the hotel.'

I knew that religious orders had been selling off property all over Ireland in recent years, but profit-sharing in hotels was a new one on me. 'Are they a Catholic order?'

Crean nodded. 'The abbey is some kind of retreat house. I don't even know what the order is called; even though it's near Donore, they never had much to do with the community. All you ever hear is rumours about them.'

'What kind of rumours?'

'Well, there's been a lot of workmen coming and

going up at the abbey in the past while. All foreign. It's not that I have anything against them as such, it's just you'd wonder why no locals are getting work. My father thinks the nuns have something to hide.'

A waitress asked if we wanted dessert, which apparently was served at the tables. I declined and asked for more water; Crean ordered apple pie and cream and a cup of tea.

'Seamus, this idea that Monashee is haunted …' I looked him squarely in the eyes. 'You don't really believe it, do you?'

He sat back, less concerned about eavesdroppers now. 'I do and I don't. All I know is what I told you. It's always in shadow in the day, people don't like passing it at night, there's strange lights seen over it from time to time.'

Always in shadow in the day? Odd place to build a hotel … 'Anything else you can remember?'

'Some say you'll see the souls of the dead in white grave-clothes rising up out of the field, hear them moaning and groaning.'

'When are these apparitions seen?'

'Mainly this time of year. My father knows all about it. I could ask him for you.'

'That would be great, Seamus.' There might be something in it for Finian to add to his collection of folklore.

'Time to be off, so.'

I put my hand up to hold him a moment. 'Look, Seamus … I feel bad about you losing your job. If we get the go-ahead to excavate at Monashee, I could have some work for you.'

'It wasn't your fault, Missus. But thanks.'

Outside, the sleet had stopped but the traffic was still heavy. We were about to part when I saw a silver Mercedes nudging its way out of a parking bay on the far side of the street. There was a woman in the passenger seat. I grabbed Crean by the arm and nodded in the direction of the car.

He dipped his head down, the better to see the driver. 'It's Traynor, all right,' he said, 'and some woman I don't know – maybe a solicitor on the way out to Monashee with him ...'

It took a few seconds before I realised Crean was staring at me. 'Talking about ghosts, Missus, you look like you've just seen one yourself.'

I was fairly certain the woman in the car was Muriel Blunden, Director of Excavations at the National Museum.

'Hold on for a second, Seamus.'

I took out my mobile phone and rang Terence Ivers at his office. 'Terence, I've just seen Frank Traynor in Drogheda with Muriel Blunden – at least, I'm nearly sure that's who it was.'

'It wouldn't surprise me. Traynor is a sharp operator. We stymied him today for a while, but he's out-manoeuvred us again. He managed to get a request into the High Court in Dublin this morning to have the injunction lifted. Decision in the morning. I think he'll win it.'

The High Court could overrule a District Court decision. I put away the phone and told Crean about our reversal of fortune. I didn't want him going away with false hopes of a job.

Chapter Seven

Following the meeting with Crean, I sat in my car in Drogheda reading through the latest survey data that Gayle had given me earlier. These findings would form the basis of my company's input into the Environmental Impact Assessment commissioned by the National Roads Authority. And I intended to have the report written before the Christmas break.

Between reading and making notes, I spent nearly an hour in the car park, so before leaving for the hospital I rang Malcolm Sherry to tell him I was running late – only to discover he was in the same situation and would probably get there after me.

When I arrived at the bicycle shed, Gayle and Keelan were still working away but the original block of peat had been greatly reduced.

'Looks like you won't be here much longer,' I said.

'No. We're expecting someone from WET to arrive soon to collect this lot,' Gayle said, handing me the key to the morgue and pointing to the stack of numbered packages.

'Don't know if we should give them this as well,' said Keelan, picking up one of the Ziplocs and handing it to me. I noticed he was wearing fingerless woollen gloves over a pair of latex ones. 'Found it close to where those seeds were.'

Inside the transparent bag was a thin coil of leather tapering to a point at each end, like stretched licorice.

I knew immediately what it was. 'I'll hold onto this for now,' I said, starting to walk away.

'Hey …!'

'Gotta go, Keelan,' I said, quickening my pace.

'At least tell us what it is,' he called after me.

'Can't explain now. Later.'

'And what about the EIA?' added Gayle.

'I'll call you,' I shouted, and rounded the corner of the shed.

The first thing that struck me when I got back into the morgue was that the smell of the place had changed – or, to be more precise, something had been added. It was sweet, familiar and yet disturbing for some reason. The harder I tried to identify it, the more evasive it became.

I looked around to see if anything had been touched. Both tables were still covered by sheets. Nothing seemed out of place. The sketch-pad and pencil I had left on the table beside Mona were undisturbed ... And then I saw it. The sheet on the other table had slipped further down towards the floor on the side nearest me. It looked as if someone had lifted it off and spread it unevenly when replacing it. It could have moved of its own accord, but it added to my suspicion that someone had been in the morgue. Archaeologists are used to making sizeable deductions from fragments of evidence.

I dug out my mobile and rang Keelan.

'What's up, Illaun?'

'Were you guys in the morgue while I was away?'

'Us? No way.'

'Did you let anyone into it?'

'Not to my knowledge. Hold on and I'll ask Gayle ...' I heard him repeat the question. 'No.'

'And no one asked you for the key?'

'No one asked us for the key,' he said slowly, for Gayle's benefit. 'Gayle's shaking her head, so that goes for the two of us. And now that we've cleared that up, what's the significance of the piece of leather?'

'I'm about to find out,' I said, and pressed the End button.

I was gingerly folding back Mona's sheet when Sherry came through the door, reading the contents of the yellow envelope he had been handed earlier. 'No question,' he said, continuing the conversation as though we had never left the place, 'the tannin did its job thoroughly …' He came over to the table and looked at Mona admiringly. 'This lady's skin is *all* leather.'

'Malcolm, have you been back here since we left?'

'No.'

'Can you smell … perfume?'

He sniffed the air. 'No.' Then he laughed. 'We're not dealing with a preserved saint here, you know.' He rolled up the envelope, stuffed it into a pocket of his duffel coat and pulled a pair of surgical gloves from a blue cardboard box in the sink at the end of the table.

I decided, for now, to forget about who might have been in the morgue and why. There were other things to think about. News of the extent of the tanning process had raised my hopes for Mona's antiquity by another notch. And there was this latest find. 'Speaking of leather …' I said, holding up the plastic bag.

Sherry's face lit up. 'From the peat in the shed?'

'Yes. Want to see if it fits?' I handed him the bag.

Sherry opened it and took the thong out carefully, holding it between finger and thumb and letting it dangle so we could see how long it was. It unwound a little but remained in a curve. I could see that the ends were stretched and twisted, as if they had snapped under pressure. Sherry straightened it out; it was about fifty centimetres long.

He drew back the sheet fully and placed the strip of leather into the groove in the side of Mona's neck. It fit perfectly. 'No doubt about it,' he said.

Then he examined the ends of the ligature. 'This wasn't done by the digger; the break is old. It must have snapped when she was being strangled.' He handed the thong back to me. 'But I would have expected a noose to be longer.'

'Maybe she was garrotted by winding this tight from behind?'

'Hmmm … yes, with a stick, perhaps. That would explain the ends being twisted the way they are.'

'She might even have been wearing it.' I held it up to the light and twirled it slowly. 'Although there are no awl-holes where it might have been sewn … no sign of it having been knotted, either.'

'I guess a knot could easily have come undone with the amount of force being used. So you could be right. She may have been murdered with her own necklace.'

'No way we'll ever be sure, I suppose.' I put it back in the sample bag. 'You're finished with Mona now, I take it.'

'I have no reason to hold on to "Mona", as you call her. And no justification to spend any more time or money on having her examined, though I will have her X-rayed for you.'

A tinny version of Mike Oldfield's 'Tubular Bells' began playing somewhere in the morgue. We looked at each other in some puzzlement. Then Sherry realised:

'Damn,' he said, 'it's my mobile.' He pulled the rolled-up envelope out of his overcoat pocket and lifted the phone from beneath it. 'Yes?'

As he listened to the caller, I smiled to myself. Was it by accident or design that Malcolm had music from *The Exorcist* as his ring-tone?

In my mind I began to itemise what we knew about Mona, but it quickly became a catalogue of things we *didn't* know about her. We had no idea of how she had really looked; no remains of her last meal to analyse; no teeth to record her lifelong eating habits; no body decorations, clothes, jewellery or possessions of any kind – unless you included the leather garrotte. And I began to wonder just how much scientific scrutiny the National Museum would foot the bill for, if Muriel Blunden had her way. Carbon-dating? Possibly. A CT scan? Unlikely.

Sherry was speaking in hushed tones. 'Can't just now ... have someone with me ... have to finish ... Well, all right – I'll be there in five minutes.' He pressed the End button and said, 'Illaun, I have to go to the reception desk in the main building. I'll only be a few minutes. Do you mind holding on here? We'll go through the other post-mortem as soon as I return.'

'No problem. I have a bit more sketching to do anyway.'

Sherry put the envelope and his phone in separate pockets and left the morgue. My phone read 18.10; I rang Keelan's mobile and left a message to say it was time for them to go home, if they hadn't done so already. I added that I would work on the EIA over the weekend and would call or e-mail if I needed to check anything with them. Staff from WET would by now be loading the bagged peat and other samples into a van – except for the leather thong, which I would leave in its bag with the body.

I walked around the autopsy table and selected an angle that provided me with a good view of Mona, taking in the ligature mark and the positioning of both her arms. The leathery flesh was already drying out and a patch on her shoulder had lightened in colour – an effect that made the pores highly visible, like puncture marks created by a tattooist's needle. While drawing her face, I saw that her nose was perfectly preserved and dainty – something I hadn't taken in before, with the shock of seeing her mutilated features. It somehow counterpointed the brutality that had been visited upon her: her delicate beauty still evident despite the efforts of her assailants.

It occurred to me that Sherry had not said whether there were any defence marks on her arms, which would indicate she had tried to protect herself. I examined first her outstretched arm, then the folded one, but could see nothing. Then I noticed properly, for the first time, that the hand over her breast was clenched into a fist. Taking her hand for the second time, I inspected it from every angle. She seemed to be holding something.

My heart racing, I squatted down to the level of the table and, raising her hand against the light, tried to squint through her bunched fingers. Not a sliver of light shone through.

I dug into a pocket of my jacket, found my penknife, opened it and gently inserted the blunt side of the blade between two of her fingers. It scraped against a solid surface.

Mona was indeed clutching something.

As I stood up again, I accidentally brushed against the second autopsy table behind me and swept the already lopsided sheet to the floor. Turning to lift the sheet back up onto the table, I was unable to avoid seeing what had been lying underneath it.

One day in class, Finian Shaw had posed the question: what single action distinguishes humans from all other creatures? Aware that he had phrased the question carefully, we tried our best to interpret what he meant by 'action' and answered 'writing' or 'playing a musical instrument', or even resorted to 'making tools'. But not one student provided the answer he sought, nor had he expected that anyone would.

'The answer is,' he said, 'we are the only creatures who bury our dead.'

I had smiled at that, not only because it was unexpected but because it reminded me that, as children, my brother Richard and I had practised ritual burial – not of people, of course; but, with great ceremony, we had interred numerous small animals in a flowerbed at the end of our garden. Our first burial was a bumblebee, laid on cotton-wool inside a matchbox. There were others of that ilk, a ladybird, a moth; then a newly hatched nestling, scrawny and pink with paper-thin purple eyelids. Eventually we graduated to a kitten, the runt of a litter, too weak to survive. I asked our mother to provide a coffin, which she did – a shoebox lined with white satin. The two of us walked in procession, me in front holding aloft the cardboard casket, both of us chanting some out-of-key hymn. We dug, knelt, prayed, buried, and set up a cross with ice-pop sticks.

Then our pet dog died of old age. Wookie was a black-and-white mongrel with fur like an acrylic toy's. Dad wanted her disposed of by the vet, but with our experience as undertakers my brother and I insisted on burying her in the flowerbed. There was no box – it would have been too big and awkward; we laid her on her side on a newspaper and put her into a shallow grave.

Two weeks later, for some reason I can't recall – maybe to see a real skeleton – I proposed that we exhume her with a spade. What we unearthed was not what I had expected to see. Wookie's usually fluffy coat was glistening wet, plastered to her body. I thought she was sweating from the heat and explained this to Richard. Then, confirming my theory, I noticed she was panting. We had buried Wookie alive!

But some instinct must have told me not to touch her. I told Richard to stay there while I went for my father, wanting to be the first to tell the news.

'Dad, dad, she's alive – Wookie's alive! Come quickly!'

When I returned, dragging my father by the hand, Richard was standing there with a stick. He had just poked it against Wookie's belly. A heaving mass of maggots was teeming out of the cavity he had created. We children stood back in confusion as the stench hit us in the nostrils.

Dad quickly grabbed the spade and piled the soil back on top of the body. 'Don't ever do anything like that again,' he said crossly. 'Some things are not meant to be seen.'

Some things are not meant to be seen. In archaeology, I had chosen a career in which what is hidden is brought to the surface again, and every so often my father's words have caused me to reflect on the appropriateness of bringing certain things to light. And this moment in the draughty morgue was one of those occasions.

Sherry had cut through the leathery casing and opened the creature's abdomen from sternum to pelvis. The ribcage was splayed out in a double fan; adhering to its outer surfaces were thick, suety deposits coated in a leathery rind. Beside it on the table were what had once been the soft innards – a cheesy, brown-green mass of unrecognisable organs and tubing, which, like the rest of the body, had been converted to what I assumed was adipocere. So had the tiny brain: it had been removed and sat like a lump of putty in the upturned skullcap on the table.

The tannin-dyed, uptilted visage was impossible to reconcile with that of a human infant. Reddish, downy hair covered the forehead, surrounding the finger-length horn of skin and below it the slit from which Sherry had removed the transparent plug. Two eyes fused together occupied the socket, their irises black, the sclera stained a nicotine yellow. Where the mouth should have been there was merely a groove in the suety face; the chin was attached by a fleshy membrane to the chest, just above Sherry's incision. Spreading out from the back of the skull and onto the shoulders was another scarf of skin anchoring the head to the torso.

I looked away, my eyes searching for something else to engage their attention for a moment or two. I glanced over at the other table, noting that various fittings were missing, including the taps and attachments that would have been used to hose down bodies, the slight tilt of the table facilitating the flow of fluids into the sink at the end, under which the waste pipes were now corroded and broken.

In the dusty sink beside me were the box of surgical gloves and a roll of Elastoplast. I busied myself putting on a pair of gloves. I didn't think I'd be using them, but it helped to pass another few seconds before my gaze was reluctantly drawn back to the object further up the table.

Two stubs of arms, each with a bud of flesh at the tip, stuck out from its shoulders, and from the hips not two but four equally short legs sprouted at a variety of angles. All of these appendages must have been in a row when the body was curled up, but Sherry had spreadeagled the limbs and taped them to the table, revealing that the four legs were joined together below the exposed pubic bone in a confused ganglion of what I took to be female genitalia. It was as if someone had plundered various parts from wax anatomy models of infants and stuck them together with no knowledge of how they should be connected.

I knew I was looking at a severely deformed human baby.

I was struck by how well preserved it was, despite being a biological wreck. I had heard of the mummifying properties of adipocere – literally, 'fat wax' – but had never imagined it to be so effective. Nor had I anticipated the rancid smell wafting from the table, which made me turn away again just as Sherry came back into the morgue, a little out of breath.

'Ah, Illaun – sorry about that … local coroner knew I was in Drogheda. A man's body was just found in suspicious circumstances. I said I'd get there as soon as I could. I see your curiosity already got the better of you.'

'Not really.' I had my hand clamped over my nose. 'I accidentally uncovered it.'

'I should have warned you,' he said. 'It must have come as a shock.'

'No, it's OK. Just wasn't expecting an odour, that's all.'

Sherry approached the autopsy table. 'Yes. It's fascinating. Odourless in one case, smelling like bog butter in the other.'

'Adipocere, you mean?'

'I keep forgetting you've done some forensics.' Sherry was being snobbish, but I didn't mind. A year spent studying forensic archaeology after my PhD certainly didn't qualify me as a pathologist.

'Doesn't mean I entirely understand the chemistry involved.'

'No one does.'

Something from my student days came to mind. 'Newborns are good candidates for it, aren't they?'

'Yes, because there are practically no bacteria in the intestines to start the process of decomposition.'

'Why does it have an extra pair of legs?'

'The second set are from a conjoined but undeveloped foetus. Sometimes called a parasitic twin.'

'Like they had in freak shows and circuses.'

'Yes. The odd one survives beyond infancy. In times past they mostly ended up in the specimen jars of teratologists, anatomists and collectors of curiosities who specialised in "prodigies of nature" – in a word, monsters. And maybe that's where we'll leave it for now.' Sherry removed his surgical gloves and in the process knocked against the infant's body, which trembled like the carcass of the face-hugger in *Alien*.

And that triggered the memory of where I had seen a creature like the one on the autopsy table. Fran and I had been on holiday in Tuscany two months earlier and had seen it in a museum in Florence, on a stone carving. At first sight it had looked like a crustacean, but in fact it was a depiction of twins, joined at the pelvis but with a head at each end, unlike the incomplete version born to Mona. Apparently it was a recording of an actual monstrous birth that had occurred near the city in 1317.

We were saying goodbye in the car park when it occurred to me to ask, 'The man's body – where was it found?'

'Oh, I'm not absolutely sure. The Gardaí will bring me to it. Somewhere near Donore.'

'Tubular Bells' chimed again. Sherry lifted his phone.

'Sherry here. What? … Say again … Are you sure?' He listened while his caller confirmed something. Then he slowly lowered his phone from his ear and looked at me. 'The dead man … it's Frank Traynor. He's been murdered. At Monashee.'

Chapter Eight

Three yellow-striped squad cars had lined up in single file down the gravelled causeway, where Traynor's silver Mercedes was parked about halfway between the road and the river's edge. Reflected headlights and the narrower beams of flashlights occasionally penetrated a mist that was rolling up from the river. Garda radio chatter crackled from the cars. Figures conversing in low voices came and went, flitting past the headlights.

I was behind Sherry as he strode past the Garda cars and briefly shone a flashlight into the Mercedes. The beam bounced off blood-smeared windows, but I saw enough of the sodden interior to know the upholstery was covered in blood too. Sherry walked to the front of the car and called a name into the hazy darkness.

A grim-faced man in a suit and tie emerged from the mist. Sherry looked at him inquisitively for a moment, then lost interest: he had been expecting someone else.

I recognised Sergeant O'Hagan and murmured a greeting; he grunted in reply. I sensed he didn't remember me – my head was bare on this occasion – and I used the opportunity to fire a question at him as he passed. 'Sergeant O'Hagan?'

O'Hagan paused and scrutinised my face.

'Was there anyone in the car with Mr Traynor when he came here?'

'Who the hell are you?'

'Well, was there, Sergeant?' said Sherry, at my shoulder.

O'Hagan scowled. 'We have an eyewitness report. Frank stopped for petrol in Donore on his way here between four-thirty and five. He was alone.'

'Thank you, Sergeant,' Sherry said sweetly.

O'Hagan continued on his way. I decided to say nothing about Muriel Blunden for now.

A cough made us turn to see a gaunt, elderly man whom I took to be the coroner, sucking on a cigarette and beckoning Sherry towards him. We followed him a few metres beyond Traynor's car, into a haze criss-crossed by beams from at least four flashlights, all aimed at a figure lying face down. His upper torso was partly supported on his arms, which were tucked under him; his hands cupped his face as if he had died while weeping or praying, or both. I recognised Traynor's silver tie – it was draped over his shoulder.

'I take it you found him in this exact position?' said Sherry.

'Yeah, must have been trying to escape from his attacker.' The coroner inhaled again and coughed, a long-time smoker with bad lungs.

'Or maybe he was deposited here.'

'Why would anyone do that?' sighed the coroner, who would obviously have preferred the State pathologist to handle this from the beginning.

'Have you turned him over?' Sherry asked, kneeling down beside the body.

'No, I could see the throat wound plain as anything. Saw the amount of blood he'd lost. There was no question about cause of death. I decided to leave the rest to you.'

'And you're sure it's Traynor.'

'Y–' The coroner coughed up the phlegm. 'Yes. That's Traynor, all right. This was sticking out from underneath him.'

He held out a bloodied white envelope for Sherry to see. I could just make out 'Frank Traynor' typed neatly on an address label.

Sherry handed me his flashlight and pulled on a pair of surgical gloves he took from his coat pocket. 'Point that for me, please, Illaun.'

He took the envelope from the coroner, saw that it was unsealed and deftly extracted what looked like a Christmas card. I shone the light on it. A stylised gold spiral design on a purple background surrounded the words, 'The Peace of Earth, Air and Water be with you, and may the returning Sun rekindle all your hopes this Midwinter.'

Sherry opened the card. Another address label stuck on inside read, '*Sic Concupiscenti puniuntur.*'

'Mean anything to you?' Sherry asked me.

I shrugged my shoulders. 'Latin. "Thus are punished … those who are … concupiscent"?' I was kicking for touch.

Sherry grunted and handed the card and the envelope to a nearby Garda. Then he shoved his hand under the body, rolled it over and beckoned to me to shine the flashlight on Traynor's face.

For a second or two the dead man's hands remained in position, covering his face, but his throat was visible – a glistening scarf of dark red and, embedded in the flesh below it, his blood-soaked necktie. Then his hands slipped from his face.

'Good fuck,' said the Garda, who had pushed in front of me, partially blocking my view.

'Jesus Chr–' The coroner took a fit of coughing.

'Illaun,' Sherry said gently. 'Come here. I want you to see this.'

I hunkered down beside him, but what he was pointing out didn't register with me at first. I could only see the horror – the cavernous eye sockets, the bared teeth rimmed by an oval of raw flesh. And then I noticed an oddly familiar scent.

'And look here ...' said Sherry.

There was a wound in the side of the head – *a gunshot?* Sherry turned the man's head to show me the other side. Another wound, with a hole in the middle.

It finally clicked.

Traynor's body would not be on view while relatives and friends paid their last respects. His eyes had been cut out, his ears and lips sliced off. Just like Mona's.

Then I saw something in the corner of his mouth. His blood seemed to have congealed into a balled clump, like beads of candle-wax. My stomach began to issue nausea warnings.

'What's that?' I said, pointing it out.

Sherry bent closer. 'Good Lord,' he said, inserting a gloved finger between Traynor's still unstiffened jaws and poking out something from his mouth. 'Can you believe this?' he asked, rising to his feet with the thing held between finger and thumb. 'What kind of sick joker are we dealing with here?'

There was no mistaking the dark, needle-tipped leaves, the cluster of bright-red berries.

Sherry had parked beside my car at Drogheda Hospital before another word passed between us.

Although both of us encountered the dead in our line of work, I dealt with the remains of people whose deaths had taken place a long time ago in circumstances I understood only dimly. OK, in my year studying forensic archaeology I had participated in the dissection of a cadaver, a man's body donated to science by its owner. But it had been easy to remain detached from the anonymous corpse, to regard it as a fascinating structure of tissue and bone.

Since then, in the course of my work, I had dealt with the remains of many dead people, and it was easy to keep your distance when they had been reduced to bits of bone or even stains in the earth, and you learned too that even entire skeletons or intact mummies were no more than the long-vacated scaffoldings or shells of once-living human beings. Even the bodies of my own deceased relatives, on view in open coffins with their rosaried hands clasped, always looked like waxworks poorly impersonating the aunts and uncles I had known.

But it was only a short time since I had seen Frank Traynor alive and well on the streets of Drogheda. Now he was dead in a field beside the Boyne with his throat cut. And what I had seen there was the man murdered – not his corpse, somehow. It brought to mind something I had heard before: the soul doesn't leave the body immediately.

The brutality of the killing was also deeply shocking.

'Even down to strangling him,' said Sherry, out of the blue. He was dwelling on it just as I was. He turned off his lights but left the engine running. 'Obviously he was sitting in the driving seat when his assailant grabbed him from behind, choked him with his tie until he passed out and then cut his throat. Whoever did it would have been drenched in blood.'

The smeared windows, the flashlight beam on the sodden upholstery. 'But how did Traynor make it out of the car?'

'I think my first hunch was right. He was hauled out and then mutilated.'

I saw Traynor lying with his hands up to his face. 'He also regained consciousness, I think.'

'Afraid so. But, with such rapid blood loss, it would have been only briefly. What beats me is that whoever did it inflicted exactly the same wounds we saw on the body in the morgue. Which means they must have got in.' He looked at me in alarm. 'We left the key with your team this afternoon for a while. We'll have to check –'

'I already did. They didn't give the key to anyone. But, yes, someone did get into the morgue while we were gone. Frank Traynor.'

'Traynor? That doesn't make sense. What makes you so sure?'

'His aftershave. I noticed it again when I knelt down beside him – same scent I got in the morgue, remember?'

'But what was he doing there?'

'That's also puzzling me. I don't think he went there

to look at Mona.' I explained how the sheet over the infant had been disturbed.

'But *why*?'

'Let's talk about the child again. Had it been born?'

'It was delivered, yes – there's no sign of placental attachment, although it's hard to tell from the umbilical stump whether the cord was severed or had just shrivelled away. Stillborn or live birth – it's hard to say. But, even if she was technically alive at birth, what's certain is that the poor thing never drew breath – it would have been physically impossible for her.'

'So how do you define cause of death?'

'Multiple structural anomalies incompatible with life.'

'And what gave rise to these ... anomalies?' Monashee itself was an anomaly, according to Finian.

'Lack of formation of the brain, to begin with.' I remembered the grey lump sitting in the sawn-off saucer of bone. 'It failed to separate into two hemispheres; in the developing foetus, there's a two-way interaction between brain and skull formation, so this resulted in mid-line defects in the symmetry of the face – a single eye socket being the obvious one.'

'But it had two eyes, not one.'

'True, but fused together. It used to be thought that our eyes formed separately from each other, but research now indicates that the eye field in the foetus begins as one and then divides in two. If that process fails we get cyclopia – a socket with a single eye, or maybe two fused together as in this case, or occasionally a slit with no eye at all. And, as you've seen, the socket may be positioned where the nose would normally emerge from the face, with the nose above that … I say "nose", but it's really only a tube of flesh with no opening.'

'God, it's like some horrible genetic joke.'

'In a way, it is. And that poor thing had more than its fair share of tricks played on it. Remember the condition of its limbs?'

'Just stumps with buds at the ends,' I said.

'It's known as phocomelia; the long bones hadn't developed. And her fingers and toes were fused together – a condition called syndactyly. It seems to be one of nature's cruel kindnesses, piling on multiple congenital abnormalities to ensure malformed infants won't survive. With this one, it didn't even end there. The retroflexion of the skull, forcing the face upwards – that's iniencephaly, which would have caused severe problems for the mother in giving birth as well.'

Giving birth. The idea of being delivered of such a creature sent a shudder through me – an atavistic female fear, perhaps. 'You still haven't said what causes the defects.'

'Sometimes it's simply a random mutation – they happen more often than you'd think, but usually the foetus is miscarried quite early in the pregnancy. Sometimes it's hereditary, a recessive gene that surfaces every few generations in a family. Sometimes it's caused by drugs or radiation. We'll do a DNA test and see if we can find out what the specific chromosomal problem is here.'

'That may be tricky. The same process that preserves bog bodies also leaches them of DNA.'

'Hmm … I'd forgotten that. But maybe the adipocere will have kept some of the infant's cells intact.'

'Maybe, but I doubt if we'll get DNA from Mona, so we won't be able to prove they're mother and daughter.'

'And daughters, technically speaking.'

'Establishing their age would be a start, wouldn't it?'

'I can tell you have something in mind, Illaun. What is it?'

'AMS. In my line of work we're happy to wait weeks, months even, for carbon-14 dating … but AMS can really speed things up.' Accelerated Mass Spectrometry is a process in which a milligram of carbonised matter can be dated in an hour, in contrast to the conventional method of measuring several grams over a number of days. 'You have priority access to AMS at UCD's radiocarbon lab. You could get tissue from both sets of remains analysed.' If Monashee was to be secured as an archaeological site, the sooner I had this information to hand the better.

'It's damned expensive. I would only request it if it had a bearing on some crime.'

'It does. A possible copycat murder. Which means you need to be absolutely sure the body in the bog is as old as it seems.'

Sherry sighed. 'I'll do it, but who's going to pay?'

'The National Museum. But they don't know it yet. Another thing: I think Mona has something in her hand.' I explained how I had inserted the blade of the penknife between her fingers.

'Ah, I was wondering why her fist was closed,' he said. 'I tried to prise her hand open, but I didn't want to risk breaking any bones. I think we should wait for the X-rays before deciding what to do.'

'Let me know as soon as you have them.'

Sherry nibbled his forefinger. 'Remember, Illaun – one good turn deserves another.'

What did he mean? 'Sure.'

He glanced over at the old morgue, a black oblong silhouetted against the halogen glow of the sky. 'So someone else besides Traynor must have been in there today. Traynor may even have had them with him.'

'It's possible, I suppose.'

'Any more thoughts about the message inside the card?'

It had been at the back of my head, queuing for attention. I thought about it for a few moments. 'Concupiscence has to do with lust, I think – physical lust, but also acquisitiveness in general. I think the sense of the phrase on the card is, "This is the penalty for those who are guilty of lust."'

'Well, I don't know anything about Traynor's libido or his business methods, but I'm pretty sure it was digging up that field that got him killed.' Sherry turned his lights back on. 'And whoever killed him is unlikely to want you doing it either.'

'You're saying I'm in danger?'

'I just think you should go easy where this field is concerned.'

'I appreciate your concern, Malcolm,' I said, and climbed down out of the Range Rover. As he drove off and I hit the Unlock button on my car remote, I discovered something odd. The doors were already unlocked. Had I left them like that? I stood away from the car for a few seconds, looking in through the front and back windows.

There was no one inside. *You've watched too many scary movies, Illaun. Just get in the car.*

Then I heard someone breathing. An icicle of fear raked along my back. I turned to look back at the morgue. The entrance to it was in deep shadow. The breathing sound was coming from there. And it was strange – like someone with a stuffed nose and a swollen throat drawing in air with difficulty, sucking it in. Was it an animal? A dog?

I saw movement, a vague white shape coming towards me. But I couldn't move. The icicle had run me through, staking my body to the ground.

Get in the car, Illaun – now!

I ripped myself free of the icy stake, wrenched the car door open, threw myself inside and slammed it shut, at the same time elbowing the button to lock all the doors. The ignition key refused to go in. *Shit!*

I paused and took a deep breath. The key slid into its slot.

Revving the engine to a scream, I hit the lights and fishtailed across the car park towards the exit, projecting a distorted moving shadow onto the morgue as I shot past. Of all things, it reminded me of a crab or a scorpion, with its pincers held out to defend itself.

Chapter Nine

On the way home to Castleboyne, I kept having to shake off the sensation that there were two entities in the car with me. At times they were sitting together in the back seat, Mona with her rubbery, misshapen face, Traynor with his blood-smeared grin and empty eye sockets; then I would imagine the presence of one or the other in the darkness right beside me, and I feared that the lights of an oncoming vehicle would reveal one of them actually sitting there.

So when the phone rang and I heard my mother at the other end, I was so relieved that I pulled in on the side of the road and let her rattle on without interruption about all she had done during the day, the people she had met while shopping, the gossip she had heard, and what present she was thinking of buying her grandson for Christmas.

'... What do *you* think?'

I realised I had not been concentrating on what she was saying, but finding comfort purely in the sound of her voice.

'Are you there, Illaun?'

'Yes, Mum. The reception went bad there for a second. What was it you were thinking of giving Eoin?'

'A pop-up tent. He can play with it in the house as well as the garden.'

'I'm sure he'd love that. But maybe check with Greta in case he has one already.'

'I'll do that. And I'd like to leave decorating the tree until he comes; I'm sure he'd enjoy that.'

'Yes, I'm sure he would.'

'And you know that Richard really wants your dad to be here at Christmas, even if it's only for the day.' She had tacked it onto the list so that it sounded like an afterthought; but that was part of her strategy.

'Yes, Mum. But it's not going to happen, you know that.'

'I feel so bad about it, Illaun.' Her voice was quivering. 'It was always Paddy's favourite time of year ...'

'We've been through it all a hundred times. I'll talk to Richard, OK?'

She sniffed. 'All right, dear. I really rang to ask if you had eaten. I've got some pork fillet left over. I could have dinner ready for you when you get in.'

I'd had roast meat already today, thanks. And my stomach was still in turmoil after what I'd seen. 'Leave it in the fridge, if you don't mind. I may have it later.'

'How was work?' My mother was homing in on the fact that my appetite vanishes when things are not going well.

'That's not the reason. I had a pretty solid lunch today.'

'That's all? Are you sure?'

The presences were materialising again. She had banished them; now she was summoning them up.

'Oh, Mum. Just leave it alone, please.'

'All right, dear. No need to snap at me.'

'I'm sorry. Have to go now – see you later.'

I switched the phone to silent, turned on the radio and started to pull out onto the road. To the accompaniment of 'The Ride of the Valkyries' blaring from the speakers, a huge figure loomed out of the trees and hurtled towards the car. I nearly swerved into the ditch to avoid it, but I realised just in time that it was only the shadow of a telephone pole cast by the headlights of a truck coming around a nearby bend. My heart was thundering. I jabbed the volume control and cut the radio.

Illaun, get a hold of yourself.

This was not like me. As well as being spooked by

shadows, I was allowing my mind to entertain some outlandish notions: that Mona had taken revenge on Traynor for disturbing her place of rest, for example, or that she was settling the score for the crime done to her.

But these thoughts seemed no more ridiculous than suggesting that Malcolm Sherry or I had killed Traynor. And that was a reasonable conclusion to draw, since we were the only living beings who knew just what injuries had been inflicted, centuries before, on the body in the bog. Unless Sherry was right and someone else had visited the morgue with Traynor.

Or unless ... I knew the idea was crazy, but I had to consider it. Unless we had completely misread Mona's age, and she had actually been murdered and dumped in the field in recent times. Which meant there was a serial killer on the loose. My fingernails dug into my thumbs as I gripped the steering-wheel more tightly. No, that wasn't possible. It relied on too many improbabilities.

In the end, wasn't it far more likely that Traynor had been killed over some business deal that went sour? Maybe his latest hotel venture had attracted the attention of a criminal gang and he had rejected their demand for a share of the profits.

Would the nuns, who themselves had stood to profit from the hotel, have been aware of any approaches made to Traynor? That would be worth looking into. There was even an outside chance that they still had a say in the fate of Monashee. I was also interested in what kind of rights they could have passed on with their land, and if this had implications for other parts of the Boyne valley.

My mind was in a labyrinth, racing up one cul-de-sac after another. I was sure Malcolm Sherry, conducting another post-mortem as I drove, was wrestling with the puzzle too, trying to explain to himself how the body on the autopsy table could have the same wounds he had pointed out to me earlier in the day.

I needed a change of subject. I reached into the glove compartment and took out an Emmylou Harris CD, *At the Ryman*. I slipped it into the player and turned up the volume. Country music was my secret vice, a love that dared not speak its name. I wasn't ashamed of it, but I had grown tired of people not just sneering at my taste, but treating me as if I had a social disease: 'So you're a country-music fan, eh? Don't worry, there *is* help available.'

I was nearly home and harmonising with 'Cattle Call' at the top of my voice when I noticed my phone was flashing. Flipping it open, I made out Finian's name. At the same time my headlights hit an opaque wall of fog.

I slowed down, switched off the music and held the phone to my ear.

'Are you all right, Illaun? I've just seen it on the TV news – the murder near Newgrange. They said a man's body had been found. Do you know who it is?'

'Yes,' I said wearily. 'A businessman named Frank Traynor. The one who was going to build the hotel there.'

'You didn't do it, did you?'

'Oh, Finian, don't joke about it. I saw the body, and it was pretty horrific. And what's really strange ...' I was steering with one hand, phone held illegally in the other, and the fog was making driving difficult. 'Look, I'll call you when I get in. And here's a question you can be mulling over: what kind of property rights could an abbey or convent have held since Norman times that would take precedence over modern planning laws?' I pressed the End key, no doubt leaving Finian with ammunition for some jibe about the bewildering speed with which women's brains jump from one thing to the next.

I drove into a Castleboyne enveloped in river fog, in which softly glowing street decorations, detached from their moorings, seemed to be floating.

Boo was on the rug, lying on his back in a dead-cartoon-cat pose: front paws bent and hanging in the air, hind legs akimbo, his expansive angora-wool belly on full display. I knelt down to tickle his tummy, and he promptly stood up and walked away with an indignant flick of his tail. Cats are great levellers. Just when you think you've learned their language, they tell you there's another meta-level to be reached and that, at the rate you're going, you're unlikely to attain it.

Maybe that's why more people like dogs – they never spurn us. And right now Horatio was what I needed. But he was in the extension with my mother, and I couldn't face an inquisition about my appetite.

I thought a shower would help. I went into the bedroom and saw on my locker the bunched-up scrap of yellow paper I had found under the bed that morning. Pulling it apart again, I saw my father's scrawled handwriting: 'ILLAUN'S ROOM'.

So simple, yet so difficult for him at the time; eventually impossible. I sat on the bed and burst out crying.

I cried for my dad, and for my mother, who hadn't deserved to end up with her funny, brilliant, gentle life's companion inhabiting the limbo of Alzheimer's disease. I wept for Mona, so callously maimed and slaughtered, and I mourned for a man whom I had had every reason to dislike but who, whatever his faults, had not earned such a shockingly brutal end to his life.

Tears still staining my cheeks, I raised my face to the showerhead and let the water mingle with them. After standing under the hot stream for ten minutes, I felt better. I stepped out to hear the phone ringing in the hall; without haste, I went to it and lifted the handset.

'Hello?'

'Are you sure you're OK?' It was Finian.

'Yes, I'm –' A leftover sob came surging up from deep down and took my breath away. 'Yes, I'm fine.' Then I remembered I had been meant to call him.

'You're not at all fine, Illaun. Do you want me to drop by? Take you out for a drink?'

'No, thanks. I just need to chill out here for a little while and get to bed early. Sorry I didn't call when I got in. I just completely forgot.'

'And did you also forget what you asked me to think about?'

'Eh …' I certainly had. *If only your memory was equal to your imagination.*

'Frankalmoign.'

'Come again?'

'Frankalmoign. Norman French for "free alms" or something along those lines.'

'What are you talking about?'

'Ancient rights, monasteries, convents, ecclesiastical property … remember? My, your brain can switch from max to min in a very short space of time.'

It came rushing back. What Seamus Crean had said about Grange Abbey. 'But what's frankalmoign?'

'It's a feudal term. It means property and privileges granted to the Church by the local lord in exchange for certain services, usually prayers for him and his family. Have you a particular case in mind?'

'Yes, Grange Abbey – the nuns who sold Monashee to Frank Traynor. They're some kind of nursing order.'

'Catholic nuns?'

'As far as I know, yes. "Came in with the Normans," to quote my source.'

'Then they've been here since the twelfth century.

Hard to know how they could have held out since then, considering they'd have been under pressure from both sides.'

'Both sides? How do you mean?'

'Well, on the Catholic side you'd have to sidestep something called *Periculoso*. It was a canon law decree issued by Pope Boniface in 1298, making it practically impossible for women religious to be in anything other than a completely enclosed environment. It wasn't until the nineteenth century that they were allowed out again; that's why most orders of nuns we're familiar with date from then. On the other hand, cloistered or not, you'd have to survive the dissolution of the monasteries under Henry VIII, then Cromwell's property confiscations and finally the Penal Laws against Catholics. That's some obstacle course.'

'Well, obviously this lot managed it.'

'Maybe they were just lucky.'

'I doubt it, Finian. I think they were tolerated for some reason, all the way from the time of the Normans until now.'

'Hmm ... Maybe the fact that the nuns were of English origin kept them protected, to a degree, when the Reformation began to kick in. Even if they were Catholic, at least they weren't the uncivilised, rebellious Irish. What's the order called, by the way?'

'Dunno ...' I pulled the handset away from my mouth and yawned. 'Question for you. Does frankalmoign still have legal standing?'

'Um … not sure. According to what I've just been reading, it disappeared from English law in 1925. But I guess it had become an irrelevant concept here long before then.'

'Why so?'

'Because nearly all Catholic ecclesiastical property had been confiscated by the middle of the eighteenth century, and the Protestant aristocracy didn't patronise monasteries and the like. That doesn't mean that frankalmoign won't pop up in property deeds from time to time, as it may have in this case. But, apart from the property itself, I'd imagine that Grange Abbey could hardly sell on whatever rights or privileges they'd gained in return for services rendered.'

'Fascinating, Finian. But I'm afraid that there we'll have to end our chat. I'm whacked.' A wave of almost aching tiredness had overwhelmed me.

We said good night and I wobbled unsteadily to the bedroom. As I drifted off to sleep, my last thoughts turned to what kind of services the Grange Abbey nuns might have rendered, for which they had received over eight hundred years of undisturbed tenure. Prayers for the dead? It seemed like a very good deal.

In the darkness there was nothing to see, only sensation: something poking me in the side of my stomach; two paws steadily kneading me in turn. And a noise: purring.

'Ah, dammit, Boo, go to sleep, will you?' I whined.

He had hidden somewhere in the room before I went to bed; I would inevitably have to get up and scoot him out. But for once, maybe, he would settle down … I dozed off again.

Some time later – an hour, two hours, it was hard to judge – I woke again. I listened for the sound of purring, waited for the soft punch of his paws, his tiny mew, even the heavy thump as he threw himself sidelong against the bedroom door. Nothing. Boo was asleep. What had woken me?

Horatio barked. And I knew it wasn't the first time. If this continued, I would have to get out of bed and shut him up; but I was so tired that I waited, hoping his mood would pass.

The dog barked again, the sound piercing my skull like a piece of shrapnel. 'Bloody hell,' I muttered, and rolled out from under the duvet. I padded down the hall to the utility room, where I slipped on a pair of bright-red rubber gardening clogs and threw on an old green fleece that was hanging there. I could hear Horatio snuffling at the door on my mother's side. When I let him through, he didn't greet me, just aimed himself at the patio door and waited to be released, his body rigid with anticipation. At least I knew we didn't have an intruder *inside* the house.

'Something out there, boy?' I whispered, trying to convince myself it was a fox or a rabbit. He was agitatedly scraping the patio door, but I was nervous about opening it, and I couldn't see out through the frosted-glass window. The alternative was to go into the living room and draw back the curtains on the sliding glass doors that also opened onto the patio; but that would have made me feel more vulnerable, somehow. Horatio was whining now, tearing at the door with his paws.

The door was locked and bolted and had a chain, which was dangling from the jamb. I slipped the chain into its catch and unbolted the door. Taking a deep breath, I turned the Yale lock, with the intention of opening the door just wide enough to peek through; but this made the dog even more frantic. Suddenly he forced the door open and rocketed out through the gap, growling into the dark.

Caught by the chain, the door swung back almost closed. I put my ear against it, expecting to hear snarls and screams as Horatio made contact with his quarry. But there was no sound.

I switched on the patio light from inside and opened the door as far as the chain would allow. Dense fog obscured the garden, the light penetrating only a few metres across the tiled patio. On the very edge of visibility I could make out Horatio, crouched on the terracotta tiles. He was facing out but creeping backwards, head to one side and looking up, ears flat against his head, teeth bared, the hairs on his neck spiking. And, instead of growling or snarling, he was wheezing strangely. Was he hurt?

Above him was a figure in a stained white robe or

overalls of some kind, slowly receding into the fog. I blinked the sleep from my eyes. I couldn't make out a face; it was veiled.

The figure disappeared.

Horatio turned back in retreat, silently wagging his tail. It was not he who had been wheezing.

I let the dog in, slammed the door shut and shakily jiggled the bolt into place as late-arriving adrenaline set my heart pounding. Keeping my shoulder pressed to the door, I tried to make sense of what I'd seen. The apparition in the fog had been wearing a hat with a veil hanging from the front. White overalls. White hat and veil.

My nocturnal visitor seemed to have been wearing a beekeeper's protective clothing. A beekeeper. In midwinter.

December 18th

Chapter Ten

It was Saturday morning. I knew because I could hear my mother in the kitchen preparing breakfast; it was the one morning of the week when we ate together. The events of the previous day started to re-run in my brain like an old newsreel, culminating in the scene in the fogbound garden. I sat up in delayed shock. How had I been able to get back to sleep after that? I hadn't even bothered to call the Gardaí – and I was the very one who would yell at stupid people in suspense movies when they refused to take the most basic precautions. I reckoned that my depleted coping system had simply switched off so it could recharge overnight.

'Illaun? Are you awake? It's ten o'clock.'

'Mmm … getting up now.' I slid back under the duvet, rolled it around me and tried to catch the 10 am flight back to Dreamland.

'Illaun!' I awoke again, nerves a-jangle. That voice could drill through kilometre-thick lead. 'Breakfast's ready. Up you get.'

'I'm up, I'm up.' *Please don't call out my name again.*

I unrolled from the duvet and found myself staring up at a pair of eyes as yellow and round as lemon slices. Boo was perched on my pillow, gazing down at me. 'Hiya, Boo Radley. Have a good night's sleep?'

The cat blinked. I blinked back. Well-informed cat owners do that kind of thing. It's meant to help inter-species communication. Sometimes I get the feeling they're just indulging our weird behaviour.

Boo came with me towards the kitchen but slipped out through the cat-flap as we passed the door to the patio. I paused, unlocked the door and looked out. The fog had cleared. The patio tiles were greasy, the drooping shrubs and flower-stalks in the garden dripping; all the trees were bare, apart from a single Cordyline palm. I shook off my slippers and stepped into the red clogs. Late-fallen leaves were slick underfoot as I crossed to where the figure had stood. There were no footprints on the wet tiles. Surrounding the patio and the raised beds was a scree of decorative gravel – no hope of prints in that. But anyone who came into the garden from the front of the house had to walk across a grassy boundary.

I clopped to the end of the patio and examined the patch of lawn that rose gently from the edge of the gravel and sloped down, along the side of the house, to the cobble-lock driveway. The grass was wet, the earth beneath it no doubt saturated – and slippery, it seemed. I could see a number of places where someone's footwear had failed to grip and they had slid on the grass, crushing the blades and gouging out some of the soil beneath. It was hard to make out if the footprints had been made on entering or leaving, except that they led straight in the direction of my car, parked in the driveway.

Pulling my dressing-gown tighter against the cold, I started up the short slope, the grooved soles of my rubber clogs finding purchase with no difficulty. Standing on the crest of the grass, I could see the damage. The passenger window of the Jazz had been smashed in. There were some shards of glass on the cobbles; the remainder I saw strewn over the seats when I looked in. The radio and CD player were intact, no wires hung from the ignition, the glove compartment was closed. Nothing had been taken and no further damage done, as far as I could see. I checked on my mother's red Ford Ka, which was parked around the corner, near the front door: the windows were all intact, the doors locked.

I called Castleboyne Garda station from the phone

in the hall and reported the incident. The officer on duty said that youths on a drunken spree had broken into several cars on the outskirts of the town, and that mine had probably been another of their targets. According to him, my ghostly visitor had been all too human, probably wearing a hoodie, and the fog had played tricks with my vision.

My mother was sitting at the kitchen table, a newspaper open beside her breakfast things. 'What were you doing out in the garden, love?' she said, looking over her reading glasses at me while simultaneously managing to pour tea from a green teapot into my cup. I could tell she had been at Snips the day before; her greying brown hair was in that tight perm hairdressers insist on giving to all women over sixty.

'Someone broke into the car last night.'

She set down the pot and clutched at the pink blouse she was wearing under a dark-blue cardigan dotted with red sequins. 'Lord save us, Illaun. What were they looking for?'

'Oh, the usual, I guess – CD player, radio. But they didn't get anything. Horatio heard them and woke me up just in time.'

She smiled. 'Paddy always maintained he was a great watchdog.' Then her expression became one of concern. 'You didn't go after them, did you?'

'No, I just heard them running off,' I lied. 'I didn't think they'd broken into it until I went out just now.'

'Have you told the Gardaí?'

'Yes. They said there were several cars broken into around here last night. People leave gifts on the back seat at this time of year.'

'Well, thank God they got nothing of value from yours. Now, the best thing is to forget about it and have some breakfast. I've got some lovely bread for you, and that nice salami from Yore's.'

My mother spent a year in Germany and Austria in the 50s, after her Leaving Certificate exam. Whatever about the small amount of German she picked up, the experience formed her breakfast habits, and we had been brought up accordingly: pickles, wurst, cheese and rye bread were always on the table in the morning, even at a time when some of these items could only be bought at Magill's delicatessen in Dublin, usually by my father at weekends. As a treat he'd occasionally bring home bratwurst, which we fried with eggs or ate cold with potato salad. And there was always my mother's crab-apple jelly, which she flavoured with cloves. That was all I wanted now; but, to show my appreciation, I spread some Hellman's Light onto a piece of bread, slapped a slice of salami onto it and began to chew.

'Will you listen to this article,' she said in an outraged tone; and then, quoting: '"Christmas is yet another pagan feast about which the Church kept you in the dark."' She rattled the newspaper and looked at me fiercely over her glasses. 'That's nonsense. We learned it in the Liturgical Catechism at school fifty years ago. I can remember the exact words: "Why was the twenty-fifth of December chosen for the feast? Answer: To counteract and destroy the influence of the pagan festival of the Unconquered Sun, the period of the winter solstice." That's open and honest, isn't it?'

I mumbled agreement and kept eating. My mother was vigilant about this kind of thing. And there was no doubt that the pagan roots of Christian festivals were gleefully recycled in the media at Halloween and Christmas, but I wasn't in the mood to discuss it.

And then it hit me. The card found under Traynor's body – the greeting on it. *The Peace of Earth, Air and Water be with you, and may the returning Sun rekindle all your hopes this Midwinter.* It had more to do with the winter solstice than with Christmas Day; it was inspired more by Newgrange than by Bethlehem.

My mother had returned to the article, reading out lines here and there and muttering darkly about the media's role in undermining Catholicism in Ireland. As I half listened I wondered whether there was some other religious significance in the choice of the two callously ironic messages on the card.

Thus are the Concupiscent punished. Both had a religious ring to them, but the contrast couldn't be more stark – one was a bland New Age platitude, the other like a sentence handed down by the Inquisition. And why did '*Concupiscenti*' have a capital 'C'? A slip of the keyboard, or a proper noun? If it wasn't a mistake, then the 'Concupiscenti' had to be a recognised group, an organisation even.

'Did your catechism have anything to say about concupiscence? And before you ask why I want to know, I'm not telling.'

'I'm sure I don't want to know. And it wouldn't have been in the Liturgical Catechism anyway. But I do remember it from Christian Doctrine class. There were two kinds, I recall – concupiscence of the eyes and concupiscence of the flesh. Concupiscence of the eyes is the inordinate desire to accumulate material possessions.'

Was I hearing the definition of Traynor's offence? 'And the other?'

'Concupiscence of the flesh is when sensual pleasure is desired as an end in itself.'

'Hmm …' If philandering had been his crime, he had paid an outlandishly heavy penalty.

'Both sins, of course. Though not many people believe they are nowadays.' My mother sighed and removed her glasses, letting them hang from their chain onto her chest, and folded away the newspaper. 'On a different subject, I spoke to Greta last night, as you suggested – about the tent for Eoin.'

'Oh, yeah? Well?' I drank some tea. It was at that ideal temperature, too hot if you gulped it but perfect to sip.

'She said he'd love it. Oh, by the way, they're off to Boston first thing this morning to visit Greta's family for a few days. Then they'll be on their way here.'

'Mm-hmm.' I got the message: *Call your brother about that other issue.*

The thought of ringing Richard didn't appeal to me in the least, so I let my mind wander. Who or what had been out on the patio, and was it the same presence that had been lurking in the doorway of the old morgue? Why would someone dress up like that? Maybe the fog *had* played tricks with my vision. What was the point of breaking the car window but taking nothing? Intimidation. perhaps? I recalled Sherry's warning.

'… the phone last night …' My mother was back on our conversation the night before.

The mental equivalent of a shrill smoke alarm went off inside my head. 'Blast – my phone. Excuse me.'

I left the table and ran into the bedroom. The bathroom. Back into the hall. Finian had rung the land line, I recalled. I went out to the car again. My mobile was not on the seat, where I remembered I had left it. I checked to see if it had slipped underneath, but I already knew it wouldn't be there.

It was maddening, but in a way I was also relieved. The theft made it easier to believe that a marauding gang had included me in their seasonal shopping spree.

Peggy didn't work weekends, so I sat at her tidy desk in preference to my own, which was cluttered with spiral-bound survey reports, County Council and NRA documents, digital and Polaroid photographs, printed e-mails and internet downloads – my desk hadn't heard the news about the paperless office.

First I dialled my stolen phone to see if the thief wanted me to pay a ransom for its return. It rang a few times and then my voicemail message came on, which meant that it hadn't been powered off but also that whoever had it wasn't negotiating. Next I rang my service provider to disable my phone. Then I rang a local garage, to be told they would have to order the replacement window and would have it at midday on Monday at the earliest.

After that I checked my e-mails and found one sent the previous evening by Keelan O'Rourke, with an inventory of what he and Gayle had found in the peat matrix. There were no surprises, no jewellery or beads or scraps of clothing, nothing apart from the leather strip; but the preserved matrix might yield more in time. I forwarded their report to Ivers at WET, adding a summary of what I had learned about Mona and recommending that further inquiry into the circumstances of her death be carried out, since to my knowledge she was the first certain victim of ritual execution to have been recovered from an Irish bog. And, in case Ivers hadn't heard, I added a P.S. informing him of Traynor's murder. It would probably be Monday before Ivers saw his mail, but, irrespective of whether the injunction was lifted or not, I assumed that all parties would cease work at Monashee over the weekend: ironically, it was now an official crime scene.

Then I rang Brookfield Farm and got Finian in the middle of a late breakfast. 'I'll call you back,' I said.

'No, come around; I've something to show you. I think you'll be very interested.'

'I'll be there in an hour or so; I have a few more things to do.' I put down the phone, lifted it again and dialled a long-distance number. This was the call I had been putting off, pretending that it was because of the time difference and that I would be calling my brother too early – it was coming up to 7 am in Chicago; but, knowing him and Greta, they were probably booked on an early flight from O'Hare Airport to Boston and would be up and about their apartment.

Richard is a paediatrician who specialises in keeping premature babies alive; the earlier the 'premmie', the greater the challenge and the more satisfaction he derives from his job when he succeeds. It had struck me of late that he was approaching our father's case in much the same way, except the challenge here was arresting a mature adult's regression to an infantile state.

Greta answered and, after we had exchanged pleasantries, handed me over to my brother.

'Hiya, big sister. What can I do for you at this hour of the morning?'

'Mum was telling me you were hoping Dad could join us on Christmas Day. The thing is –'

'Just for a few hours, I said. I can't imagine Christmas without him. I'm sure you can't either.'

Stop trying to manipulate me. 'It's not possible, Richard.'

'Of course it's possible. He's not *dead*, Illaun.'

I resisted the urge to say something I would regret later. 'I know it's hard for you to accept, but his condition has worsened to the point where he's ... beyond us.'

'You mean mentally?'

'And physically too.'

'So he's doubly incontinent, is that it? Surely we can cope with that for a day? He wiped our arses when we were kids, and when he brought me to the bathroom to pee, he used to aim my willie at the pan. Surely I can do the same for him now.'

This was more difficult than I had thought it would be. It was ultimately selfish of Richard to want our father at home for Christmas. He wanted a picture-perfect scene that morning – carols on the radio, everyone opening presents with the Christmas tree in the background, his son climbing on Granddad's knee, Grandma in the kitchen cooking the turkey.

'It's not that at all. It's that he's ...' I thought for some reason of Mona's decalcified body. '... He's just a shell. It wouldn't be Dad you'd have at Christmas, but a stranger who'd stolen his clothes and looked vaguely like him.' There was silence at the other end. That had been the left jab; time for the knockout blow, though delivering it would give me no pleasure whatsoever. 'And then you'd have the disruptive behaviour. Can you imagine how Eoin, a three-year-old kid, would respond to seeing this weird guy jump up and roar at the top of his voice – or, worse still, wandering into a room and finding him masturbating?' I had my eyes squeezed shut, but I could feel the tears escaping and wetting my lashes.

'I think you're being extreme, Illaun.'

'Oh, please, Richard. Do you think I'd exaggerate something like this?' I could hear Greta in the background calling him.

'Listen, gotta go,' he said. 'And will you do something about that damned dog?'

'Horatio?' I said deliberately. He could at least give the animal its name.

'Yeah, Horatio. And where Dad is concerned, we can talk about it when we get over there. Maybe some extra medication will do the trick on the day.'

I held the phone out and looked at it as the click of disconnection sounded distantly. What a waste of time that had been. And I would have to do it all over again. I slammed down the phone and swore at my brother for his unwillingness to face the truth.

I was on the point of leaving the office when the phone rang. Thinking it might be Richard ringing back, I hesitated; then I picked up, ready to do battle again.

'Couldn't get you on your mobile,' said a male voice. Not Richard's; Malcolm Sherry's.

'Hi, Malcolm. It's been stolen, I'm afraid.'

'Bad luck. Anyway, I'm ringing you from Drogheda. The Gardaí are questioning Seamus Crean about Traynor's murder.'

'Seamus? That's ridiculous! No way would he have killed Traynor.'

'He had reason to dislike him.'

I saw Crean and myself standing in the street, observing Traynor. Me dashing Crean's hopes of employment. Traynor the cause.

'Oh, come on, Malcolm. So did I. So did a hundred others, I'll bet.'

'There's also the question of how the bog body's injuries came to be inflicted on the victim. Crean had ample time to examine the remains last Thursday before anyone else arrived.'

'But she was packed inside half a ton of wet turf.'

'He could have dug out some of the soil around her head and then replaced it.'

'But why would he inflict the same wounds on Traynor?'

'Maybe, in Crean's mind, death in itself wasn't sufficient punishment for what this man had done to him.'

'He'd only been fired from casual employment; it wasn't the end of the world.' As soon as I said it, I knew it was a weak argument. It obviously had been a big issue for Seamus Crean. I was a witness to the fact that he had been in St Peter's Church praying for a job.

'And there's something of a pointer in the card left with the body, the sprig of holly stuffed in the mouth – payback for firing him at Christmastime.'

I didn't think Seamus capable of a theatrical flourish like that, but I let it pass. There was something far more unlikely. 'The Christmas card was written in Latin, for God's sake.'

'I had a problem with that too, I must confess. But, according to the detective I've spoken to, it seems Crean's mother is an old-style Catholic and a devotee of the Latin Mass.'

'So she writes a murder note in Latin for her son. Are they seriously suggesting that?'

I hoped Sherry was squirming.

'They think it's more likely he just found it at home and used it without knowing what it meant.'

'But … oh, forget it.' What was the point of arguing over such an absurd idea? 'Have they found the murder weapon yet?'

'Not so far. No sign of blood-stained clothing at the scene or in Crean's house, either. Nothing to link him directly with the killing. But Forensics have lifted plenty of prints, and they'll be checking them against his.'

'But they've only taken him in for questioning at this stage?'

'Yes. He's been detained under Section 4 of the Criminal Justice Act, which gives them up to twelve hours before charging or releasing him. But they can always have that extended.'

'Thanks for the call, Malcolm. I just wish I could do something for him.'

'No doubt the Gardaí will be in touch with you. I'd leave well enough alone until then. And, by the way, I've had the bog specimens put into cold storage here until we hear from whoever's taking charge of them. I'll be talking to you about the X-rays next week.'

I put down the phone and reflected on the series of events that had occurred since Mona had been unearthed. A more superstitious soul than I would already have formed the opinion that some kind of malevolent force had been released along with her.

Chapter Eleven

When Bess came padding around the side of a red-brick outhouse to greet my car, I knew Finian was working somewhere nearby, probably in one of the greenhouses. We went in search of him together. I watched, amused, as a flock of starlings crowded into a birdbath and energetically whirred their wings, spraying water over their backs and out onto the frosted garden, the drops falling like shards of glass through a shaft of afternoon light. I guessed Finian had poured hot water into it to melt the ice for them. Further on, a blackbird was turning over some old leaves at the edge of a still-frozen fishpond, occasionally venturing out onto the ice to approach the vegetation from a different angle. Above him, greenfinches and coal tits were clinging to a basket of peanuts hanging from a branch.

I strolled past the gable ends of the first three greenhouses with Bess for company; as we neared the fourth, she shot through a partially open door. I followed, closing it behind me. 'What's the point if you don't close the door?' I shouted, knowing Finian was not far away.

'Makes little difference when this happens,' a voice said from behind some shrubs over-wintering in tall terracotta pots.

Finian was on a stepladder, fitting a pane of glass into one of the overhead frames. He was wearing gardener's standard-issue clothing – checked Viyella shirt, padded green body-warmer and tan cords. He seemed as much a part of the place as the plants, the sunlight, the chlorophyll-scented air; he is one of those people who inhabit the Earth with the confidence of a native, making the rest of us look like apprehensive visitors.

'Just replacing a broken one,' he said, smoothing putty around the edges of the frame with a small trowel. 'It fell in last night, in the early hours of the morning …' He studied his handiwork for a moment. 'Needs a tiny bit more just here; could you pass me up that, please?' He pointed to a plastic tub on a potting bench.

'How do you know?' I asked, handing him the tub.

'That I need more of this?'

'No! That your glass got broken early this morning.'

'I heard it from the bedroom as I was about to turn off the light. Around one or so.' He dug out a small portion of putty with the corner of the trowel and handed me back the tub.

'Funny. I had my car window bashed in at about the same time.'

'Were they trying to steal it – the car, I mean?' He applied the putty to a corner of the frame, then pressed it in further with his thumb.

'I don't think so. They got my phone, though.'

'That's a nuisance. And I thought stealing mobile phones was a thing of the past now that the service providers can disable the handsets.'

'That's a point. And what I saw last night was pretty strange anyway.' I described the scene out on the patio, including Horatio's behaviour.

Finian stopped what he was doing and looked down at me, his face full of concern. 'That must have been very frightening. Who the hell could it have been? What was he up to?'

'I don't know. But I'd seen someone in white outside the morgue in Drogheda earlier in the night, when we came back from the scene of Traynor's murder.'

Finian backed down the ladder, laid the trowel on the bench and wiped his hands on a cloth. Just there, just then, in the greenhouse with the man-smell of putty from his hands, I wanted him to hold me.

'Seeing someone who'd been murdered must have been a dreadful experience,' he said. 'Is it possible that it had more of an effect on you than you realised? Was what you saw partly your imagination?'

Once again I considered the possibility. My famous imagination does not run to hallucinations, but it does do exaggeration, on occasion. The misshapen figure at the morgue could have been the play of light and shadow. 'I didn't imagine the person on the patio, obviously,' I said. 'But the beekeeper suit … I don't know; maybe. The fog didn't help. It was scary, though.'

Finian reached out and brushed back a curl from my cheek. 'You've been having a bad time, my love. Let's try to banish it. How about some mulled wine?'

'I'd like a hug first.'

'Of course. How stupid of me.' He put his arms around me, and I melted into him for what seemed like ages.

'I can't be drinking wine at this hour of the day,' I said eventually, smiling up at him.

'Oh, come on, it's Christmas!' He hooked his arm through mine and marched me from the greenhouse while Bess, wondering what the excitement was, leaped and barked around us.

Finian picked up a photocopied newspaper article from several he had laid out on the table. I could tell from the layout and the absence of photographs that they were from the nineteenth or early twentieth century. '*Voilà!*' he said, handing it to me. 'I'll go heat up the mulled wine. You read these, starting with this one.'

He left me alone, and I started to read the article he had tinted with a green highlighter. It was from a weekly paper, the *Meath Chronicle*, dated February 1898.

STRANGE OCCURRENCE AT NEWGRANGE

A body believed to be of great antiquity was found floating in the Boyne near Drogheda last week. The find was made by a pair of fishermen casting for salmon at a weir downstream from Newgrange. Having hauled in the ebony-skinned corpse, the men, noticing it had been severely maimed, alerted the constabulary at nearby Donore, who in turn notified Dr Wyatt, also of that village. The medical practitioner allayed fears of foul play by declaring the body to be of great antiquity, surmising that it had been loosened from a marshy field in the townland of Monashee by the recent flood-waters that have risen to unprecedented levels this winter and are only now receding. The Curator of Antiquities for County Meath, Mr Canty, was subsequently informed of the discovery, and the body, believed to be that of a male person, was removed by the police for inspection by his officials.

The next cutting was dated April of the same year. It was a letter to the editor of the *Chronicle* from a Rev. Mr Reginald Maunsell, a representative of the British-Israel Association, which, he explained, held that the 'Anglo-Saxon-Celtic peoples' were descended from the Ten Lost Tribes of the House of Israel. His letter began:

> *In these days when science disputes the irrefutable truths of the Bible (I refer to the late Mr Darwin et al.) it is unfortunate when an opportunity is lost to reinforce those eternal verities. Such an occasion was the recent discovery of the body of a Nubian slave in the River Boyne.*

He went on to explain that a Jewish Egyptian princess called Tea-Tephi had come to Ireland in 585BC, married the High King Eochaidh at Tara ('which should surprise none, for Druidism is a sort of halfway house between Sinai and Calvary') and, having 'planted the seed of David in these islands', eventually imported a gang of masons and slave workers from her native land to build her tomb on the banks of the Boyne, in imitation of the Nile pyramids. The body found floating in the Boyne, which was of 'Negroid appearance', must therefore have been that of a Nubian slave who had been working on the construction project.

151

So it was this reverend gentleman's letter that had given rise to the myth of the Newgrange Nubian, in all likelihood a dark-skinned bog body. Apart from the far-fetched theories, his chronology was completely skewed – the Newgrange passage tomb was built hundreds of years before the pyramids – and he also reflected the view, popular at the time, that the native population could not have done it by themselves, much in the way that aliens are invoked today to account for mysterious artefacts. But, however outlandish his views, the Reverend Maunsell had made a practical effort to track down the bog body, and a brief account of this attempt brought his letter to an intriguing conclusion.

I should add that, having travelled to the area in the past month in expectation of seeing the body for myself, I was disappointed in that hope. Rumour had it that the remains were spirited away by a nearby community of Roman Catholic nuns to be given a Christian burial, although when I inquired of the abbess if this were so she denied it, whether from reluctance to share the truth with a representative of the Reformed Church or to spare the community the attentions of antiquarians, I cannot say.

The similarity of the circumstances was striking: a mutilated body accidentally freed from Monashee, and the Grange Abbey nuns – for who else could the 'nearby community' have been? – entering the picture. It was becoming more urgent that I visit them.

Finian came in, bearing a tray with an antique silver punch bowl hung with several mugs. As he began to spoon out the steaming wine, its spicy aroma filled the room.

'Mmm …' I closed my eyes and breathed it in. 'Just the scent of it is enough.'

'Well, you can sit here just smelling it. It'll mean more wine for me.' He pretended to pour one of the mugfuls back into the bowl.

'No way. Hand it over.' I reached out for the mug, wrapped both hands around it and took a sip. It was delicious.

'These clippings are fascinating,' I said. 'How did you manage to track them down?'

'When I heard my father mention pyramids and Nubians, it struck me that there might be a connection with the British Israelites. They carried out a dig at Tara around 1900, looking for the Ark of the Covenant.'

'Found little or nothing, as I recall.'

'But stirred up lots of what we'd now call "media coverage" about the Bible, Egypt and so on. So I asked my father what age his own father might have been when he heard the story, and we narrowed it down to a few years either side of the turn of the century. I drove over to the *Meath Chronicle* office in Navan yesterday for a rummage in their microfiche archives. I worked backwards from 1902 and found Maunsell's letter after about an hour.'

'Did you show it to Arthur?' Finian's father was in another room, watching horse-racing on TV.

'I did. But he thought I was talking about Noah's Ark, which he said could certainly have sailed up the Boyne before – you guessed it – the bastards meddled with the river.'

'Don't be so smug. The idea of either of the Arks turning up in Ireland is no more bizarre than some of the recent theories about Newgrange I've been reading up on for this interview.'

'Like what?'

'How about the one that suggests Newgrange was built during a mini-Ice Age, as a conduit for the heat of the sun to warm the Earth?'

'Pass.'

'That Newgrange, Knowth and Dowth are sited over geological faults that produce magnetic emanations?'

'New Age wishful thinking.'

'That the mounds are early prototypes designed by people who then travelled to Egypt and South America and built the stone structures there?'

'Reverend Maunsell in reverse. I'll grant it the same level of credibility.'

'There are one or two I find intriguing, though.'

'Such as?'

'That some of the circular patterns inscribed on the stones represent sound waves, for example.'

'How would Neolithic people know what sound waves looked like?'

'The unusual acoustic properties in the chamber can set up a series of wave pulses that become visible in certain lighting conditions, when you get mist or smoke being penetrated by the sun's rays. Add in another theory that the solstice light was reflected back out of the chamber and bounced off the river below, and you've got the makings of a megalithic sound-and-light show.'

Finian chuckled. 'So you had genuine *rock* concerts thousands of years before U2 played at Slane Castle. Which reminds me – you're not the first of your family to have a fine voice. I came across this while looking for the Nubian.' He handed me another photocopied article, which had been set aside from the others. It was dated November 1898.

BALL IN CASTLEBOYNE

A very successful ball was held in the Courthouse, Castleboyne, on Monday evening last for the purpose of raising funds for the purchase of coals and provisions for the poor of the town at Christmas. The Castleboyne Amateur Musical Society worked energetically to ensure its success and provided an opening programme of vocal and instrumental music, the

*highlight of which was Mr Peter Hunt's rendition
of 'A Little Golden Ring' with violin accompaniment by Miss Marie Maguire.*

'There's only one family of Hunts in Castleboyne,' said
Finian.

'My mother's.'

'So I assume Peter Hunt is one of your ancestors.'

'Yes. I've seen his signature on books and sketches
at home. And we have an old violin that I think
belonged to him.' The instrument had come down
through the family, and my mother was its present
curator; but it spent all of its life in the attic, the wood
drying out, the horsehair of the bow fraying, the
strings disintegrating.

'Given the date, it would make him – what, your
grandfather?'

'No, my great-grandfather.' I continued reading the
article, which revealed that 'Mr Brittain's string band
gave universal satisfaction' and that the dancing was
kept up with 'unflagging zeal till the small hours of
the morning'. There were close to '40 couples'
present: the attendance was listed, ladies first, each
with her home town or village in brackets beside her
name. It was possible that Peter Hunt's accompanist,
Miss Maguire (Celbridge), had eventually become his
wife; distant cousins of mine still lived in the once-tiny
hamlet, thirty kilometres away in County Kildare. I
was possibly reading about the early stages of a

relationship between a couple from whom I was descended.

'Thanks, this is wonderful.'

'I like the fact that it's seasonal, too. Lets you know what your forebears were up to at this time of year.'

'Sounds so civilised, doesn't it? A fundraising ball, a programme of vocal and instrumental music – and look …' I read from the clipping: '"The candlelit hall was beautifully decorated with evergreens and golden drapery hung with ferns."' I looked up at Finian. 'Now, isn't that just the business?'

There must have been something wistful in my tone, which I hadn't intended, because he took my hand in his. 'You'd like to have lived back then, wouldn't you?'

I gave him a sharp look. 'And be listed as Miss Bowe, brackets, Castleboyne – accomplished at sketching and singing, obviously on the lookout for a man, and eventually to be saddled with seven children and a drunken husband into the bargain? I'd probably end up being the beneficiary of coals and provisions myself in no time. No, thanks.'

'Oops, sorry. I get the message.'

In my attempt to disabuse him of the notion, I had probably veered too far in the opposite direction; but something told me Finian didn't really believe me. 'While we're on the subject of Christmas decorations, talk to me about holly. Why do we use it – what does it symbolise?'

'That's not an idle question. Why are you asking?'

I told him about the holly in Traynor's mouth.

'Good grief. Sorry I asked. Now, let's see ... There's lots of lore attached to the holly tree – that it sprouted leaves to hide the Holy Family from Herod's soldiers and has been evergreen since then, that Christ's crown of thorns was woven from its branches and that the original white berries were turned scarlet by His blood. There are superstitions, too – it's meant to bring good luck to men, just as the ivy looks after women. Virgins hung it around their beds on Christmas Eve as protection against incubi ...'

There was nothing that I could connect with Traynor's murder.

'The early Christian Church didn't much like holly: it was used in the Roman festival of Saturnalia to ward off evil, and it was sacred to the Celtic druids, who linked it with the Sun God since it was particularly noticeable in the bare forest at this time of year. They also thought of the berries as the menstrual blood of the Goddess. Let me see ...'

I looked at my watch. I was hoping to do some of my Christmas shopping, and there was another carol practice after seven o'clock Mass.

'There's an English tradition of placing holly around beehives ...'

I thought I had misheard. 'Did you say *beehives*?'

'Beehives, yes. Because of the humming of the bees.'

'The humming?'

'Yes. It was believed that, on Christmas Eve, the

bees in their hives hummed in honour of Christ's birth. They were said to be obeying the first line of Psalm 100 – "Make a joyful noise unto the Lord."'

Finian had not made the connection with my experience the previous night. It gave me an eerie sensation for a moment or two, but I quickly dismissed it as mere coincidence.

'Which reminds me, that's what I'm meant to be doing shortly – making a joyful noise.'

When I left Brookfield I was feeling a lot more upbeat than I had been when I arrived. The wine accounted for some of it, but Finian's concern for me had added to my sense of well-being. Moreover, on a professional level, the documentary evidence of another bog body at Monashee was just what I needed to challenge Muriel Blunden's denial of the site's importance.

Chapter Twelve

After seven o'clock Mass, the choir stayed on for our carol practice. Gillian Delahunty was out with a head cold; replacing her on the organ was the bespectacled Sister Aloysius McNeill, a member of the Mercy Order, who had taught generations of Castleboyne schoolchildren. A handful of elderly Sisters, retired from teaching, their convent now a hotel, still lived in the town.

As we were putting away our hymn folders afterwards, I engaged Sister Aloysius in conversation and accompanied her down the stairs, which were just wide enough for the two of us to descend side by side.

'Fran wasn't with us tonight, I noticed.' They still liked to keep tabs on us.

'No. She's on night duty.'

'How is your father keeping? I still miss him on the television.'

'As well as can be expected under the circumstances, I suppose.'

'It's a cruel thing for anyone to have to suffer, but even worse for the likes of your father.'

'The loss of memory, you mean?'

This observation had been made so often, in one form or another, that it hardly registered with me any more. Behind it was the fact that many people felt they knew my father because of his role as a genial shop-keeper in a long-running drama series on television. It was this very notion of being public property that had made him decide to go back into theatre. And then one night, playing Vladimir in a production of *Waiting for Godot*, he had exclaimed, 'I can't remember my line!' and lapsed into silence. The audience took this to be part of the script until the curtain came down. And for P.V. Bowe it never rose again. No theatre company would take the risk.

'Yes, how sad,' she said. 'And here's the likes of me still on the go, apart from the usual aches and pains. It's hard to put a bad thing down, as they say.'

'You never seem to age at all, if you ask me.' My turn for a platitude. But it was true: apart from her shrunken veil, Sister Aloysius looked the same to me as she had when I was in her classroom in primary school, down to the Buddy Holly horn-rims and the perfect false teeth.

'Oh, go on out of that, Illaun,' she simpered.

As we reached a landing two men emerged from a storage room, carrying between them a life-size plaster statue. By the turban on his head, his dark features and the golden incense jar in his hands, I identified him as Balthasar, one of the three Magi, on his way to be installed in the crib. We let them go ahead of us; as they struggled past, Balthasar's kneeling posture made it seem for a moment as though he was hovering in mid-air and in need of no help from his handlers.

As we slowly followed them down, I seized the opportunity to quiz Sister Aloysius. 'I wonder, Sister, if you're familiar with a religious order I've been hearing about in the past few days. They have a retreat house called Grange Abbey.'

She paused, leaning on my arm for support as she searched her memory.

'Between Slane and Drogheda,' I added.

Sister Aloysius squeezed my arm. 'Ah, yes ...' We continued down the bare wooden stairs. 'Grange Abbey are Hospitallers – an old nursing order. Snooty, too. I think their mother house was in or near Dublin, but they're gone from there now. Not many of them left in Grange, either, I'd say.'

'No. I think they're selling up.'

'Like all of us, Illaun. That's the way it is now. They don't want us in education or in the hospitals.'

'What kind of hospitals were the Grange Abbey order involved in?'

We came to a halt again, the old nun looking at me suspiciously. 'It's not another of society's crimes being blamed on the religious yet again, is it?'

'No, Sister. It has mainly to do with getting an archaeological site preserved. And idle curiosity, I admit.'

We took the last few steps of the stairs and went out onto a tiled porch, as the men backed through the swing doors into the church and disappeared with their burden.

'Lying-in hospitals, they used to be called,' she said. 'Maternity homes, in other words. Except, in the case of the Hospitallers, it was the daughters of the rich they looked after.' Our breath was visible in the chill air that had invaded the porch; the door to the outside had been left ajar. Sister Aloysius gave me a cynical smile, unusual for her. 'Well-off Catholics who didn't want it known that their young one had given birth to an illegitimate child.'

'So what happened? The baby was given up for adoption?'

'Yes. The Hospitallers looked after that as well. I don't know how they managed to evade canon law on the other subject, but they did.'

'What do you mean, the other subject?'

'Nuns were always prohibited from becoming midwives or having anything directly to do with gynaecology. Other religious orders that took in girls when they began to "show" were only providing privacy; the births took place in regular maternity homes. I can only presume it was because of the Hospitallers' influence in high places that they were allowed to look after pregnant girls up to and including delivery.'

'Hmm … that's very interesting, Sister. Thank you.'

I walked home; I had decided against bringing the car, minus its window, and freezing myself solid. So now I knew what the nuns of Grange Abbey had devoted their lives to. And I assumed it was the reason why they had been granted their lands in the first place.

When I got home, there was a message flashing on the answering machine in the hall. An American-tinged Donegal accent identifying itself as Detective Inspector Matt Gallagher of Drogheda Garda station was anxious that I contact him by phone or call in person to the station as soon as possible.

But first I rang Finian. 'Remember we were talking about frankalmoign? I know what services Grange Abbey rendered in exchange for their property.' I told him what Sister Aloysius had said.

'Intriguing. Now are you happy?'

'What do you mean, am I happy?'

'You seem a bit obsessed with this Grange Abbey place. Isn't it time you gave it a rest?'

'You don't understand, Finian. If they're involved with the hotel development, then we may be able to persuade them to put it on hold until Monashee is properly investigated. It would save us having to go the legal route.'

'Then why not go and see them? Ask them yourself, in person.'

It was the final shove I needed. Plus, tomorrow was Sunday and I had no other commitments; I could visit the Abbey and then drive on to Drogheda Garda station.

Finian and I said good night, and I set about finding a number for Grange Abbey. Directory Inquiries said there was nothing listed under that name.

I decided to ring the number left by Detective Gallagher. The fact that he answered took me by surprise. I had intended to leave a message for him.

'You're the archaeologist brought in by Newgrange Visitor Centre to examine that woman's body?'

Strictly speaking, it had been WET who brought me in, but it wasn't worth disputing. 'That's right. Look, I –'

'I need to ask you some questions.'

'Yes, I know, but not now. I'll see you in person. How about tomorrow? I know it's Sunday, but I'll be in the area in the evening.'

'What time?'

How long would I be at the abbey if they agreed to meet me? 'Say between four and five.'

'Hmm ... I have to be in Slane at six, and I've arranged to see someone who works at Newgrange Visitor Centre on my way there. I guess I could call in a wee bit earlier, get that over and done with, and then meet you there as well. What do you say?'

'The Centre closes at five in the winter.'

'I'll bribe them to stay open for us, if necessary.'

'How will I –?'

'I'm a police detective, Miss Bowe. You'll have no trouble.' Was he being funny or serious?

'I'll try and get there around half-four. Just one thing: do you have a number for Grange Abbey? The nuns who sold the land to –'

'I know who they are. Why do you need to contact them?'

'I believe they're involved in the hotel development at Monashee, and I want to see if they'll give us the go-ahead for a survey before any more work is carried out.'

'I doubt if they have any say in it.'

'Have you spoken to them?'

'One of the team here telephoned them to say we'd be calling around at some stage, to interview whoever it was negotiated with Frank Traynor.'

'So you'd have the number on your database, then ...'

'A bit pushy, aren't you?'

'Don't mean to be, Inspector,' I said sweetly. 'But I'm sure you're anxious to get on with the investigation.'

Gallagher muttered something under his breath and

then read off a number. 'And I take it you know who to talk to?'

'Well, no, actually.'

'The abbess. Her name is Geraldine Campion. I'm told you should avoid Sister Roche, the bursar. Tough cookie, apparently.'

There was definitely a sense of humour lurking in there somewhere. 'If you say so, Inspector, I certainly will,' I said, hung up and dialled again.

'St Margaret's?' A cultivated voice, contralto-deep. Indefinable age.

For an instant I thought I had been given the wrong number, but that was evidently the proper name of the Abbey. 'I'd like to speak to the abbess, please. Er, Abbess Campion.' I was floundering. Were they Mothers or Sisters? I'd never addressed one before.

'This is she. Sister Geraldine Campion. And you are?'

'Illaun Bowe. I'm an archaeologist.'

'What can I do for you?'

'It's about the field at Monashee. I believe you sold it to Frank Traynor – the late Frank Traynor.'

'Yes. What a dreadful thing to happen. We did indeed sell Monashee and some other plots of land to him. Is that the answer you require?'

I hadn't actually asked a question. 'It's not as simple as that. And it could take a bit of time to explain over the phone. Is there a chance we could meet? I could call in to you tomorrow.'

'But what would be the purpose of our conversation?' Steely. *Don't lose her, Illaun.*

'To discuss surveying and possibly excavating the site.' How to put this delicately? 'I understand you may be able to bring some influence to bear on its future development.'

She laughed, or she made a low sound in her throat that could have been an ironic comment on what I had just said; I wasn't sure. 'What time tomorrow had you in mind?'

'Er – three o'clock?'

'Make it four on the dot. No earlier, no later.'

I almost said, 'Yes, ma'am,' but she hung up before I embarrassed myself.

I watched TV for a while but found nothing was holding my attention, so I decided that an early night would do wonders for my health. I didn't need to make myself anything to eat, either, because I'd had a snack while shopping in town. Before getting into bed I picked out clothes for my appointments the next day, settling on a white cashmere polo-neck and grey trousers with an oxblood leather jacket and matching handbag I had bought in October, when Fran and I had spent the second week of our holiday in the walled city of Lucca. Finally I checked to make sure that Boo wasn't in the room with me. I wanted an unbroken night's sleep.

But after only half an hour I awoke drenched in perspiration, my heart slamming against my chest, certain that some entity had its face right up to mine. It didn't breathe, it had no body temperature, no smell – that was how it climbed up close in the dark without you knowing. If I moved even a hair's breadth I would brush against it, and then the terror would be such that my already hammering heart would not survive it. But I had to do something, or it would devour me anyway. Holding my breath, I reached out for the light switch.

The creature evaporated instantly into the shadows, leaving me sitting up and breathing rapidly, convinced I had caught a glimpse of a monstrous winged insect with scorpion's claws and the face of a human infant.

December 19th

Chapter Thirteen

It was a clear, frost-tinged afternoon, with only a single wisp of cloud floating in the pale-blue sky, when I set off from Castleboyne. After ten minutes on the road I got out to re-seal the clear sheet of polythene I had taped across the passenger window. Looking up, I realised the insubstantial fragment of cloud was actually the gibbous moon, so wafery thin that the sky seemed to have almost dissolved it. I took a deep breath of cool, sun-kissed air and gave thanks for the day, and for the fact that the nightmare of the previous night was finally loosening its grip.

It was only when I had turned off the main road near

Monashee that the surroundings became gloomier, a combination of the short December day and a veil of mist along the Boyne. The temperature dropped too, and the battle between the car heater and the cold breeze flapping in past the polythene sheet, which had been evenly balanced, tipped in favour of the damp, clinging air. I was chilled to the bone by the time I pulled into a gateposted driveway to check my map in the dying light.

I hadn't thought to ask anyone for directions, but I had consulted a monastic map of Meath before leaving. On it I spotted a cross on Redmountain Ridge, across the river from Newgrange, that I took to represent Grange Abbey. According to my calculations, as I traced my journey on the map with a gloved finger, I was just about there now.

No earlier, no later. The abbess's words rang in my ears. I looked at the clock on the dashboard – 15.50. It was getting perilously close to four o'clock. Why had she been so specific about the time? I ran through the possibilities in a futile effort to stave off the prospect that I was going to miss the appointment. Then, from somewhere, I dredged up a memory. At sunset on the day of the winter solstice, the rays of the sun light up the south chamber of Dowth passage grave, lending symmetry to the morning event at Newgrange. I had been in the chamber with a small group of other archaeologists on one such occasion, and I remembered that the light had faded at exactly five past four – midwinter sundown.

Shrugging off a sudden sense of disquiet, I got out of the car to look around for a tower or a castellated roof. An ivy-covered wall stretching away from both sides of the gate blocked my view of the valley, so I walked a few metres inside the entrance. Fields on either side fell gently away down a rolling hill, and here and there in the distance I saw coils of smoke from farmhouse chimneys suspended in the still air. Lower down and about two kilometres distant, I could see Newgrange; even in the dimness it was clearly visible, the ring of quartz enclosing its grassy dome glowing like a crown of pearls.

I looked at the nearest gatepost: no plate or inscription on it, nor on the one across from it. Only then did I see a pair of rusting wrought-iron gates, hanging from the posts but completely pushed back into the driveway, where they had become ensnared in some bushes. They were decorated with a leaf-and-branch design, and running across the top in faded gilt were some words in French. On the left, '*La Croix du Dragon*'; on the right, completing the sentence, '*Est la Dolor de Deduit*'.

It looked like an heraldic motto, probably of Norman origin. 'The dragon's cross is the sorrow of – something' was the best I could do with my school French. But what was this medieval inscription doing on the gates of an estate in the Irish countryside? Then it dawned on me that I had been at St Margaret's all the time.

The avenue led downwards into a wooded part of the hillside that was evidently hiding the abbey. As if pointing the way, a great sickle-shaped flock of starlings came wheeling overhead, then swept down into the trees in an elongated stream, like a genie summoned back into its lamp.

I jumped into the car and sprinted along the tree-lined avenue. The clock on the dash read 15.59 as I crunched to a halt on gravel outside an ivy-clad three-storey residence. There was a vintage cream-and-blue Land Rover parked to one side of the forecourt. I pulled in beside it and stepped out in front of a lawn sloping down to a dark sweep of conifers.

The starlings that had descended on the trees bubbled and chittered noisily behind me as I walked up the steps to a painted black door under a leaf-shaped arch. I pressed a brass bell on the right door-jamb; I couldn't hear it ringing inside, and after a minute or two of trying I decided that neither could anyone else. I had just lifted up a heavy dragon's-head knocker to hammer on the door when I paused. Mingled with the hubbub of the birds was the far-off lilt of women's voices.

Thinking that perhaps I had come to the wrong entrance, I backed away from the door, checking the windows for any sign of life; but there was nothing to indicate that anyone was at home. Then I noticed that the windows, though Gothic in style, were not original. The entire stone façade had a restored appearance.

Some outbuildings were set back to the left of the residence, the connecting wall pierced by an archway. Probably they had once been the coach-house and stables, I reflected, walking through the arch and finding myself in an enclosed space, its left side bounded by a high, red-brick garden wall and the other two by the nave and north transept of a medieval abbey church. In the centre of the west gable was a Romanesque doorway, its warm sandstone tones contrasting with the sooty grey limestone of the rest of the building. The north transept projected at right angles to the nave – both featured round-headed windows – and rising above the pitched roof was a square tower with slender, stepped battlements indicating a later construction date.

Far inside the church, the nuns were engaged in a form of rhythmic chanting unfamiliar to me. As it was dusk, I presumed that the community was observing vespers; that would explain why nobody had answered the doorbell.

I strolled along the outside of the nave towards the north transept, taking in the damp smell of old stone and noting how the coating of lichen at the base of the building gave off a luminous green glow. Above me in the gloom, faces peered out from the carved foliage forming the capitals of the windows. I stood for a moment to examine a pair of the carvings. The foliate faces were reminiscent of the Green Man carvings found in some ancient churches and often regarded as the pagan Lord of the Forest who is reborn in winter; but these looked more like the faces of children.

Standing there, I began to pick up some of the words the Sisters inside were singing.

'*Ecce mundi gaudium ...*'

Behold the joy of the world ... At least my understanding of Latin was better than my grasp of medieval French.

'*Procedenti virginis ex utero ...*' Delivered from the womb of a virgin ...

'*Sine viri semine ...*' Without male seed ...

'*Novus annus est ...*' This is the new year ...

'*Sol verus in tenebris illuxit ...*' The true sun has lit up the darkness ...

The community of St Margaret's were having their own carol practice, albeit with earthy, almost secular medieval material. And the unaccompanied voices I heard were young and sturdy, not the tremulous cadences of elderly women. The carol ended in a hearty shout, and then there was silence.

Thinking they were finished, I walked back to the main door in case they exited that way. As I retraced my steps along the cobblestoned ground, I noticed that I was walking uphill and that, to compensate for the sloping ground, the wall of the nave decreased somewhat in height towards the west end. Just as I reached the door the nuns launched into another vigorous hymn, this one accompanied by hand-clapping and what sounded like a bodhrán.

I took a few moments to examine the door, which was recessed inside a round-headed triple arch, each arch and its supporting columns decorated with deeply incised patterns and carved figures. It was an impressive example of a twelfth-century Romanesque portal. The reliefs were mainly of fanciful creatures, among which I easily identified a manticore (a creature with a man's face, the body of a lion and a scorpion's tail) and a cynocephalus (a dog-headed man). There were others that were unfamiliar, and I made a mental note to ask the abbess about the provenance of the arch should the opportunity arise.

I pushed against the heavy, studded doors; but not only were they locked, they bore a patina of grime and dust suggesting they hadn't been opened for a long time. Tendrils of ivy crisscrossing the top of the doors confirmed it. The nuns would not be coming out this way.

I walked around to the south side of the church, where the nave formed part of a square surrounding the cloister, the other three sides being the domestic buildings of the convent. An opening led into a covered walkway around the cloister, whose pointed cinquefoil arches looked onto a grassy garth. At the far side the south wing of the convent merged with the transept, presumably to allow the community to go to and from the church in all weathers.

In the dusk I could just make out a door in the transept and one of the nuns emerging from it. She spotted me and signalled for me to wait while she locked the door. As she hurried to join me, I saw she was a tall, elegant woman in her mid-forties, wearing a grey two-piece suit and a white blouse. Her black hair was swept back severely from her forehead and held in place by a white headband, attached to which was a short veil matching her suit. She was brown-eyed, with jet-black eyebrows, a pale complexion and delicate cheekbones; her poise and appearance put me in mind of a prima ballerina.

'I'm so sorry,' she said. 'I didn't realise the time. We decided to have a carol practice after vespers.'

I recognised the voice.

'And I haven't even introduced myself,' she said apologetically. 'I'm Geraldine Campion. You must be …?'

'Illaun Bowe. No need to apologise, Sister; I was enjoying my stroll – and the singing, too.' I could hear the congregation starting another carol, this one less frantically paced than the others.

Sister Campion tapped her watch and smiled a little nervously. 'Shall we go?' I had a sense that she didn't want me to linger any longer within earshot of the choir. I wondered if that had had something to do with her insistence on the precise time of my arrival. But what might I have heard if I had come any later?

'It's a fine church,' I said as she led me away. 'I'm

estimating twelfth century for the nave, with some later decoration. The tower over the crossing – thirteenth century. Fifteenth for the cloister? And the building out front is a neo-Gothic restoration.' I wanted her to see that I was interested in the architecture of the abbey. I intended paying another visit, to examine the west door in greater detail. And who knew what was to be seen inside the church itself?

'You've got a good eye,' she said as we walked under the arch of the coach-house. 'The west wing suffered fire damage in the nineteenth century and was rebuilt afterwards. We have all the restoration plans, if you'd like to see them.'

'I'm much more interested in the Romanesque ar–'

Sister Campion laid her hand on my forearm. 'Do archaeologists have to know everything about architecture as well?' The coldness of her hand penetrated the sleeve of my leather jacket.

'Not necessarily. For my Master's degree I studied the archaeology of art and architecture.'

'I see,' she said, losing interest. 'Now, what's this you want to do at Monashee?' We were straight down to business without having even reached the house.

'Well, ideally what we call research excavation.'

'As distinct from?'

We mounted the steps side by side and paused outside the door. It crossed my mind for a moment that we were going to finish our discussion there.

'As distinct from rescue or salvage excavation,

which has to be done under pressure when a site is threatened.'

'And is the site – is Monashee threatened in some way?'

'Well, with the hotel being built –' I saw her perplexed look. 'Do you mean ... you didn't know about the hotel?' Was she for real? What about the profit-sharing scheme?

The abbess found a key in her pocket and inserted it in the lock. 'You'd better come in,' she said.

The residence was sparsely furnished, dimly lit and poorly heated, and my breath was visible in the air as we marched through parquet-floored reception rooms and along tiled corridors. Instead of the smells I had been expecting, polish mixed with the lingering aroma of Sunday roast, there was only the odour of must and damp. The bare walls were relieved here and there with wreaths of intertwined ivy and conifer branches, sprigs of berried holly and an occasional hank of mistletoe. 'That's what kept us late for choir,' Sister Campion said, flicking up a hand towards the foliage: 'putting up the decorations.' As I followed behind her, I noticed a wine-red stripe bordering her veil. I had practically dressed myself in the colours of the order.

Sister Campion ushered me into a carpeted, green-walled room with a high ceiling, a pair of metal filing cabinets and a desk on which a goose-necked lamp provided the only artificial light. At least it was warm. This was obviously her office, and I guessed that a window behind the desk allowed her a view into the now-dark cloister.

She was closing the door behind us when a mobile phone rang discreetly and briefly. Sister Campion took the phone from her jacket pocket, looked at it but didn't answer. 'Please take a seat,' she said. 'I have to assign some duties; I won't be long.'

As her rubber-soled shoes squeaked into the distance, I took in my surroundings. There was only one chair apart from her own. The carpet was threadbare, and the warmth was being supplied by an electric fan-heater. There were no ornaments on the desk, no paintings or prints on the walls – just a single framed photograph of a group of nuns. There were no signs of wealth, not even of comfortable living. The abbey's spartan interior suggested a run-down institution rather than the convent of a well-to-do order.

So what had you been expecting? A luxury guest-house? I admitted to myself that I had imagined them being better off. *Be honest – you thought these nuns were money-grabbers.* That was true; but I was more concerned about something else. And I couldn't put my finger on it.

I looked around the room again. And then I figured it out. Apart from that picture on the wall, there was nothing inside the Grange Abbey residence to suggest that it was a religious establishment of any kind.

I stood up to examine the photograph. It looked fairly recent and featured two rows of smiling women in grey attire, about twelve in all, most of them in their thirties, some of Asian or African extraction – the typical mixed-race mosaic of a modern religious order. They were standing on the very same steps I had walked up a few minutes before. Once again my speculations had been out of joint with the reality. St Margaret's was a small but thriving community.

Then something caught my eye. On top of one of the filing cabinets, outside the circle of light thrown by the lamp, was the tiny skeleton of an animal mounted on a plinth. It was half-upright on two spindly legs, but its most remarkable feature was the skull: the bones flared outwards above its empty eye-sockets like the flagging petals of a tulip at the end of its days. It looked like a miniature alien.

A knock on the door made me resume my seat. I turned around as the door opened and a nun stuck her head in. 'Where has she gone now?' the head demanded imperiously. Steel-wool hair stuck out under the front of her veil. In many ways her face was similar to Geraldine Campion's, but it was like a coarse sketch of the original.

'Er … she said something about assigning duties,' I said timidly, flashing back to my days as a pupil of nuns just like her.

The woman flung open the door and stood there sighing heavily. 'It's all been done; that's why I was ringing.' She had her mobile phone gripped in her hand like a weapon. She added, with obvious exasperation,

'Why won't she just leave it to me?' I felt guilty, as though I had colluded with the abbess to make this woman's life more difficult.

The nun slammed the door with a bang that made me jump. That must be the bursar, Sister Roche, the one Gallagher had warned me to avoid. I could see why.

For the next few minutes I strained my ears as voices called out to one another at intervals in the recesses of the convent. I couldn't make out what they were saying. Soon they subsided, and once again I heard the squeak of rubber soles on the parquet.

The abbess entered and strode purposefully to her desk. Sitting down gracefully, she leant forward, drew a full breath and addressed me. 'Once again, my apologies. A matter of internal administration. Managing a religious community, however small, is not always plain sailing.' She sat back in the chair. 'I can assure you of my full attention now.'

'Thank you. How many of you are there here, as a matter of interest?'

'There are a nice metric ten of us, plus myself and Sister Roche – Ursula, that is. I think she paid you a visit?' Her smile hinted that we both thought the same of Sister Roche. I nodded but did not accept her invitation to smirk. I was a stranger. Whatever their differences, they were closer to each other than I was to either of them.

'About Monashee,' I began. 'I take it you know there was a woman's body found there on Thursday.'

'Yes, I heard. From the distant past, I believe. So Frank told me.'

'Frank Traynor?'

'Frank and I were old friends. That's how we came to do business with him. Now, about this body that was unearthed ...'

I wondered if Sister Campion had heard how Traynor was killed. 'We're not sure just how old it is yet. If it's as old as I hope, then it could shed new light on the builders of Newgrange or those who occupied the valley after them. It's also possible the site may contain artefacts or other human remains.'

She frowned. 'Other remains?'

'Yes. There's documentary evidence to suggest that a body in similar condition was flushed out of Monashee by flood-waters over a hundred years ago. In fact, it may have been subsequently re-buried by the nuns here at the time.'

'Really? Well, I'm not aware of that. And I'm still not sure I appreciate what exactly you want of me.' Sister Campion's voice was striking a harsher note.

'The problem is that Mr Traynor was planning to strip the entire covering of peat from the field to make way for a hotel.'

'Oh, I don't think so,' she said, her voice softening again. 'And, in any case, I would be totally opposed to that.'

Something in me relaxed. Monashee might be safe

after all. And it seemed as though the abbess had been unaware of Traynor's true intentions.

'But I understood you knew what Frank Traynor was up to? There's even a rumour going round that the order was in for a share of the profits from the hotel.'

The abbess rotated her chair so she could gaze out into the darkened cloister, taking her time before answering. 'We live in changing times. For a thousand years the Hospitallers of St Margaret of Antioch have provided nursing care to those we now call "single mothers".' Again that harshness coming to the fore. 'We trained as midwives and worked in the order's lying-in hospitals, providing a discreet service without any interference from Church or State. Now, almost overnight, we have no demand for our services. Apparently there's no longer any stigma attached to pregnancy outside marriage; and, in any case, abortion can be availed of without fear of haemorrhaging to death ... or going to hell.' She laughed low in her throat, but without any mirth. 'So what's the result? An order that survived for a millennium is left without any source of income.' She turned back towards me. 'Can you blame us for trying to source funding for our work?'

I shook my head, more in perplexity than in absolution. 'But I thought ... Didn't you say there was no role for the order any more?'

'Oh, no; you misunderstood me. There will always be a role for us among the poor, as there always has

187

been. You see, we have traditionally used our income from the better-off in society to fund our charitable activities.'

Was it just cant, or was she being truthful? 'Even though you have a reputation for caring only for the wealthy in society?'

'It may be true that, from time to time, we have lost sight of our vocation and had to remind ourselves of it. And for the order to survive, to escape persecution, we've had to be pragmatic on occasion. But we've been doing that since *Periculoso*, when we revised our constitution and became a so-called secular order, a pious society. This means that, in theory, we don't take perpetual vows – in reality we do, but we're free of them one day a year – so we get off on a technicality, as they say.' A smile began to tug at the edge of her mouth. 'That's why ...' She was about to explain something but switched to another subject. 'Did you know that Henry II came over to Ireland in 1171, at Christmastime?'

I nodded, with a vagueness that matched my awareness of the event.

'He was determined to show the Norman barons who had recently invaded Ireland – and the native Irish too, of course – that he was their overlord. But there was something else on his mind. He was in trouble with Pope Alexander, for the murder of Thomas Becket in Canterbury Cathedral ...' Sister Campion leaned her elbows on the desk and tented her hands in front of her mouth, tapping her lips lightly with her forefingers. She seemed to be weighing up what she was going to say next.

'Anyway – long story short – ours was one of the first charters issued by Henry when he arrived in Dublin. There were several other properties granted to the order in Ireland, but I was shown the Grange Abbey charter when I became abbess here, so I know its contents. It was originally in Latin, of course.' She closed her eyes and began to recite from memory. '"Let it be known to all good Christians that I have given these lands and the fields, woods, waters, mills and fisheries thereof, wholly, entirely and in perpetuity for whichever purposes they deem fit, to St Margaret's Abbey and the nuns there serving God, to hold same in frankalmoign, free and quit of all secular exaction."'

Finian had been bang on.

'Frank Traynor must have thought he could acquire those rights too,' I said.

'That's as may be. The legal ins and outs of what we signed over are more the bursar's area than mine. But one thing is sure.' She leaned forward, slammed her palm on the desk and fixed me with her eyes. 'We never agreed to a hotel at Monashee.'

She quickly sat back again, as if to correct an imbalance in her body language. 'Elsewhere in the area, yes, but not in a field across from Newgrange. We're not out of touch with the world outside these walls. That part of the Boyne Valley is a protected area, and rightly so. And I'll use whatever' – she picked the word carefully – '*influence* I can to have our understanding enforced.'

I noticed a gold ring on one of her fingers. A bride of Christ? But what was more interesting to me was the appearance of her fingernails. They were carefully manicured, buffed to a sheen like the inside of a seashell. Sister Campion, I suspected, was not averse to a bit of pampering.

The abbess abruptly pushed back her chair and stood up. 'So there we are. I'm afraid I have to say goodbye to you. Duty calls, and all of that.'

'Of course. Thank you for your time.' What had she actually promised? I wasn't sure it amounted to much. 'Just one more thing ...' I rose slowly and looked around the room. She followed my gaze as it rested for a moment on the mounted skeleton.

'A tarsier, I believe it's called,' she said. 'Full-grown, apparently.' Gesturing to the group photo, she added with a hint of disdain, 'A gift from our friends overseas.'

'I see. But that wasn't what I wanted to ask you ...'

She had moved past me and was standing with the door open.

'Mr Traynor seemed to be in such a hurry. Any idea why?'

'No,' she said, ushering me out into the corridor.

We had reached the main hall when Sister Roche, still gripping her phone, came rushing down the stairs and intercepted us. 'Martha Godkin has a high fever.

Temperature of thirty-nine. She's asking for a doctor, but I said –'

The abbess had raised a hand to silence her. 'Wait a moment, Ursula.' She looked annoyed. 'I'm just saying goodbye to …'

'Illaun,' I filled in for her.

'Illaun, that's right.' She left Sister Roche standing in the hall and led me to the door. 'Goodbye, now; nice meeting you,' she said with a brittle smile.

'Just before I go, Sister, I'm curious – who was St Margaret of Antioch?'

'A fourth-century virgin martyr. Refused to have sex with a Roman official, who then betrayed her Christianity to the authorities. They tried unsuccessfully to burn and boil her to death, so in the end they beheaded her.' The abbess opened the door. It was dark outside.

I had another question. 'And the motto on the gate – something about a cross and a dragon?'

'*La croix du dragon est la dolor de deduit*?' She stood holding the door open. 'St Margaret again. The words have appeared at the entrance to each of our houses since Norman times. "The dragon's cross is pleasure's pain" is how we translate it. I believe the word "deduit" first appeared in the *Roman de la Rose*. It refers to sexual pleasure, of course.' Her tone implied that I could hardly be ignorant of the fact.

I nodded. 'Of course. And what does "the dragon's cross" refer to?'

'Legend has it that St Margaret was swallowed by the Devil in the form of a dragon, but she used her crucifix to jab at his insides, so he spat her out whole and entire. Hence Margaret became the patron saint of labour and childbirth. Sounds quaint now, if a bit on the macabre side.' Sister Campion began to close the door.

A virgin who was the patron saint of pregnant women? But at least it reminded me of something I'd meant to bring up in our conversation.

'One more thing,' I said. 'There was another body found beside the bog lady at Monashee.'

'Oh?'

'A baby.'

'How odd.' Sister Campion's face was half hidden behind the door, making it difficult to read her expression.

'Yes, it's puzzling,' I said, and stepped outside. A light came on automatically, distracting me for a second. 'Well, thanks for your time, Sister, and ...' I turned to shake her hand, but she had already closed the door.

I sat in the car, observing the residence. Most of the upper rooms in the front – presumably the dormitory – were lit up, but the area around the archway was in darkness. I waited for a while, thinking about, among other things, the order's motto. Sister Campion had told me what it literally meant but had skirted around what message it was intended to convey. It was a warning: the pains of childbirth are the consequence of lust.

I searched in the glove compartment, found my digital camera, thought about taking my flashlight but decided it would be an encumbrance. I set the camera to high resolution, then clicked the overhead light so it wouldn't come on when I opened the door. I tiptoed across the gravel, through the arch and over the cobblestones towards the west door.

It was just possible to make out the gable end of the church, with a darker patch in the centre where the door was. I stood slightly to one side so as not to obliterate the details of the carvings in the full glare of the flash – some shadow would give them more definition. I aimed the camera at the doorway without being sure if I was getting it all in the frame, and took the photograph. From ground to sky the world around me was lit up for an instant, and I decided to get out of there before anyone came out of the convent to investigate.

As I turned to go, I heard a noise nearby like someone snoring and wheezing at the same time. For a moment I thought of the wheezing figure outside my home. But then I remembered being startled by this same noise, years before; and this was the ideal location for a nesting barn owl.

But just before I went through the arch, I paused to take another photo of the façade, just in case. My retina was still a little dazzled from the reflection of the first flash; looking through the viewfinder, I had the momentary illusion that there was someone dressed in white standing between me and the west door.

Chapter Fourteen

Emerging out of the long avenue, I was uncertain which way I should go, after all the twists and turns I had taken to get there earlier in the afternoon. Once again I climbed out of the car and tried to get my bearings. Despite the darkness, there was still a glow from the semicircle of quartz around Newgrange. In the far distance I could see what looked like a multi-coloured brooch attached to the hummocky landscape; it was the village of Slane in its Christmas array, the electric garishness of the living streets contrasting with the spectral luminosity of the place of the dead. But of nearby Grange Abbey's existence there was no sign whatsoever. *A light shone in the darkness and the darkness grasped it not.*

I sat back in the car. It was coming up to five and I had no mobile phone to ring Detective Gallagher. But the Visitor Centre wasn't all that far away if I chose the right road, and now I knew the general direction.

There were few vehicles in the car park when I drove in. I pulled down my sun visor and used the illuminated vanity mirror to quickly apply some mascara and lipstick. I had decided against make-up for my visit to Grange Abbey. I remembered Sister Campion's fingernails. She was entitled to keep up her appearance, of course; and it was far from being a fashion statement.

The walk to the Centre was under a wooden pergola, along flagstones glittering with frost. To my right the Boyne was flowing in the opposite direction; over it a suspension footbridge led to the minibus departure point, from where tourists were shuttled to Newgrange and Knowth and back again. On my left was an artificial waterfall, which shrank to a trickle just as I was passing it. Closing time.

I explained who I was to a member of the staff, who was waiting inside the main entrance for a couple of tardy souvenir shoppers to leave. She told me I was expected and pointed downstairs to the restaurant. As I descended the winding steps, I saw a lone figure sitting at one of the tables reading a Sunday newspaper.

The man looked over his newspaper as I headed in

his direction. His moustache, his close-cropped hair and a burly frame straining to burst through his nondescript grey suit said 'detective', just as he had predicted. But for some reason he had failed to mention his most obvious feature – his hair. There was no euphemistic way of describing it: 'red' was a complete misnomer, 'carrot-red' was getting there, and the yellow-orange shading of a sliced carrot was closer still. His complexion spoke of a recent sun holiday: not a tan, but an angry red forehead and a peeling nose.

I stuck out my hand. 'Illaun Bowe. Sorry I'm late.'

His grasp swallowed my hand up to the wrist. 'Matt Gallagher. I was getting worried. But I assumed you'd ring me if there was a problem.' The soft Donegal accent was at odds with his wrestler's physique. I estimated he was in his early forties.

'I should have called you anyway, but my mobile phone was stolen early yesterday morning.' I looked at his half-empty cardboard cup and got the urge to have a strong coffee.

'Oh? How did it happen?' He folded the paper and laid it on the table, partially covering what looked like a scanned copy of the Christmas card found under Traynor's body.

I told him about the intruder and the smashed window.

'Expensive phone, was it?'

'Not particularly.' I glanced over at the service area, which was in semi-darkness.

'Hmm ... well, that's why we tell people to leave nothing visible in their cars.' He reached into his jacket and took out his jotter and ballpoint. 'I think it's closed,' he said, indicating the service area, 'but if it's just caffeine you want, you could try a bit of burglary yourself. I'd say the Coke dispenser is still operational.'

His sense of humour put me at ease. 'Encouraging me to commit a crime, Inspector?' I went to the dispenser, picked up a cardboard cup and filled it to the brim. Then I fished a coin from my purse and left it beside the till.

I sat down at the table and sipped the cold Coke, waiting for Gallagher's first question. Instead he lit a cigarette – breaking the law himself – and leaned back in his chair, which wobbled slightly as his ample frame put it to the test.

'When I heard Frank Traynor'd been murdered, I reckoned he'd been doing business with the wrong kind of people – foreign criminals, maybe. When I heard it was a stabbing, I wondered if he was just a victim of our wee country's latest blood sport ...'

He watched my eyes, which must have registered a question; I had no idea what he meant.

'Random killing – a pastime for scumbags on drink and drugs. But then I saw his body and thought, *What the hell are we dealing with here? A psychopath? A serial killer?* I had to admit I was baffled. Then I remembered a basic principle ...' He leaned forward again and gulped down the remainder of his coffee.

'When someone's trying to outsmart you, they'll make it seem complicated.'

'Meaning?'

'Frank Traynor was killed by someone he knew. Someone with a grudge. Plain and simple.'

'But why such … brutality?'

'As I said, to make it seem like something other than what it is.' He tapped some ash into his cup.

'What do you mean?'

'It'll become clear as we go along.' Gallagher flipped to a fresh page on his jotter. 'Where and when did you last see Frank Traynor?'

'On a street in Drogheda, on Friday, between two-thirty and two-forty-five pm.'

'Was Seamus Crean with you at the time?'

'Yes.'

'Why were you meeting him?'

I explained that I had been anxious to find out as much as I could about Monashee and to mention the prospect of short-term work to Crean.

'Was killing Frank Traynor the job you had in mind, by any chance?'

I had been about to take another sip of Coke, but the cup didn't reach my lips. 'You can't be serious?' I knew I was suddenly blushing, as though he had slapped me in the face. This guy was good cop and bad cop all in one.

Gallagher's expression was cold. 'Answer the question, please, Miss Bowe.'

He knew he had me flustered. I had to regain my balance quickly. For some reason I focused on the peeling skin of his nose. 'Of course not. I thought there might be some excavation work on the site for him. We sometimes use JCBs to clear topsoil or dig trenches.'

Gallagher laid his cigarette on the edge of the table and thumbed through the jotter until he found the entry he was looking for. 'According to Dr Sherry, only he and you knew the exact pattern of the injuries that were on the body found in the field and that were later inflicted on Mr Traynor.'

'As far as we know, that's true.' I wasn't going to tell him my suspicions about Traynor's visit to the morgue just yet.

'But he couldn't rule out the possibility that Crean had examined the woman's body before anyone else arrived – maybe removed some of the soil covering her face, then replaced it. It's also possible that you passed on the details to Crean when you met him.'

I saw red. 'Oh, yeah. Did a quick sketch and said, "Do me one of these, will you?" And, while we're at it, have you asked Dr Sherry if he perhaps passed on the details to whoever he met at lunchtime on the same day? I'll bet you haven't. And what about this?' I dragged the scan of the Christmas card from under his newspaper and waved it at him. 'If Seamus Crean had anything to do with this, then I'm Santa Claus – and Mrs Crean works for the Spanish Inquisition.'

Gallagher shifted uncomfortably in his chair. 'We're

keeping an open mind on the card,' he mumbled, snatching back the sheet and hastily slipping it under the paper again.

I stood up from the table. 'This investigation is going nowhere. You're looking in the wrong direction.' I said it louder than I'd intended.

Gallagher's moustache twitched. He glanced nervously at a cleaning woman who had started to mop the floor. 'What do you mean?'

I lowered my voice. 'It has to do with the field at Monashee, all right. But you have to ask why Traynor was in such a rush to rip it up the week before Christmas. He was hardly going to get any more work done on the site until after the New Year, so he could have waited. Then there's the body of the deformed infant ...' I wasn't sure I wanted to share my thoughts.

'Go on.'

I prayed my reputation for flights of imagination had not gone ahead of me. 'I'm convinced Traynor saw it in the morgue – went there to see it, even. We've all been concentrating on the way he was murdered and mutilated, but that's distracting us somehow. Then there's the fact that I'm being followed ...' My voice caught momentarily. I was under more strain than I had realised.

The cleaning woman's mopping had slowed down as she angled her ear in our direction. 'Look, will you please sit down?' Gallagher said quietly, taking a last drag on his cigarette and dousing it in the bottom of the cup with a sizzle.

I slid back into the chair. 'The night of the murder, there was someone dressed in white outside the morgue, watching me. Then I saw this weird-looking individual standing out on the patio, the same night my phone –'

'Describe "weird".' Gallagher seemed interested all of a sudden. He was even taking notes.

'Wearing white overalls or a robe of some kind, and a hat with a veil hanging from the front – like an old-fashioned beekeeper's outfit. Then there's today. I think I may have been followed to Grange Abbey by the same individual.'

'Who you believe is the murderer.'

'I don't know what to believe.'

'Do you think your life is in danger?'

'I think it could be, depending on how close I get to knowing why Frank Traynor was killed.'

'Well, then I suggest you don't pursue it any further. Make sense?'

'But if you have the killer locked up, what have I to worry about?'

He smiled properly for the first time, showing a fine display of American dental work. 'You're smart. But in fact Crean *isn't* in custody right now. So the warning still stands.'

'You haven't formally charged him with the murder?'

looked him straight in the eye and hoped he was worried.

'Sit in,' he said, jabbing his thumb towards the back of the car.

I opened the rear door and got in behind him.

'What the fuck do you want?' The buffoonish mask had slipped, revealing vicious fangs beneath.

'We can trade,' I said. 'You tell me about the progress of the investigation. I'll forget the incident I've mentioned ever happened.'

'Go fuck yourself.'

I pretended I had another card. 'Then there are the other favours done over the years, the nod-and-a-wink business relationship between the deceased and the local sergeant … The newspapers would love to hear about that.'

O'Hagan stiffened. As a passing car lit up the interior, I caught his eyes in the rear-view mirror. He was weighing it up.

'You know we hauled in Crean,' he said, almost under his breath.

'And you know Crean didn't do it. What else are you working on?'

'There were two untraced calls made to Frank's phone shortly before he died. One from an un-registered mobile in Drogheda. The last one from a phone-box in Slane. There's nothing else to go on.'

'There has to be. There was a woman in the car with

'Not yet.'

'Have you spoken to the woman who was with Traynor that afternoon? Maybe she knows who he was meeting at Monashee.'

'Hmm, this mystery woman. Crean mentioned seeing her. But the next reported sighting we have of Frank Traynor that afternoon was on the outskirts of Drogheda, and he was alone in the car.'

'So he dropped her off somewhere.'

'The uniform lads have been interviewing anyone who might have passed along that street at lunchtime on Friday – shoppers, office workers, schoolkids. Some recall seeing his Merc parked on the street, but that's about it. We've more or less eliminated the woman from our inquiries. But, just in case, we've appealed for anyone who was with Traynor that day to come forward. So far your lady hasn't made contact. Who was she, anyway? Do you know?'

'Her name is Muriel Blunden. She's Director of Excavations at the National Museum.'

I couldn't read his expression. He was looking down at his notebook, slowly turning it over to find a blank page.

'She had taken his side in a radio interview that morning, so presumably they were close. And, as I said, she may have overheard something.' I stood up to leave.

'Thanks for coming,' he said mechanically.

'I can't say it was a pleasure.'

Gallagher waved me away and continued writing.

'I disagree,' he called after me, as I put my foot on the first stair. 'Let's have a proper cup of coffee together one of these days.'

Only if I can pour it over your head, I thought.

On the way to meet Gallagher at the Visitor Centre, I had come down a road from Redmountain Ridge without passing Monashee. Now, on the way back along the valley floor, I slowed down behind a line of cars and, rounding a bend, saw a Garda checkpoint about five hundred metres ahead, positioned outside the field. I assumed they were asking drivers if they had passed that way on Friday evening. I was surprised by the large number of cars in this rural area until I remembered that the shops in Drogheda were open on Sundays for Christmas trading.

Creeping along in first gear, I thought about my meeting with Sister Campion. I felt that there had been something stage-managed about it, and that, in those moments when I had unsettled her, she had revealed that all was not as it seemed at Grange Abbey. In the same way, while she had appeared to be open and honest about her relationship with Frank Traynor, I felt there was some aspect of it she was deliberately concealing.

And then there was the atmosphere of the place. It was hard to describe exactly, but it definitely wasn't an air of sanctity – and not just because there wasn't a single cross, statue or religious painting to be seen.

To the best of my knowledge, Grange Abbey was not in any gazetteer of Romanesque buildings. Was that because it was in continuous use as a religious establishment? Or was there some other reason? I was wondering what that might be when I saw Gallagher flash by in a white Ford Mondeo. He overtook the entire line of traffic, blue light flashing, paused briefly to talk to someone at the checkpoint and then streaked on at speed.

The checkpoint was manned by a couple of young uniformed Gardaí who were standing in the middle of the road, facing the traffic in each direction. There was a squad car parked on the grass verge to the left, and as I edged closer I spotted a familiar face in the front passenger seat. I pulled out of the line of cars and parked in front of the Garda vehicle. The bareheaded officer inside looked puzzled as I walked towards him; then recognition dawned, followed by a frown. He rolled down the window.

'Sergeant O'Hagan?' My breath condensed in the frosty air.

'What can I do for you?' he said sullenly.

'I've just had a meeting with Inspector Gallagher. He asked me if I was aware of any unusual activity at Monashee on the day Frank Traynor was murdered.'

'What's that to do with me?'

'Well, it has only come back to me now that there were no Gardaí from Donore present here that morning, despite the order to enforce an injunction.' I

Traynor in Drogheda that afternoon. Why hasn't she been traced and questioned?'

'There was no woman.'

'You're not playing ball, Sergeant. I know who it was.'

A sharp intake of breath.

'Her name is Muriel Blunden.'

'Shite,' he said, breathing out. I had finally pressed the right button.

'Go on.'

'I talked to her. She's in the clear. I knew that anyway, but I wanted to see if she had any idea who might have murdered Frank.'

'And?'

'All she knows is that he took a call on his mobile when she was with him in the car. It had to have been one of those untraced calls. He arranged to meet whoever it was at Monashee. Muriel is convinced it was a woman.'

'Why didn't you give that information to Gallagher?'

'Because I want to find Frank's killer myself. Apart from which, I wouldn't give Gallagher the steam off my piss.'

No wonder Gallagher hadn't known about Muriel Blunden. O'Hagan had used his position to make sure no reports of her reached his eyes.

'So you said nothing and allowed Seamus Crean to be arrested.'

'Gallagher won't be able to make it stick. The fingerprints in the car aren't his.'

'You've got fingerprints?'

'Yeah, we've got lots of prints, all right. Fucker didn't care.'

'What other leads have you got?'

'Elvis or the banshee, take your pick.'

'What do you mean?'

'A woman driving past Monashee claims she saw someone dressed in white getting into Frank's Merc. The lads in the station are laying bets that it was the banshee, or else Elvis on his way to a gig.'

I had the strange experience of finding something both funny and chilling at the same time. But now I realised why Gallagher had become so interested when I mentioned the visitor on the patio.

'I'm betting Gallagher will hire a psychic to find out,' O'Hagan said.

'Why do you say that?'

'Because he's already using some shrink to tell us what we already know about the killer.'

'Which is?'

'Fuck all.'

I clicked open the car door. 'Well, at least he'll know soon enough about the call Traynor took while Muriel Blunden was in the car.'

'You're going to tell him?'

I got out of the car, then leaned back in for a

moment. 'I won't have to. He'll find out when he interviews her.' I closed the door.

It was past seven when I got home. I hadn't eaten since breakfast, which had consisted of tea, cereal and a slice of toast. Then I remembered the meal my mother had prepared on Friday was in the fridge. As I put the plate in the microwave, I heard Boo come through the cat-flap. My mother had taken Horatio with her to my widowed aunt Betty's house, ten kilometres out the Dublin road; she sometimes spent Sunday night there with her sister, after they'd had a couple of gin and tonics.

I checked the answering machine. There was only one message: Finian asking me to give him a call. Right now I wanted my privacy and a chance to purge my mind of things associated with Monashee and Traynor's murder.

I discarded my clothes in the bedroom and threw on a dressing-gown and slippers. With my dinner on a tray, I shuffled into the living room, turned on the TV and selected a nature programme. But, despite the comfort food, the amazing behaviour of land crabs and a purring cat beside me, the hoped-for switch-off didn't occur.

Why had O'Hagan been protecting Muriel Blunden? The only possible answer was that she was involved with him, Traynor and the Grange Abbey nuns in the hotel development. She had probably been lured into the partnership because they needed a heavyweight batting for them among the myriad of State agencies responsible for conservation. But as a senior executive with the National Museum she stood to lose her job if this was discovered, and the likelihood of that had increased with the investigation into Traynor's murder.

And, if Geraldine Campion was protecting Muriel too, then perhaps she was only claiming to be against the hotel at Monashee in order to persuade me not to pursue the issue any further.

And then there was the Minister for Tourism and Heritage, Derek Ward. I'd almost forgotten his connection with the scheme. But now it all fitted neatly together. As the minister responsible for the National Museum, he must have turned a blind eye when Muriel was headhunted – his way of providing practical support while seeming not to be involved. It would be in his interest to ensure she was not exposed.

I pushed the tray to one side of the couch and turned off the TV. What strange bedfellows they made – the Nun, the Hotelier, the Civil Servant, the Garda Sergeant, the Politician; like Chaucer's assortment of medieval pilgrims in the *Canterbury Tales*. *Ther was also a Nonne, a Prioresse ...*

The notion of 'bedfellows' slithered back into my mind, half-word, half-image; and then – bang! – it was centre stage, demanding attention. Muriel Blunden and Frank Traynor had been lovers! That had to be it. From that primordial fact sprang everything else – his smug radio interview, her dismissal of the find, their being in the car together, and now the determined effort to shield her. She didn't have to be induced into the project; she had been there from the start.

Excited by my new vocation as an armchair sleuth, I went to the drinks cabinet and poured myself a glass of wine from a half-empty bottle of Australian Shiraz I'd opened the night before being called to Monashee. That was ... I counted back – four nights ago. I'd inserted a rubber stopper and pumped air out of the bottle.

It was OK, if not in the first flush of youth. *A bit like yourself, my dear.* A familiar voice inside my head was seizing these opportunities to ambush me of late.

This is no life for a woman of your age – eating leftovers, drinking out of last week's bottles ... The voice bore an uncanny resemblance to my mother's, with a touch of cackling hag added for effect.

'Begone, Satan,' I said aloud, and bunged the stopper back in the bottle.

I sat back down, glass in hand, and resumed my sleuthing. What if you entertained the idea that it was a disaffected member of the business partnership who had, if not actually carried out the murder, at least commissioned it – maybe even lured Traynor to his meeting with the hired assassin? But which one? Muriel Blunden? Even if she and Traynor were lovers, that didn't rule her out as a suspect. She could also have lied about him arranging to meet a woman. On the other hand, if she was telling the truth, then who had Traynor gone to meet at Monashee? The abbess? Sister Campion had said she and Traynor were friends, not just business partners, and had also given the impression that she wasn't directly involved in the transaction: 'The legal ins and outs are more the bursar's area than mine ...'

Of course – Sister Roche! I had left her out of the picture altogether. Maybe she had pulled a fast one in the land deal to provide herself with some personal funds, and Frank Traynor, having found out about it, had been going to expose her. But how could she have described Mona's injuries to the assassin? It kept coming back to that. Unless ... who *did* Malcolm Sherry meet for lunch that day?

Whoa there, Illaun, take it easy.

My brain had become a runaway train, picking up speed as each new theory flashed in and out of view like another railway station on the route. Despite having had only half a glass of wine, I was thinking as if I were drunk, accusing ordinary, decent people of carrying out a particularly nasty murder. My efforts at crime investigation were liable to land *me* in jail before anyone else. Best to leave it to the experts. I leaned back in the couch and closed my eyes.

When Boo landed on my lap I knew I had been asleep, but for how long I couldn't estimate – maybe seconds, maybe half an hour. At least the express train in my head had pulled into a siding. Outside, the wind had risen higher. I could hear it rattling the flap of the post-box.

The phone rang in the hall. It was Finian, a little tetchy with me for not ringing him back. I explained I'd wanted some time to myself.

'Does that mean you're not coming with me tomorrow night?'

Jocelyn Carew's party! I'd completely forgotten to confirm it with him. I wondered briefly if my bad memory was a sign of early Alzheimer's, part of my genetic inheritance. But I dismissed it just as fast: I mightn't recall where I'd left my car keys a minute ago, but my long-term memory was like a vice – or so I told myself.

'Sorry, Finian. Of course I'm going with you.'

'Too late – the offer expired yesterday.'

I knew he was teasing. 'It just went out of my head, with all the things that have happened. By the way, were you thinking of staying the night in Dublin?' I bit my lip. Why had I blurted *that* out?

'No ...' he said, sounding a bit puzzled. 'Why would I want to?'

'Oh, you know ... drinking and driving, having to travel fifty kilometres home ...' I knew it sounded lame.

'Would you like to stay in Dublin for the night?'

'Eh ...' I knew there was some impediment. Or perhaps I was looking for one. 'What date is tomorrow?'

'The twentieth.'

'Oops. Means it's the eve of the solstice. I have to be at Newgrange early next morning, all bright-eyed and bushy-tailed.'

'Well, let's leave it at that. We just need to arrange what time we're leaving at.'

We talked briefly and then said good night. I put down the phone wondering how I'd managed, in our short exchange, both to reveal more than I wanted him to know and to sabotage an opportunity for us to be together.

I threw back the wine in the glass and picked up my dinner tray. Leftover dinners and leftover wine – it sounded like a line from one of those country songs I pretended not to like.

And now all I've got in this sad life of mine
Is just leftover dinners and leftover wine ...

And, in a way, Finian was a leftover man.

As I came into the kitchen, a gust of wind knocked a plastic plant pot off the windowsill outside and sent it skittering around the corner of the house. Horatio would usually be barking on a night like this, the wind skewing his ability to distinguish real threats from imagined ones. But he was with my mother in Aunt Betty's.

Feeling isolated and vulnerable, I went around the house making sure the external doors were locked, the alarm set. As I stepped into the utility room to check that the patio door was bolted, something scraped against the windowpane.

I couldn't move. Spicules of fear had entered my blood and were turning it to ice.

The door rattled; a gnarled silhouette appeared at the window, and the talon raked along the glass once more. I realised it was a branch of the overhanging wisteria that was being buffeted against the door by the wind.

I reached for the bolt and rammed it home, then stood with my back against the door as my heart worked overtime to send the blood flowing freely through my veins again.

December 20th

Chapter Fifteen

'Morning, Illaun. Did you have a nice weekend?' said Peggy brightly when I arrived in the office. She was leafing through the morning papers.

I sat down and attached my laptop to a large display screen. 'Not exactly brilliant ...'

But Peggy wasn't really listening for an answer. 'I see the bookies aren't expecting a white Christmas. Someone could make a fortune if it snows.' She brought me over the *Times* and the *Independent*. It seemed all the yearly clichés were being trotted out. 'Prospect of White Christmas Fading' ... It had snowed once at Christmas in my lifetime, and maybe even that was a false memory. 'Stores Expecting Bumper Week' … I had never seen one that said, 'Stores Expecting Poor Sales.'

The *Times* also carried a colour photo of a group of young carol singers: 'Members of the Piccolo Lasso choir at their annual Christmas concert in the National Concert Hall last night.'

'That would make such a nice Christmas card, don't you think?' said Peggy, going back to her desk. 'I know you're fussy about what you like.' This arose from a comment I'd made on a card that had arrived the previous week: 'Happy Holiday!' accompanied by a photograph of the Dublin Spire. Peggy's own preference was for jokey cards; her preferred newspapers were the red-top tabloids, one of which she had open on her desk.

Ignoring her reference, I scanned down the sidebar listing the main news items in the *Times*. There was nothing to suggest there had been any progress in the murder investigation.

'I don't believe it. You haven't sent any cards yet, Illaun. You're a disgrace.' Peggy had taken my lack of response as an attempt to avoid the subject, which was partly true.

Let me describe Peggy. Plump, big-breasted, fifty – or, as she might put it, voluptuous, curvaceous and free. (The last referred to her having reached an age when childbearing was no longer an issue and she could indulge her voracious sexual appetite without chemical or prophylactic intervention. Not that she was promiscuous: Peggy's husband Fred was the sole object of her desires, and those who knew this were inclined to snigger at the man's beanpole appearance and perpetually harassed look.) She was constantly changing her hairstyle and its colour – at present it was a shiny jet-black helmet *à la* Louise Brooks, with kohl eye make-up to match. Peggy was a devotee of herbal remedies for every ailment, avidly followed all the TV soaps and was encyclopaedic in her knowledge of the lives and loves of 'celebrities'. She was also the most organised human being I had ever encountered – exactly what I needed in a secretary.

'I suppose you've forgotten our staff lunch is on Thursday, as well.'

'Of course I haven't.' That was a lie. 'We'd better book a table somewhere.'

'Ah, Illaun. Do you really think there's a restaurant in Castleboyne would have a table available in this of all weeks?' She gave me a mischievous smile. 'Don't worry. I booked the Old Mill for the four of us a month ago.'

See what I mean?

'I'll get some cards for you this morning and print out the address labels. All you'll have to do is sign the cards.' She folded away her newspaper. 'All right with you?'

'Great. Any mention of the murder in the paper, by the way?'

She looked puzzled. 'What murder?'

'Sorry, I thought you knew.' I'd wondered why it wasn't the first topic of conversation.

It turned out Peggy hadn't heard about Traynor's death, despite the fact that it had been on every news bulletin on radio and TV over the weekend, not to speak of the tabloids of which she was so fond. But no doubt she had been finding better things to do with her time. I tried to give her as brief an account as possible of events since Friday – which wasn't easy, given her numerous requests for gruesome detail.

'... Which brings us to this morning,' I said almost half an hour later, glancing at the office clock to indicate the subject was about to be closed. 'As you can imagine, I'm trying to get back to some semblance of normality. But cast your mind back to last Thursday and Friday for a moment. Did anyone call the office looking for information on the find at Newgrange?'

'No journalists, if that's what you mean.'

'I mean anyone. Particularly if they didn't identify themselves.'

'No. I'd remember a call like that. In fact, the only other person I spoke to about it was Keelan. That was Thursday, when I told him he was to go to the hospital next morning.'

'OK. If you do get any calls from the media, just redirect them to Detective Inspector Matt Gallagher at Drogheda Garda station. Or, better still ...' I was thinking of how anything that would make Muriel

Blunden's life uncomfortable would greatly please me. And then I thought of her mourning her dead lover, and of how isolated she was probably feeling, as the mistress usually does on such occasions. 'No, forget it,' I said. 'Now, let's see what has to be done.'

I had to summarise the most recent data from the motorway interchange survey, include it in the report and write an introduction. I wanted to follow up on Mona's X-rays, that of her clenched hand in particular. I also needed to load the digital images from the morgue and the abbey into my PowerBook. At some stage I would have to pick out what I was going to wear to Jocelyn Carew's soirée. And, if there was time after all of that, I would try and put my mind to what I might say in the following day's interview with *Dig* magazine.

Faced with this daunting list, I proposed that Peggy drive my car into Castleboyne; while the window was being replaced she could buy the cards and pick me up a new mobile phone. By the time she had opened the post and left, I was immersed in the motorway survey. The proposed interchange and the roads converging on it would be passing through a crowded archaeological landscape, the history of the county in microcosm. Among the features we had identified were a prehistoric stone circle; several raths or ring-forts, early medieval homesteads; the remains of an Anglo-Norman manor house including earthworks and enclosures; two cemeteries, one of which was a *cillín*, a burial ground for unbaptised children; and an area of farmland where a skirmish had occurred in advance of the Battle of the Boyne in 1690 – a test trench here had unearthed three pike-heads, a plug bayonet, musket and cannon balls, and a couple of intact mortar bombs. Finding evidence of this hitherto unknown encounter between the Williamite and Jacobite armies was a good example of how archaeology could help historians gain a more accurate picture of the past.

I had just started writing the introduction to the report when the phone rang. I let it ring out, but when I heard Malcolm Sherry's voice leaving a message I grabbed the handset.

'I'm here, Malcolm. Just trying to get a survey report written up before the Christmas spirit takes over.'

'I understand, Illaun. Same goes for me. That's why I want to put your bog lady to bed, so to speak. I've been looking at the X-rays. Nothing remarkable to report – no obvious pathology or skeletal deformity, no signs of injury to the skull. But she has something in her hand, all right. It looks man-made.'

'Metal or stone?' I held my breath. Mona's age could be quickly determined by this artefact, if such it was.

'Neither. I think it's made of bone.'

'Bone?' Mona seemed determined to keep us guessing. A bone ornament could be from any period. 'I've got to see it as soon as possible, Malcolm.' I might be able to interpret its age from the way it was carved.

'I'm shipping off the two sets of remains today. Chap called Ivers has arranged for them to be put in the climate-controlled unit at the National Museum for the time being ...'

Ivers had managed to bypass the Director of Excavations. But Muriel was probably out of the office anyway.

'And you should be hearing something back from the UCD radiocarbon lab by the end of the week. I've also been thinking about the cause of the deformities in the infant. Assuming the body isn't from the modern era, we can rule out drugs and radiation; but perhaps inbreeding could be a factor.'

'In that it increases the likelihood of severe malformations?'

'Yes. And it would be taboo – within the immediate family, anyway – which might account for the killing of the mother. Maybe the birth was used as evidence to convict her of incest, and her brother or father, whichever was responsible, suffered the same fate.'

Which could account for the 'Nubian'. But I knew that incest wasn't always taboo in ancient cultures. Among ruling castes, if no female of suitable rank was available, a king might marry his sister rather than a woman of lower social status – an option institutional-ised by the Egyptians of the New Kingdom.

'It's an interesting thought, Malcolm. I'll bear it in mind.' But I was more excited at the prospect of seeing the artefact Mona had been clutching in her hand. Where was Sherry, anyway? 'You sound as if you're still in Drogheda. How come?'

'I decided to stay the weekend. Went on a little tour of Meath with a friend.'

The same friend he had met for lunch on Friday? *Forget it. Stick to the subject.*

'Could I ask a favour, Malcolm?'

'Go ahead.'

'That piece of bone – I'd like you to remove it from her hand. I'll have someone collect it and the thong from you within the hour, if you can hold on. It'll be OK with Ivers.'

'I'll do it. But, as I said last week, one good turn deserves another. How about it?'

'Em …' *Why was I nervous about this?*

'Illaun, are you still there?'

'I'm here.'

'The solstice event at Newgrange tomorrow morning. Can you get me in there … plus one?'

I was surprised. But then, what had I been expecting?

It wasn't going to be easy. Sherry knew well that tickets for the day and the two days either side – a hundred passes in all, for the five days during which the light comes through the roof-box – were allocated by lottery in October, with a handful being reserved for VIPs. I had witnessed the solar phenomenon myself some years previously, but on this occasion I would be outside the chamber.

'If I can't do it, what about the following day, or Thursday?'

'Won't be around, I'm afraid. I'm going away for Christmas.'

That was really narrowing the odds. 'I'll do my best. Can't promise anything.'

I put down the phone wondering why he had left it so late to ask me. I rang Keelan O'Rourke; his mobile responded with an agitated bleeping. Out of order? Keelan lived in Navan – also on the Boyne, but not as picturesque as my hometown. His landline was in our database, but, as he was scheduled to be out at the interchange site with Gayle and was utterly dependable, there was no point in trying it.

Gayle had neither a mobile phone nor her own transport. About the latter I could do little, as she didn't know how to drive, but her refusal to accept a paid-for company phone was more frustrating; it made little sense in a working environment where the mobile phone was an extremely useful tool.

Irritated at not being able to reach the team, I redirected my stress into steeling my nerve to ring Con Purcell, Director of Newgrange Visitor Centre. I hated putting him on the spot, but he was my best hope for gaining admission for Malcolm Sherry.

Purcell was at his desk. I explained the situation briefly, adding that Sherry had been very helpful in connection with the find at Monashee.

'Nothing I can do unless we get a cancellation,

Illaun. And then officially we have to draw from our panel of applicants.'

'I understand. Maybe if one of your VIPs bows out?'

'Doubt it. But you never know.'

I had no sooner put down the phone than it rang again. An unfamiliar number came up on the screen.

I answered as Peggy would. 'Illaun Bowe Consultancy, how can we help you?'

'Keelan O'Rourke of the Away Team checking in, Captain. How is everything on board the *Enterprise*?'

'Keelan! Am I glad you called. Where are you ringing from?'

'Don't tell the boss, eh? I'm in a pub down the road from where I'm meant to be working.'

I laughed. 'So why are you there?'

'Had my phone stolen on Friday night.'

'That's odd; so did I.'

'How?'

'My car was broken into.'

'Sorry to hear that. In my case it was just stupidity – I left it behind on the counter in my local. When I went back on Saturday, they said it hadn't been handed in.'

'Well, look, get yourself a new one and bill the company. Ask Peggy later for an order number or whatever it's called. In the meantime I want you to pick up something in Drogheda for me and bring it here.'

'What is it?'

'Remember that strip of leather? That and something else. From Dr Sherry. He's waiting for you at the old morgue.'

'Will do. How's the report going?'

'I've got it more or less laid out, and I'm doing the introduction as we speak. Let's wrap up the survey now, and I'll get the report to the NRA today. I'll e-mail it to you and Gayle, and you can both take a look at it over the holidays. We can always send them an addendum if it's needed.'

'When do I have to collect the stuff from Dr Sherry?'

'Your little blue Micra should be halfway to Drogheda by now, that's when.'

He chuckled and hung up.

I liked Keelan for many reasons, not least because he kept me on my toes. With renewed determination, I went at the report. I had spent no more than twenty minutes on it when Con Purcell rang back.

'Well, Illaun, funny you should have mentioned VIPs. Derek Ward's secretary just rang to say the minister and his wife are going to a friend's funeral and won't be able to make the solstice. Did you know something I didn't?'

'No, Con. Just a coincidence, I guess.' But I was fairly certain whose funeral Ward was attending. And that gave me an idea.

'Tell Dr Sherry to be outside the site at eight am.'

I thanked Purcell and reflected, as I dialled Sherry's number, that it was far more of a coincidence than I had time to explain: Derek Ward's place would be taken by the man who had carried out the post-mortem on his friend.

Sherry was fulsomely grateful and said he would see me there. I looked at the clock. Just gone eleven.

The phone rang again. 'Hi.' The caller had no need to identify herself.

'Hi, Fran.'

'Just reminding you about lunch today.' She knew my form.

'I know. Twelve-thirty. The Old Mill.'

'Walter's.'

'Walter's it is. Hey, I forgot to tell you: I'm going to a rather special event in Dublin tonight.'

'The Spinsters' Ball?'

'Jocelyn Carew's "At Home", as we say.'

'I'm so jealous it hurts,' she said facetiously. 'Who are you going with – Wolfman?' Wolfman was her nickname for Finian; it had its origins in a conversation with me in which she'd referred to him as a sheep in wolf's clothing, an inversion she found hilarious because as far as she was concerned it also described his appearance.

'Don't give me that; you'd love to be there,' I said, evading her attempt to engage me in a discussion about Finian.

'No way. I'd prefer a night with the handsome electrician who said he'd like to switch on my fairy lights.'

'He wasn't dressed in red and sporting a white beard, by any chance?'

'Come to think of it … yeah, he was. He also promised he'd come down my chimney on Christmas Eve.'

I told Fran she was obscene, which she seemed to take as a compliment, and put down the phone.

I had been working on the report for another five minutes when the phone rang again. I answered it immediately, rather than have to listen to the pre-recorded message and the caller's response. Where *was* Peggy?

My irritation subsided when I heard Seamus Crean on the other end.

'Seamus, how are you?'

'Not great today, Missus. The asthma is at me.'

'Sorry to hear that.' I suspected it had been brought on by the stress of being taken in for questioning.

'Anyway, I'm ringing to say I talked to my father …' He paused for breath. 'And it's fixed for tomorrow at four.'

'Fixed? What's fixed?'

'He'll meet you in Mick Doran's bar here in Donore. It'll be quiet at that time.'

I was lost.

'You said you were interested in hearing about the apparitions.'

In the vaguest possible way, as I recalled. But I hadn't the heart to refuse. And, as far as I knew, I had nothing else scheduled for the afternoon of the twenty-first. 'Thanks, Seamus. I'll be there at four. What's your father's name, by the way?'

'Jack Crean.'

'Jack – right, so. And now that I have you on the line – and I'm sure the Gardaí made you go over it a thousand times – would you mind telling me what happened at Monashee from the time you found the body to the time I arrived?'

'No problem. I remember the first thing I done was ring the Visitor Centre. I was put through by Directory Inquiries and I asked to talk to the boss. Then Mr Purcell came on and said he'd drive down to Monashee. I'd say he arrived about ten minutes later …' He paused again for air.

It had never occurred to me that Con Purcell had been at the site because my first point of contact had been Terence Ivers, who had been alerted by Purcell. 'What happened in the meantime?'

'Nothing, except the dump truck that had been hauling away the soil came back for another load, but I sent it away.'

'Did the driver take a look at the body?'

'No, Missus. He was as rattled as I was. Drove off like a scalded cat.'

'So then Mr Purcell arrived. What did he do?'

'He took a good look in the bucket, said it was definitely a body that was stuck in the turf and had probably been there a long time … Then he said he'd arrange for someone to examine it properly because he was very busy.'

'And then he went away?'

'Yeah. He asked me to stick around until the experts arrived.'

'So before I came on the scene, you were hanging around there for – what, forty minutes? And you never went near the body?'

'No way. I had some sandwiches, so I ate them in the cab, listening to the radio to pass the time. Then some fella stopped his car at the side of the road, and I went up and had a chat with him.'

'Who was he?'

'Dunno. He was just passing by, saw the digger and wondered if there was a car park being laid for people to view Newgrange.'

'What did he look like?'

'He had a bit of a beard, I remember. Well spoken.'

'He didn't get out of the car?'

'No. He drove off. And that was all that happened until you came.'

'And when you were sitting there in the digger waiting, what was going through your mind?'

'To be honest, I was a bit scared. I kept remembering a prayer you were supposed to say passing Monashee.'

'Oh? What was that?'

'Let me see or hear no evil as I pass; and, if I do, please God, let me never speak of it to anyone.'

It couldn't be a coincidence. No eyes to see, ears to hear, mouth to speak. I caught a glimpse of the mutilated apparitions that had been with me in the car that night. 'Seamus, did you recite that … that prayer for Inspector Gallagher?'

'No. Because I didn't hear about the cuts to Traynor's face until I came home after being in custody.' Seamus had spotted the connection.

'But you'd heard the prayer before that.'

'Sure. I learned it from my mother.'

Just as well it wasn't in Latin, I thought. 'Well, if Gallagher questions you at any stage in the future, don't volunteer it. It could land you in trouble all over again.'

'I won't, so. But I'm glad I remembered it that day, because it worked.'

'How do you mean, it worked?'

'It protected me, like. They say the evening Mr Traynor was killed there was a figure in white seen in the field … My mother says it must have been the soul of that poor woman we found, and that she's upset because we haven't given her a Christian burial.'

'I see. Well, tell your mother …' Tell her what? That Mona would probably end up on exhibition in the National Museum? 'Tell her I wish her and the family a happy Christmas.'

Twenty uninterrupted minutes later, I sat back and scrolled through the completed report. I had come across one item on the inventory that I had considered querying: I thought we had found three pike-heads at the skirmish site, but only two were catalogued – but I decided it was better to get the report to the NRA before Christmas, as planned; in the meantime, when I met Keelan and Gayle I would ask them about the apparent discrepancy. I clicked the report off to the NRA, with copies to my two field staff.

Only then did I notice the small stack of opened post that Peggy had left on my desk. I picked it up and quickly flicked through to see if there was anything urgent.

When I came across the Christmas card, my mouth went instantly dry. An abstract, purple-hued landscape with a spiral motif in gold running across it, and the words 'The Peace of Earth, Air and Water be with you, and may the returning Sun rekindle all your hopes this Midwinter.'

My fingers trembled as I opened it. Blank. I turned it around: nothing on the back.

It was a warning: *You're getting close. But come any closer and it will cost you your life.*

I shot out of my chair over to Peggy's wastepaper basket, lifted it onto her desk and started searching for the envelope.

Peggy arrived just then, talking as she came through the door. 'I waited until they replaced the window. Took an early lunch. Saved both of us having to drive back –'

'Tell me which envelope this came in, will you?' I held up the card.

'Goodness, you look upset. What's the matter?'

'Just help me find the envelope.'

Peggy put down her handbag and waved me aside. 'Should be easy. The envelope was blank too.'

'What do you mean, blank?'

'No name or address. Not even a stamp.'

Which meant the card hadn't been posted. I remembered the lid of the post-box rattling the previous night. There had been someone outside. I felt suddenly weak and slumped back into my chair before my legs buckled.

I must have had my head in my hands, because I didn't notice Peggy approaching the desk and placing the half-crumpled envelope in front of me.

'I knew you disliked certain kinds of cards,' she said when I finally looked up, 'but I had no idea just how much.'

She looked so glum I had to laugh. 'Oh, Peggy. I dislike this card for sure, but for other reasons. Let's just say someone used it to send me a particularly nasty message.'

Peggy went back to her desk, probably baffled at my interpretation of what seemed a perfectly benign greeting. But that moment of levity had helped me recover my strength.

I found a pair of tweezers in a drawer and held the

envelope up to the light. There was nothing inside. I pulled a Ziploc bag from another drawer and dropped the envelope and the card into it.

Peggy had been following this procedure, and she tried her best to pick up her earlier conversation. 'The phone you wanted isn't in stock, by the way. They'll have it in later this evening or first thing tomorrow morning. I did get your ... em ...' She had taken a number of cellophane-wrapped packets from her capacious handbag and was pointing at them in order to avoid using the C-word. 'Not in the mood for writing them, I'd imagine.'

'Not right now. And I'm meant to be on my way to meet Fran. One or two things before I go. Keelan will be dropping in some items for me and going back to Drogheda.' I held up the bag with the card in it. 'Will you ask him to bring this to the Garda station there, to be given only to a Detective Inspector Matt Gallagher? In the meantime, ring Gallagher and tell him there's evidence on its way that was left in our post-box last night. And finally ...' I took the digital camera out of my backpack and set it on my desk beside the PowerBook. 'Load these into the laptop. Call the folders "Morgue" and "West Door".'

Chapter Sixteen

The place Fran had suggested for lunch was near the massive curtain wall of the Anglo-Norman castle from which my hometown took half of its name. Unlike the office-party revellers filling the more chic restaurant next door, Walter's clientele were mainly people with shopping bags and parcels tucked under their tables. But the table Fran was at had a small gift-wrapped box sitting on top of it – which, I realised with some embarrassment as I sat down, was for me.

'I mightn't see you between now and the twenty-fifth, the way things are going. I thought I'd give you your present today.'

'Well, you know me, Fran. I'll be giving you yours closer to the time.'

She flashed a grin. 'As is traditional, Illaun.' Fran knew that I sometimes ended up, in a panic, still hunting down presents on Christmas Eve. For that reason, she had forced me to buy Finian's Christmas gift in Lucca in October. It had seemed unnatural at the time (*October*?); only now did I fully appreciate her forward planning.

I put the box to one side, leaned over and gave her a kiss on the cheek. 'Thank you, Fran.' My voice sounded flat.

'Merry Christmas. Now let's have something to eat.'

As we read the menu we chatted about Daisy and Oisín. Fran was separated from her alcoholic husband and had custody of their two children. She tended to speak little of him but endlessly about them. Both looked like her, but in different ways; if you could reassemble them into one person, you'd have Fran. Her son Oisín had inherited her green eyes, Daisy her red hair; Oisín got the freckles, Daisy the long legs; and both had her wicked smile.

We gave our orders and continued to talk about family matters, but I found myself growing increasingly detached from the conversation. I became aware that Fran was staring at me.

'You're upset about something, Illaun. What's wrong?'

'I think I'm having a delayed reaction …'

The waitress arrived with our orders – smoked salmon and cream-cheese bagel (hers) and avocado and prawn salad (mine).

'Delayed reaction to what?'

'A death threat.'

'Jesus, Illaun. Who's threatening you?'

'I don't know.' As we ate, I filled her in on what had transpired since we'd last met. 'It's obvious I've overturned a stone under which something nasty was hiding,' I concluded, 'but the question is, what did I do, say or hear in the past few days that disturbed it?'

'I'd be suspicious of O'Hagan,' said Fran, after giving it some thought. 'For one thing, he's been hampering the investigation; and now you've probably got him into deep shit with Gallagher. Apart from which, he sounds like a right bastard.'

Heads turned towards us as Fran emphasised the word with obvious relish. Her subliminal feelings towards her ex-husband sometimes found unexpected outlets.

My reply was barely above the level of a whisper. 'I can see where you're coming from, Fran. And I do believe O'Hagan's embittered about life for some reason – but a sadistic killer? I don't think so.'

Fran sighed. 'OK, then it's the Ghost of Grange Abbey – whooo!' She wiggled her hands in the air to complete her impression of a ghostly apparition.

'I wouldn't be surprised,' I said, discovering the ability to smile again. 'But seriously, there's something just not right about them. It's as if they've always hidden in the shadows; now they're suddenly thrust into public view, and all they really want is to drop off the radar screen again.'

'I could help you find out more about them.'

'How?'

'We have one of them in the nursing home. A patient, I mean.'

'You're sure she's a Hospitaller of –'

'St Margaret of Antioch, yes. And she was at Grange Abbey. She reminds us of these facts every day.'

'Is she … all there?'

'No more or no less gaga than any of our other old dears.'

'I'd have thought a medical order would care for their own?'

'The mother ship flew off and this one got stranded. Like E.T. And just as many wrinkles.'

'Does she get visits from any of the Grange Abbey community?'

'No. I think they were having an influx from their missions a few years ago, when Sister Gabriel was about to check out: mostly younger nuns, strangers to her, I suppose.'

'But the abbess …?'

'Don't think Gabriel saw eye-to-eye with the boss lady. Look, why not go and ask her yourself? I'll arrange a visit for you.'

I couldn't let the opportunity pass. And the sooner the better. 'When?'

'It'd be best if I was around. Next Monday, maybe? That'll give me time to talk to her, get her prepared. Having a visitor is a rare event.'

Monday was a full week away. Not exactly what I had in mind. 'I'd really like to talk to her before then if possible.'

'If she's *compos mentis* when I go back on Saturday evening, I'll try and fix it for the following day.'

St Stephen's Day. Only a day earlier. Still not ideal, but I wasn't going to push Fran any further while she was off work.

'Now, about you and Wolfman ...'

I looked at my watch. 'Hey, it's gone two and I have to pick out my clothes for this do tonight. Let's go.'

'You're not getting away that easily,' she said. 'When I come back from the loo we're gonna *talk*.' She excused herself and headed for the toilets. That gave me an opportunity to pay the bill without having to argue with her. Fran was proud of her independence, and any gesture that encroached on it, however small, was suspect. Her spiky personality also masked a generous and protective nature – hence, anyone she suspected of not being good enough for me got the sharp end of her tongue.

We had always been an unlikely pair. As a child she had been a diligent Barbie-groomer, while I liked to poke under rocks in search of creepy-crawlies. As a teenager she'd metamorphosed into a lanky, chalk-faced Goth who hid fishnet tights in her schoolbag to wear on the way home, while I became a Pre-Raphaelite pixie mooning about in Héloise-like daydreams about Finian. In time our paths had diverged as we predictably followed different careers. But when I came back to live in Castleboyne we had simply picked up where we'd left off.

The waitress took my credit card, and while waiting for her to return I decided to unwrap Fran's Christmas present. It made me blink in disbelief at first; then it put a broad smile on my face. She had given me a six-CD box set of seasonal country music – from Alison Krauss and Union Station all the way back to Bob Wills and his Country Playboys. It was probably more Christmas country than even I could take during the festive period, but it was a lovely thought – not least because, when Fran and I had renewed our friendship, she'd been alarmed to discover I'd been 'converted' to country music, as if some cult had brainwashed me. When I explained that, even if it was a Church of sorts, it was a broad one, my argument fell on deaf ears. Not even when alternative country became cool with rock critics (I tried to turn her on to the spooky Handsome Family without success) or when her pinup George Clooney helped to make old-timey mainstream with the soundtrack of *O Brother, Where Art Thou?* could she be persuaded it was anything other than Hicksville.

Just then she came back, and at the same time the

waitress returned with the receipt and my card. I gave her a tip and short-circuited Fran's protest by standing up to leave. 'All done,' I said.

'Thank you. But it's not who's paying for lunch I'm concerned about. It's you and that wolf who's really a sheep.'

'Hey, come here,' I whispered, forcing her to lean closer to hear what I had to say. When she was within range, I kissed her on the cheek. 'Thank you for the pressie,' I said, and moved towards the door. 'It's very sweet of you.'

'Don't worry, I wore a burqa going into the record store,' she said, catching up. 'So when are we going to discuss you and Finian?'

'Another time, eh? All I'll say is, he has from now to Christmas Eve to make some kind of move. Otherwise, that's it.'

'Oh, yeah? And reindeer will fly.'

The polythene bags delivered by Keelan were on my desk. Peggy had left the office early to do some Christmas shopping. At this time of year, the working environment was laid back. If it wasn't urgent business, forget about it; if it needed planning and concentration, start on it afresh in the New Year.

I sat in my swivel chair and opened the bag, which was packed with sheets of soft foam protecting and separating the thong and the piece of bone Sherry had removed from Mona's fist. The bone carving – I knew it was an artefact immediately – was about the size and shape of an extended lipstick. There was some dried-out soil adhering to it, but I could make out a number of indentations along its length, and the flat end had been formed into a kind of plinth. For a moment I thought it might be a chess piece.

I took a toothbrush from the top drawer of my desk and began a gentle flicking motion, which dislodged most of the crust. In the same drawer I found a toothpick, another implement of incalculable value to an archaeologist, and I began to tease out the grime from the grooves carved into the bone. As I worked I considered the difficulties of dating the object – not in terms of its absolute age, carbon-dating would establish that, but in terms of its usage. For example, was it an heirloom that had been in circulation for some time before it ended up in the mire with Mona? And why was it that, when so much of her own skeleton had been dissolved by the bog acids, this item had survived along with the hand that clutched it so tightly in death?

When I'd finished cleaning it, I counted ten parallel grooves that circled around the bone to join up with a single groove running from the base to the smooth conical top, which was like an unopened mushroom cap. The artefact was of such a familiar design that I didn't even need to look it up, but it added to my excitement when, a couple of minutes later, I compared the object in my hand with an illustration in a book on the Boyne Valley. Among the ceremonial artefacts found inside the passage tombs is a carved stone phallus about twenty-five centimetres long; and a miniature replica of it had been buried with Mona.

I was stunned. I finally had a direct link between Monashee and Brú na Bóinne across the river, between Mona and the Neolithic people who had built Newgrange. And this once more raised the issue of her age, something I had almost given up on.

Turning the carving upside down, I noticed a perforation under the plinth, scooped out to leave a tiny arch of bone. I picked up the thong and saw that I would have no difficulty threading it through the hole.

Mona *had* been strangled with her own necklace, from which this pendant had hung – until the ligature snapped. In her death throes she'd somehow managed to keep the pendant in her hand. But had it been the death-grip of a desperate woman trying to tear the ligature away from her throat, or had Mona delibe– rately taken the phallic carving with her to her grave?

Later than I had hoped, I found myself sliding open the door of my wardrobe in search of something to wear to the Carews' soirée. My taste in clothes is eclectic, to say the least: gypsy girl from *Carmen* one day, power broker from the City the next. And, chameleon-like, I tend to match them to my mood, even to my surroundings. This is sometimes planned (as in the

Christmas-cracker effect) but more often accidental (as on my visit to the abbey, when I could have said 'snap' to Sister Campion).

I wondered if Miss Marie Maguire had been anxious about her appearance that night in Castleboyne over a century earlier. Unlike our modern anxiety caused by too much choice, in her case it was probably a matter of hoping that her one good dress would be suitable. And what of my great-grandfather? What would have been his concerns? Not what he wore, unless his suit was threadbare. He might have been hoping to walk Miss Maguire home. No: she lived in Celbridge, at least two hours' journey by horse-drawn coach. She must have stayed the night in Castleboyne – not with him, of course; with friends of the family. Did he leave her home, and did they get to embrace downstairs while all were asleep above? A hug, a kiss ... what else? Were they aroused by each other? Had they then to deny their passion, telling each other that it would show a lack of respect and that they should remain virgins until their wedding night?

And was that such a bad idea? I wondered, flicking through the hangers on the rail. In a very real sense, it made you totally each other's on that occasion – and forever more, if you remained faithful. But it provided no other guarantees.

I selected a couple of garments and laid them on the bed. One was an ivory satin blouse with a high neck that buttoned on the side. No. The other was a red jersey dress with a pleated bodice and a mandarin collar, close-fitting, soft on the skin; seasonal and sexy. But which shoes? I drew the mirrored door closed and opened another one.

The idea of staying overnight with Finian began to preoccupy me. It had awoken desires that had been dormant for quite some time. But was I just focusing my sexual needs on him because he was the nearest available attractive male, or was it something deeper? And, if so, why now?

Boots? Not with that dress. With a black three-quarter-length flounced skirt I had rarely worn, and that blouse I'd rejected – plus another leather jacket I owned, black, looser than the one I had worn on Sunday. I slipped on the jacket and held the blouse and skirt up against it in the wardrobe mirror. Getting there.

Hair? In the mirror I could see my half-wet hair had divided downwards into two scraggy sections. It suited the Romany look I was aiming for perfectly, and I could keep it intact with some gel. No need for the hairdresser. If the total look wasn't right, I would revert to the red jersey dress – or maybe not: by the time I was finished accessorising it, I'd probably look like something Jocelyn Carew could hang on his Christmas tree.

I sat on the edge of the bed. If Maria and Peter had married, then they were responsible for my presence in the world. But no one in the future would ever owe their existence to me. And that suddenly seemed so important. *Because time's getting on, dear, that's why.* The witchy version of my mother's voice was at it again.

I was getting broody. But it was easy to dispel. I just thought of the genetic experiment nature had conducted on the infant buried at Monashee.

Chapter Seventeen

The evening was cold but dry. Arm-in-arm, Finian in a full-length black coat, we strolled towards Fitzwilliam Square from Leeson Street, the vista provided by the elegant lines of Georgian terraces drawing our eyes towards the outline of the National Maternity Hospital in the distance.

'Last time I was there was when Jennifer was born,' said Finian. Jennifer was one of his sister Maeve's three children.

The subject of children was never far away these days, it seemed. We had been talking about how family politics can be tricky at this time of year. Maeve was of the view that their father would be better off in a nursing home, and Finian was interpreting her decision not to formally invite them to her house in Galway for Christmas – as had been traditional since their mother's death a decade ago – as a way of making her point. It made little difference to Finian, but he knew Arthur would miss seeing his grandchildren on the day. So both of us were feeling the pressure applied – although in different directions – by members of the family living away from home.

'My advice is to *assume* you're invited. So ring Maeve tomorrow and ask her what time she's expecting you on Christmas Eve.'

'Wow, you can be scary sometimes,' he said, hugging me closer. 'I'll give it a go. Now, on the subject of "lying-in homes", as they used to be called ...' He waved a hand in the direction of the maternity hospital. 'Allowing for the fact that a considerable part of Ireland's history was lost in the fire in the Public Records Office in 1922, I can find no trace of a maternity home run by the Hospitaller Order in any part of the country. And that's from the Middle Ages right up to the foundation of the State.'

'I got the impression it was in or near Dublin.'

'Can't have been.' Finian shook his head firmly. 'It's estimated that by 1700 there were no nuns *at all* in the city of Dublin. That's how successful the Penal Laws were. And in the following century there were only two communities recorded on the entire island – and

251

the Hospitaller Order wasn't one of them. Most of the religious orders for women, the ones we're familiar with, were established in the nineteenth century after Catholic emancipation.'

'Curiouser and curiouser, eh?'

'But, then again, Grange Abbey doesn't officially exist either.'

'I'm not surprised. Go on.'

'Medieval land ownership in the bend of the Boyne is reasonably well documented, but your nuns don't turn up on any deeds or charters. As you know, practically all of the land around there was owned by the Cistercians until the Anglo-Normans arrived.'

I nodded. Mellifont Abbey had been founded by the Cistercian Order, and it was they who introduced the idea of granges, separately run farms on their estates – one of which was Newgrange.

'After the Normans took control of the area, they granted some land to Augustinian canons from a Welsh monastery called Llanthony. But I can find no reference to the Hospitaller Order of St Margaret being endowed with any property.'

'It was granted directly by Henry II, according to the abbess. Maybe that explains it.'

'Hmm. That would make their non-existence in the records even more mysterious. Especially when every monastic settlement was inventoried for Henry VIII's confiscations.'

'Maybe they were deliberately overlooked – something

252

to do with the reason they got a royal charter in the first place. Also, Sister Campion said they were technically a pious society. That might have got them off the hook.'

'The people who framed the Penal Laws against Catholics wouldn't have been impressed by technicalities. No – the Grange Abbey nuns were an exception to the rule. A big exception ...'

We had paused outside a discreetly lit shop window with a display of gold jewellery based on Celtic designs.

'We could ask Dr Carew,' I said. 'He's good on the history of medicine in Ireland, and they're a nursing order, after all ... Oh, that's stunning.' I was pointing at a ribbon torc, a neck decoration consisting of a strip of hammered gold twisted into a continuous spiral. 'It's so simple, so beautiful.'

'Wouldn't you prefer a bone pendant?' said Finian facetiously. I had told him about the find on the way to Dublin.

'And end up in a bog-hole? No, thanks.' I dug him in the ribs affectionately and we moved on.

'Joking aside, I wonder if that carving had something to do with her death. And, if so, is it wise for you to be in possession of it now?'

'You're not being superstitious, are you?'

'No, I'm just urging caution, considering the threat you got this morning.'

'But whoever sent me the card didn't know the carving even existed.'

'The same way as Traynor's killer couldn't have known about the pattern of injuries to the body found in the field? Yet somehow he or she did. I don't know who or what you're dealing with here, but I think you'd better take it for granted that they probably know more than you about that woman and why she died.'

All the rooms of the house, including the staircases and landings, were thronged with writers, journalists, artists and especially environmentalists, many of whom had worked on Jocelyn Carew's election campaigns. Some guests were gathered in small groups, talking and laughing; others, singly or in pairs, glasses of wine in hand, wandered around admiring the paintings and prints covering the walls, and the sculptures that seemed to occupy every available space.

We eventually got to the drawing room on the second floor and headed for a quiet corner between a baby grand piano and one of the Georgian windows looking out on the street. Finian was wearing a plum-coloured bow tie – outrageously colourful for him – and a charcoal-grey silk jacket. We chatted for a while, and then he said, 'I must go and find Jocelyn so I can introduce you.' Our host had been downstairs, deep in conversation with the country's Attorney General, when we arrived.

'Before you go, who's she?' I had been observing a woman, dressed in brown, flitting in and out of the company like a wren in a hedge. It had taken several sightings of her to establish that she had her hair in a chignon and that her jacket and skirt were almost Edwardian in style.

'That's Edith, Jocelyn's wife,' Finian said discreetly.

'I'm going to get myself a glass of wine,' I said. 'Meet you back here.'

I eased my way past people and furniture, but found my passage momentarily blocked as the crowd parted to make way for a group of four young people, two of each sex, each one carrying a folder of sheet music. They took up a position in a corner near the fireplace, and I decided to stay and listen. There was no need to go into the next room for drinks – a woman came past with a tray, and I took a glass of red as the ensemble started to sing 'The Holly and the Ivy'.

Nice touch, I thought. *Carols to remind us of the reason for our festivities.* The singing was sublime, the harmonies complex but unforced. After the applause they introduced their next choice, 'The Wexford Carol'.

Good people all, this Christmastime,
Consider well and bear in mind
What our good God for us has done,
In sending His beloved Son …

Just above the applause when they had finished, I could hear Finian laughing. He was out on the landing with Jocelyn Carew.

'Yes, that was the Rotunda ...' I heard Carew saying as they came into the room.

Finian led him over to me. 'As I was saying, Illaun is trying to ... well, something's rotten in the Royal County – she can explain it herself. Jocelyn Carew, Illaun Bowe.'

Carew held my fingertips and bowed. 'Delighted to meet you.' He was wearing a razor-sharp, double-breasted navy suit. His accessories were a bright-red cravat, ruby cufflinks in his crisp white shirt and a tiny red rose in his lapel. He stood to his full height and looked me over lecherously – in a theatrical way, of course. 'Pulchritude in pursuit of putrescence, eh?' His lips were red and sensual, and made more prominent by a close-shaven white beard and moustache. His colourful, well-preened appearance was in marked contrast to his wife's drab plumage.

'Well ... yes, sort of.' *Bons mots* are difficult to reply to. 'I'm trying to find out as much as I can about an order of nuns who ran a lying-in home – '

'Ah, what wonderful terminology ...' Carew affected the pose of someone hearing sublime music. 'Sounds so benign, too. Much more reassuring than some of the other places still trading when I was a boy. I mean, would you like to have been carted off to a place called the "Hospital for Incurables" or even "Rest for the Dying"? Or how about, saints preserve us, a place known as "the Colony for Mental Defectives"? But I digress. Sorry, m'dear.'

'If you don't mind,' Finian interjected, 'I'll leave you both to it.' He slipped away and mingled with the crowd.

'Please continue,' said Carew.

'This was a home for well-off girls who became pregnant.'

'Up the pole, m'dear, to use the medical term. Daddy's little filly fucked by some stable boy and about to drop a foal.'

'Eh, yes. But they also claim to have provided the same care for the poor.'

Carew snorted and made an outlandish gesture with his arms, reminiscent of a pantomime dame. 'Who are these paradigms of virtue? Do tell.'

'The Hospitallers of St Margaret of Antioch.'

Carew raised his eyes to the ceiling and squinted, his habit when calling on his reputedly extraordinary memory. 'According to my father, who was a Church of Ireland clergyman, Catholic nuns were always to be treated with the utmost respect, particularly an order of midwives – an anomaly within the Roman Church – that had a house on the Dublin–Meath border near where I grew up … because, he told me in the gravest tones, they carried out a duty for which all Christians should be grateful.'

'And they were the Hospitallers of St Margaret?'

'Indubitably. And that was their lying-in home.'

'Not in the city, then?'

'No, no, dear heart. Goodness me. It had to be away from prying eyes.'

'And did your father tell you what this duty was?'

'The strange thing is, it never occurred to me to ask him. I assumed they provided a discreet service to protect reputations, arranged for the products of sexual indiscretion to be sent for adoption and so on. And I took my father's words to imply that they looked after our crowd as well.'

So that was it. The order had been able to come through the vicissitudes of Church and State un-molested, because both sides of the religious divide were beholden to them. The rich were always prepared to pay to smooth over domestic difficulties, especially illegitimate pregnancy. The religion of those who could assist in the cover-up became irrelevant. In the case of the Protestant aristocracy, it was probably an additional safeguard against claims on their property if infants were spirited away to the Catholic side, from where there was scant hope of legal redress. The silence of both sides was the deal that sustained the system.

Carew suddenly frowned and peered into my face as if examining me for signs of fever. 'Are you Paddy Bowe's daughter, by any chance?'

'I am, yes.'

'I thought I saw a resemblance. How is he? Bloody fine actor in his day.'

My father was already being eased into the past tense.

'As well as can be expected under the circumstances.'

'Pity he wasted so much of his talent on that TV rubbish.'

I felt like saying, 'Well, acting's a notoriously precarious way of making a living, and he did have a family to feed, clothe and educate.' But instead I thought of Sister Aloysius and smiled: she was a reminder of how he had brought pleasure to many people's lives. 'And that's as much as you know about the Grange Abbey nuns?'

'Afraid so. Never heard tell of them again until – Did you say "Grange Abbey"?'

'Yes. It's in the Boyne Valley.'

'Hmm. I remember a couple of years back I was given a report by a group protesting against illegal dumping of medical waste near Duleek. They were worried about groundwater contamination, among other things. For some reason Grange Abbey was mentioned in the report – don't ask me why. You'd need to talk to someone in the locality. May I ask why you're researching the order, by the way?'

'There was a mummified body found last week on land they had owned. It's near Newgrange. Then the man they had sold it to was found murdered in the same place.'

'Frank Traynor, the property developer.'

'Yes. You obviously know about the case. My interest as an archaeologist is the preservation of the site, and the nuns may have some say in that. But I'm also intrigued by the order's history. They're something of an enigma.'

Carew drew me away from a knot of people standing within earshot. Then he spoke quietly and forcibly. 'I can't tell you much more about the nuns, I'm afraid. But I would advise you to do a little digging – if you'll pardon the pun – on the connection between the late Mr Traynor and Derek Ward.'

'The minister?'

'Yes.' He looked about him again. 'Ward has been dancing to Traynor's tune for quite some time now, especially where rezoning of land is concerned. The puzzling thing is that there's no visible benefit for Ward – no big house, flash cars, expensive holidays. He seems to have kept his hands clean.'

'Or else he's got a big stash of brown envelopes he's never opened.'

'Well, certainly as Minister for Tourism and Heritage he was able to put a lot of pressure on Meath County Council to sanction this hotel of Traynor's. One has to ask, did money change hands? And isn't it odd that, as soon as the issue hit the headlines, Traynor was murdered? Was it about to get uncomfortable for Ward?'

'You're not suggesting …'

'No, I'm not saying Derek Ward personally took a knife to Traynor. But there may have been some among the minister's entourage who interpreted his wishes *à la* King Henry and Archbishop Becket.' He was referring to the knights who interpreted Henry's displeasure as a cue to kill the 'turbulent priest' Thomas Becket in Canterbury Cathedral in 1170.

'That could bring down the government,' I said.

'Yes, m'dear. That's how serious it could become. But, then again, this government has reeked of corruption for so many years that they're no longer capable of smelling their own ordure. They did nothing when –'

'Jocelyn!'

We turned to see a loud-voiced, overdressed woman bearing down on us.

'It *is* you,' she gushed, reaching out to envelop him in a swirl of perfumed drapery. And, before I could say a word, she linked her arm through Carew's and dragged him away.

The carollers launched into a hearty version of 'Ding Dong, Merrily on High'. I looked around for Finian, but he must have drifted off to one of the other rooms while Carew and I were conversing. I moved through the crowd to get nearer the singers and had just begun to sip another glass of wine when someone poked me in the back. I turned around, expecting to see Finian, and was surprised to find an ex-boyfriend grinning at me.

'Hi, Tim,' I mouthed, and turned back to the singers.

He nudged me again, but I didn't respond. Then I felt his breath on my cheek as he leaned in to say something.

'You look great,' he whispered.

I nodded in acknowledgement and stared straight ahead. Tim Kennedy was an archaeologist with the Heritage Service, and he and I had broken up at least three years previously. It was not an amicable split.

Although we hadn't lived together, it had been quite a passionate affair. Most weekends he travelled from Dublin to Castleboyne or we went away together, sometimes to Irish country houses, occasionally to London or Paris – until I eventually discovered that during the week Tim maintained a relationship with his secretary, who seemed to tolerate him disappearing from her life at weekends.

'I've broken up with Karen,' he mumbled in my ear.

This time I recoiled, indicating my desire to listen to the carol. But Tim inserted his thin, angular frame between me and an elderly man and woman with whom I was sharing a cramped space between two armchairs. I would have to escape somehow.

'Yes, it's all over,' he continued, oblivious to my lack of interest. 'How about you? Any developments in your love life?'

I was about to say something sarcastic when I saw Finian out of the corner of my eye, standing on the far side of the elderly couple. The carol was coming to an end. Here was my chance.

'Have to go, Tim. Sorry.'

The quartet reached the short hymn's last chorus of 'Gloria, hosanna in excelsis', and as we applauded I excused myself to the white-haired couple and squeezed past them. Finian saw me, smiled and raised his glass.

I heard Tim's voice from behind. 'Go back to Daddy, then.'

It was as if he had thrown a knife into my back. It had always been his contention that I was too much of a 'daddy's girl' and that my friendship with Finian looked suspiciously like a surrogate relationship. Had the remark been uttered by anybody else, I would easily have shrugged it off.

'What's wrong?' Finian asked as I joined him.

'Oh, nothing,' I lied.

'Wasn't that Tim Kennedy?' Finian had met him once or twice. 'Did he say something to upset you?'

'He's had too much wine,' I said.

I looked over in Tim's direction. He had disappeared. I gave Finian a hug. In all the time I had known him, Finian had never said a hurtful thing to me. He could be critical of my views, he might get annoyed with me sometimes, but he would never insult or offend me.

'Time to leave, do you think?' he said gently.

'Let's wait until the carols are finished.'

'Like another glass of wine?'

I said yes, and he went to fetch it. While he was away I gave my full attention to the singers, their vocal skills and arrangements. From time to time I was aware of Edith Carew somewhere in the room, but always just on the edge of visibility.

Two more carols had been sung by the time Finian came back. 'It's getting to be quite a squeeze in there,' he said. 'I'm glad we arrived earlier rather than later.'

'Mmm ...' I sipped some wine. 'I'm so pleased you asked me to come, Finian.'

The choristers announced their final selection, 'The Coventry Carol'.

Lully, lullay, thou little tiny child,
By, by, lully, lullay ...

'It means a lot to me that you did,' he said. He put his arm around my waist and gave me a gentle squeeze. We stood there, my head resting on his shoulder, listening to the soothing cadence of the much-loved Christmas lullaby.

Oh, sisters too, how may we do
For to preserve this day
This poor youngling, for whom we do sing
By, by, lully, lullay ...

I was familiar with the words of the carol, but they seemed a little strange to my ear, as though I were hearing them for the first time. I noticed Edith Carew standing in the crowd, still for once, listening intently.

Herod the king, in his raging,
Chargèd he hath this day
His men of might, in his own sight,
All young children to slay ...

The Slaughter of the Innocents, always more a subject for a painting than a real event to me, was becoming disturbingly vivid in my mind.

> *Then woe is me, poor child, for thee,*
> *And ever morn and day*
> *For thy parting, neither say nor sing*
> *By, by, lully, lullay ...*

The mother is singing to her newborn infant, lulling him to sleep, in the full knowledge that a horrific fate awaits him at the hands of Herod's men. The melancholy look on Edith's face told me she was fully aware of the import of the words.

> *Lully, lullay, thou little tiny child,*
> *By, by, lully, lullay ...*

'Let's go, Finian,' I whispered, my sense of unease growing.

'Better say good night to one of our hosts,' he said, heading in Edith's direction. But when he saw she was dabbing tears from her eyes, he bowed briefly and mumbled a quick 'Thank you' in passing.

As I approached, Edith put on a brave smile, but her soft brown eyes betrayed her – they seemed designed to express sadness. 'Don't mind me,' she said, as I shook hands with her. 'It does this to me every time. It's a carol for the dead, you know.'

On the way down the stairs we passed a mirror, and I noticed what I was wearing: the black jacket and skirt, the ivory blouse. An odd combination of colours for a festive occasion. They reminded me of funerals and last rites, of shrouds and ashes. They were the colours of death.

December 21st

Chapter Eighteen

At seven-thirty there was a rosy tint in the sky to the southeast, over Redmountain Ridge. Birds flitted from one side of the road to the other in front of the car as I drove. Behind occasional gaps in the hedges, grey fields were forming out of the dark, and the river flashed pink and silver like the salmon that once thronged its weirs. For the third time since leaving Castleboyne I played 'The Coventry Carol' from a Loreena McKennitt CD I had brought with me. I was still astonished that I had missed the true pathos of it over all the years.

On the way home to Castleboyne, Finian had

sensed my mood and interpreted it as concern over the threat I had received. He offered to stay the night, but I said I'd be happy if he just took a look around the house. While he was outside doing that, I listened to a recorded message from Gallagher: he was having the card examined by the Forensics team and would be in touch. Finian had refused to leave until I promised to ring him immediately if I thought anything was wrong. But the night had passed uneventfully.

By the time I parked beside a number of other cars near the outer entrance to Newgrange, thick folds of underlit cloud were sitting above the ridge. As I put the CD back in its case it flashed the light into my eyes, and that gave me an idea for the magazine interview.

A wedge of swans rowed out of the still-dark western sky and, keeping in formation – I counted seven as they passed – flew down to the river in the valley below. I walked over to the winter-thin hedgerow and looked down at frosted fields still in semi-darkness, plough marks outlined in some of them. There was little or no breeze, yet the air was penetratingly cold. I zipped up my parka and pulled on my gloves, wondering if, on this morning five thousand years ago, people had gathered on the slopes below and in the meadows across the river. The terraces carved out by the Boyne as it ate into the valley floor over the aeons made a vast natural amphitheatre. But perhaps the side of the river with its sacred temples was reserved for the elders or priests or whoever conducted the ceremonies. So how did they get from one side of the river to the other if they needed to? There was a ford a short distance upstream, but it would have been frequently unusable during winter floods. By boat was the obvious answer.

I turned around to look up the hill at the grass-topped dome. Already, the bow-shaped quartz façade around it was picking up the available light and a knot of people had gathered outside the entrance of the mound.

A vehicle came down the road towards me as I walked to the gate leading into the sloping field on which the mound had been built. I recognised the black Range Rover only when the driver dimmed his headlights and I could see beyond the glare. Malcolm Sherry was sitting behind the wheel, a woman in the passenger seat beside him. He waved at me as he passed by. I returned the gesture and continued to the gate, where Con Purcell was standing with some other members of the Visitor Centre staff.

'Morning, Con,' I said. 'And many thanks. Dr Sherry is just behind me.'

He opened the gate to let me through. 'A journalist and photographer have gone up to the mound already with one or two of your colleagues.'

I started up the path to the mound as the light in the sky increased dramatically. Looking towards Redmountain, I could see the cloud had separated into parallel strips of grey, unveiling a glowing sulphur sky.

Among the group outside the entrance I spotted two of the three women who, along with me, were the subjects of the magazine article. They were standing apart from the people who would be shortly going into the mound to witness the sun's rays coming through the roof-box and along the passage to the floor of the chamber deep inside. The two archaeologists were chatting to Hebe Baxter from *Dig* magazine; closer to me as I walked up the path was the magazine's photographer Sam Sakamoto, in paramilitary gear, aiming his lens at one of the standing stones that once formed an outer ring around the mound – the remains of the largest stone circle in the country.

'Hi, Sam,' I said, passing him by.

'Hi. Hey, can you tell me if these stones were erected at the same time as the mound?'

'No, long afterwards. Hundreds of years.'

'What for?'

'Not sure. One theory is that they represent a "fencing in" of the older religion of the tombs.'

'So this place was the centre of two religious cults in its time?'

'Or maybe more,' I said, moving on up the hill. I could have told him that even later, in the Iron Age, Brú na Bóinne had become the legendary burial place of the High Kings of Ireland. Although no archaeological evidence has borne this out, it nevertheless proves that a mystical aura surrounded the mounds long after their original purpose was forgotten.

Hebe Baxter saw me approaching and called out, 'Hi, Illaun, we're over here.' She was dressed, as we all were, for the cold. But her neon-pink padded jacket, with lipstick and shades to match, helped to set her apart.

'Good morning,' I said to the three women. 'It's looking good for the occasion, isn't it?'

They each glanced towards the sunrise and murmured something.

Hebe gestured to the two women with her. 'You know Mags and Freda, don't you, Illaun?'

'Indeed I do. And who's the fourth member of the gang?' Hebe had interviewed us separately the previous week, and while I had made a mental note of the other names at the time, I had forgotten one of them. She wasn't an archaeologist; that was all I recalled.

'Isabelle O'Riordan. And she's right behind you.'

I spun around to see Malcolm Sherry giving the woman he was with a kiss on the cheek, then turning to join the others going inside the passage tomb. Isabelle came towards us smiling and flushed in the face.

'I'm not late, am I?' she asked in a squeaky, baby-doll voice that set my teeth on edge. Full-lipped, doe-eyed, her yellow curly hair carelessly sticking out of a dark-green bucket-shaped hat, she was wearing a crimson, calf-length velvet coat from under which peeked what could have been the lacy hem of a slip but was probably a skirt. There was no doubting who would stand out in the photographs. But while I admired her panache – envied it, even – I had taken an instant dislike to her.

'Not at all,' said Hebe. *Not that it would have mattered to Isabelle if she had been,* I thought. 'I know that the rest of you are probably wondering why Isabelle is here. I thought it was fair that, on the occasion, we should hear an alternative point of view about Newgrange. Perhaps, Isabelle, you'd like to tell the gang where you're coming from.'

'Sure. I'm a member of the Fellowship of Orion. We believe that Newgrange and the other structures on the hillside here are portals to the stars … and a lot more besides.' She stuck out her pretty chin determinedly. 'We also intend to open the closed minds of archaeologists to the true nature of these monuments.'

One of my academic colleagues reacted with a shrug of the shoulders, the other with a polite cough.

I wanted to throttle her.

Hebe, unaware that anyone's nose was out of joint, droned on. 'I want to do a short piece on Newgrange with each of you. I've brought a recorder to make it simple. Sam will also take some pics of you all together, which we haven't had a chance to do until today.'

Just then there was a clamour of excited voices around the entrance as Con Purcell arrived to open the gate into the mound.

'I'm off to keep someone company inside. He's a bit claustrophobic,' said Isabelle.

'But ...' Hebe watched helplessly as she skipped away. 'Oh, what the hell; she can join us later.'

Sherry, waiting for Isabelle at the entrance, gave her a hug, and they proceeded into the mound. The rest of us drifted towards it. Sam Sakamoto joined us, clicking off random shots as we formed into a semicircle with our backs to the quartz façade. The cloud had thinned out above the opposite ridge and the sky was molten gold.

Sam lowered his camera for a moment. 'Hey, you guys, that wall behind you is just amazing.'

We looked around and saw that the retaining wall around the mound was aglow with light. The disc of the sun had edged above Redmountain Ridge, but it would take another four minutes for the shaft of light to enter through the slit above the entrance.

We all waited in silence, checking our watches. Then, from inside the mound, there was an audible murmur – a remarkable effect in itself, since the crowd within were nearly twenty-five metres from the entrance and beneath a two-hundred-thousand-tonne cairn of earth and stones.

'Right,' said Hebe, taking out a minidisc recorder. 'Let's get this done while the sun is doing its business inside the chamber. And we'll start with ... how about you, Mags?'

I was relieved it wasn't me. I had given the subject little thought, even though in the past few days my life had been closely linked to it. Mags Carney's area of expertise was passage-grave art and she could talk forever on the subject if required. Indeed, both she and Freda Dowling were venerable figures in the world of Irish archaeology and had been my lecturers at one time or another.

Mags swept her hand around in a gesture that included the massive original entrance stone with its flowing spirals and the huge inscribed kerbstones supporting the mound. 'It's estimated that two-thirds of Europe's megalithic art is inscribed on the stones of the Boyne Valley ...'

I could predict what she was going to say, and so I could gather a few thoughts while she was talking, without really paying attention. But my mind kept returning to Isabelle. It irked me that she was the reason why Malcolm Sherry had put me under pressure for the tickets. But that wasn't the only issue.

'... Others ascribe the swirling patterns to drug-induced shamanic insights of some kind ...'

Isabelle was the one Sherry had been meeting in recent days. But, even if he had described Mona's injuries to her, she wasn't anyone's idea of a murderer. Still, the Christmas card with the New Age greeting was just the kind of thing she would send to someone.

'... and why the remains of only a few individuals were buried here. Were they the bones of the tribe's ancestors, playing their part in the cycle of birth and death?'

Or, if not Isabelle herself, maybe another member of the Fellowship of Orion. I could sense Mags was coming to the end of her talk and tuned in to what she was saying.

'... is to ask, what will be made of Chartres Cathedral in five thousand years? Even now its role in the lives of people at the time it was built is becoming foggier with every passing year. But let's imagine that some great catastrophe in the future not only collapses the cathedral but wipes out all knowledge of Christian civilisation. What would archaeologists five thousand years hence make of the rediscovered ruins of Chartres, do you think? They'd find some human bones there, of course – but they'd be far off the mark if they decided Chartres had been only a tomb, wouldn't they? So that's why we have to be careful about jumping to conclusions where Newgrange is concerned.'

Mags got a round of applause.

'Thank you, Mags Carney,' Hebe said into her microphone. 'Now let's hear from '... Oh, heck – Mags was first here this morning, so let's do it in order of your arrival. Freda, over to you.'

Freda Dowling was an authority on Neolithic farming practices. 'I'm just astounded at how it was done. Newgrange on its own would be remarkable, but think of all of Brú na Bóinne: Knowth and Dowth and the forty other unnamed mounds and henges in this area, some of which we know are interconnected ...'

Again I knew roughly what ground Freda would be covering.

'... Without the wheel, without metal devices of any kind, they lugged hundreds of boulders weighing up to ten tonnes each across several kilometres from where they were quarried ...'

I decided I'd have to talk to Sherry. Then a guilty feeling came over me that I was jealous of Isabelle O'Riordan, not because of her relationship with Sherry but because she was free to spout any notion that came into her head about Newgrange without having to subject it to any academic rigour. And for all I knew she would one day be proved right.

'... They brought cobbles here by water from the Mourne Mountains, chunks of quartz from Wicklow, just to enhance the appearance of the place. And then they inserted a finely tuned astronomical device that's still working after five thousand years. Just think, my friends, we're standing outside the oldest solar-aligned structure on the planet. I think Newgrange is a place that can teach us to be less arrogant about the past. Thank you.'

Another round of applause. Now it was my turn.

'Thank you, Freda. Illaun?'

Even now, at nearly forty years old, I felt nervous in front of my former lecturers – who would, no doubt, be assessing my contribution in the light of what they remembered of me at university. 'A good imagination is essential in an archaeologist, Illaun,'

Mags used to say, 'but if you want to be another Erich Von Daniken I suggest you study hotel management.' That was the profession's attitude to the ex-hotelier who wrote *Chariots of the Gods*. 'Imaginate, don't hallucinate,' was Freda's pithier, if grammatically quirky, version.

I took a deep breath. 'Picking up on what Freda just said, visitors to Brú na Bóinne often ask why only one of the mounds has a specially designed sun window. I can't rid myself of the feeling that the answer is very obvious and that we'll see it if we just look at things from a different perspective.

'Supposing that, rather than trying to interpret the intrusion of their world into ours, we do the opposite, by projecting something from our world back into theirs – in our imaginations, that is.' *There's that word.* I looked at the faces of the two older women. Their expressions hadn't changed. *Keep going.*

'If we could time-travel back with something from our own era to give to the people gathered here this morning five thousand years ago – this, for example...' I took the CD from my pocket and held it up so it caught the light. 'Better still, hundreds of them, one for everyone in the audience – what would they assume they were to do with them?'

'What you've just done,' said Hebe. 'Mirror the sun.'

'Exactly! So the people assembled on the slopes here and on the far side would be treated to an even more spectacular display.'

I could see some puzzlement on the faces of my colleagues.

'I guess I'm making two points. One is that what went on at Newgrange on ceremonial occasions was probably far more impressive than we can envisage. The second is that people then were probably no different from us in the way we make things fit in with our own beliefs and practices. Just as they could never conceive of the CDs playing music, we will remain blind to the true function of Newgrange unless we think ...' I looked around at the roof-box, engineered to facilitate the entry of the rising sun's rays into the mound. 'To use the type of pun beloved of a friend of mine – unless we think outside the box.'

The applause, when it came, was generous. They surely knew I had been busking.

Hebe was about to say something when a squeaky voice behind us shouted, 'It's a womb, not a tomb!'

Isabelle came flouncing across to us as though we had been awaiting her verdict with bated breath. 'It's a womb, not a tomb,' she repeated. 'And as a woman I find it offensive that the male-dominated profession of archaeology has kept this under wraps for so long. It's just so ... so *patriarchal* to emphasise death over life, isn't it?'

'Excuse me,' I said. 'I'll be back in a few minutes.' I had spied Sherry standing with his back to us, scrutinising the patterns on the entrance stone.

'Let's go back in here for a minute,' I said, grabbing his arm. 'And keep your voice down.'

We climbed down the steps to the entrance, and as we passed a surprised Con Purcell I asked him to leave the lights on inside the mound. I pushed Sherry ahead of me up the narrow passage formed by the huge upright stones called orthostats.

'What's going on?' he called back, bewildered by my insistence.

I waited until we entered the chamber before I spoke. 'You knew you were putting me in an awkward position, asking for passes at the last minute. You could have told me why.'

Sherry looked distinctly uncomfortable. I stood with my hands on my hips waiting for him to say something, the absolute silence of the stone chamber adding to the tension.

'Em ... it was all a bit complicated,' he said eventually. 'I only met Isabelle a month ago. I found her a breath of fresh air, I have to say. Especially her views on prehistoric sites – quite fascinating, I think.'

I didn't respond.

Sherry knew he had goofed. 'Yes, well ... she found herself in a bit of a fix last week. She'd fibbed to the magazine editor that she'd been in the chamber to witness the sunrise on a previous occasion. So she travelled down to the Visitor Centre to try and persuade them to part with an invitation. No chance. We met in Drogheda for lunch and I rather rashly promised to sort something out. That's when I turned to you ...' He swallowed, and his Adam's apple bobbed up and down. 'But I can't understand why it's made you so angry.'

He had a point. It had to do with Isabelle, of course. But apart from the obvious – her brash New Age theories – why had I taken such a dim view of her? It wasn't jealousy, yet I knew it had to do with my liking for Malcolm. I put it down to protectiveness – a feeling deep down that she wasn't suitable for him, which was paradoxically coming out in my being angry at *him*, like a parent scolding a child she sees running across the road without looking left or right.

I had no time to explain any of this, even if I'd wanted to. And something else had occurred to me. 'Malcolm, this is serious. Think carefully. Did you tell her about the injuries to Mona when you met her last Friday?'

'No, I know what you're thinking and I swear I didn't. And anyway –'

'Darling?' That voice! Isabelle was on her way along the passage.

'She's getting anxious,' said Sherry. 'We're off to Munich for Christmas – a spur-of-the-moment kind of thing.' He grinned sheepishly. 'You really got me out of a tight spot, Illaun; thank you. And I'd also be grateful if we could keep it between ourselves – how I got the passes, I mean.'

I gave him a scathing look. 'You've got a damn nerve, Sherry.'

He winced.

'Malcolm!' Isabelle was almost upon us.

Sherry grabbed my arm, his brown eyes widening like a frightened boy's. 'OK, Illaun?'

Isabelle arrived in the chamber. 'What are you two up to? A girl could get jealous, you know.'

Sherry laughed nervously. 'We're just discussing a case, Isabelle. Can you give us a few more minutes?'

Isabelle made a peevish face. 'I suppose so.' But she had something to say to me before she retreated back along the passage. 'By the way, I've decided that the standing stones outside are forming an acupressure point on the Earth's surface. Put that in your next academic journal.'

Embarrassed, Sherry cast his eyes up to the corbelled roof. 'Do you believe there's another passage within the mound?'

'I couldn't care less, Malcolm. Let's talk about the case instead. What's the latest from Forensics?'

Sherry raised his hand and waggled his fingers. 'The prints. The bloodstained prints in Traynor's car ...'

'What about them?'

'They're huge. The dermal ridges are almost three times the average diameter for fingerprints. And ...'

'And what?'

Sherry started to move along the passage. 'I'm a bit claustrophobic ...'

'Tell me what it is.'

He stopped and turned. 'It's hard to define, exactly.

When prints are found, they can range from a single digit to an entire set of fingertips, including the thumb – that's a possible ten. In Traynor's car, prints from both hands were found, often in pairs and from four different digits. But only those four.'

'What's remarkable about that?'

'Watch.' Sherry showed me his left hand. Then he brought his thumb and forefinger together and, with his right, bunched together the remaining three digits and pulled them well away from the others. 'This gives you a very rough idea of what I'm talking about. It's as if the killer has only four digits in all.'

Sherry set off along the passage again, ducking his head under a wooden beam wedged between a pair of orthostats to keep them upright.

I followed him into the final stretch of the passage. 'What could account for that?'

'It's just a suggestion. Remember in the mortuary in Drogheda I pointed out the congenital deformity of the infant's hands? Syndactyly. It's sometimes called "mitten hand" – two or more fingers fused together. Usually they're separated by surgery in early childhood, but it's just possible that an adult ... What I mean is, if it were left untreated –'

'Darling!' Isabelle was waiting at the entrance. As we stepped out into the daylight she hooked her arm into Sherry's. 'We really must go if we're to make the flight in time.'

'Hi, you two ... I'm freezing my ass off here.' Sam

Sakamoto was stamping his feet to keep them warm. 'Let's get this over with.'

Isabelle ran across to the others, which gave me the chance to have a final word with Sherry. 'Malcolm, you owe me – big-time. Keep in touch while you're in Munich.' I handed him my business card. 'E-mail me if there's any news. And in the meantime, suggest to Isabelle that maybe the best way to think of Newgrange is as both a womb *and* a tomb. Sex and death – always a great combination.' I winked at him. 'As you well know.'

Sherry and his new girlfriend left as soon as the photographs were taken, and while the others debated going to Donore or Slane for a hot whiskey I pleaded another appointment, said my goodbyes and started down the path. Across the valley a flight of starlings rose up from a wooded part of the ridge. Could they be the same ones I had seen funnelling down into the trees on Sunday?

Sam was hunkered down on the path a couple of metres behind me, dismantling his camera. I walked back to him.

He glanced up at me. 'Hey, that was some sunrise.'

'Yes. Pity you couldn't see it from inside.'

'It still works Christmas Day, doesn't it?'

'It should, just about. But it's not open, un-fortunately.'

He smiled. 'So it's gonna be something special for our partners, then. A treat for not being home at

Christmas …' He noticed I was staring at his camera. 'What can I do for you, Illaun?'

'Could I use your zoom lens for a minute?'

'What are you trying to see?'

'See the flock of birds over there? Just below them.'

He squinted through the viewer and quickly adjusted the focus. 'Here – should be just about right.'

I aimed the lens at where I'd seen the starlings flying up. The woodland was mostly deciduous and bare of leaves, but within it was a stand of conifers that hid Grange Abbey from view. Unless you were looking for it, as I was, you'd never notice the tower, its stepped battlements merging with the serrated outline of the trees. As I saw it from the far side of the Boyne, it struck me forcibly that the abbey was directly across from Newgrange.

Chapter Nineteen

As if to mark its return, the noonday sun was sending out gold and silver streamers of light that glittered like foil. Its low position in the sky made shoppers on the streets of Drogheda shade their eyes and drivers snatch sunglasses from glove compartments as they edged along in the traffic.

The already congested streets were almost at a standstill as a flood of mourners exited from St Peter's after the funeral Mass for Frank Traynor. I had arrived in the town just before the end of the service and pulled into an empty loading bay outside a shop across from the church. To avoid getting a ticket, I stayed in the car and observed the people coming down the steps. I was expecting to see Muriel Blunden.

After Traynor's mourning widow and her teenage children had seen the coffin lifted into the hearse and the door closed, relatives and friends escorted them to a waiting black limousine, which a uniformed Garda waved out into the traffic. Cars began to pour out of a nearby car park to join the funeral cortege; another Garda gave them right of way, leading to much trumpeting of horns further back in the traffic as other drivers, unaware of the reason for the hold-up, vented their frustration. Among the last to emerge onto the steps of the church was Derek Ward, accompanied by his wife, who was familiar to me from various social functions in the county. I was surprised to see Ward taking a less-than-prominent position among the mourners. Then I saw a black ministerial Mercedes coming out of the car park. Ward's wife got into the back seat; he said something to her, then closed the door and headed along the footpath in the opposite direction.

The crowd had dwindled to a few stragglers, and still Muriel had not appeared. She was apparently possessed of more sensitivity than I credited her with.

In my wing mirror I noticed Ward striding away, shielding his eyes from the sun, talking into his mobile phone. He came to a halt outside the multi-storey car park and put away the phone as a man approached him. They engaged in some kind of banter that involved much hand-shaking and back-slapping – the man was probably a political supporter – but Ward's body language told me he really wanted to escape from this encounter. As soon as he could disengage himself, he looked up and down the street and slipped into the entrance to the car park.

Risking a parking ticket – or possibly clamping – I decided to follow him. Moving as fast as I could without breaking into a run, I entered the ground floor of the car park and saw one of the lifts indicating a stop at level 4. Another door opened, and I took the slow-moving lift up to the fourth floor. I didn't realise it was on the roof until I found myself in the open air, facing the sun's glare.

In the blind spot in front of me, someone started a car and pulled out of a bay. As it headed for the exit, I stepped into the shadow of a parked van and saw a blue Peugeot 307 slip down the ramp. Both occupants were wearing sunglasses, but there was no mistaking Derek Ward in the passenger seat; and the glimpse of a Jackie Kennedy coiffure across from him was enough to tell me the driver was Muriel Blunden.

I turned and ran down the stairs to the ground floor, emerging near the ticket machines as the Peugeot came around the last bend of the ramp. Out of the blinding sun, I could clearly see the pair. They spotted me at the same time and braked to a halt.

I stepped onto the island and stood beside the ticket machine they would have to use. Another car came down the ramp behind them, and they were forced to move forwards. As the car drew alongside me, Muriel had to open the window to insert the ticket into the machine.

'Muriel, I need to talk to you,' I said firmly.

She tried her best to ignore me and aimed the ticket at the slot. Ward sat in silence, staring ahead.

'Muriel, for God's sake!' I said, snatching the ticket.

'How dare you!' she screeched. 'Derek, do something.'

The car behind blasted its horn.

'We can't argue here, Muriel,' he said through clenched teeth. 'Drive around to the Estuary Hotel. We'll meet her there.'

'Did you hear that?' said Muriel, her scarlet lips twisted in rage.

'I'll be there in five minutes,' I said, handing her back the ticket. 'And I expect to see both of you.'

The barrier flew up and she was out of the car park, exhaust pipe snarling. I felt a giddy surge of power, ordering a government minister and a senior civil servant to do my bidding.

It took me at least twenty minutes to collect my car – fortunately unticketed – ask directions to the hotel, which I'd never heard of, and get there through a maze of one-way streets. I spotted the blue Peugeot in a far corner of the ample car park outside the nondescript modern hotel and drew alongside.

I had been expecting Muriel to step out, and I was

perplexed when Derek Ward emerged from the car and came towards me. He was wearing a navy-blue overcoat, white shirt and red tie. Ward's most distinctive facial feature was his eyes, or rather the bags of sagging flesh under them, which were always emphasised in newspaper cartoons. Almost as distinctive was his slick, wavy hair, black to the roots with a little help from Just For Men.

I let the window down and Ward leaned in. 'What's the problem, Illaun? Can we sort it out here and now?' The tone was measured, unemotional, used to solving intractable issues.

'There's no problem, Mr Ward. I just want to talk to Muriel about the field at Monashee. I heard –'

Ward put up his hand for silence. 'I'm aware that you sent her a threatening text message. She hasn't reported it to the Gardaí yet, but in the light of your continued harassment she has little choice.'

I was caught completely off guard. I had hoped, by certain well-placed questions, to unravel a web of intrigue involving all the participants in the Monashee development. Now I was the one on the defensive. I decided to step out of my car. I could see Muriel behind the wheel of hers applying even more lipstick.

'She may have received a text message, but not from me. My phone was stolen on Friday night. I'm only trying to get the field at Monashee preserved for a proper archaeological assessment. Muriel is opposed to the idea, and I just want to know why – that's all.'

Ward raised his hands in evident exasperation. 'I'm going for a drink. Ask her yourself.'

As I walked towards her car, I saw Muriel turn the vanity mirror sideways to observe my approach. I tried to open the passenger door but had to wait for a few seconds before she flipped up the locks and I could get in.

Muriel put her sunglasses back on and lit a cigarette. She was in a beige mohair coat with a brown fur collar; a patterned chiffon scarf to protect her bouffant hair from the breeze was draped around her shoulders. Recently sprayed scent still hung in the air. I estimated Muriel was only in her early forties, but her sense of style seemed to come from my mother's generation.

'I have nothing to say to you,' she declared, pouting her lips to check them in the mirror. Her voice was like well-worn leather.

'Whatever text message you received, it wasn't from me. My phone was stolen late on Friday night.'

Muriel remained silent, her expression unreadable behind the dark glasses and a wreath of smoke.

I opened my window, and the smoke curled its way across the roof and out of the car. 'What did it say?' I asked.

Muriel opened her window and flicked out some ash. I waited. She exhaled again; a cloud of smoke hovered above her head, momentarily unsure which window to escape through, before being wafted into the back of the car by an incoming flow of air.

I felt I was wasting my time. I clicked open the passenger door.

'I wondered how you knew,' said Muriel.

I took my fingers off the door handle.

'Knew what?'

Muriel took another drag but said nothing.

I had to make a guess. 'Knew that you were having an affair with Frank Traynor?'

Her head whipped around so fast it was in danger of flying off her shoulders. 'What!' Her smoky breath hit me full in the face. 'Don't be so ridiculous. An affair with Frank Traynor? A man who just happened to be blackmailing me?'

'Blackmailing you? Not your lover?' I looked out the window and then back at Muriel, my mind working overtime. 'So let me get this straight. It's Derek Ward you're having a relationship with …'

'Gee, you're such a bright girl, Illaun,' she said caustically. 'How did you ever pair me up with Traynor?'

'I heard your radio interview … then I saw you with him in Drogheda and put two and two together.'

She snorted. 'I did the interview. He wrote the script.'

'You weren't his business partner, then?'

'No.'

'Was Ward?'

'Not in the sense you mean.'

'You know Brendan O'Hagan, I take it.'

She nodded.

293

'Was he in some kind of business relationship with you?'

'No.'

'Have you ever heard of Sister Geraldine Campion?'

She shook her head. 'No.'

'Ursula Roche?'

'No.'

While I was digesting this, Muriel stubbed out her cigarette in the ashtray, leaned back against the head-rest and sighed. 'Derek and I met last summer at a two-day conference which he opened – "Tourism versus Heritage", or something. We hit it off like that' – she snapped her fingers – 'and went to bed together that night in the hotel where the conference was being held. Bad move. Traynor was at the conference as well, and he sussed what had happened. And he was well aware that Derek, being the minister responsible for the Museum, is technically my boss.

'Traynor bided his time, kept his eye on us. Then, when this damn bog-body issue came up, he pounced – got on to me immediately at the Museum, threatened he'd have us all over the papers at the weekend if I didn't dance to his tune ... But I wasn't to tell Derek he was putting pressure on me. Which made me suspect Traynor was already extracting something from him.' She slipped another cigarette from the packet and lit it without lifting her head off the head-rest. 'Excuse the cancer sticks; I'm a little on edge today. I'd only just given up the bastards, as well.'

'That's OK.' I could sympathise. Though I'd been off cigarettes nearly three years, I still felt the tug. 'So he asked you to go on national radio and play down the significance of the find.'

'Which is exactly what I did. But later that morning I came down from Dublin to persuade him to get off our backs, now that I had gone public about Monashee on his behalf. Traynor was leaving me back to the train station when you saw us.'

'What happened at your meeting?'

'He tried to make out he wasn't a blackmailer. No money would ever be demanded, just the odd favour – that kind of crap. He even hinted that he had occasionally paid Derek for services rendered. I knew then there was more to Traynor's hold on Derek than our relationship. So I put it to him that, in the scheme of things, a minister having an affair with a civil servant is not really tabloid fodder and that, having done him his so-called favour, I wasn't going to stick to what I'd said in the radio interview.' She took a drag on her cigarette.

'How did he react?'

'He laughed. Said something had come to his attention that meant Monashee was no longer an issue, and that he couldn't care less what action I took.'

'Oh? Did he say what had changed his mind?'

'No. He just renewed his efforts to push me into a corner – said that, if I didn't want to hear unpleasant things about Derek aired in public, I'd better go along with him. All I'd have to do was turn a blind eye if it came to my notice that he was buying or selling the occasional historic artefact.'

'Illegally, you mean.'

'Of course. I said if it was outside the law I wouldn't do it. His response was, "We'll see about that." I knew he would probably put pressure on Derek again.' She sat upright in her seat, adjusted a straying strand of hair she had spotted in the mirror and patted the back of her coiffure into place. 'But he never got the chance, did he?'

For a moment I thought she was implying that she'd had a hand in his murder. 'Be careful how you phrase that to the Gardaí.'

'Don't worry. I've already had a visit from Inspector Gallagher.'

'And you told him about the call Traynor took while he was with you.'

'Sure.'

'Tell *me* about it.'

'It was no big deal. I was in the car when his phone rang. He made an arrangement to meet the caller. Monashee was mentioned. He used the caller's name – I can't remember it, but it was a woman's name. End of story.' She flicked her cigarette out the window.

'Did you tell Gallagher that Traynor was blackmailing you and Ward?'

'Of course not. Traynor's dead, isn't he? He can't threaten us now.'

'And where does Sergeant O'Hagan fit into this? His role was ultimately – what, guarding the minister's reputation?'

'Wrong again. O'Hagan was protecting his own interests. And Traynor's, too, in a way.'

'I don't understand.'

'Traynor is – was – his brother-in-law.'

'You mean Traynor's wife …'

'Is O'Hagan's sister, yes.'

I was on a steep learning curve today.

'It seems Traynor kept the sergeant briefed on how he was manipulating me. He must have contacted him on Friday, after seeing me off. Following the murder, O'Hagan came to see me and said he'd make sure I wasn't questioned by the investigators if I promised not to reveal what his brother-in-law had been up to. There was a veiled threat that he could make me look like a suspect, as well, but I assumed he was just protecting his sister and her family, so I agreed. Now I realise he was also covering his own ass. In fact, he rang me yesterday to make sure I hadn't talked to the official investigators. Claimed he was making progress by himself and didn't want it screwed up by Gallagher – with whom I was having a conversation at that very moment.' She chuckled deep in her nicotine-husky throat.

'O'Hagan takes a dim view of Gallagher, for some reason,' I said.

'I'd say it works both ways. And I think Gallagher

ust have hauled him in for questioning. O'Hagan didn't turn up at the church today, according to Derek.'

'Didn't attend his brother-in-law's funeral? That's odd.'

'Maybe he's done a runner. Who knows?' Muriel reached for another cigarette but thought better of it and rolled up the window instead.

'When did you receive the text message you thought was from me?'

'Early Saturday morning.'

'What did it say, exactly?'

'"License a dig at Monashee or Ward's career is over."'

'Hmm. Not my style. Far too ambiguous.'

Muriel ignored my attempt at levity. 'I don't have your name in my mobile phone, so I had no way of identifying who it was from, bar ringing the number. It wasn't until yesterday morning, when I was able to ask my secretary to check the number against our database, that I found out it was you. Then I thought, *The bitch. I'll see she never gets work from any source over which I have influence.*'

'Which, apart from the question of morality, is why it would have been business suicide for me to threaten you like that.'

'How the hell did I know what was going on in your mind?'

She had a point. 'OK. But let's think this phone

thing through. Someone steals another person's phone to send a threatening text message that can't be traced to them. It's a clever idea – beats having to cut and paste letters from newspapers and magazines. But why from my phone?'

'Because it has my number stored in it.'

'Right. I probably had entered "Nat. Mus." or some contraction, with your name or initials. But it still doesn't make sense, because if I hadn't left my phone in the car and turned on, they wouldn't have had it to use.'

'Then it was just opportunism. Probably means they were looking for something else at the time.'

I saw the figure melting into the fog. 'But what?'

'Your notes, photographs, camera, whatever. Maybe they thought you had the bog body in the boot.' Muriel was beginning to thaw a little.

'Or they could have been coming for *me*, but the dog scared them off.' I described what had happened in the early hours of Saturday morning and told her about the Christmas card I'd since received.

'You're giving me the heebie-jeebies. And who the hell are *they*, anyway?'

'Someone who knew that you were involved with the minister and that he had even more to hide.' And how had they found that out?

Muriel sighed. 'Which is why I decided to meet Derek today and have it out with him – find out what hold Frank Traynor had over him, what favours he had extracted over the years. I was also going to discuss what to do about you. But I guess that's off the agenda now. So I don't feel I'm being bullied into making a decision which I would probably have been in favour of anyway.'

'About Monashee?'

'I'll be proposing that we issue a licence for the site to be surveyed with a view to excavating it, yes.'

I tried to show professional restraint, but my expression betrayed me.

'Your smile tells me that meets with your approval.'

'It certainly does.'

'Well, at least somebody's happy.'

Then the answer to the question I had asked myself clicked into place, and I wasn't smiling any more. 'I'd be happier if I hadn't come to a conclusion about something just now. Whoever sent the text from my phone must have extracted the information about you and Ward from Traynor. So ask yourself: when did *that* happen? Did he seem like a man under that kind of pressure when you were with him on Friday?'

Muriel lowered her sunglasses and looked at me with fear in her rather attractive brown eyes. 'No. As I said, if anything, he was in high spirits. So someone must have forced the information out of him after ...'

'After you'd left him. In other words, his killer.'

We both sat in silence for a while.

I broke it first. 'Muriel, go back to the first conversation you and Traynor had about Monashee. Presumably he told you he was building a hotel there. But did he explain why he was in such a hurry to dig up the field before Christmas?'

'No. But, thinking about it now, maybe something was buried there.'

'Something he needed right away – to use as blackmail material, perhaps. But what?'

'Evidence of a crime?'

'Then what could have happened on Friday to make him lose interest in ripping up the field?'

'He had found the incriminating evidence.'

'Let's assume for the moment you're right. What's the next question that occurs to you?'

Muriel splayed out her fingers and admired her bright-red nails. 'I'm getting bored with this. Let Gallagher figure it out.'

'No, no – go on. We're getting somewhere. What's the obvious question?'

'Was Traynor killed by the person he was going to blackmail with that evidence?'

'That's the question, Muriel. And, if that's what happened, why does the killer now want Monashee excavated?'

'It doesn't make any sense.'

'Let's make another assumption. Suppose the killer forced Traynor to part with the evidence before murdering him.'

'Then it makes even less sense to have the field dug up.'

'Unless … unless the killer was worried that Traynor had told someone else about what was buried in the field. So he planted false evidence that will put him in the clear if it's found. That's why he wants the dig to go ahead.'

'Smart thinking, Illaun. But we don't know of any crime being committed in the first place.'

'There were two bodies found, don't forget.'

'Yes, but –'

A loud rap on the driver's window made both of us jump.

'Jesus, Derek,' said Muriel, letting her window down, 'you didn't have to scare the wits out of us.'

'Are you coming in for a drink?' he asked impatiently.

'I will when I'm ready. Get in for a minute.'

Ward swore under his breath, opened the back door and flopped into the seat.

Muriel removed her sunglasses and caught his eyes in the mirror. 'It looks like the text message was sent to me by Frank Traynor's murderer,' she said without expression.

'Oh, come on, Muriel. You know if it wasn't this woman here then it was some lunatic tree-hugger; we've already discussed –'

'Minister, I think Muriel should go to the Gardaí as soon as possible,' I said firmly.

'Why should she do that?'

'To tell them that Traynor was blackmailing her.' I turned to look at him for a moment. 'The same way he'd been blackmailing you.'

Ward sat forward and grabbed the back of my seat.

'That's an outrageous statement. I don't have to listen to this bullshit.'

Muriel shifted around to address him face-to-face. 'Derek, Frank Traynor more or less told me he had you in his pocket.'

'That was a lie.'

'Well, he had some means of controlling you.'

'For Jaysus' sake, Muriel, shut the fuck up.' Ward was becoming incensed. He was certainly not going to divulge anything while I was listening.

'Hold on, hold on. You can have it out between you when I'm gone. I just think the Gardaí should be told that Traynor was more than likely murdered by someone he was blackmailing; and it will have to come from a credible source.'

I got out of the car, put my head in the window and addressed Muriel. 'I'll contact you after Christmas to talk about Monashee. And – you'll love me for this – I've asked UCD to carbon-date the bodies, on your behalf.'

Muriel waved me away impatiently. She had bigger fish to fry right now.

Walking towards my car, I reflected that Derek Ward, freed of Traynor's yoke, was not going to reveal what it had been – not even to his lover – for fear he might be burdened with it again. I sensed that a relationship already in crisis was about to take a nose-dive.

Chapter Twenty

I checked the time as I left the car park and saw I had well over an hour to spare. There was another relationship that needed thinking about, and for that hour or so I was going to squeeze everything else out of my mind.

At the party the previous night, Finian and I could have passed for a long-married couple. And that worried me. It was as if the thrill of the chase, the ups and downs of courtship, the novelty of spending time together, the frisson of sexual anticipation, were all behind us – except that we had never experienced them in the first place.

Focused on these thoughts, I inadvertently travelled out of Drogheda along the Dublin road; I didn't realise it until I saw a sign for Bettystown. On the spur of the moment, I turned left towards the seaside village. A walk along the beach would clear my head. By the sea thoughts become clearer, the universe more explicable.

I turned off the road and parked behind the sand dunes for which this stretch of coast is famous. I grabbed my parka from the boot and zipped it up as I climbed the first ridge. The sea was still invisible from the summit, so I slid down the other side and began my ascent of the next ridge, skirting a deep hollow surrounded by marram grass.

The sheltered hollow in the dunes reminded me of a rainy summer's day when Tim Kennedy and I had taken a detour to this same place on our way to Carlingford Bay, further north, where we were spending the weekend. The sun had been making one of its brief appearances as we strolled hand in hand across the dunes, and the only other people in sight were some golfers on the nearby links.

We began to kiss, hungry for each other. While wondering how to escape the curious gaze of the golfers, we came upon a similar grass-fringed depression punched into one of the peaks of sand. With lustful urgency spiced by the risk of being discovered, we stripped off our clothes; and with them strewn under us and our bodies partly hidden by the grass, we made love, Tim lying on his back, the heat of the sun on my shoulders, pleasure rippling through me like the waves I could see running towards the shore. Even now I felt a quickening as I remembered it.

Would Finian ever be so uninhibited? He had the capacity to love intensely; that I knew. What most people – my friend Fran included – were unaware of was that the break-up of a passionate affair when Finian was still a teacher had been one of the factors in his decision to give up his career and devote himself full-time to his garden. It was something he hadn't shared with me until after I had graduated, but even then his pain was still acute. It was only as time passed and the garden took shape that it had eased. And, as that process continued, the relationship between Finian and me had deepened into something more than friendship.

I would be meeting him shortly, and then probably on only one other occasion before Christmas. Was the deadline I had set in my mind for a quantum leap in our relationship unrealistic? Probably. But I knew that if, between now and then, he treated me more like a sister than a lover, then my New Year's resolution would be to end it.

I reached the summit of the second ridge and found myself looking out on several kilometres of flat sand stretching to my right and left. Even in front of me, the tide was so far out that there was only a slim blue ribbon of sea along the horizon. It wasn't the thought-clarifying watery expanse I had been expecting, but it was still the sea. And, anyway, I'd done enough reflecting. I wanted to zone out completely for a while.

I descended to the base of the dunes and onto the upper shore, which was coated in crushed seashells. I picked up a bleached branch of wood and walked parallel to the dunes for a while, occasionally turning over an intact shell that caught my attention. Further out, a line of curlews were making their plaintive penny-whistle calls.

When the sun dropped lower in the sky and glared into my eyes, I turned away from the dunes in the direction of the sea, across an expanse of corrugated flats topped by thousands of spirals of sand ejected by burrowing lugworms. The curlews had no doubt been probing for them with their long, curved beaks. I reached a tidal stream and walked back along it in the direction from which I had come. I stopped to poke at one of the lugworm casts with my stick. The plump worms, used as bait by sea anglers, occupy vertical U-shaped tubes under the sand; one end is marked by the cast, the other – the entrance – by a depression in the sand about a hand's length away.

Something began to take shape in my head – or, more accurately, tried to find three-dimensional expression. From the edge of the tidal flow I carved a semi-circular furrow in the sand, looping it around the cast and back to the stream again. It filled with water, which encircled the mound of ejected sand like a moat. Just by my foot, on the near side of the furrow, was a barely detectable depression, the entrance to the lugworm's lair. The entrance and exit were on opposite sides of my moat, the tube underneath it.

Feeling a bit like Richard Dreyfuss in *Close Encounters of the Third Kind*, I knelt on one knee and stared hard at the marooned coil of sand, just as he stared at the mountain of mashed potatoes on his plate. Dreyfuss eventually went on to sculpt the Devil's Tower in Wyoming – which must make mine a subterranean structure of some kind ... *Well done, Illaun. But a bit obvious, what with you being an archaeologist.*

So much for the sea making the universe more explicable. I looked at my watch. It was time to go.

Before climbing the dunes, I whirled the stick over my head and flung it into the distance. It startled the curlews, who rose up and headed further down the beach. I followed their flight until their silhouettes were consumed by the sun's glare.

But my thoughts had gone back underground, to Monashee and what lay beneath it. In his encounter with Muriel, Traynor had raised the subject of trafficking in artefacts. Maybe it wasn't evidence of a crime he had dug up, but something extremely valuable in a different way – a treasure hoard, perhaps. On his own land. How convenient.

That's a rubbish idea, Illaun, and you know it. Yes, I knew. In my heart of hearts I knew that what had changed Traynor's mind that day was something he had seen shortly before meeting Muriel Blunden: the remains of the infant in the morgue.

As I drove towards Donore village, the sharp-etched shadows cast by the bright sun grew longer. I switched on the radio to get the three o'clock news headlines. The second item was terse in the way that initial reports about a murder usually are.

'The body of a man believed to be a Garda sergeant has been found in a field behind the prehistoric monument of Newgrange in County Meath. Detectives from Drogheda have launched a murder inquiry.'

I knew it was O'Hagan.

Mick Doran's bar seemed to be empty when I arrived. There was a coin-phone on the wall near the door; I found some change in my purse and asked an operator to put me through to Drogheda Garda station. Gallagher wasn't there, so I left a message for him to ring me at the number printed above the phone.

Next I rang Peggy, who was quite agitated when she answered. 'Oh, Illaun, I was going out of my mind wondering how to contact you. Inspector Gallagher called, left a strange message for you: don't arrange to meet anyone you don't know or are in any way suspicious of. He said you'd know what he was talking about. Are you in some kind of danger?'

Out of the corner of my eye I saw a movement. Then I realised I wasn't alone after all: on the far side of the oval bar, a man whom I took to be the proprietor was leaning on the counter. He had his back to me and had just turned a page of the newspaper he was reading.

'I can't talk now, Peggy, but if Gallagher rings again tell him I'm at this number.' I asked her for Gallagher's mobile number, and then I told her to let Terence Ivers at WET know that Muriel Blunden was giving us the go-ahead for Monashee. I wondered vaguely why he hadn't been in touch with me since Friday, but I let it pass. I finished by asking her to pick up my new phone – the shop hadn't been open at the early hour I'd left Castleboyne. As I should have guessed, Peggy had already collected it.

I found some more coins and got through to Gallagher's voicemail, on which I left a message including Finian's mobile phone number. Then I sat on a stool at the horseshoe-shaped bar. Gallagher's warning worried me, and I was glad that I'd invited Finian to come to Donore on our way home the previous night. I even wondered if I should cancel the meeting with Jack Crean, which, by Gallagher's criteria, I shouldn't be having. But that would be taking caution to an extreme, I thought.

I tapped on the counter to get the proprietor's attention.

'I'm here. What do you want?' Doran said without raising his head. His tone was sharp, almost aggressive.

'What do you have in the line of food?'

'Soup, sandwiches, toasted sandwiches,' he said brusquely, still keeping his back to me. Finian wouldn't be greatly impressed with our lunch venue, but I hadn't promised him more than a snack.

'There's someone joining me shortly; I'll wait until he arrives.'

Doran grunted something in reply and disappeared from sight. I surmised that he had known Sergeant O'Hagan and that his mood was a response to the news of his murder, which would have spread quickly through the village.

There wasn't a sound. Old-fashioned paper garlands hung in loops from the ceiling. They reminded me of the ones we had at Christmas when I was a child. Taking them down afterwards with my father, I would stand on a chair, hold one end of the decoration above my head while the other dropped to the floor, and then let it concertina downwards until it was a flat slab of paper.

Minutes dragged past. At last I heard an engine idling outside, followed by a car door opening and closing. Finian came in, strode across to the bar and embraced me. 'Sorry I'm late. I got Hugo to drop me over.' Hugo was an odd-job man at Brookfield Gardens. 'Hey ...' He was still holding my shoulders. 'You're trembling, Illaun. What's up?'

'I'm a bit scared. There's been another killing, and I'm sure it was Sergeant O'Hagan. I'm just waiting –'

''Twas O'Hagan, all right.' Neither of us had noticed Doran standing behind the bar. 'They found him over the far side of the river, in a field behind Newgrange. Word has it he was butchered the same way as his brother-in-law.'

I started to tremble so hard I had to lean my hand on the counter to steady myself. It came to me that I hadn't paid full attention to the news bulletin earlier. In my mind I'd made Monashee the scene of the crime, but O'Hagan had been found not only across the river but fifteen kilometres away by road, a fact that seemed significant for some reason that eluded me.

Finian put his arms around me. 'Let's go sit somewhere else,' he said, and led me gently over to an alcove. We didn't talk, just held hands while the last light of the fiery afternoon came through a window behind us. In my mind I said a prayer for O'Hagan's wife and family.

Eventually Finian looked around the pub, still empty apart from ourselves, the owner nowhere to be seen. 'There was no need to book out the entire place for us, you know,' he said in an obvious effort to raise my spirits.

I went along with it. 'No problem. Just wait until you hear what's on the menu.'

'Let me guess. For starters, a choice of oysters, *foie gras* or caviar.'

'Close,' I said. 'How do you like them done, plain or toasted?'

312

Finian sighed. 'And it's ham or cheese, I suppose.'

'We have chicken,' muttered Doran, who had magically appeared behind the bar again.

'Just what I was hoping for,' said Finian. I couldn't tell if he was joking. 'From the toasted menu, if you please. And a pint of Guinness. You, Illaun?'

I didn't feel like eating.

'Go on, it will do you good.' Finian was determined to get me back in full working order.

'All right. Toasted cheese for me, please. And I'll have tea.'

Doran vanished.

I asked Finian for his mobile phone, explaining that Gallagher might be ringing me at any time. He handed me the phone and then removed his coat, slipping a slim, gift-wrapped parcel from an inside pocket as he did so. 'This is a sort of pre-Christmas present,' he said. 'I think you'll like it.'

I blushed. 'Why, thank you. Should I open it now?'

'Yes, that's why I said it was a pre-Christmas gift. You're allowed.'

At that moment, the sun blazing through the glass, the rural stillness all about, Finian beside me, I felt a million miles away from the scary place where my head had been over the past hour.

'Thanks again,' I said, kissing him on the cheek.

'You still haven't opened it,' he said.

I rested it on my lap. 'There's no need to,' I said. I

knew my eyes were glistening, but I didn't care; I was happy.

Doran arrived in the alcove with our sandwiches and drinks on a tray. The moment had passed. But I would treasure it.

Finian thanked the proprietor as he distributed the contents of the tray. 'What's the name, by the way?'

'Mick.'

Finian introduced us both. Doran grunted and went off again.

'Grand man,' said Finian. Then he pointed at the parcel still in my lap. 'For God's sake, open that!'

I undid the gold foil wrapping. A newspaper column under glass in a black frame: the *Meath Chronicle*, dated December 1898.

CHRISTMAS IN THE INDUSTRIAL
SCHOOL FOR BOYS, CASTLEBOYNE

Once again, when mirth and good cheer are prevalent all over the land, the inmates of the above institution lacked none of the good things which are associated with the festive season of Christmas. At dinner, roast beef and plum pudding were provided, such as everyone, both rich and poor, partakes of at this time. After dinner the master distributed apples and oranges to the boys.

Then the boys were agreeably surprised by a

performance for their benefit ably carried out by the members of Castleboyne Amateur Musical Society. The string overture was splendidly played by Messrs M. Maguire, P. Hunt, W. Dalton, J. Olohan, J. Nugent, T. Butler and V. Kitts.

I read on down the column, which listed the various compositions played and sung on the occasion; they included 'Kitty of Coleraine' and 'The Banks of the Nile'. These were interspersed with hornpipes danced by members of the company, and there were 'jokes and conundrums' which the children 'loudly applauded'. The final song, performed by all members of the Society, was 'Let Erin Remember the Days of Old', following which:

An encore was called for, and Mr Hunt, accompanied by Miss Maguire, outdid himself in his rendition of 'Mona', which was the song of the night. It was also notable that under the Castleboyne man's tutelage Miss Maguire's playing has reached a standard of excellence rarely heard on the amateur stage.

So was the season of Xmas spent in Castleboyne Industrial School, and if it were as pleasantly spent everywhere else, Christmas should have been a very happy one indeed all through the world.

Mona. I smiled at Finian. 'You spotted the song title, I take it?'

He nodded. 'I found that piece on Friday, so the name was fresh in my mind from the night before. I thought it was worth getting framed.'

'It's such an odd little coincidence,' I said. 'I'll have to track down the song someday and learn it.'

'Interesting, too, that not only was Miss Maguire from Celbridge, but your great-grandfather – if it was he – seems to have been her tutor.' Finian was hinting that there was a parallel between them and us.

'I really must ask my mother about them.'

We finished our sandwiches and sat for a while in a comfortable silence as the descending sun got caught in the hooks of a blackthorn tree outside the window. Then we heard the door of the bar squeak open, and a man whom I took to be Jack Crean ambled up to the bar.

He was of similar build to his son and had the same ruddy complexion, but his had a more purplish hue. He was wearing a flat cap and a sports jacket that was several sizes too small, so that he seemed to be stuck inside it.

I went across to the bar and introduced myself.

'Hello, Missus,' said Jack, extending a hand with jumbo-sized fingers.

'And that's a friend of mine,' I said as he pumped my hand, 'Finian Shaw.'

Finian saluted him. Jack released my hand on one of

the upward movements, so that it flapped out like a butterfly.

Doran arrived behind the counter from wherever he had been. 'Evening, Jack. Jemmy and red?'

Jack made the slightest movement of his head and Doran poured him a glass of Jameson, adding a splash of red lemonade from a plastic litre bottle.

'There'll be frost tonight,' said Jack, putting a note on the counter. He sipped his drink, gathered his change and then came with me to the alcove. 'I suppose you've heard about them finding the sergeant dead,' he said as we sat down.

'Yes. It gave me quite a shock, hearing it on the radio.'

'O'Hagan wasn't all that popular with the people here, but nobody would have wished that on him.'

'Does Seamus know he's dead?'

'He does. Lucky for him, his asthma got bad on Sunday and he's been in bed ever since, so the Gardaí will have no excuse to haul him in this time.'

'It's an ill wind, as they say. Tell Seamus I was asking for him.'

'I will, Missus. He's going into hospital tomorrow for tests, so maybe they'll have him better by Christmas.'

I glanced at Finian. *Time for you to talk.*

Finian rooted in one of his coat pockets and produced a digital voice recorder no bigger than a mobile phone. 'Your son told Illaun that Monashee is haunted.'

'Aye, the Bog of Ghosts is what we always called it.'

'Do you mind if I record our conversation?'

'No problem.'

Finian turned on the voice recorder while I switched his mobile phone to silent, noting that there had been no contact yet from Gallagher.

'This is a time of year when ghosts are more active, isn't that so?' Finian began.

Jack took a sip and savoured it for a few seconds. 'At Christmastime, yes. That's because the souls in limbo are allowed to visit the living, so it's a time for apparitions – water sheeries, especially.'

'Water sheeries?'

'They're a sort of spirit that you'd see floating over bogs and marshy places, usually at half-light – dawn or dusk. On a foggy morning they might look like glowing lights inside in the mist. You have to keep your eyes closed, because the lights could lure you into the field and you'd be drowned in the river.'

'And Monashee's the place to see them?'

Jack nodded. 'Or you might hear one singing. High and mournful, like one of them boy sopranos.'

'Have you heard one?'

'I have. I'd been out playing poker one night and got back to Donore very late, but Mick's father' – he nodded in the direction of the bar – 'was still serving drink. It was raining and I had a good distance still to walk, so I stayed put in the pub, fell asleep in a corner and let myself out early the next morning. And as I was going past Monashee I heard it. I can tell you it sent the shivers up me.'

'What did you do?'

'I hurried past, looking straight ahead and saying the prayer we were taught when we were young: "Let me see or hear no evil as I pass, and if I do, please God, let me never speak of it to anyone."'

Finian gave me a glance that said, *I'm getting some good stuff here.* 'And what were you afraid you might see?'

Jack swallowed the rest of his whiskey. 'It was said that, if you saw one up close, a sheerie would have the face of a child. Crying.'

The back of my neck began to prickle.

'Crying?' said Finian.

'Yes. They're sad because Christmas reminds them that the gift they desire most, which is eternal life with God in Heaven, can never be granted because they're in limbo.'

'And why are they in limbo?'

'They're the souls of unbaptised infants.'

'But why do they inhabit Monashee?'

'I don't know,' said Jack. 'I only know it's haunted.'

Finian turned off his recorder, and we all sat in silence for a while. Then Jack asked if anyone wanted a drink, but Finian said the round was on him and went to the bar to order it. I took the opportunity to ask Jack what relations were like between the people in the village and the Grange Abbey community.

'Nonexistent,' he said emphatically. 'There was never much contact, and they got even more remote when that Sister Campion became the abbess, although she's the first woman from this area to get that job. Even getting a bit of work from them nuns is a rare event. As far as I know, the only people they've hired in the past year or two were a gang of builder's labourers – all foreign.'

'Why foreign workers?'

'Cheap labour, I suppose. Next thing you know, it'll be only them that gets work from people like yourself excavating the caves,' he said glumly.

'The caves? What do you mean?'

He jerked his thumb in the direction of Newgrange. 'That's what we call the mounds around here. Because the old name for Newgrange was "the Cave of the Sun".'

A roar of laughter from the bar distracted both of us. Finian had said something the proprietor found amusing – a rare enough event, I was sure. When he came back with the drinks I excused myself and went to the ladies, where I checked to see if Gallagher had rung Finian's mobile. There were no missed calls or text messages, and the public phone had not rung in all the time we had been there.

Fixing my hair in the mirror, I realised that it had been less than twenty-four hours since 'The Coventry Carol' had made such an impression on me. Now the subject of dead children had come up again. It was as if their souls really were trying to make contact with the living.

When I went back out, a handful of other customers had arrived. A dark-haired young woman with a pale face, whom I took to be Mick Doran's daughter, had come out to serve them; Finian had returned to the bar and sat conversing animatedly with her father.

Jack greeted me with a gap-toothed smile, his already ruddy cheeks now alight. There was yet another round of his favourite tipple waiting on the table, and I suspected Finian was plying him with doubles.

I went back to the conversation we had been having. 'These people hired to work up at the abbey – what have they been doing?'

'Pick-and-shovel work, from what I can gather. Nothing special.'

'Then there must be another reason why the nuns didn't hire people from the locality.'

'Maybe they have something to hide, something they don't want known locally. Because of what happened a few years back.'

Was it possible he knew about the report Jocelyn Carew had mentioned? 'Had it something to do with illegal dumping?'

Jack finished one glass and took a sip from the other before answering. 'You're right, Missus. About two years ago there was medical waste found dumped near Duleek, which isn't far from here, as you know. The contractor was identified and brought to court. He'd been collecting it from various hospitals and dumping it illegally – used syringes, blood-bags, dirty dressings … you know yourself. That was bad enough; but they found some old jars as well, with organs and body parts in them, all from babies. There was even a whole … foetus. Terrible. When it came to court, the contractor who dumped the waste couldn't account for the jars and none of the hospitals identified them as theirs. But a pal of mine who works in the County Council sanitation department said that, even though during the trial only the medical institutions the contractor had dealt with came up, he had also been collecting domestic waste from other places like schools and convents, including Grange Abbey.'

'And why do you think the jars had something to do with the abbey?'

'The nuns ran a maternity hospital once, didn't they?'

There was more loud laughter from the bar as Finian and Mick Doran shared another joke. I wondered what button Finian had pushed to get the proprietor in such good form – although I had been coming around to the opinion that the man had a sense of humour, if one worthy of an undertaker.

At this point Jack said he had to talk to another man who had come into the pub and would rejoin me shortly. It gave me an opportunity to reflect on what I'd heard. I reckoned I knew what had given rise to the stories of child apparitions: Monashee was a children's graveyard.

At one time, stillborn infants and babies who died before they could be baptised were interred in isolated, unconsecrated graveyards known as *cillíní*. Occasionally women who died in childbirth were buried there too. From early medieval times up to the 1960s, unbaptised children were not entitled to a Christian funeral. The location chosen for a *cillín* to hold these unmarked graves was often marginal land, liminal – the seashore, or a patch of bog.

Had the Hospitaller sisters used the boggy field at Monashee as a burial ground for the babies who died in their maternity home? Had Traynor threatened to expose that, and was the infant in the morgue the evidence he needed? It made sense, except for the fact that burying dead babies in such places had at one time been common custom throughout the country. That a religious order of midwives had practised it too might make them seem unenlightened by today's standards, but was hardly the stuff of scandal.

The illegal dumping of children's body parts or entire foetuses was in a different league. But the retention of organs by hospitals was already in the media as a controversial issue and a new story on the subject was unlikely to cause much of a stir, unless it threatened to destroy the reputation of some venerable institution. That a little-known medical order had in the past dissected or preserved body parts belonging to the stillborn babies of anonymous mothers would be of scant interest to anyone. And anyway, it was going to be difficult to prove it was they who had dumped them.

It was hard to see how any of this could be linked to the deaths of Traynor and O'Hagan. But, just as Jack Crean hadn't made the connection between water sheeries and an infant burial ground, perhaps I was failing to grasp something too.

Chapter Twenty-One

As we got into the car, Finian was rambling on about his chat with Mick Doran. Not much of it made sense, so I chose to ignore him. Before driving off I checked his mobile phone once more, in case I had missed Gallagher's call, but it was blank. Hardly surprising, since he was dealing with a second murder; but that didn't stop me feeling exposed, unprotected somehow. I wished Finian hadn't drunk so much – he had bought another round, 'one for the road,' before bidding numerous Merry Christmasses to Jack Crean, Mick Doran and his daughter, and several complete strangers at the bar.

But, as I drove to the car-park exit and waited for a van to pass by on the road outside, I couldn't help tuning in to Finian's monologue.

'He told me about this local farmer known as "the Bat". Asked me to guess how he'd earned the nickname. My best shot was, maybe he had worn a long black coat all his life – get it? A bat?'

The van passed, and I turned right onto the far lane.

'Guess what the answer was? The guy had played cricket in his youth – an answer that might have come to mind had he lived in Surrey, not in rural Ire–' Finian hiccupped.

'That's very interesting, Finian. Now why don't you lie back and get some sleep?' I needed to think.

'No wonder I was stumped – get it? *Stumped*.'

'Hmm …'

Finian mumbled something as he reclined his seat. It sounded like 'Gerampion's father'.

'What did you say?'

'I said that man – the Bat – was Geraldine Campion's father.'

'Why didn't you say so in the first place?'

'Was getting round to it.'

Jack Crean had said Geraldine Campion was from the area.

'Her father was what they used to call a "strong farmer", but his fortunes were in decline. Brought Geraldine up very strictly … mother died young. Girl had a wild streak, though …' He petered out again.

'Finian!'

'Oops, sorry … Where was I? Ward and Traynor … both from Drogheda. Mick Doran … went to school together …' Sleep overtook him.

'Oh, come on, Finian,' I said, poking him in the ribs. 'Who went to school with whom?'

He blinked awake. 'Mick Doran … was at school in Drogheda with Derek Ward and Frank Traynor. He said Ward and Traynor were inseparable. Also upwardly mobile and very competitive. Doran went into the family pub business while they went to college. At weekends the other two used to come out to the pub together for a drink and talk about how they were each going to make it big in business and politics. Then they began to bring along Geraldine Campion, who was a student nurse at Drogheda Hospital. They were both keen on her. New money chasing old stock. It eventually caused a rift between them. Then something happened that took Geraldine out of the picture altogether …' He relapsed into silence.

'Keep going.'

Finian perked up again. 'Story at the time was that, when she realised she had soured the relationship between the two men, Campion opted for the religious life rather than be the cause of her two friends falling out.'

'Sounds rather unlikely, doesn't it?'

'Yeah, fairy-tale stuff. Mick told me what really happened …'

327

'Go on.'

'At the hospital, Geraldine got involved in the Charismatic Renewal movement – it had just come to Ireland from the US. By the time she qualified, she was all fired up with religious zeal ... decided to join the Hospitallers. That gave her an outlet for her nursing skills, too.'

I had to give Finian credit. While apparently indulging in idle pub talk he had uncovered the roots of the relationship between Traynor and Ward, and something even more intriguing: the fact that Geraldine Campion was linked to both of them.

'What else did Doran tell you?'

I was answered by a snore. Finian was fast asleep.

Approaching Monashee, I dipped the headlights for an oncoming car; when it had passed, I noticed how bright the night was. I pulled in to the side of the road and turned off the lights. Everything around me was bathed in a silvery glow.

I climbed out, quietly pressed the door closed behind me, leaned back against the car and looked up. Almost directly overhead, a startlingly radiant moon was beaming from the centre of a clear, almost glassy, cupola of sky that was in turn encircled by a vast, misty halo. In the limpid zone between the moon and the glowing ring of ice particles, there was just one other object – a single star. I remembered Mags Carney telling us, in a lecture, that one of the designs on the decorated stones of Brú na Bóinne was thought to be the moon in the centre of an ice halo – exactly what I was witnessing.

I had one of those dizzying moments when you get a glimpse of just how much time has elapsed between events. The observers who made the astronomical calculations for Newgrange were looking up at the skies more than three thousand years before the Three Magi set out on their journey from Persia to Bethlehem. That meant there was a greater gap in time between the Magi and the Boyne Valley farmers than there was between the Wise Men and me. And yet there – just across the river – was the farmers' temple, still intact ... I felt I was getting close to some greater insight; but it slipped away, and I was left with the Magi still in my head.

It made sense, I reflected, that the three astrologers would have been out and about at this time of year; there would have been no shortage of stellar or lunar phenomena to observe. In summer we notice the landscape; in winter, the sky.

Yet, for all its charm as part of the Nativity story, the journey of the Wise Men has its dark side. Their visit to Herod, alerting him to the birth of a king whose star they had seen, led indirectly to the Slaughter of the Innocents. And the gift of resinous myrrh – a staple ingredient used in the embalming process at the time – was a reminder to the infant of His last end. Caspar, Melchior and Balthasar were harbingers of death.

Across the road from where I stood, it was the embalming properties of bog water that had preserved Mona and her child. And I, like a modern Herod, was beginning to wish they had never been found. Two people were dead as a result, and whoever had killed them had me in his or her sights too.

I walked across the frozen road, its surface glittering like the Milky Way fallen to earth. Boann, the goddess of this place, in the guise of a white cow, was said to have formed that great river of stars by sprinkling her milk across the heavens. Leaning on the gate, I looked down into the field. Here and there, frost-sided tussocks of grass were picked out by the moonlight, but most of the field was invisible and dark as a pit. It seemed to have the capacity to absorb light, like a black hole.

Was I really looking into a *cillín*, or had my overactive imagination got the better of me? But I had seen the proof: the remains of two typical *cillín* occupants – Mona and her malformed infant. There was even a plausible explanation for the 'Nubian' being there – if I allowed for a moment, as I was already doing with Mona, that he was from the Christian era: a stranger who died in a rural area and whose religion was unknown would have ended up in the nearest *cillín*.

I looked beyond the black void of the field to where the Boyne flowed past like mercury, and beyond that again to the top of the moonlit hill, where Newgrange seemed to be emitting its own phosphorescent light. I wondered what had led Brendan O'Hagan, determined to find the killer of his brother-in-law, to a field *behind* the mound. Once again, the matter of distance seemed important somehow. Newgrange was less than a kilometre from where I stood, but fifteen kilometres away by road. And a few hundred metres up the ridge behind me was Grange Abbey.

The only sound was the whispering of a weir downstream and the occasional clack of bare elder branches in the icy breeze. That was when I realised I was not alone.

Fists raised, I whirled around and nearly clouted Finian in the face.

'Damn you, Finian!' I yelled. 'You shouldn't have sneaked up on me like that. Someone's murdering people around here, you know.'

He gave me a lopsided smile. 'Sorry about that. I need to pee.' He glanced up at the sky. 'Wow, fantastic,' he said, and wandered unsteadily a few metres along the road until a tree presented itself.

'It's so easy for guys, isn't it? Just take it out and off you go.' Not that I was averse to going outside myself, if necessary. Facilities on digs aren't always up to scratch.

'I thought you were having one yourself,' he called back.

'Went before we left,' I said.

'What were you doing out here, then?' he said, coming back to join me at the gate.

'Just trying to figure out what went on in this field.'
I stared back into the darkness.

Finian shot me a quizzical look. 'Maybe they grazed
cows in it.'

I laughed. 'I'm sorry, I should have told you. We're
at Monashee.'

Finian drew back from the gate. 'Monashee,
where…?'

I nodded.

He looked up at the sky, then into the field once
more. 'Jesus, it's pitch-black in there,' he said.

'An anomaly, as you said bef–'

We both heard it at the same time: a distant moan.
We glanced at each other, then peered in the direction
from which it had come – across the river.

We waited.

'It was a fox,' whispered Finian.

We heard the noise again.

'It's a cow,' he said.

'What is it with you and cows tonight?'

He was about to answer, but I put up my hand.
'Shh, listen …' This time it was louder: a plaintive,
bleating sound that put me in mind of Chewbacca.

'It's human,' I said.

'No, I know what it is. It's a deer. They raise them
somewhere near here.'

'For God's sake, Finian, are you going through some
kind of wildlife directory?'

'If it's human, then where is it coming from?' His

question was oddly put but still required an answer.

'Newgrange.'

I checked for any movement in the fields sloping up from the far riverbank to the mound: nothing. I stared for what seemed like an age at the quartz façade. Then I noticed a shadow that hadn't been there before.

'Quick, look!' I said, pointing. 'Do you see that shadow to the left of the entrance?'

Finian squinted into the distance. 'I think it's being cast by one of the standing stones,' he said, with the air of an astronomer correcting an over-enthusiastic stargazer. He seemed to be sobering up.

I peered at it. Maybe he was right.

We heard the bleating again, louder this time. For a second I saw a pinprick of light in the recessed entrance area. When I looked back at the façade, the shadow had disappeared. And then for a brief moment we saw, standing in front of the darkened entrance, a figure dressed in white.

'And you *did* see it?' I asked Finian as we got into the car.

'I've told you several times now, Illaun: yes, I did. OK?'

'And you think it was a Garda in forensic overalls.'

'Makes sense, doesn't it? Combing the area around Newgrange after the murder.'

It was a reasonable conclusion. 'What about the strange noise?'

'I have no idea. It probably came from somewhere else along the river.'

I said nothing.

'You think whoever was up there was making that sound?'

'Yes. And I also think we were looking at the same individual I saw that night in the fog.'

'How can you be sure it was the same person? Whoever we saw just now was very far away.'

'The headgear – some kind of veil. Couldn't you see it?'

'I couldn't make out any details, not at that distance. But don't those forensic overalls have hoods as well?' That was true. 'It wasn't a water sheerie, at any rate,' he added.

'Speaking of which,' I said, turning on the engine, 'remember what Jack Crean was telling us about sheeries, children's souls and so on?'

'Sure.'

'I think it points to Monashee being an infant burial ground, a *cillín*.'

'I've heard of them.'

'I think the Grange Abbey nuns used to quietly bury dead babies from the maternity home in there.'

'Which could mean it was used for centuries.'

'That's possible.'

'But, if that's the case, why did Seamus Crean only unearth the remains of one infant? You'd imagine there'd be hundreds of them.'

'I think I know why.' I told him about the items found in the illegal dump.

'Are you saying they cut up the bodies, kept parts of them in jars?'

'I think so. Presumably for medical research. And I think Traynor discovered that – and something else about Monashee.'

'But, if they weren't burying babies there, then it's not a *cillín* after all.'

'They buried some of the babies there. But it had another function – as a place of execution for people like Mona.'

'Then surely that's the real story: ritual execution of the living, as opposed to random burial of the dead. And two men ending up dying in a similar fashion.'

'It should be, in theory. But Traynor had no interest in Mona, only in the infant. We're being made to think that it's all got to do with Mona in order to lead us away from the child. That's the reason for the copycat injuries.'

Finian ran his hand through his hair. 'Illaun, that's so convoluted it's giving me a headache just thinking about it.'

'No, Finian, that's just your hangover starting to kick in.'

'Let's go home,' he groaned.

'No – let's go up to Grange Abbey,' I said, pulling out onto the road.

Finian laughed. Then he realised I was serious. 'This is an absurd idea, Illaun.'

'Why?'

'Because …' I saw him looking at the clock on the dashboard. 'It's after twelve; they'll all be in bed.'

It was my turn to laugh. 'Even better,' I said, making a sharp left turn and heading uphill.

'But why go there – for what? To ask them to own up to pickling babies in jars?'

'There's something about the place that doesn't ring true. In fact, I'm finding it hard to believe I was actually there at all. It's like a dream.'

'They'll have the place locked, you'll see.'

But the gate was open, and the avenue snaked downwards like a sequinned white ribbon into the dark wood below. There were no tyre-marks in the frost, a fact I found surprising for some reason.

'Well?' Finian was half-hoping I would abandon my plan. And if I had been on my own I would have.

I drove through the gates.

'Oh, shit,' he muttered.

'Watch this,' I said, and turned off the lights of the car. Finian sank into his seat and closed his eyes. But the light of the moon was sufficient to drive by.

The abbey was there, all right, but there wasn't a single light on, outside or inside. And the Land Rover was nowhere to be seen. I pulled off the drive and parked on grass under some leafless lime trees about thirty metres from the edge of the gravel forecourt.

'Happy?' said Finian, anxious to leave.

'There's no sign of life whatsoever,' I said.

He sighed heavily. 'Illaun, it's half-twelve on a winter's night. What were you expecting, a garden party?'

'Shh,' I said. 'I can hear something.'

I let down the window on my side. Two, maybe three voices. Outdoors. And I knew, from the way sound was behaving on this crystalline night, that they were not as close as they seemed.

'I think those voices are coming from somewhere around the church,' I said.

'Probably the nuns coming back from matins or whatever they sing at midnight. Can we leave now?'

'I'm going to take a look.'

'You're crazy, Illaun.'

'Are you coming?'

Finian's cautious nature tended to spur me in the opposite direction, and the more uptight he was about what I wanted to do, the more daring I would often become. It had been a feature of our relationship since our teacher-and-student days, and tonight a certain amount of schoolgirl giddiness had entered the picture as well – perhaps because I knew that all he wanted to do was get home to bed.

Finian swore and reluctantly climbed out of the car. We squeezed the doors shut, and I led the way towards the archway into the abbey close.

The sharp outline of the moon was blurred by an

inner halo that had formed around it, the orb within looking like the core of a vast galaxy. Reaching the side of the archway, we hugged the wall and listened for any sound from the area around the church. In the minute or so it had taken to get there we had heard the voices once or twice, but now there was silence.

I peered around the side of the arch. The moon was just above the battlements of the tower, carving the square into angular sections of shadow and light. I thought the square was empty until I noticed the moonlight glinting off something, which turned out to be the abbey's Land Rover. It was parked between the church and the side of the walled garden.

'There's nobody around,' I whispered, trying to sound convincing. 'They must have been parking their Land Rover for the night. Probably went into the residence by the cloister.'

'So, once again, what the hell are we doing here?' As Finian returned to complete sobriety he was becoming a little cantankerous.

I had brought the flashlight from the glove compartment. 'I want to show you the west door and some of the other carvings, to see what you think.'

'I'll arrange a tour for myself with the abbess – preferably during daylight.'

I turned the flashlight on my face so that he could read my expression. 'I'm serious about this, Finian. I don't think people get to see this place unless they drive in here by accident. I think they had their own reasons for letting me come here.' I turned off the light again.

He breathed deeply a few times through his nose. It was his way of de-stressing. 'All right. Let's do it.'

We walked through the arch, keeping to the shadows until we were standing opposite the west end of the church. The entire façade was pitch-black, so I switched on the flashlight.

The shock made me grab Finian's arm.

The door was wide open. Both leaves of what had been a seldom-used entrance were agape, and I could see the circular beam from my flashlight playing on the wooden ceiling inside the church.

'Oh, shit,' said Finian under his breath. 'Let's get out of here.'

I had already switched off the flashlight and was on my way when something made me turn around, like Lot's wife in the Bible.

'Look,' I said, pulling Finian about by the arm.

We could see a glow deep inside the church.

'Come on,' said Finian, grabbing my hand.

'Wait …' I didn't believe the light in the interior had just come on. So why had it been invisible as we approached the doorway? I remembered the uphill slope back to the west end.

'I know why we couldn't see it until now,' I whispered.

'What are you talking about?'

'The floor slopes downwards – they had to follow the contour of the bedrock. So the east end isn't visible until you come close to the doorway.'

'Fascinating. Now get your ass in gear.'

'OK, let's go.'

Then we heard a sound that froze us to the spot. It was the sound of applause, like a small audience welcoming someone on stage.

The clapping subsided, and far inside the church a lone voice started to sing.

O the holly she bears a berry
As red as the wine
And we worship Lord Sol
Our saviour divine ...

'What the hell's going on in there?' whispered Finian, just as astonished as I was – and not just because it was an unlikely choice of material for whichever of the canonical hours was being observed.

Several voices began to harmonise, in the robust, nasal style of English folk singers.

And we worship Lord Sol
For our saviour is he
And the first tree that's in the greenwood
It was the holly ...

Finian gripped my arm and propelled me away from the church. 'I don't understand,' he said.

Neither did I. Because all of the voices were male.

Chapter Twenty-Two

We drove at speed up the avenue, saying nothing to each other until we had passed through the gates and out onto the road.

Finian was the first to speak. 'That was so weird. Maybe it's just the shock of the unexpected – men singing in a convent chapel late at night. What did you make of it?'

An annual fertility rite was the first thing that entered my head. The order had become self-perpetuating by breeding its own members. Never having to openly recruit, thereby drawing no attention to itself ... that was how it had managed to survive. But what did they do with the male offspring? They must be sent for adoption through the same channels as the children born in the order's maternity hospital – but not all of them: some were kept for mating purposes. And that would result in inbreeding – guaranteed to produce defective births. Which was why they needed outsiders to join from time to time …

'Illaun, that silence tells me your mind is working overtime. Share your thoughts before your imagination runs away with itself.'

He knew me well. I was on a roll. Then a slightly less lurid idea occurred to me. 'When the abbess talked about the vows taken by the order, she said they were free of them for one day in the year …'

'And you think they were getting up to something naughty on their day off. A midnight orgy, possibly?'

I avoided mentioning my wilder speculations. 'A celebration. The abbess said Henry II issued his charter at Christmastime; maybe they mark it in some way.'

Finian chuckled. 'Imagine if the good Sisters were simply holding a carol concert with invited guests. Raising funds for the restoration of the church roof, perhaps. For all we know there were even posters in the pub tonight advertising it.'

'Finian, as you said yourself, it was half-twelve on a winter's night. On the night of the solstice, as a matter of fact. Fundraising? I don't think so. Whatever it was, it had something to do with the turning of the year – and nothing to do with Christmas.'

'I guess I agree. Just trying to see it from a different perspective, that's all.' He sat in silence for a while, then said, 'That carol had more than a whiff of paganism about it, I'll admit.'

'That about describes everything in that place. And the idea that holly might be playing a prominent part in their rituals is really scary, considering what I saw stuffed in Traynor's mouth.'

'Look, let's not go too far with this. It's been a long evening; give your brain a rest.'

'It's been a long *day*, but it's not finished yet. You're coming home with me.' Just in case there was any chance of him misinterpreting my intentions, I added, 'To help me decode the enigma of Grange Abbey.'

Finian groaned again.

While he made tea, I went to the office to print off some of the images I had loaded into my laptop. Having chosen a high-resolution setting, I was able to enlarge segments of the west-door shot while maintaining perfect clarity.

I took the A4 sheets into the kitchen along with a magnifying glass. Finian had poured out two cups of tea and was sitting at the table, reading Saturday's newspaper and idly stroking the cat.

'Let's look at these under the light,' I said, sitting down at the dining table, pushing Boo out of the way and spreading out the prints. I have a yellow Tiffany-style lampshade featuring green-winged dragonflies with glowing red carbuncles for eyes, and they seemed to be peering over our shoulders to examine the photos.

'You're the expert on this stuff,' Finian said, sifting through them. 'I can see the reliefs are in good condition, but don't ask me to interpret them.'

'It helps me to think a bit more clearly when I have someone to bounce ideas off. Just bear with me for a while.'

'I'm all yours.'

Tracing my finger along the curve of the outermost of the three arches, I began to point out various reliefs. 'We're into the medieval bestiary in this frieze,' I said. 'This fellow that's part lion, part eagle is a griffin; that two-legged dragon is a wyvern; here's a cockatrice – also known as a basilisk; and here's a manticore, with its scorpion's tail.'

Finian peered through the magnifying glass. 'What are they doing outside a church?'

'These guys probably had what's called an apotropaic function – warding off demons on the principle of meeting like with like. They made sure nothing evil came into the church.'

'There seems to be what looks like an actual scorpion in the middle of them.'

I took the glass from him and confirmed his opinion. 'Moral finger-wagging. As far as I recall, the scorpion was equated with lust. See – it has a female face, the idea being that it seduced you with its beauty only to poison you with its sting.'

'Carvings like these would have been painted, wouldn't they?'

'Yes – and brightly, too. Probably a bit like the colours on the lampshade.'

Finian studied the dragonflies for a moment and gave a noisy yawn of approval.

'Now let's look at the two innermost arches,' I said. 'They're the best preserved from the weather; the carvings are still nice and crisp.'

'What have we here?'

'Products of the medieval imagination again: the fabled inhabitants of far-off lands. I haven't had time to study them carefully, but I recognise several more than I did at first glance. Here's a representative of a monstrous race called the blemmyae – men with no heads, or, to be more precise, with their mouths and eyes on their chests. Next to him there's a cyclops, and then some others I have no names for: a thing that looks like an octopus; a man with claws for hands, another with the head of a lion. And see this almost-human fellow here, with the wide division between his eyes and the long snout? That's a cynocephalus, a dog-headed man. There's a mermaid here as well ...'

'These were all meant to be different races?'

'Yes. Now, here's something I'm only seeing properly for the first time myself – the designs on the capitals supporting those arches ...'

'They're not in high relief like the other carvings.'

'No. They're incised, a little more difficult to make

out. Foliage of some kind on one pair of capitals …
and winged insects on the other.'

I shared the picture with Finian and we peered at it
together.

'Look closely at the insects. See – they're striped,' I
said.

'They're honeybees.'

'Hey, you're right …' The figure out on the foggy
patio immediately entered my mind. I shivered.

'You OK?'

'I'm fine. Just a bit tired. Where were we?'

'Talking about bees again.'

'Yes. Any idea what they symbolised at that time –
in religious terms, I mean?'

'Well … there's the obvious appeal they would have
had to monastic leaders because of their social organisation. Communities of nuns were often compared
to bees.'

'Uh-huh … interesting. Keep going.'

'The bee is a symbol of death and rebirth because it
was believed to die in winter and return in spring …'
He was screwing up his eyes as he retrieved the lore
from various recesses in his memory. 'Also, its honey
represents Christ the merciful, its sting Christ the judge
and … There's something to do with the Virgin Mary,
too, but I can't recollect what it is.'

'Try.'

Finian snapped his fingers. 'Her chastity – that's it.
Because it was thought that bees collected their

young from flowers rather than hatching them from eggs.'

'Hmm. So they weren't involved in the messy business of sexual reproduction.'

'But you do know how bees actually breed, don't you?'

'Remind me.'

'In the hive the workers are all female, while the males – the drones – have only one purpose in life: to mate with the queen. But a curious thing happens when the drones fertilise the queen's eggs.'

'What's that?'

'All the eggs develop into females.'

Finian had no idea how eerily this paralleled my earlier conjectures about the Grange Abbey community. I picked up the magnifying glass again. 'OK, let's take a closer look at the vegetation on the other pair of capitals.' I looked through the lens. 'I don't believe this,' I said, handing it over to Finian.

'Leaves ... berries ...' He looked at me in surprise. 'It's holly, isn't it?'

'Damn right, it's holly,' I said grimly.

'Honeybees and holly together. A nice decorative touch, or something more? Are they to be taken separately or are they linked in some way?'

Finian seemed to have forgotten the connection between holly and the dead men, but I thought it best to keep on the course he had set with his questions. 'I guess we've lost the ability to grasp how the medieval mind would have read them, just as they might not be able to understand certain signs in our culture. Take a simple thing like ... like a circle – no, even better, a ring. If I asked you and a medieval man what a ring symbolised, you would probably both say "eternity". That's one that's common throughout the ages. But if I showed you a white flag with five interlinked rings coloured blue, yellow, black, green and red, it would mean nothing at all to him but lots to you.'

'The Olympic Games.'

'Of course. And not just the concept of the Games, but a whole bunch of TV images and memories as well, and also the range of issues that the Games regularly throw up: drugs, definition of amateur status, commercialisation and so on. And then the big aspiration: the five continents represented by the rings, unified through sport. All of that can be tapped into once you see those interlaced rings.

'So when medieval people looked at stone sculptures or images in stained-glass windows, they could read not only the obvious meaning of any given one, but probably several layers of significance attached to it. And when images were presented together they interacted in various ways, so the potential for complex messages was multiplied. Holly, for example – as you told me before, it protected the Holy Family from Herod's soldiers, its berries represent the blood of Christ, it warded off incubi from the beds of young women and so on. Blend those meanings in with the symbolism of bees, and what do you get?'

'Beats me,' he said.

'For a start, in Romanesque architecture the church door was a favourite site for judgement scenes and warnings about the consequences of various vices. So it's a fair bet we're in that territory. This particular stone sermon seems to be very much concerned with promiscuity and loaded with warnings about the fruits of original sin.

'On the incised capitals alone – what we've just been looking at – there's an entire lesson about the struggle between paganism and Christianity: the blood of Christ has replaced the blood of the Goddess, who is herself replaced by the Virgin Mary; the endlessly dying and rising Lord of the Forest has been superseded by the gentle God who died and rose once and for all, but whose judgement will be severe on those who don't appreciate what He's done for them. The question now is – why this lesson on this particular doorway? And how can we better interpret the figure carvings on the arches?'

I heard a snore and looked across at Finian. I had thought he was scrutinising one of the photographs, but he was fast asleep with his head resting on the table, the magnifying glass still in his hand.

I sat back and continued the discussion within my mind.

The reason for Grange Abbey's existence was, I

believed, in those stones. I had already known the nuns delivered young women of their illegitimate babies, hence the warnings about the consequences of lust; but there was something more in the stones, something I wasn't getting.

And something else was gnawing at me. When I had visited Grange Abbey there hadn't been a single religious statue or picture to be seen; there was plenty of holly and ivy, even mistletoe, but no sign of a crib. The Latin hymn I had heard the community singing on my first visit might as well have been welcoming the returning sun as celebrating the Nativity. And there wasn't the slightest ambiguity about the words we'd heard sung tonight – 'we worship Lord Sol, our saviour divine.' The place didn't just have a faint aroma of paganism; it stank of it.

I allowed my darkest thoughts to rise to the surface. I believed that the nuns of Grange Abbey had not only abandoned their Catholic beliefs and practices, but had done something to reverse the balance of power in the struggle portrayed on the doors. *The blood of the Goddess is reddening the berries again, and it is she and the Green Man who are now in the ascendant. The evil that was being warded off is now within.*

There was one last thing, but I was reluctant even to think it.

Frank Traynor and Brendan O'Hagan had both found out far more than it was safe to know about the nuns of Grange Abbey. And I already knew too much as well.

December 22nd

Chapter Twenty-Three

Early on Wednesday morning mild westerly winds blew in from the Atlantic, bringing squalls of fine rain that billowed around the street like lost fishing nets as I battled my way on foot towards the Dean Swift Hotel and Leisure Centre. I was on my way to find Fran.

December in Ireland was proving typically variable and the weather forecast was, as always, mocking Bing Crosby's dream. 'White Christmas', worn out from endless repetition, dripped drearily from the speakers in the lobby, where its jadedness was matched by the fake tree that had been blinking there since mid-November.

Finian had been completely sober when I woke him up and had insisted on staying in the house for my protection. I was not inclined to argue, so after we had locked up he went to sleep in the guest bedroom and I eventually collapsed into my own bed at 3.30 am.

I had left him sleeping. I'd taken time over my breakfast to clear my head and get things in perspective, which I needed to do before talking to Gallagher. For a start, I would have to keep my ideas about Grange Abbey in check. I had conjured up scenes worthy of inclusion in a sequel to *The Wicker Man*. All I needed to do was have a sexy Britt Ekland type play Sister Campion and I'd have a cult classic on my hands. No – will-o'-the-wisps out on the bog and stone carvings on a church were not the first items I should draw to the attention of a double murder investigation. I needed more information about Grange Abbey; and that was why I had come to the leisure centre.

Emerging from the dressing-rooms, I took in the scene: two women and a man lane-swimming in a section of the pool roped off for that purpose. Nobody else. Then I saw Fran, in a blue one-piece a shade lighter than my own, exiting from the steam room at the far end and taking a shallow dive. I stepped in and swam towards her. Fran surfaced near a sculpture of a giant fish streaming water from its mouth. She let it play on the back of her neck, holding up her chin, her eyes closed as it massaged her. I waded right up to her and waited until she opened her eyes.

'Aaah!' she cried, and jerked backwards, losing her balance and floundering in the water. She gargled some obscenity at me as she regained her feet, wiping water away from her face with both hands. 'What are *you* doing here?'

'Same as you,' I said, starting to swim away from her. It felt good.

'What is it, Illaun?' she said, catching up. 'You didn't come here for the good of your health.'

She was right, of course. 'I rang but you weren't in. Daisy told me you were here.'

We reached the end of the pool and, like members of a synchronised-swimming team, turned on our backs and began to pedal underwater with our necks resting against the lip.

'There's been another murder at Newgrange,' I said.

'Heard it on the news.'

'Then you know it's not O'Hagan I've to worry about.'

'Yeah. Wrong call.'

'I think when you said it was the Ghost of Grange Abbey you were nearer the mark. I called in there last night, actually.'

Fran sniggered. 'Know something, Illaun? I think you've got a late vocation.'

'It was late, all right,' I said. 'Past midnight, in fact.'

I was staring up at the ceiling high above us, but I could feel Fran's eyes boring into the side of my face. 'Stop teasing and tell me the story.'

By the time I had finished we were both standing like people chatting on a street, oblivious of our watery environment. I ended with a question that I should never have put to Fran if I wanted a serious response. 'So what do you think the men were doing there?'

She didn't seem to give it much thought, but her answer was intriguing. 'Entertaining the pope.'

'What?'

'So Sister Gabriel says. At this time of year, she prattles on about some feast at the abbey in honour of the pope. She gets it confused with one held in Rome centuries ago. The problem is she has lucid spells, too, so you can't tell fact from fiction –'

'Fran …' I said, grabbing her by the shoulders.

She looked surprised, alarmed even. 'Yes?' she gulped.

'I have to see that nun. Like now!'

'Oh my God,' she said, 'that's OK.' She mopped her brow exaggeratedly. 'I thought you wanted to kiss me.'

'Not likely. You're not my type.'

'Don't I know it. The only thing you want near your G-spot is a green finger!' She splashed water in my face and swam away.

I dived down; before she reached the steps I had climbed out, picked up her flip-flops and thrown them in the pool.

We were the only occupants of the women's dressing-rooms. Fran plucked off her swimming cap and shook her hair. 'I'll get back to you as soon as I can about Sister Gabriel.'

'Thanks. I really need to talk to her.'

'How did the party go?' I knew she really meant, *How did it go with Finian?*

'Great. The only downside was bumping into Tim Kennedy.' I told her what had happened.

'I always thought he was a creep. Just as I think Finian is repressed.' Fran knew that, although Finian expressed his affection for me in many ways, he had never made sexual advances.

'I don't think so, Fran. He's unsure because of the age thing. He doesn't want to embarrass either of us by making the wrong move.'

'"Faint heart never won fair maid," as they say. But, then again, Finian is just a sheep in wolf's clothing.'

'He's not faint-hearted,' I said, 'he just has his own way of doing things. Yesterday he gave me a gift that spoke for him in a very subtle way.' I explained the teacher-student relationship between Peter Hunt and Marie Maguire. 'I guess he was saying that here was evidence that a relationship like this could turn into romance and marriage as well.'

Fran looked at me with a pitying expression. 'Romance and marriage, is it? Can the pair of you not just have a good shag and get it over with?'

'Kissing would be fine at this stage.'

'You mean you haven't even …' She shook her head disapprovingly and zipped up her sports bag. 'Seems to me if you don't take the lead yourself you're not going to get anywhere with this guy. But do you really want someone who has to be coaxed into your knickers?'

'It's not like that, Fran. And I've given him until Christmas in my own mind.'

We left the dressing-rooms and strolled towards the lobby. *This is bizarre,* I thought. *Here we are discussing my love life while I should really be worrying about actually staying alive.* But it was a welcome distraction.

'Listen to me,' Fran said forcibly. 'Getting things sorted out with Finian between now and Christmas may be expecting too much, especially if he doesn't know he's on trial – Jesus, I can't believe I'm saying this. So give him until the end of the year. But *tell* him, for God's sake. If he hasn't come up trumps by then, forget him and move on. And I mean *move on*. Life's too short.'

I hadn't the heart to point out how inappropriate her last comment seemed to me at that moment. 'Sure,' I said.

We had reached the car park. 'And one more thing,' said Fran, unlocking her car. 'I saw a TV documentary on Abelard and Héloise last week. She never wanted to marry him, you know. She'd have preferred to be his mistress.'

'Really? But, if memory serves me, she ended up as neither his wife nor his mistress, but locked away in a convent. And, like you said, I could have a late vocation!'

The leisure centre was beside a shopping complex and so, on the basis that a little retail therapy would help me re-establish a normal existence, I decided to catch up on my Christmas-present shopping. Two hours later I was carrying two large bags packed with gift-wrapped items and heading for the exit when my new phone rang for the first time. I dumped the bags on the ground and answered it. It was Fran.

'Hi, Fran. What's the story?'

'Sister Gabriel will see you this afternoon. I think she liked the idea of someone paying her a Christmas visit.'

'Well done. Thanks.'

'I'll have to go with you. She's nervous about anything new. It'll help if I'm there.'

'No need. I'm sure one of the other nurses will be on hand.'

'To hang around while you two have a chinwag? Yeah, that's the way the Health Service works. One nurse for every conversation.'

'OK. I appreciate you coming along. I'll drive. What time will I collect you?'

'Three o'clock. Means we'll get there about half past. And I've promised the kids we'll be back before six.'

Peggy ran through a list of people who had tried to contact me the previous day: Matt Gallagher, Keelan O'Rourke, a couple of clients including the National

Roads Authority and, to my surprise, Muriel Blunden – in the late afternoon, according to Peggy.

'Did she say why she was ringing?'

'Just checking that she had the right e-mail address.'

Had she found out more about Frank Traynor and Derek Ward? I postponed my call to Gallagher and scrolled through our e-mails until I found one from Muriel. It had been sent from the National Museum at 5.35, which meant she had gone back to her office after meeting Ward.

> *Have a preliminary C14 report (full AMS data – and invoice – to follow, apparently) from the radiocarbon lab at UCD. Am e-mailing same to Dr Sherry at his request. Seems he told the lab the Museum would stump up and quoted you as having the requisite authority. While deploring the methods you use, I admire your audacity. Consider this – and the full report to come – a Christmas gift.*

No mention of Ward; but, reading between the lines, it didn't look as if her mind was exactly preoccupied with him. Had they called it a day? For her sake I hoped they had.

I opened the attachment. 'C14/AMS Prelim. Uncalibrated Results – Not For Publication ...' My eyes ignored the preamble that followed and went straight to the lines of figures that really mattered.

Sample No. 4678/Woman
(Age: Yr BP +/– 50)
750 yrs

'BP' stood for 'before present' – 'present' being 1950, a date fixed by scientific convention for the purposes of carbon-dating. The margin of error was fifty years on either side of the estimated age of the organic material submitted for analysis. And the '750' was how many years before 1950 Mona's ability to process the radioactive isotope carbon-14 had ceased – how many years ago she had died.

The woman I had named Mona had died between AD1200 and AD1300, four thousand years after the builders of Newgrange had passed into prehistory. She was not Neolithic, not even from the Iron Age. She had more than likely been buried at Monashee at a time when the Anglo-Normans had established themselves as lords of Meath.

I was disappointed about Mona's age but not entirely unprepared for it. The infant was another matter entirely.

Sample No. 4679/Infant
Age: 1950 +11 yrs

The child whom we had assumed to be Mona's offspring had been given what is sometimes called a 'future' calculation. She had come into the world and

363

died in 1961. Not only were she and Mona unrelated: one was medieval, the other from the modern era. Their burial together had been purely accidental.

And somehow Traynor had known this.

Peggy was working on the end-of-year accounts in the office; so as not to distract her, I went into the house and rang Gallagher from there.

'Matt Gallagher. Who's speaking?' I could tell he was under pressure, already sounding impatient.

'Illaun Bowe here. I need to talk to you.'

'Look, I can't do any more than give you the same advice.'

'What do you mean?'

'I can't provide you with round-the-clock protection.'

'That's not why I'm ringing you, Gallagher. I have information for you, but I want some in return.'

'I suggest you try the Golden Pages,' he said tartly. 'Now, if you don't mind –'

'But I do mind.'

'I'm a busy man, Miss Bowe. And right now, where information is concerned I'm a one-way system – in, not out.'

'If you were listening, I said I have information for you.'

He sighed loudly. 'Oh, let's get it over with. What do you want to know?'

'When I got your warning, I assumed you had confirmed that the card was sent to me by the killer.'

'Do you want the long or the short answer?'

'The short one will do.'

'The answer is no.'

'But I thought …'

Gallagher sighed again. 'What I'm saying is we don't know for definite. Ten thousand cards with that design and serial number were distributed in packets of ten throughout Ireland, but only one outlet in this area had them for sale – a newsagent's in Drogheda. It's therefore reasonable to conjecture that the killer bought them there. But the till receipts show that all the packets they sold up to last weekend were bought for cash. We also looked at footage from a security camera in the shop, but it's of such poor quality that you'd wonder why they installed the thing in the first place. In the meantime we've sent the cards and envelopes for DNA analysis, which may link them – if the killer has obligingly left traces on both. That's police work, Miss Bowe. Painstaking and tedious a lot of the time, and what makes it even more tedious is having to spend time talking about it.'

Gallagher's condescending tone infuriated me. It was time to stop him in his tracks.

'How's this for police work? Up until his death Frank Traynor was blackmailing Derek Ward, the Minister for Tourism and Heritage.'

Silence at the other end. Then a clearing of the throat. 'Traynor? A blackmailer?'

'Who not only forced Muriel Blunden of the

National Museum to go on radio last Friday morning, but dictated what she should say.'

Gallagher spluttered. 'And he was blackmailing the minister?'

'Yes. And Sergeant O'Hagan knew exactly what his brother-in-law was doing. That's why he made sure no reports of a woman in Traynor's car reached your ears – in case you stumbled across their dirty little secret. Now, is that enough to convince you to take me seriously and not be so bloody obnoxious?'

'I'm sorry. I apologise. It's just that, with O'Hagan's murder, our own top brass is breathing down my neck as well. Whatever else about him, O'Hagan was a cop, and we don't like to see one of our guys getting hacked up like that. Pax, OK?'

'OK, then. And, while we're in Latin mode, have you had someone check out the writing on the card?'

'Yes. A lecturer in Maynooth College. He thinks "*Concupiscenti*" is a term like "paparazzi" or "literati", that it refers to a group who practise something or have a fellowship of some kind.'

My thoughts too.

'So what hold did Traynor have over Derek Ward?' he asked.

'That's what you'll have to find out. From the minister himself, I suggest.'

'But you're not saying he had anything to do with the killings, are you?' I could tell that Gallagher was already anticipating the skull-crushing weight of sky falling on his head should he accuse a government minister of involvement in homicide.

'I don't know. But my hunch about Traynor has proved correct.'

'Which one is that?' There was no trace of sarcasm in his voice.

'That he was interested in the infant found at Monashee. He may have been actually looking for its remains, because after paying his secret visit to the morgue he told Muriel Blunden the field wasn't an issue any more.'

'What possible interest could he have had in a baby hundreds of years dead?'

'He knew it wasn't. I have scientific proof that it died in 1961.'

'What? Why the fuck wasn't I told this?'

I hadn't heard him swear before.

'I requested fast-track carbon-dating of both sets of remains. And, before you ask, the woman is from the Middle Ages. Ergo, no link with the child.'

'Latin-speaker, eh? I should haul you in, you know.' Gallagher had loosened up considerably.

'Did I not hear you say "pax" a couple of minutes ago?'

'*Touché.*'

'Hey, what's this? Language soup? While we're at it, let's add in the word *cillín*. Ever heard of it?'

'Em … you've got me there.'

'It's a burial ground for unbaptised infants.'

'Come again? There are special graveyards for kids who die without being baptised? Why, for God's sake?'

'Let's not go into that now. I think Monashee was used by the Grange Abbey nuns for that purpose. They may also have dissected the bodies of stillborn infants, for research purposes. Frank Traynor and Derek Ward were at one time keen on Geraldine Campion, now abbess of Grange Abbey. Should I go on?'

'Jesus, you've been digging up a lot of dirt. No wonder you were sent one of those cards.'

'Then I must be digging in the right place. What about you lot? What have you been coming up with?'

'We believe the killer has an archaeological background.'

Now it was my turn to be surprised.

'I don't necessarily mean a qualified archaeologist; it's just as likely to be a New Age type who's into Earth Mysteries – those are new to me, but apparently they're something to do with all of these ancient structures we can't account for. Anyway, we noticed something when we marked the positions where the two bodies were found on the map. O'Hagan was in a field to the north of Newgrange, Traynor to the south. If you draw a line from one to the other, it cuts through Newgrange itself.'

'So?'

'That didn't happen accidentally. O'Hagan's body was moved from wherever he was killed, and dumped at a spot that marked the line of intersection exactly.'

368

'You may be on to something.' I wasn't too impressed by their analysis, but I wasn't going to argue. I wanted to tell him about the text message sent to Muriel Blunden. 'Remember I told you my phone was stolen?'

'Hmm … it just doesn't make sense,' he said when I'd finished. 'Everything else points to the killer *not* wanting Monashee to be touched.'

True. I was about to tell Gallagher how Muriel Blunden and I had been speculating about the killer planting evidence when an entirely different thought struck me. If Gallagher had been unaware of the existence of *cillíní*, why should I assume that Traynor had been any better informed?

If he had known it was a burial ground, then he would have realised it was unlikely that the digger would conveniently unearth the one body – the incriminating evidence – he was interested in. If, on the other hand, he had been unaware that Monashee might be a *cillín*, that would better explain his response to the unearthing of the infant. In other words, he had been expecting to find a child's body – and a deformed one at that.

I had started to suggest this to Gallagher when I heard him muttering to someone in the background.

'Sorry about this,' he said, coming back on the phone. 'I have to go to the County Council offices in Navan. We're trying to establish how Traynor obtained planning permission for this hotel he was going to build. I'll call you later.'

'OK. And I have a new mobile phone, by the way. Same number.'

'I'd appreciate it if you didn't approach any journalists with this allegation that the minister was being blackmailed by Traynor. Or that O'Hagan was suppressing evidence.'

'As long as I know you're going to pursue it.'

'You have my word,' he said, and hung up.

Chapter Twenty-Four

I switched on the kettle and went back out into the hall. I listened for my mother's radio, then went into a porch with a skylight overhead and tapped on her door – my official entrance to her place, but less used than the one from the utility room at the back of the house. I could have opened it, but I liked her to feel she had a say in whether she had company or not.

Horatio woofed once at half-volume, then snuffled a bit at the bottom of the door. I could hear my mother talking to him as she approached, gently persuading him to stand aside. When she opened the door she looked like a hobbit beside the giant dog.

'Cup of tea? My place?'

'Thank you, dear, that would be very nice. I'll be there in a few minutes. Just listening to the end of a short story.'

She knew that 'cup of tea' was the invitation to a round of negotiations that was going to take the best part of an hour.

'In your own time. Large dogs not admitted, of course.' I said it jokingly, but Horatio was not allowed into my part of the house on days when I might have clients visiting. It wasn't just that his size might intimidate them; he was inclined to leave gloops of saliva lying around for them to slip on. It was a feature of the breed I wasn't too keen on myself, but my mother had no problem cleaning up after him. Richard, however, wasn't too keen on his son squishing his fingers into pools of animal saliva, and that was why Horatio was part of the negotiations that, if successful, would make Christmas run smoothly.

As if making a point about this, Boo was on a rug in the living room posing as a sphinx: forelegs parallel and stretched out in front of him, rear legs tucked under his body, haunches high, head facing straight ahead, half-closed eyes focused on something not in our world – a quick lesson in why the Egyptians believed in the divinity of cats.

A few minutes later my mother arrived. I didn't want the conversation to seem like a big issue. 'Just wanted to sort out the plans for visiting Dad at Christmas. What do you want to do?'

She kept her head down.

'Come on, Mum. Don't make it harder. We have to decide.'

She raised her face, and her eyes were brimming with tears. 'Paddy's favourite time of year ... but of course you know that. He got such joy out of seeing your faces on Christmas morning when you were showing us what Santa had brought ...'

I looked away, not wanting her to see my emotions.

'And then, when you were older and we'd all exchange our presents after midnight Mass ... your father ... always put so much thought into mine ...' She sobbed quietly.

I fought against the urge to do likewise. 'I know, Mum. Those were special times, and always will be to us. But things aren't the same. You adapted to change once – we grew up; now things have moved on again. Dad's no longer at home with us. But we can go to him, can sit with him a while and maybe even talk about our memories so he can listen.'

She wiped away her tears and sat upright in the chair. 'God has given you the strength to see us all through this. It's a great gift, Illaun, and a great burden. I promise I'll put my mind to it today – even make out a roster of visits, so we don't drain ourselves or him. And I'll support you when it comes to convincing Richard.'

Like a woman healed of some paralysis, she approached me with her arms outstretched.

'Oh, Mum,' I sighed, hugging her. 'Richard's so determined to have his way. And he treats me as the enemy. It's like waiting for a showdown.'

'I won't have any dissension in the house over your father at Christmas. It's something he would utterly abhor. It will all be sorted out. Take my word for it.'

After tea and biscuits, lots of chat and a phone call to my Aunt Betty, arrangements were finally in place for Richard and Greta's arrival. Later that afternoon Betty would drive into Castleboyne, pick up my mother and Horatio and take them to her place, where the dog would be boarded over Christmas. My mother would stay with Betty overnight to settle Horatio into his holiday home; tomorrow evening Richard and Greta would arrive in Dublin airport, pick up a hired car and drive to Betty's, from where they would all travel home at around eight. Then we would have to attempt to resolve the issue of our father. I didn't want it to be still hanging over us on Christmas Eve.

After my mother had gone back to her part of the house, I headed to the office. Peggy had left to get something for her lunch, so I took the opportunity to check my other e-mails. There was one from Malcolm Sherry, another from Keelan O'Rourke, and a sticker on my screen from Peggy, telling me that Finian had left a 'call me' message on our voicemail while I was talking to Gallagher. Finian had been gone when I returned to the house, and he probably thought I was still without my mobile phone.

I opened Sherry's e-mail first.

> *Illaun,*
>
> *I've been informed of O'Hagan's murder and briefed on the post-mortem. The plot thickens.*
>
> *Just saw the AMS dates. I'm sure you're disappointed, but who knows – your 'Mona' may yet yield some fascinating insights. Where the infant is concerned, the dating would seem to correspond with what a colleague of mine, Dr Gudrun Walder, pointed out to me here at dinner last night: that phocomelia was a widespread phenomenon among infants born throughout Europe in the early 1960s (West Germany – as it was then – in particular).*

The term 'phocomelia' sailed right over my head – the difference between hearing and seeing a word, I suppose. But as I read I remembered: the draughty morgue in Drogheda, Sherry pointing out the infant's stunted limbs.

> *The limb defects were caused by Thalidomide, a drug widely prescribed to pregnant women as an antidote to morning sickness. As phocomelia*

375

*is not a typical feature of the set of other
syndromes we witnessed in the neonate, my guess
is that she suffered the effects of Thalidomide
poisoning – as if the poor creature weren't in
enough trouble already.*

Poor creature, indeed. It seemed the only decent thing
that had happened to her was having Mona for a
companion in the black earth in which they had both
been laid.

Was Thalidomide the reason for Traynor's interest
in the infant? On reflection, I realised that he would
have been hardly more than an infant himself in 1961.

I rang Finian.

He came straight to the point. 'Who'll be in the
house with you tonight?'

'Em ... no one, actually.'

'Well, either you come here or I stay with you. You
decide.'

'Thanks. I'll let you know later.'

'I'll be on your case. And, by the way, I also took
your advice and rang Maeve – and guess what? It
worked. Dad and I are travelling down on Christmas
Eve as usual, so I'd love if you could come around here
before we go. We're leaving around six.'

'Sure. I'll see you then.'

I was glad for Finian and even more so for Arthur.
But it reminded me once more that my confrontation

with Richard was still on schedule. If only I could sort out my own family as easily as I had Finian's.

'I've also been giving some thought to why Mona ended up in that field. I need to do just a little more research.'

'Well, then I should tell you I've just got the dating results from the radiocarbon lab. She's medieval, circa 1200.'

'That's music to my ears. Fits in with the way I'm thinking. Now, remember – you're not staying on your own tonight.'

'I get the message. See you later.'

I put down the phone and it rang again. Gallagher. 'Just on my way out of the County Council offices. I had to cut you short earlier just as you were about to say something about Traynor and Monashee. What was it again?'

'That he probably didn't know it was an infant burial ground. So he might have been looking for something specific, and assumed the unearthed remains were what he was looking for.'

'Hmm ... interesting you should say that. Because he certainly had no intention of building a hotel there.'

'I ... I don't understand.'

'It'll take a wee while to explain. Look, I'm only fifteen minutes away from Castleboyne and there are some other aspects of the case I'd like to discuss with you, so why don't I call around?'

377

I looked at the clock. 'You'll have to come straight away.'

'Any chance of a good cup of coffee when I get there?'

I laughed. 'Sure. I'll give you a plastic cup and you can fill it yourself from the dispenser.'

I went back into the kitchen and put on some coffee. Then I saw Peggy parking outside and went into the office to meet her.

'I'm expecting an Inspector Gallagher to arrive here shortly,' I said. 'But I'll talk to him in the house so you can keep at the accounts.'

'Fine. Have you read Keelan's e-mail?'

'Haven't had a minute.'

I knew Peggy was giving me a disapproving frown, even though it was hidden under her black fringe. 'He seemed really anxious for you to see it.'

'OK, I'll do it now.'

I sat at my desk and opened Keelan's e-mail.

Rang contact in WET. Preliminary results from Monashee indicate high level of grass pollen, so we're in a post-woodland clearance period. Also evidence of ribwort plantain (Plantago lanceolata) – a weed associated with pasture farming in the surrounding area (the Cistercians?). There's much more material to be examined, but I thought you might like to know how it's shaping up.

About the macro-botanical samples, I'm sure you'll agree the most significant so far, for obvious reasons, are those seeds we found, which turn out to be the fruit of Ilex aquifolium *– pretty festive, don't you think?*

The pollen indications were backing up the radio-carbon date for Mona. But I could see why Keelan wanted me to know about the *Ilex* which by comparison was stunning news. The seven peppercorn-like pellets found beside her head were mummified holly berries. And it was a fair bet that they had originally been in Mona's mouth.

Whoever had killed Traynor and O'Hagan had replicated a detail unknown to any of us, one that sophisticated technology had only just confirmed. It was as if Mona had sent us another reminder from the Middle Ages that her death and those of the two men were connected – and that she and the infant repre-sented two mysteries that were separate and yet bound together.

Chapter Twenty-Five

'According to the County Council officials, planning permission was never sought for a building at Monashee.'

Gallagher and I were having coffee at the counter in the kitchen. His orange hair was even brighter under the beam of a light directly over his head, but his sunburn looked less angry and his nose was no longer peeling. He was wearing a brown check suit, a white shirt and an apple-green tie.

'So where was he planning to build his hotel, then? He was going to build one, wasn't he?'

'Not exactly. He had applied for change of use of an existing building.'

'Oh?'

'Yeah – Grange Abbey, apparently.'

'What?' I shook my head in disbelief. What exactly had Sister Campion said when we discussed it? *We never agreed to a hotel at Monashee ... elsewhere in the area, yes ...* And she hadn't mentioned a hotel being *built*. I should have been listening more closely.

'You're saying he bought Grange Abbey to convert it into a hotel? Had he approval from the County Council?'

'Yes. And the minister was very much behind the project. Off the record, the Council officials think Ward stood to gain from it in some way.'

'Or was being forced into supporting it.'

'Hmm. This blackmail theory of yours, Miss Bowe – or can I call you Elaine?' Gallagher slipped his notebook from the inside pocket of his jacket.

'Please don't. It's Illaun. "Ill" as in "hill", "aun" as in "dawn". OK, *Matt*?'

'Got it. Now, as I was about to ask you, this blackmail theory –'

'Look, Matt, let's get this straight: it's not a theory. Frank Traynor was up to his neck in using information against people.' I reported what had passed between me and Muriel Blunden in Drogheda, and how defensive Derek Ward had been.

'I hadn't realised Ward was having an affair; not a clever thing for a man in his position,' said Gallagher

381

when I'd finished. He had filled up several pages of his jotter.

'Yes, but, as Muriel herself knew, Traynor must have had much more on Ward. Jocelyn Carew, the independent TD, thinks so too.'

'You said that Traynor and Ward were both keen on Geraldine Campion at one time.'

'"Rivals for her affection" is how it was once expressed, I believe.'

'So you think there's something in their past that led to all of this.'

'It's all about the past, Matt. The relationship between those three people in the 1970s, a Thalidomide baby a decade before that … But it stretches back as far as the Middle Ages. It may even have something to do with Newgrange, I can't be sure.'

'Hey, hang on a minute. A lot of stuff just zipped past there; you'll have to fill me in on it. But Newgrange I can handle. O'Hagan was found there – or as close as makes no difference.'

'Was he murdered there?'

'No. He might as well have been dropped from a chopper.'

'What do you mean?'

'A farmer out shooting on his land found the body in a ditch. There were no signs of a struggle in the immediate area. O'Hagan was fully clothed, but the material of his uniform had been scuffed and torn, indicating he had been dragged for some distance, but not through the field – there were no traces of grass or mud. No sign of footprints in the field, either, but that's probably because the soil is well drained, even at this time of year.'

'And his injuries were the same as Traynor's?'

'In every detail. Holly left in the mouth as well. We think his belt was used to strangle him, but we haven't found it. He'd been dead for about twelve hours, but the pathologist estimates he was in the ditch for less than half that time – there were no signs of animal interference with the corpse. No card left with the body, but it may have blown away.'

'What do you know about his last movements?'

'His wife said he went to meet someone in Slane late on Monday night after Traynor's removal to the church. She was staying with her sister-in-law – Traynor's wife – so when he didn't arrive back there, she assumed that he had gone home to sleep in his own bed and that they'd see him at the funeral next morning. When they didn't, she raised the alarm. We found his Vectra in the car park of a pub in Slane. No reports of him being seen there or in the village. We're assuming that, after driving to Slane, he voluntarily went somewhere with whoever murdered him.'

'Another question: if his body had been moved from another location, why wasn't it dumped just inside the entrance? Why carry it all the way to the far side of the mound?'

'We can't establish from which direction the body

was carried into the field. We only know it was deliberately positioned there.'

'Hmm … This alignment you spotted – that makes the murder even more ritualistic, you think?'

'It's why we're working on the basis that the killer has some knowledge of archaeology.'

'I hate to rain on your parade, but the alignment has no ritual significance that I know of. It's probably accidental.'

Gallagher scratched his head. 'But aren't these so-called sacred sites connected by all kinds of lines?'

'Yes. For example, some people believe Newgrange and the Great Pyramid lie along a major ley line. But you can draw a line between any two points on a map. That proves nothing. Even the fact that the line runs through a third, fourth or maybe more ancient structures along the way is of no significance if the cultures that erected them were widely separated in time.'

'Damn.' Gallagher couldn't hide his disappointment.

'Unless someone wanted you to think it was significant,' I said.

'Exactly,' he said, clutching at the straw. 'The killer is playing a game with us. His success in baffling us with the copycat ritual injuries spurred him on to set a more elaborate archaeological puzzle with O'Hagan's body.'

'Doesn't sound like someone with a simple grudge, which was what you were saying on Sunday.'

'Well, you have to adjust,' he said blithely. 'Our

thinking now is that this guy's a save-the-environment type who's probably been nursing a hatred of property developers and their ilk for quite some time. He's likely to be a loner who doesn't share his feelings with others – doesn't go on protest marches or write letters to the papers. But his emotions finally erupted into a murderous rage focused on Traynor. And the reason he mutilated O'Hagan as well is because he's starting to enjoy the ritual itself, for its own sake.'

'Is this the kind of thing your shrink comes up with?'

'Shrink?'

'O'Hagan said you had enlisted what sounded like a psychological profiler, who he said had contributed nothing to the case.'

Gallagher gritted his teeth. 'He was referring to me. But I'm no profiler. He just seemed to resent the fact that I spent six months at a cop college in the States. Maybe he thought I was on a hotline to them every night, getting advice. And maybe he didn't like departing from the tried and tested methods.'

'The ones that got him killed, as it turned out.'

'Yeah. For example, he was carrying around a hard-backed notebook belonging to Traynor – we found it in his car this morning. Soaked in blood, pages stuck together. O'Hagan must have taken it from the Merc the day Traynor was murdered. We'd found Traynor's electronic organiser in the car, so it didn't occur to us he went around with a notebook as well. From what we can make out it seems to be mainly drawings of things, antiques – fittings for his hotels, maybe. No contact names or numbers on the few pages we've been able to see so far, just a title or code name for each item. We'll cross-check the contents against his organiser after we get all the pages separated.'

'I'll bet they're not antiques – not legitimate ones, at any rate. According to Muriel Blunden, Traynor was trafficking in stolen historical artefacts.'

'Well now … if that's the case, then maybe he had a falling-out with a supplier or someone he was trading with. O'Hagan figured out who it was from the notebook and foolishly arranged to meet them. But I can't see someone like that bothering to make the crimes this complicated. This feels more … personal, somehow.'

I looked at my watch. It was nearly time to pick up Fran. I would have to leave Gallagher trying to fit square theories into round problems. And, just to make it more of a challenge, I decided to tell him about the e-mail from Keelan.

'There's another thing. The woman in the field had holly berries placed in her mouth too – seven centuries ago. They've only just been analysed. None of us knew – apart from the killer, that is. How?'

'If I weren't sure you were going to provide me with a rational explanation, I'd say you were telling me the killer had come back from the dead.'

'But that's precisely the problem, Matt. I *have* no rational explanation.' I stood up to leave. 'I've got to go, I'm afraid. But I'm meeting someone who may be able to answer some of the questions I have about Grange Abbey. When I get a chance, I'll brief you on that and the rest of what I've learned.'

Gallagher frowned. 'My warning about meeting strangers still stands.' He put away his jotter and drained the last of his coffee. I realised he hadn't smoked during his visit.

I walked him to the door. 'This is a very elderly lady. I don't think she's a threat.'

'Be careful all the same,' he said.

As soon as Gallagher drove off, I gathered up my things: handbag, keys, mobile phone. I stuck my head into the office and told Peggy I wouldn't be back. It was only when I was getting into the car that I realised that something had begun to ruffle my sense of order. I'm one of those contradictory people who are tidy in some things and not in others – my desk is hopeless, my underwear drawer immaculate. But, tidy or not, I always know where everything is – or should be. In the past few minutes I had seen or heard something that wasn't right, a dissonant note, something out of place. I made a space in my mind for it to come forward and own up, but nothing materialised. No doubt it would pop up when I least expected it.

I collected Fran just after three. The darkness had set in early and the electrical decorations were coming on outside the houses in her estate – icicles dripping from eaves, strings of pulsating colours framing windows and doors, snowmen and Santa Clauses glowing in front gardens. Light defying the dark.

The nursing home had some things in common with the centre where my father was being cared for – the central heating was set at maximum and the volume on the TV in the day room was at full blast. Even though Fran had told me that many of the patients were hard of hearing or prone to hypothermia, I still thought it must be hell for the others.

We went through the day room, where a handful of elderly men and women sprawled on couches in front of the blaring TV, looking stupefied by the heat, and along a corridor with bedrooms to the left and the nurses' station, bathroom, toilets and storerooms to the right. Fran knocked on the bedroom door at the end of the corridor and, with a finger up to me to hold on for a moment, went inside. I could hear her talking; then she poked her head back out and beckoned me in. 'I was just sitting her up and reassuring her you were a friend of mine,' she whispered.

Sister Gabriel's face was the colour of unbaked pastry, and her hair looked like a few wisps of sheep's wool had accidentally settled on her head. She was in a pale-blue flannelette nightdress and propped up on pillows. Her bony hands clutched the edge of the duvet, under which her body made hardly any impression.

'This is my friend, Illaun ...' Fran gestured me to a chair beside the bed. The only other furniture in the room was a bedside locker on which sat a small oval clock. Fran had told me that Sister Gabriel was allowed neither TV nor radio, as they made her excitable and she was inclined to shout at them. I had brought a purple hyacinth in a pot as a small gift, and I placed it on the locker.

'Illaun, this is Sister Gabriel. I'll leave you two to talk.' Fran went to the door and whispered back to me, 'If you need me, I'll be at the nurses' station down the corridor.'

I sat on the straight-backed chair and looked into eyes paler than the washed-out blue of her nightdress. 'Thanks for agreeing to talk to me, Sister Gabriel.' A waft of scent came from the hyacinth, reminding me of home.

Sister Gabriel lifted a finger in acknowledgement and began to speak. As she tried to form words, the lines radiating from her colourless lips moved about like the pleats of an accordion. I couldn't hear anything; I leaned closer.

Her voice gained power from somewhere and emerged as a gravelly croak; her tongue darted in and out of her mouth. 'It's the Beekeepers, isn't it? You've come to ask me about the Beekeepers.'

It was as if some entity had taken control of Sister Gabriel's body and was speaking through her. Fran hadn't mentioned that the old nun had mediumistic powers, so my mind scrabbled frantically to grasp what she was talking about. And just as I did, Sister

Gabriel confirmed it for me. 'The Beekeepers. That's what we were called before Vatican II.'

'Because of the habit you wore?'

'The veil, really. Came down to the chin. Headdress of a third-century martyr, from a drawing in the catacombs. Pope Adrian recommended it ... What are we talking about?'

'The Hospitallers' veil.'

'Yes, yes, I know. The veil. The rest of the habit was quite plain, with a red cincture around the waist – to represent the umbilical cord ... We were midwives, of course ...' The border I had noticed on the abbess's veil was probably a vestigial reminder of this. 'But from early on we were referred to as the Beekeeper nuns, so the bee became the emblem of the order. Of course, the veil did have a purpose. I've forgotten what it was ...' She peered into my face for inspiration. 'Could it have been protection from the sun? You know, when we went abroad on the missions?'

I doubted it, but decided to humour her. 'Oh, yes. Of course.'

Sister Gabriel pursed her mouth in annoyance, the pleats forming into tightly bunched striations. 'What are you trying to say to me, you stupid girl?'

I had made a mistake. I shouldn't have patronised her.

'You know quite well that we had to be unseen. No embarrassment for either party should they meet at social gatherings ... Christmas parties and such. Like the papal dinner. Did you know the popes used to have a big feast at the abbey on Christmas Eve, between vespers and midnight Mass? Wonderful, it was, wonderful. I was there myself. Corelli, Scarlatti – they all composed choral music for it ... something to do with the shepherds, I recall ...' She began to hum a tuneless hymn in a quavering voice, eventually breaking into words. '*Quem pastores laudavere, quibus angeli dixere, absit vobis ... absit vobis* ... Oh dear, I've forgotten the words.'

'Did men ever sing in the church on such occasions?'

'Men? Don't be silly, child. Only men ever at the abbey would be priests from the parish for Mass and confessions. Or workmen.'

'So, apart from the nuns, there was no one else living in the abbey.'

'No. Unless you count the church sacristan. A lay Sister, deaf and dumb. Still wore the old habit. Only one who did.'

'She was the only one who wore the Beekeeper habit? Are you sure?'

'Are you questioning me, girl?'

'I'm sorry – I was just making sure I heard you right. Tell me, was Grange Abbey always a retreat house for the order?'

'Oh, not just that. It was a training centre for postulants. And at one time we had other ... responsibilities.'

'Other responsibilities?'

She frowned. 'They used to say you could read about them in two places, besides the charter – the order's special duties: on the west door and in the crypt. One in stone, the other in glass.'

In glass? A stained-glass window, perhaps – but in the crypt? 'Did you see what was in the crypt for yourself?'

'No. From the time I was a postulant it was out of bounds. Part of the roof had fallen in, they said. But Campion and Roche got workmen in. They found something ... Three Sisters who came with me from the lying-in home have died at the abbey since then, all poisoned by it. That's why I escaped here.'

I could see what Fran meant. Fact and confabulation were difficult to separate, as they were delivered with equal conviction. 'How long ago was that?'

'It's my second Christmas here, I think. Frances will know. I'm tired now – must say prayers for the benefactors of the order ...' She lay back and began muttering, '*Oremus pro benefactoribus nostris ...*'

'I understand, Sister,' I said, and rose to leave.

But Sister Gabriel sat up again. 'Where are you off to, you silly thing? It's time for bed.'

'I know, and that's where I'm going. Tell me, do the abbess and the bursar get on with each other?'

'Have to now; nothing left to quarrel over.'

'What do you mean?'

'They were rivals for the position of abbess. Both

quite young at the time, too. Campion was appointed and Roche was made Head of Training, which was a powerful position when there were dozens of postulants coming there. But that was twenty years ago.'

'So how many were in the community when you left?'

'How should I know? Kept myself apart, you see. Bad arthritis in my hips, as well. Couldn't attend the Divine Office. Too far to go.'

'To the church, you mean.'

'Didn't like it, either. Built on unholy ground.'

'What makes it unholy?'

'The reason the church was built there in the first place. It's all in the charter.'

'Just one last question. What do you know about Monashee?'

She lay back down, plucking nervously at the duvet cover. 'There are things buried there.' Her voice had thinned, the power draining from it.

'What kind of things?' I asked gently, about to open the door.

She gathered a loose part of the cover and pulled it up to her chin. Her eyes were darting about in her head. 'Monsters. Freaks of nature born at the lying-in home and sent to Grange Abbey to be disposed of without trace. That was where they buried them.' She was whispering now. 'Please don't let them put me in that Godforsaken place.'

'It's all right, Sister. I won't let them do anything to you.'

I opened the door, saw the shadow on it as she raised her arm and ducked just before the clock slammed into the door at the level where my head had been. It clattered onto the floor, losing its battery, which rolled under the bed.

'You stupid, stupid girl!' Sister Gabriel screeched. 'You couldn't even resist taking a man into your bed, and now look what you've got for your few seconds of pleasure – a painful birth, a child you'll never see again and a lifetime of regret ...'

I skipped out before something else was thrown.

Fran was already coming down the corridor, looking worried. 'What's the problem?'

'No problem.' I gave her a smile. 'We just ran out of time ...' I slipped the clock into Fran's hand, and she looked at it in surprise. Then I noticed it had stopped at exactly 4.05. The last rays of the setting sun were leaving the south chamber at Dowth.

Chapter Twenty-Six

On the way back to Castleboyne I didn't tell Fran much of what Sister Gabriel had said; I explained that it would take me time to separate out the various strands before I could make any sense of it.

Fran understood only too well. 'I know. She'd do your head in. Listen to her long enough and your brain ends up as scrambled as hers.'

As I was dropping her off I presented her with two gifts, wrapped and tied with red ribbon. One was a DVD of The Cure videos and live performances; the other, to amuse her, was a lavatory brush with a base shaped like a wide-open mouth, allowing the user the pleasure of imagining whose throat they were ramming the brush down on any given day.

'Before Christmas?' said Fran. 'I'm impressed. Can I open them now?'

'No. Just because you have them is no excuse to break with tradition.'

Fran laughed.

'And these are for Daisy and Oisín.' I had found some patchouli-scented bath stuff I knew Daisy liked, and for Oisín I had bought a CD by a rap artist his mother disapproved of.

Fran kissed me on the cheek. 'Thanks. Gotta go. I'm bringing the pair of them to a movie and McDonald's as a reward for putting up the decorations while I was out – I hope!'

When I got home the entire house was in darkness, telling me that both Peggy and my mother had left. I turned on the lights in the kitchen and immediately saw the sticky note on the fridge: 'GILLIAN RANG. CHOIR PRACTICE IN CHURCH AT 7 PM.'

It hadn't been scheduled; I suspected it was because Gillian hadn't been present at the previous rehearsal and wanted to satisfy herself we were in shape for midnight Mass on Christmas Eve. I checked my watch. It was almost 6.30. I had promised Finian to let him know where I was spending the night. I realised I was putting it on the long finger because, with the house to myself, I was anticipating that delicious sense of free-dom that comes with having only your own company for a while. Which would be fine until I awoke in the middle of the night terrified that someone was breaking in. Still, I rang Finian and said I'd decide where I was staying after choir practice.

I entered the church through a side door that led directly to the stairs up to the choir loft. The lights on each landing were on, but when I reached the loft it was lit only by the lamps in the nave below; a small number of them were left on, for the convenience of people dropping in to say a prayer or to light a candle beside the crib. The loft was in semi-darkness. I was the only one there.

As was my habit, I had arrived early, so I didn't take the absence of other choristers as anything unusual. What was unusual was the fact that Gillian Delahunty wasn't there ahead of me.

'Hello?' I said softly, feeling for the light switch on the wall. Perhaps my mother had written down the wrong time. The sound of footsteps down in the church made me pause. *Don't signal your presence.*

I crept past the rows of benches to the balcony overlooking the nave. Down below, the only movement was from the shadows being projected onto the pillars by candles flickering on the offerings tables. I was sure I had heard someone padding swiftly along the centre aisle. *Padding.* An animal?

Whoever or whatever it was could be already rushing up the stairs to attack me, or waiting on one of landings to jump out – but it didn't matter: I couldn't stay trapped where I was.

I went back down the stairs, my heartbeat picking up speed at every step. When I reached the door leading into the porch I took a deep breath, opened it, crossed the porch and grabbed the circular brass handle on the outer door. It moved, but the door wouldn't budge. It was locked.

I wasn't going to be cornered. Pushing through the swing doors into the church, I stood for a moment with my fists raised, prepared to defend myself. Nothing. No one.

I surmised it must have been Mrs Dowling, the sacristan, on her rounds – locking up, turning off the lights, preparing to douse the candles. And running? Not sixty-something Mrs Dowling. One of her grand-children, perhaps.

I crossed under the balcony of the choir loft. Now I had a choice: try the door in the opposite porch and find it locked too, or head for the sacristy, where I would probably find Mrs Dowling, who would let me out.

I turned down a side aisle towards the sacristy. My adrenaline pump had slowed down, but I was still keen to get out of the building; I didn't pause to admire the crib with its life-size Mary and Joseph and infant Jesus, standing shepherds, kneeling kings. I had just passed it when something made me glance back. I was sure one of the shepherds had moved. Probably to do with the shadow-dance created by a nearby offerings table, I thought.

The shepherd's back was to me, but as I looked he turned around. Then I heard him, panting and snuffling. His face was in deep shadow at first, but as he emerged from the gloom and came towards me I saw it. And I screamed.

In sheer terror I turned to run and smashed the side of my head against the sharp corner of a plinth projecting from one of the pillars. My strength drained away and I staggered against a pew, holding on to it for support.

I heard him snarling, coming closer. Somehow I found my voice and began calling for help.

'Illaun!' Someone shouted out my name.

Willing my legs to carry me, I stumbled down the aisle. People came towards me from the sacristy, led by Finian. I fell into his arms and passed out.

I looked up and saw Fran sitting on the bed. Not my bed. Not even my room.

'Where are we?' I said.

'Better than "Where am I?" but not entirely original,' she said, lifting up my wrist and feeling my pulse as she looked at her watch.

'That's fine,' she said after a moment. 'And you're in my house. We thought it was best to take you here after the doctor had seen you. I'm a nurse, after all. Also, Inspector Gallagher thought it would be a good idea.'

I tried to sit up but my head swam. That, and a throbbing pain in my temple, convinced me to lie back down. 'Do you mean Gallagher was here? What doctor are you talking about?'

'Dr Walsh examined you, same as he has for the best part of forty years,' Fran droned with exaggerated patience. 'And no, Gallagher wasn't here, he was on the phone.' She looked towards the door. 'Hey, what do you know – you've got a visitor.'

Finian came into the bedroom and pulled over a chair. 'Glad to see you back in the land of the living.'

'What made you come to the church?' I looked from face to face. 'And why aren't you at the cinema?' I said sternly to Fran.

'Finian called to the house just as I was going out the door. He was wondering if I knew about a choir practice.'

'Gillian Delahunty drove past me, heading out of town, as I was coming into Castleboyne at about quarter to seven,' he explained. 'I thought, "That's odd," so I decided to swing by Fran's and double-check – see if she'd gone to the choir practice as well.'

Fran placed a cold, damp cloth on the side of my forehead. 'But I hadn't heard anything about any practice, so we headed for the church pretty damn fast. We were talking to Mrs Dowling in the sacristy when we heard you scream.'

'And did you find ... him?'

Finian looked at Fran. 'You seemed to be trying to get away from someone, all right ...'

'But there was nobody there,' said Fran.

'Yes, there was. The shepherd in the crib – the animal ... He was snarling –'

They glanced at each other.

'I think Sister Gabriel scrambled your brain entirely,' said Fran.

'No, no! You're not listening. The beekeeper had taken off his ... her veil ... It was waiting for me to go past so it could attack ... It has the face of – the face of a wolf ... a dog ...'

Finian held my hand. 'Well, we didn't have the pleasure of introducing ourselves. Mrs Dowling had locked the door to the choir porch but not the one on the opposite side, so that's how he or she must have escaped.' Despite his reassuring bedside manner, I could tell he thought I was raving.

'There was a note from my mother about choir practice,' I said. 'I didn't make it up. Let's ring and ask her who she was talking to.'

They eyed each other again.

'I think it's best not to alarm her at this hour of the night,' said Fran.

I realised I had no idea of the time.

'Yes, I think Fran's right. It's after eleven,' said Finian.

'And you need to rest,' added Fran.

'Rest? I've been out for four hours. Who needs

bloody rest?' I was angry at not being in control, at being treated as though I had lost my marbles.

I struggled to get out of bed, suddenly noticing that I was wearing a lemon-coloured nightdress that wasn't mine. Fran had evidently undressed me and put me to bed. The thought of Fran and Finian united in their protectiveness hit me like an ocean wave.

I lay back once more and closed my eyes, but I knew the tears had escaped and were streaming down my cheeks. 'I'm sorry,' I whispered.

'What's to be sorry about?' said Fran. 'We just want you fully recovered.'

The last thing I remembered was Finian gently squeezing my hand.

December 23rd

Chapter Twenty-Seven

Gallagher arrived at the house just before 10 am. With what I thought was a reasonable bribe from me, Fran had already driven Daisy and Oisín off to Blanchardstown Shopping Centre to have breakfast and then catch an early showing of the movie they had missed the night before.

'That's a nice bump you have there,' said Gallagher, stepping inside. 'What were you up to last night?'

I led him into Fran's living room and we each sat down in an armchair.

'I've just been on to my mother. A woman claiming to be Gillian Delahunty rang shortly after five to remind me there was a carol practice. Whoever it was must have known I wasn't there at the time. It was a way to get me up in the choir loft on my own, but they hadn't reckoned on me getting there early. And then Mrs Dowling locked the nearest door, which interfered with their plan. So the killer hung around the crib. From there he could see which way I left the building and attack me from behind.'

'But you weren't actually attacked.'

'No. Hearing Finian shout scared him – or her – off.'

'Why do you think it might have been a woman?'

'It was dark, hard to see. But the habit was the same I saw on the patio that night. I think it's the old habit of the Grange Abbey nuns.'

'The nuns again.'

'Yes. And, just for a moment, consider a few other things. For a start, Muriel Blunden says Traynor arranged to meet a woman. Then there's the Latin message inside the card left with Traynor's body: the nuns' charter is in Latin, they even sing all their hymns in Latin. And what about the connection between Geraldine Campion, Traynor and Ward; the possible use of Monashee as a *cillín*; the fact that someone near there was storing infants' body parts; and the fact that Traynor seems to have been expecting to find a deformed baby? We even know that, in the past, the nuns were suspected of spiriting away a mutilated bog body that had originally been buried in Monashee – which links them to Mona, and ultimately to the pattern of injuries inflicted on Traynor and O'Hagan. And, lastly, holly appears as an emblem on the church at Grange Abbey. Did I say consider a *few* other things?'

'Whew! That bump on the head hasn't slowed you down. But now it's time for me to rain on *your* parade. Everything you're saying is speculation, one way or another. Mixing partial truths with unrelated facts is not how we do business, I'm afraid. And then there's the matter of what you actually saw last night ...'

I knew what was coming.

Gallagher looked at his jotter. 'According to your friends, when the shepherd in the crib came to life ...' He paused deliberately. 'He or she – you weren't sure – had the face of an animal ... and it snarled when it was chasing you?'

'Look, it was dark, I was scared. Maybe my imagination went into overdrive, but there *was* someone there, and there was definitely something weird about the shape of the face.'

'I don't doubt you. And I wasn't being a bastard just now. I just wanted you to realise how hard a job I'd have convincing my superiors, not to mention my team, to take the rest of what you say seriously.'

'Then leave it out, for God's sake.'

'No. I'm doing something a lot better. Bit by bit, I'm following up on what you've told us. Here –'

He held up the newspaper so I could read the headline: 'GARDAÍ TO INVESTIGATE MINISTER'S LINKS WITH MURDERED HOTELIER.'

'See what I mean? But it will take time. We'll start with a visit this morning to Traynor's place. Then we'll be talking to the minister. And, depending on how we get on, we may be giving the good Sisters a call after that.'

'If they're still there. The place has been sold, after all.'

'They probably agreed a get-out date with Traynor. Not till the New Year, I'd say. But I'll have someone give them a call.'

After Gallagher left, I rang Peggy and told her I would meet her and Keelan and Gayle at the Old Mill for our Christmas lunch. I didn't mention what had happened or explain why I wasn't coming into the office; I hadn't told my mother about the incident, either.

I went upstairs to the bedroom. I stretched out on the bed, fully dressed, with the back of my head on the soft pillow, and tried to think, without distractions, without irrelevant details cluttering my brain. Just to keep myself on the straight and narrow, I bore Gallagher's lofty principle in mind: *Mixing partial truths with unrelated facts is not how we do business.* Sure.

Sister Gabriel …

I drifted off with Gallagher's voice echoing in my head and awoke to it rasping into my ear. Without consciously hearing my mobile phone, I had managed to pick it up.

'What … ?' I wasn't following him at all. 'Say again?'

'I said we're out at Traynor's place. You should see what he had stashed away, not only in his garage but in the outbuildings as well. All sorts of antiques. And some really old … junk.'

'Junk?' I noticed the time on the clock-radio beside the bed: 11.34. I had been asleep for over an hour.

'There's a lot of church furniture, which his wife maintains he bought along with the abbey. It looks like the entire place was stripped – pews, benches, altar rails, candlesticks, chalices, you name it. But I think it's the stuff in the garage that will interest you more …'

I swung my legs out of the bed and sat on the edge.

'Are you with me?'

'Still here; go ahead.'

'I'll start with some items we found in a cardboard box on the floor. A bargain bin, you'd say. No labels on them or anything, just a jumble of rusting metal. Sword-blades, cannonballs, one of those spears with a hook at the back – it fitted on a long pole … a pike, that's it. And …' I could hear the clatter of iron as he lifted something out of the box. 'Something that looks like the firing mechanism of a flintlock musket or pistol. Would these be of any value?'

'Hard to say. From an archaeological point of view, they're virtually useless if you don't know where or when they were found. That's why there's a law against using unlicensed metal detectors, and why it's illegal not to report finding historical artefacts.'

'OK. Now, moving along, we come to some shelves

where the items are neatly laid out and labelled … For example, there's a knife with a broken blade – it's got a tag attached that says, "Bettystown Viking Hoard". Now that I see it up close, the handle has jewels in it. And there are other things with it – bracelets, brooches and what look like ingots of solid silver.'

'That's exactly what they are. Remember the case, by the way?'

'Vaguely.'

'The hoard was found by unlicensed treasure hunters near Bettystown strand last year, but by the time they were caught and prosecuted they had sold off a lot of the items, some of which you're describing now.'

No wonder Traynor had wanted Muriel Blunden to turn a blind eye to his activities. Even if he was just a collector of artefacts and not a fence, it was against the law merely to be in possession of them.

'What else can you see, Matt?'

'A stone head of a knight labelled "Crusader". Looks like it was sawn off a wall. Leaning up against the shelves there's a stone slab, must be nearly two metres long, with a sculpture of what I'd say is a bishop on the top. There's also an entire Celtic cross standing in the corner over there …'

It was sickening. Traynor had not only been receiving and probably selling archaeological artefacts; he was also sponsoring the destruction and theft of historic monuments.

'Hold on for a moment …' I could hear someone

else talking, Gallagher saying something unintelligible, paper being rustled near the phone. Then Gallagher came back on. 'Remember that hard-backed notebook I told you about, with the drawings? We copied some of the pages before it went for treatment. And we've recognised some of the items already. Ken has just collected the photocopies from the car so we can check them against what we're seeing … One second …' More riffling of pages. 'Yeah, it's like I said. For example, there's a wee sketch here of what looks like a shield, with a ribbon underneath it. Turns out there's a big chunk of rock here on a shelf that looks just the same. It's a coat of arms. There's some paint or colouring still on it. It has what I'd say is a dragon on his back, with a sword – a cross, really – stuck in his belly, and there's a motto on the ribbon … "*La croix du dragon est …* " I can't make out the next bit …'

'*La dolor de deduit?*'

'Hey, that's it! What does it mean?'

'The dragon's cross is pleasure's pain.'

'Come again?'

'It's the motto of the Order of Saint Margaret – has to do with the consequences of lust. What you're looking at probably came from inside the abbey, maybe from the capital of a pillar or a ceiling boss. Anything else of interest in Traynor's notebook?'

'Yeah. There's one item in particular we can't find, and we really want to, because the last entry in the notebook refers to it. It's drawn just under that last one, the coat of arms. Done by a different hand from the others, too, I'd say – not as good. It's a rough sketch in blue Biro. A circle, could be a coin or medallion of some kind – it's hard to gauge the actual size. There's a human figure inside it, no shape, just like a child's stick drawing. And beside that there's a word. Looks like Traynor wrote it. "Goldilocks." Any idea what the object could be?'

'No. But it's safe to assume that the figure depicted on it is a woman. And I'd imagine that it's made of gold.'

'Interesting. Because there's just one other word on the page, and we're satisfied it's Brendan O'Hagan's handwriting. It's written along a line he drew from the medallion to the order's shield, and it says, "Gotcha."'

Chapter Twenty-Eight

Because Finian had brought Fran to the church in his car the night before, she had been able to take my car back to her house; so, after Gallagher's phone tour of Traynor's garage, I drove home to shower and dress before our staff lunch. I decided to wear a sober black jacket and trousers with a plain white blouse; no makeup, no jewellery. I wasn't being a party pooper; it was just the way I felt – sober. Or maybe it was sombre.

Checking myself in the mirror, I saw that the skin was broken over the bruise on my temple but that it hadn't bled. I made sure to pull my hair down over it; I didn't want to be asked any questions.

Keelan greeted me as I entered the bar of the Old Mill. He had found himself the top half of a tuxedo somewhere and was wearing an open-necked, frilled shirt and a yellow paisley-patterned cravat with it.

'You're looking very chic,' he said, then whispered conspiratorially in my ear, 'You'll notice Peggy has dressed in Christmas-cake icing, while Gayle has stuck with the still-on-site look.' Gayle had a pint in her hand and was talking to Peggy; she was wearing a heavy ribbed jumper, jeans and working boots, while Peggy was in a frosted-pink dress with lots of fake pearls stitched into it. The contrast between the two women was amusing, but I thought Keelan's remark was bitchy; I attributed it to his having had a few drinks already and to how I was feeling at the time.

A couple of drinks later we sat down to eat, and the conversation inevitably turned to the events following the find at Monashee. I stuck as close as I could to the scientific details that had emerged so far – the carbon-dating results, the pollen analysis, the identification of the holly berries – giving Keelan the credit for winkling the botanical information out of WET ahead of schedule.

As the main course was being served, I moved away from the subject and talked about my meeting at Newgrange on the day of the solstice, and some of what the various people had had to say. This prompted Gayle to mention that the Temple of the Sun in the Inca city of Machu Picchu was an observatory, which at this time of year would have been used to mark the departure of the sun, just as Newgrange was noting its return. Peggy asked her to tell us more about her backpacking trip through Peru, which she did at length. The tables around us were getting louder as the diners settled into becoming drinkers. Keelan, who was sitting across from me, looked increasingly bored; I noticed him fiddling with a sprig of holly stuck in a small vase on the table.

I looked away and rejoined Gayle on her expedition. Then I had a strange sensation, as the moment of unresolved disorder I had experienced the previous day suddenly came into sharp focus and I realised exactly what had been out of place. I could see it, clear as day – Keelan's e-mail on my computer screen.

About the macro-botanical samples, I'm sure you'll agree the most significant so far, for obvious reasons, are those seeds we found, which turn out to be the fruit of Ilex aquifolium ...

Everything slowed down. Pretending to be concentrating on listening to Gayle, I observed what Keelan was doing. The hubbub of conversation around us receded into the distance as I watched him rolling the holly between finger and thumb.

Without alerting the other two, I caught his attention. 'Just to change the subject for a second, Keelan,' I said a little nervously, 'in your e-mail yesterday you said I would agree that the holly berries were highly significant, for obvious reasons. What reasons, exactly?'

He shrugged. 'I guess because you wanted the body to be as ancient as possible. Holly berries wouldn't have had anything to do with nourishment, but they could have been used in a Druidic ritual, which would make her pre-Christian – if not Neolithic, then maybe Iron Age.'

It was a plausible answer. No doubt I had expressed my hope to the team that the find might be prehistoric. But my instinct was that in the e-mail he had said more than he intended about the berries. Because the obvious reason they were significant was their presence in the mouths of the murder victims – something that was known only to me, Sherry, Gallagher's team and the killer.

'Hey, I've got to go,' Keelan said suddenly, and rose from the table. 'Have to get a present for my sister.'

The others grumbled at him for leaving the party but brightened up when he promised to return later and join us for a drink. Putting on his army greatcoat, he punched his gloves out of one of the sleeves, where he had stored them. I had seen the fingerless gloves before, but now they were different: his fingers were covered.

What was it Sherry had said? 'As if the killer had only four digits ... sometimes called "mitten hand" ...'

I waited until I had seen Keelan go out the door;

then I interrupted Peggy and Gayle's conversation. 'Gayle, those gloves of Keelan's – I wouldn't mind getting a pair for myself.'

'Oh, his mittens? They're ideal for what we do, all right. They keep your hands warm when you're working with your bare fingers; then, when you're finished, you can pull over the mitten part that's attached and hey presto! – you're fully protected from the cold.'

'Fantastic. Hey, remember last Friday – the day you were working on the mound of soil in the bike shed? Do you recall what time you left the hospital?' To the best of my memory, I had left a message on Keelan's phone shortly after six.

'About twenty past six. I was frozen stiff, I remember.'

'That late? I thought you were long gone.'

'We should have been, but Keelan had to go and collect something in town and didn't come back for ages.'

'What time did he leave you?'

'Hmm … around five. Yes, we said we'd give it until then.'

I relaxed. The coroner had rung Sherry at about 4.45, when Traynor had already been dead about an hour.

Then I noticed Gayle colouring. She blushed easily, I knew, but this was several shades brighter than usual.

'Is there something you're not telling me, Gayle?' I said gently.

'I don't want to get anyone into trouble,' she said.

'I understand. But this is vitally important. I have to know.'

'He went off earlier as well,' she said.

'Oh? At lunchtime, do you mean?'

'No. We had our lunch together in the hospital café. He drove off somewhere around three; he arrived back just before you came to see how we were getting on.'

My mouth went dry. That had been after four. Keelan had been gone for an hour at least. And that hour coincided with the time of Traynor's murder.

'Where did Keelan say he was going just now?'

'He's gone shopping for a present for his sister,' said Peggy.

'He's coming back to join us,' Gayle added.

'Peggy, could I talk to you for a minute?'

We stood up and walked together to a corner. 'The day I was called to the find near Newgrange, I asked you to ring some people for me ...'

'Yes. Let me think. Con Purcell, to say you were on your way ... Keelan, to cancel your meeting with him and Gayle at the motorway site ... and then later you asked me to contact Keelan again, to tell them to be at Drogheda Hospital the next morning.'

'In the first call to Keelan, did you tell him why I had to cancel the meeting?'

'Well, I ...'

'It's OK, Peggy. I just need to know what exactly you told him.'

'I said there'd been a body found across the river from Newgrange and you were going to examine it. Illaun, you look worried. What's wrong?'

'Nothing. I've just got to go back to the office to make some phone calls.' I headed for the door.

'Make them from here, why don't you?'

'I need to look up some notes. Won't be long.'

I got Seamus Crean on his mobile phone. He was in a hospital bed awaiting the results of X-rays and various tests, but his breathing seemed easier.

'Seamus, the man in the car who talked to you on the day you discovered the body ... You said he was well spoken, had a bit of a beard. Was he driving a blue Micra, by any chance?'

'That's right, Missus, he was.'

'And he was asking if the field was being made into a car park. Did you talk about anything else?'

'The conversation came round to the woman's body somehow. I might have said something about it, I don't know. But he was only interested in whether there had been any jewellery or ornaments found with it, and I said there hadn't.'

I thanked Seamus and made the next call.

'Muriel, this is important. The name of the woman Frank Traynor spoke to while you were in the car with him on Friday. If you can't remember it, then what makes you so sure it was a woman's name?'

'The sound of it. It sounded feminine.'

'Like "Keelan"?'

'That's it.'

She knew by my sharp intake of breath that there was something wrong. 'Have they found her?'

'Looks like it's a him. I can't say more for the moment. Just one other thing: have you heard from Terence Ivers these past few days?' Ivers's lack of contact had been worrying me, for some reason. In the light of what was unfolding, it was of minor concern, but I still needed to know.

'Not directly. I wanted to talk to him about your bog body, but it seems he's gone away for Christmas.'

That should have been something of a relief, but my stomach was far too knotted for any such emotion.

On to the last phone call, the one I had to make.

'Matt, according to Sergeant O'Hagan, Traynor received two calls on his mobile phone shortly before he was murdered, is that so?'

'Correct.'

'I'm going to read out a number to you. Tell me if it's one of them.'

I read out Keelan's mobile-phone number. I could hear Gallagher flicking pages.

'Where did you get that number?' he said eventually.

'You haven't been able to identify the caller, right?'

'No. It's a pay-as-you-go phone. An old one – unregistered.'

'It's also the phone from which the call was made to

Traynor while Muriel Blunden was in the car with him. But it wasn't made by a woman. It was from one of my team, Keelan O'Rourke.'

'One of your staff?'

'Yes, and he was absent with no explanation around the time Traynor was killed. And he wears these fingerless gloves, but they can be made into mittens, and I know the killer's fingerprints were like that – and … and I think he knows I've become suspicious. God, I can't believe this is happening.'

'Look, hold on a wee minute. Explain how you found all this out.'

I told Gallagher what had happened at the Old Mill.

'Where is he now?'

'In Castleboyne, shopping for a present for his sister. Or so he said.'

'We're on our way. The best thing you can do is behave normally. Go back to the pub if that's what you've arranged to do. Where is it?'

'Where Market Street turns onto the Old Bridge. You can't miss it.'

I put down the phone, my heart thumping. I went through into the house and sat for a moment in the living room with the lights out and the curtains drawn, trying to quell the turmoil inside. Then I felt my lunch resurfacing and stumbled towards the bathroom.

Chapter Twenty-Nine

My house is on a bend of the river, two kilometres from Castleboyne. The road from the town follows the course of the Boyne and is visible from the bay window in the living room. As I came back from the bathroom the drawn curtains were illuminated by a passing car. Or could it have been turning in? It was too early for Richard and company to be arriving. I went to the window and drew aside one of the curtains.

Parked in the drive beside my mother's car was a blue Micra. I snapped the curtain closed and ran for the phone in the hall. The doorbell chimed. I stopped in the middle of the room.

He'll hear me talking in the hall. My mobile was in my jacket, in the office – I'd have to pass through the hall … Deep breath. *Do it.*

The doorbell rang again.

He knows I'm here. I went into the hall. *Buy time, act normally.* 'Hold on, please; I'll be with you shortly.' *Horatio's not here. Damn.*

I went into the office, put on my jacket, took out my phone.

A muffled voice behind the door. 'Hi, Illaun. It's me, Keelan.'

I typed 'K AT MY HOUSE. HELP', found 'Matt G', pressed 'OK' and saw 'Message Sent' going skywards. And hoped.

I went back into the hall wondering if I should just stay put and not let him in. *She must have known her assailant.* I hated hearing that on the news. Men bent on murder, preying on trust.

Keelan thumped on the door and then shouted through the letterbox, 'I have a pressie for you. You don't want me to freeze to death, do you?'

I couldn't care less. In fact, freezing to death's too kind.

I made my decision and walked towards the door. *Use the skills your father taught you. Deep breath. Confident voice.* 'I'm coming, I'm coming. Hang on to your Santa hat.'

I opened the door and Keelan was standing there looking nervous, a smallish parcel clutched to his chest.

Maybe he'll hand it to me and go away, I thought. *Talk to him.* 'I was just going back to the pub. Came here to freshen up. I was expecting to see you there.'

'Yes, I called in but you weren't around. I told the girls I had to see you first, then I'd come back. I ... I need to explain this present to you. Can I come in?'

I had already decided to go along with whatever put him at ease.

'Sure. Would you like a drink?' I turned into the living room and switched on the lights.

'I'm probably already over the limit, so best not. I have to drive to Navan.'

'That's why I decided to phone a taxi to take me back to the pub,' I lied. 'It should be here any minute.'

Keelan showed no interest; he slumped down onto a couch and sighed heavily. 'I have a confession to make,' he said.

I sat down opposite him, tense and ready for flight.

'Best thing to do is open this first,' he said, standing up and handing me the parcel.

My hands trembled as I tried to remove the Sellotape sealing the small package. I noticed the paper was printed with holly wreaths. I tried not to speculate what the contents might be – the knife he had used to carry out the killings ... parts of the victims' clothing, or worse still ...

Keelan sat back down again, and at last I succeeded in opening the parcel. Inside was a bubble-wrap envelope. There was just a small strip of Sellotape sealing the flap, and I opened it easily and looked inside. My throat constricted.

'Go ahead,' said Keelan. 'Take it out.' He picked up the wrapping paper and began to fiddle with it.

Reluctantly, I inserted a finger and thumb and removed a piece of bone about the size of a spice jar.

'I think you can guess where I got that,' he said.

I could hear myself breathing rapidly through my nose, feel my heart rate soaring by the second. I wanted out of there.

'Go on, look at it.'

I looked down at what I was holding in my fingers and realised it was a carving of a woman. But I was too agitated to take in the details.

'Can you guess?' Keelan had crushed the wrapping paper into a tight ball.

'Was it in the peat ... in the matrix ... with the bog body?'

'Thought you'd get it straight off,' he said.

'But ... why are you giving it to me now ... like this?'

Keelan gave a nervous cough. 'I found it, you see. I said nothing to Gayle. Something came over me, and I put it in my pocket and took it home later. I've been asking myself why ever since. Just to have it for a while. I mean, we do all this digging, usually in crap weather, sometimes in old rubbish heaps or cesspits, for God's sake – and for what? To hand over things that get catalogued and stored away somewhere, never to be seen again. We – the ones who've done the dirty work – never really get to *know* the objects we've found ... to spend time with them, unhurried, unsupervised.'

'So you took this home and cleaned it up.'

'Yes. But I was going to tell you the next day that I had held on to it. Then with all that happened, the murder and so on, I copped out. That's why I'm only getting around to it now.'

Car headlights swept past the bay window, on which I had left the curtain partially open.

'Who's that?' he said, eyes darting to the door of the living room.

'Probably the taxi.'

'Shit, I want to make sure this thing is sorted out tonight, here.'

'Tell you what: I'll ask him to come back in half an hour.'

'You do that.'

I placed the carving on the couch and was about to leave the room when we both heard the sound of a key turning in the hall door.

'Illaun ...' It was Peggy. 'Hello?' she called from the hall. What the hell was Peggy doing here?

Keelan stood up. 'I want this kept private,' he said, coming towards me.

I waved him back. 'She's probably just called to collect something from the office,' I said. 'Best let me deal with this.'

I went into the hall and turned towards the door to

see Gallagher and another detective with their backs flattened against the wall. Gallagher put his hand on my shoulder and propelled me towards the door, exchanging eyebrow signals with me as I passed: *Is he inside?*

I nodded and made a downwards gesture with both hands to indicate things were reasonably calm. Peggy, her kohl-rimmed eyes wide and staring, was standing on the doorstep, in more need of help than I was, by the look of things. I put my arms around her as the two men slipped into the room, and then we heard the sound of gruff voices and Keelan's higher-pitched one remonstrating with them.

'They came to the pub,' said Peggy. 'Asked if any of our staff were there. Then they asked me if I had a key to the house; I was happy to hand it over, but they thought I should come along and open the door. What's going on, Illaun? Is Keelan drunk or what?'

'He's got a lot on his mind,' I said.

Gallagher put his head out into the hall. 'Miss Bowe, could you come in here, please? And Miss Montague, you can go now. Thanks for all your help.'

I stayed with Peggy while she got back into her car. 'I would have loved to invite you all back for an hour or two. I didn't get time to wish Gayle all the best, either.'

'I'm sure she'll understand.'

'Anyway, have a merry Christmas and a happy New Year and I'll see you Monday week.'

'Same to you ...' Peggy started the car. 'I hope

Keelan will be all right.'

'I'm sure he will.'

As she drove off, I realised I hadn't given her the Christmas gift I had bought for her – a flamboyantly coloured silk batik scarf. But the gesture, made or not, seemed insignificant now.

When I re-entered the living room Keelan was sitting in the same place, glowering. The detective who had come with Gallagher was standing behind the couch, the light from the dragonfly lamp casting his shadow over Keelan.

'I'm sure you'd like to sit down,' said Gallagher. 'This is my colleague, Detective Sergeant Ken Fitzgibbon.'

I nodded to Fitzgibbon, whose left hand was on the back of the couch, his right holding something out of sight behind it. Gallagher was a big man, but Fizgibbon was on the way to becoming a sumo wrestler; a bullet-shaped shaven head and a permanent scowl completed the appearance of someone I wouldn't want to tangle with.

'I'll sit here,' I said, pulling out a chair from the dining table and dragging it over. I wanted to be at an angle to Keelan rather than facing him.

'Were you harmed in any way by this guy?' asked Gallagher.

'Jesus, Illaun,' said Keelan, 'let's lighten up. It was only a fucking bone pendant. Why all this?'

'Mr O'Rourke here says he's made a full confession

to you. He doesn't seem to grasp that it's us he has to confess to.'

'Mr O'Rourke has admitted only to keeping an artefact, from the find at Monashee, which he returned to me tonight.' I pointed to the carving, which was still on the seat. 'We discussed no other aspects of the case.'

'The case? What fucking case?' Keelan was becoming more aggressive.

Gallagher picked up the bone carving and walked past Keelan a few times, passing it from one hand to the other, saying nothing. Then he leaned down suddenly and spoke into Keelan's ear. 'Did you ring Frank Traynor on your mobile phone on Friday last, at exactly 2.48 pm?' Gallagher sat down and observed Keelan's reaction.

Keelan looked as if he had been hit by a sledgehammer. 'Did I ring Frank Traynor ... ?' He swallowed hard. 'Did I ring ... ?'

'Just answer the fucking question,' Fitzgibbon growled from behind the couch.

'Hey, give me time to think, will you?'

Fitzgibbon guffawed loudly. 'Listen to this, Matt. He wants time to think. What does he think he's doing, a fucking exam?'

Gallagher smirked. 'Hey, you there, the thinking man. We *know* you rang Frank Traynor last Friday. But if you want to keep up this stupid act, be our guest. We'll just lock you up overnight, give you plenty of time to think, and start again tomorrow morning. On the other hand, you could tell us the truth now – the whole truth, the whole story from beginning to end; get it off your chest. It's up to you.'

Keelan put his hands up to his face and slumped back into the couch. 'OK, I'll tell you,' he gasped.

Gallagher signalled to Fitzgibbon, who pulled out another chair from the table, took a jotter and Biro from his inside pocket and sat down, placing the handgun he had been hiding on the table, within easy reach. Gallagher moved to sit near me, facing Keelan.

'Do I have to stay here?' I whispered.

Gallagher nodded and leaned towards me. I dipped my head to listen. 'Just in case we have to clarify something,' he murmured. 'Go ahead,' he said aloud, to Keelan.

'I rang Frank Traynor because I thought he would buy that from me.' Keelan pointed to the artefact, which Gallagher was still passing from one hand to the other. So much for him just wanting to have the carving to himself for a while.

'And what made you think he would?'

'I'd done business with him a couple of times before.'

'Selling artefacts from archaeological sites?'

'Yes.'

I couldn't believe it. Then I remembered the missing pike-head from the motorway survey. 'Did you sell him the pike-head from the skirmish site?'

He didn't reply.

'Answer the question,' Gallagher insisted. 'We found an item matching that description in Traynor's garage. Did you sell it to him?'

Keelan looked at me and shrugged as if to say, *What did you expect?*

I had been so wrong about the guy. In his first year out of college he had been systematically betraying one of the profession's fundamental principles. On my watch.

'Illegal, isn't it, trafficking in historical artefacts?' Gallagher looked at me, but I had nothing to contribute because my saliva glands were leaking again – the prelude to nausea. 'In fact, my understanding is that the international black market in antiquities comes third after drug-running and illicit arms-dealing.'

Keelan began sniffling.

'Wouldn't have thought this was worth much, though,' said Gallagher, squinting at the carving.

'Traynor told me to start with small things. He said it was like serving an apprenticeship. Building up trust on both sides.'

'Ah, yes. Honour among thieves. It always cracks me up when I hear that noble sentiment. Go on. Last Friday.'

'He said he might be interested in the carving. Then he asked me what we were doing at the hospital. I told him a bit about it and mentioned that the remains of the woman and the infant were nearby in the old morgue. When he heard that a child had been found, he became all interested and asked me if I could help him get into the morgue. I said I had the key, and then I drove around to the back of the morgue and waited for him. He was late, but I didn't mind – I needed to clean up the figure before he saw it. When he showed up I gave him the key and he went inside.'

'You didn't go in with him?'

'No way. I stayed in the car to keep warm. When he came out again, he leaned in the window and I showed him the carving. He seemed surprised; he muttered something like, "Fuck me, it's Goldilocks's ugly sister…" – I remember that because of the way he was mixing up the fairytales, Goldilocks and Cinderella –'

'Yeah, yeah, keep going,' Gallagher interjected, but he threw me a knowing glance.

'Then he said, "Why do you think I'd buy something that belongs to me already?" I said it was officially State property, but in reality whoever had it in his possession could call the shots. I knew he would eventually pay me something for it. Then his mobile rang and he took the call. It was short, he hardly said a word, but he seemed very pleased about whatever he'd been told. Then all he said to me was, "Go home and feed that thing to your dog." And he got into his car and drove off.'

Gallagher waited for more. 'That's not the end, is it, my wee lad?'

Keelan looked over at me. 'In a way it is. Because that was a turning point for me. And the rest of the story really has to do with Illaun.'

The other two men stared at me.

I was feeling sick to my stomach, though there was nothing to get rid of. 'Excuse me,' I said, putting my hand over my mouth. 'I need to go to the bathroom.'

One of the lesser-known advantages of a vivid imagination is that you often anticipate what life's about to throw at you. You *see* the train before it comes around the bend. You *know* there's a gigantic waterfall beyond the rapids. And, because you've already imagined it, when it happens you're prepared. But I hadn't seen this coming at all.

I dry-retched for the third time. It was as if the lies and deceit were harder to stomach than the idea that Keelan was a murderer. And I was worried about what was coming next. Why was he focusing on me? I just wanted him out of my life.

I gargled some water and spat it out, splashed my face and sank it into a hot towel from the rail. Then I looked in the mirror to brush my hair; my skin was a blotchy green, my eyes red-rimmed. 'Fuck you, Keelan,' I said.

On the way back to the living room I slowed down. Why had he come to my house with the carving? Was that the action of a frenzied killer?

'Are you OK? You look terrible,' said Gallagher when I came back in.

'I'm fine – go ahead,' I said, waving him on.

'Keelan here was just filling us in on some personal

details, so let's pick up from where he left off. Go ahead.'

Keelan had stopped sniffling and was trying to catch my eye, but I avoided him. 'At first I was annoyed with Traynor for treating me that way. But it actually made me re-think what I had been doing. I felt it was unfair to Illaun, in particular, so I made my mind up to hand over the artefact and to tell her about Frank Traynor's little business on the side.

'But I had only just got back when she turned up to see how we were getting on, and then I realised the carving was still in my car, which would have been hard to explain in front of Gayle. Before we left that evening I went to the morgue, but it was closed. So I wrote a note and put it in the bag with the carving – I was thinking of sticking it under Illaun's windscreen wiper, but then I noticed her doors were unlocked. So I put the package on the passenger seat.

'When I heard about Traynor's murder later that night, I realised the note in Illaun's car linked me to him, so I panicked. I drove to Castleboyne to beg her not to tell anyone what was in the note, but then I spotted the package still on the seat of her car. I couldn't believe my luck. I broke the window with a wheel-brace and grabbed the package. I had my mittens on, so it wasn't until I got back into my own car that I realised I had picked up her mobile phone as well. Then I heard a dog barking and a light came on, so I drove off.'

'How were you dressed?'

'Same coat I have on now. Why?'

Gallagher glanced at me for a reaction. I shook my head. It wasn't Keelan in his army greatcoat I had seen.

'Did you see anyone else near the house?'

'No. But it was very foggy.'

'OK. Let's move on. There are now two phones to be accounted for, your own and the one you took from your employer's vehicle. What did you do with them?'

'I had already dumped my own, because I knew the number would be on Traynor's call register and you guys would keep ringing it. Returning Illaun's phone would have raised too many awkward questions, so I knew I had to get rid of it as well. But on Saturday morning I was messing around with it a bit and came across Muriel Blunden's number. Traynor once boasted to me that I didn't need to worry about doing business with him, that he had good contacts in the Gardaí, that the Minister for Tourism and Heritage was eating out of his hand and so was Ward's mistress, Muriel Blunden of the National Museum. At this stage I felt so guilty about what I'd done that I thought the best way to make it up to Illaun was to fix it so she got the licence for a dig at Monashee. So I sent Blunden a text.'

'And that's it, so, is it? You make yourself out to be a guy who has more changes of heart in a day than a Bangkok whore turns tricks. And you want us to forget that you're a liar, a thief and a blackmailer into

435

the bargain. Well, chew on this, my wee boy: I'm arresting you for the murder of Frank Traynor under Section 4 of the Criminal Justice Act. Sergeant Fitzgibbon and I will be taking you to Drogheda Garda station, where you'll be formally charged and detained for further questioning. Further charges may be brought in connection with the death of Garda Sergeant Brendan O'Hagan.'

Keelan slumped back in the couch with his hands up to his face again. 'It's not true. I didn't kill anyone. This is crazy.'

Gallagher looked at me and nodded towards the door. We went into the hall, where he folded his arms and leaned back against the wall, his head rattling a framed picture hanging behind him. 'I'm sorry this is the way it's turned out. I'm sure you're shocked.'

'Shocked, and disappointed. But I'm not entirely sure …'

'Not sure of what?'

'That he's the murderer.'

'But everything fits. We knew it was someone with his kind of background.'

'That wasn't him in the church last night.'

'There's a lot more we have to question him about. I'm sure he'll eventually admit to it. Our main aim now is to help him recollect what he was up to during the period when he claims he was at the morgue.'

'But why did he come over here tonight with the carving?'

'He needed to assess how much you knew or suspected. To find that out, he had to regain your trust by owning up to the theft. Eventually he would have drawn you into a discussion about the murders. Any hint that you were a threat, and you would have become Victim Number Three.'

I shook my head. 'I know I was scared when he arrived. But I don't think he's killer material, just a petty thief. There's also the question of why – why kill Traynor in the first place?'

'Money. Traynor was acting as a fence for stolen artefacts. O'Rourke was doing business with him, either on his own or as part of a ring of looters and treasure-hunters. But he, or they, became unhappy with what Traynor was paying, so O'Rourke decided to get rid of him – cut out the middleman, deal directly with Mr Big, whoever he is. The finding of the bog body provided an ideal opportunity to confuse the investigation by introducing an element of voodoo.'

'And O'Hagan?'

'He was aware of his brother-in-law's trafficking in stolen artefacts and took the notebook to prevent us finding that out. Eventually, from what he saw in there, he put two and two together and worked out who killed Traynor. Then he had to be dealt with too.'

'But you said that, in the notebook, O'Hagan wrote "Gotcha" along a line pointing to the Grange Abbey shield.'

'Yes, but I think we may have been misinterpreting that. Here's what I think happened: after O'Rourke showed the carving to Traynor, he sketched it quickly in his diary and called it "Goldilocks", which O'Rourke has admitted was the term Traynor used when referring to it.'

'"Goldilocks's ugly sister", to be more precise,' I said.

'Matters not a damn. The main thing is, the line connects the Goldilocks carving to the Grange Abbey shield – but not necessarily to Grange Abbey. I think it's possible that O'Hagan had discovered a connection between the person who brought Traynor the Goldilocks artefact – in other words, O'Rourke – and whoever brought him the shield. Remember, there's no evidence that it came directly from the nuns; it could have passed through any number of hands. That's why I say that O'Rourke may not have been in this alone, that there may have been a whole gang of looters involved. And O'Hagan may have stumbled on a connection between two of them.'

'But if Keelan was planning to kill Traynor, he'd hardly have been trying to sell him something an hour beforehand.'

'Why not? At that stage O'Rourke probably wasn't fully committed to carrying out the murder. But when Traynor humiliated him by rejecting the carving, that made his mind up.'

Gallagher was like a medieval knight, thrusting and

parrying with every weapon at his disposal. The best I could do was set a fly buzzing inside his armour.

'Look, Matt, I have no reason to believe anything out of Keelan's mouth, any more than you have. But, by his own admission, he told Traynor about the infant's body in the morgue. And, as we know from Muriel Blunden, that made Traynor lose interest in digging up the field all of a sudden.'

'So?'

'I guess we'd also accept that Keelan phoned Traynor to try and sell him the artefact – and that's when they arranged to meet at the morgue.'

'Yeah? So?'

'So Keelan was there to witness the last call Traynor received, the one made from a call-box in Slane – probably the one that lured him out to Monashee.'

'It could have been one of O'Rourke's buddies setting him up.'

'Be that as it may, Keelan said Traynor seemed very pleased with whatever he'd been told. To me that sounds like a man who had just received a reply that was to his satisfaction.'

'A reply to what?'

'A demand. A demand he had made after confirming the existence of the deformed baby.'

'But he made no calls in between.'

'He didn't have to. He could have just sent a text.'

Gallagher's own phone rang before he could comment.

'Yes? ... What? ... The minister, you mean?' He gave me a glance that said, *This is not good news,* and went outside to continue his conversation.

I asked myself what had made me change my mind about Keelan being the killer. It was mostly instinct, but there were also pieces of contradictory evidence that Gallagher was choosing to overlook. For example, he himself had previously described the drawing of 'Goldilocks' as having been done by another hand – not Traynor's; moreover, it was drawn as part of a circular object, and Traynor's put-down of the bone carving implied that Goldilocks was quite a stunner by comparison with her 'ugly sister'. And, since I would have bet that Traynor equated beauty with monetary value, I still believed Goldilocks to be a gold artefact.

Chapter Thirty

Fitzgibbon had obviously phoned the local Gardaí: a squad car drove up to the house and Keelan emerged from the living room, head bowed, handcuffed to the detective. When he realised I was there, he looked at me imploringly. 'I may be a thief, Illaun, but I'm not a murderer. Please tell them I'm not a murderer.'

Fitzgibbon shoved him towards two uniformed Gardaí who were approaching the still-open door. Gallagher paced up and down outside, talking into his phone.

I was glad my mother hadn't been around to witness all of this because she was ... *Damn!* Richard and

Greta's flight had arrived at least two hours ago. They were all due at any moment.

The squad car drove off. I saw Keelan's pale face in the back between Fitzgibbon and one of the uniformed Gardaí, his eyes staring straight ahead. He was frightened.

Gallagher came back into the hall – which, I noticed only now, was as cold as the outside. I was shivering and I started to close the door behind him, but he signalled that he was departing straight away.

' … Right, keep me up to date.' He put away his phone. 'Derek Ward's been badly injured.'

'How?'

'Someone threw a brick through his windscreen. Random delinquency, it seems. He was in the wrong place at the wrong time.'

'Where was that?'

'Between Drogheda and Donore.'

'And they're sure he wasn't the intended victim?'

Gallagher's moustache twitched. 'That's what it looks like at this stage.'

'I thought ministers had drivers.'

'Sure. But all of us like to be on our own from time to time.'

'It means you can't question him. Odd, isn't it?'

'If he can talk at all, I'll be asking questions. Meanwhile, I've got to make sure we get O'Rourke to court tomorrow morning with all the right paperwork done. It's going to be a long night. Any news, I'll let you know.'

'Don't be too tough on Keelan,' I said, following Gallagher onto the doorstep. 'I think he's just … weak.'

I closed the door and went back towards the living room. Passing the picture Gallagher had banged his head against, I noticed it was slightly askew. A charcoal drawing of a rural churchyard blanketed in snow, it was dated 1896 and signed by Peter Hunt, the talented man I had come to accept as my great-grandfather.

The depiction of the church in the wintry landscape, isolated and alone on a hillside, the gravestones barely proud of the snowdrift, had made a strong impression on me when I was a child. But, as I adjusted the picture on the wall, I realised I hadn't looked at it properly in years. As I did, the memory of my childhood response to it – one of those defining moments when an emotional reaction is fixed for all time – flooded back. It had given me mixed feelings: a comforting sense that the dead, whom at the time I imagined lying in a form of extended sleep in an underground cave, were even more snug beneath the blanket of snow – marred by anxiety that, when it melted, the water would rain down upon them. Now that childhood recollection morphed into a presentiment similar to the one I'd had on the beach at Bettystown: that these images – water, a church, the subterranean lair of the dead – were like Tarot cards promising insights into the future if they could only be properly interpreted.

I was startled by the phone ringing beside me.

'Are you OK?' said Finian.

'I'm all right.'

'Peggy rang me. What's been going on?'

I gave him a brief account.

Finian made little or no comment about Keelan. He was more concerned about my well-being. 'Do you want me to come to the house?'

'No, the others will all be arriving –' I saw lights outside. 'They're actually here, Finian. And, by the way, I'm not telling Richard about this or about what happened in the church, OK? Got to go.'

Greta climbed out of the front passenger seat, wearing a peach-coloured jogging suit and immaculate white sneakers. 'Good to see you,' she said, with a huge, perfect smile. Greta was also tall, golden-tressed and golden-limbed into the bargain.

'Hi, sis,' Richard called from inside the car, struggling with an unfamiliar seat-belt.

'Eoin's asleep,' said Greta, opening one of the rear doors. 'He's propped up against his gran in there.' I could see my mother in the back seat, gently stroking Eoin's curly head.

Richard freed himself and came around the car to give me a squeeze before he leant in to gather up his son.

'Let's not wake him,' I said. 'Follow me – I'll show you where he's sleeping, and where you two are, as well.'

Richard slung Eoin over his shoulder and carried him inside. As we went along the hall, I could see how alike all three of us were – black curls, pale skin, inky eyebrows.

Within a few minutes Eoin had donned pyjamas, gone to the bathroom, downed half a tumbler of water and been tucked up in bed without apparently opening an eyelid. As we assembled in the living room, I wished I could have joined him in the Land of Nod. Recent events had left me feeling like a punch-bag.

But I had to make the effort. 'Well, it's great to see you all! Welcome to your first Christmas in Ireland as a family. Would anyone like a drink?'

Richard was standing with his back to the fireplace, flipping through a magazine he had found somewhere. He glanced across at Greta.

'To be honest, Illaun, we're really pooped,' she said, making the decision for them both. 'Could we leave the drinks until tomorrow night?'

'Suits me fine. What about you, Mum?'

'I'm tired too, Illaun. Talked out. You know your Aunt Betty.'

And I know you as well, Mum. Two of a kind.

'She had me going through some old photographs with her. She wants to – what's the word? – scan them and give family albums to all the nieces and nephews.'

'For Christmas? It's a bit late in the day, isn't it?' said Richard, still flicking pages.

'No, not for Christmas. It will take time. She's going

445

to have to get your dad's family to go through their collections as well.'

Richard stopped what he was doing and caught my eye. The mention of my father had distracted him.

'How far back do the photos go?' I asked, ignoring him.

'Well, your great-grandmother and great-grandfather are there. They would have been married a few years when the photo was taken, sometime early in the century.' Twentieth century, she meant. My mother had never quite adjusted to the intrusion of a new one into her life.

'What were their names? Peter and Marie?'

'No, no. Your great-grandfather's name was Willie and your great-grandmother was Julia Russell.'

I was confused. 'Then who was Peter Hunt? The man who played the violin – the one who drew the picture in the hall?'

My mother smiled wistfully. 'Ah, that was your great-great-uncle. A wonderful man, by all accounts. It was sad, though: he died suddenly at the age of twenty-six.'

I was stunned. 'Twenty-six? And what happened to his wife? His wife was Marie, Marie Maguire … from Celbridge … ?'

'I don't know who you're talking about, dear.' My mother was looking at me strangely. 'Peter Hunt never married.'

'Never married?'

'No. I heard it said he had a sweetheart, but I never knew her name.' She stood up and gave Richard a hug, then kissed Greta good night.

'We'll be on our way, too,' said Greta, slinging her arm around Richard.

'Uh, yeah,' he said, putting down the magazine. He kissed me on the cheek as he passed. 'We have to talk, you and I,' he whispered.

'Let's do that. In the morning.'

When they had left, I sagged down into an armchair and sat gazing at nothing on the wall opposite. What was the point of wishing if wishes were never fulfilled?

There was a tap on the door. I stiffened, thinking Richard had changed his mind. Instead my mother put her head in. 'You look as if you've been to hell and back. And I noticed that bruise on your head, too. What's happened?'

I beckoned her in, and she perched on the edge of the armchair.

'I hit my head against the edge of the car door,' I said. 'In the car park of the church. After the carol practice.'

'You got the message from Gillian, then.'

'Are you sure it was Gillian herself who rang?'

'Well, she didn't say her name; but she was quite curt, the way Gillian can be sometimes.'

'I know what you mean.'

'You haven't answered my question, dear.'

She would have to be told about Keelan.

'You could have been dead under this very roof,' she said when I had finished.

'I don't think so, though I'll admit I was scared at first. But now I'm just ... disillusioned, I suppose.'

She stroked my hair as she had Eoin's in the car earlier. 'We're flawed, Illaun. Weak and fickle and flawed. That's why we need God. That's why we have to call on Him sometimes. And it's not when we build impressive monuments to Him or create elaborate rituals that He listens to us. He listens when we're honest about our failings, when we admit we need help, when we acknowledge that we can't do it all by ourselves.'

'What about Dad? I don't see how God has helped him in any way.'

'God helps *me*, Illaun. That's how it works. That's how I'm able to cope.'

I had just turned off the light when my mobile rang. It was Gallagher.

'Still processing this arrest,' he said. 'In the meantime, you'll not be surprised to hear that Derek Ward may have been the intended victim of the brick thrown at his car.'

'You're right. I'm not surprised.'

'He got a call from someone and took off – left his driver twiddling his thumbs. He was driving under a flyover near his home when someone dropped a brick from above. It slammed onto the bonnet, then came through the windscreen; it would have taken his head off, except the driver's airbag inflated and took some of the impact. The car ran off the road onto the grass verge and stopped. He was lucky. Broken neck, bad bruising, but he'll pull through.'

'Who did the call come from?'

'We won't know until tomorrow.'

'Are you going to talk to him?'

'You bet. And, just in case you think this helps O'Rourke's case – the attack took place at about three o'clock this afternoon, just about the time O'Rourke was absent from your little get-together.'

Christmas Eve

Chapter Thirty-One

10.24. There was no light coming past the edges of the curtains, which partly explained my late waking. I pulled them back and looked out on the garden; it was still in semi-darkness, as if the sun had failed to rise above the horizon. The grey, amorphous clouds shutting out the light were mottled with patches of pink and purple and ivory that ran into one another like watercolours on wet paper. It looked like a snowy sky, but the weather forecast I heard while dressing said no snow was expected, at least in the east of the country.

As I headed for the kitchen Boo emerged from the

living room, his entire coat bristling as though he had been plugged into the mains. He looked at me with a mixture of terror and indignation in his huge eyes, then sat at the door to the utility room and mewed plaintively. He wanted out and was, unusually, using his voice. The reason for his tense fur came into view: Attila the Hun in blue dungarees – my three-and-a-half-year-old nephew. Eoin spotted his quarry and gave chase. Boo panicked and shot through my legs down the hall, skittering past the child and around the corner towards my mother's part of the house, where he would find himself in a cul-de-sac and become even more desperate.

'Whoa there,' I said, and collected Eoin up in one arm as he pounded by, at the same time opening the utility-room door so that Boo could eventually escape into the garden.

'Want cat,' said Eoin, struggling to get down. I put both my arms around him and asked if he would not prefer some nice hot toast slathered with chocolate spread instead.

'No – yes!' he replied.

Richard, in a red-and-blue checked shirt and jeans, was in the kitchen putting some things on a tray for Greta. 'Two treats she asked me for, on her first morning,' he said. 'A lie-in without You-know-who clambering all over her, and breakfast – to include porridge – in bed.'

Just like Goldilocks, I thought. 'Lucky girl,' I said.

'We don't like the look of what she's getting, though, do we, Eoin? We're here to get some chocolate spread and toast, aren't we?'

'Yeah! Choctoast!'

Richard swept up the tray and headed out of the kitchen. 'Enjoy,' he said.

Ten minutes later Eoin resembled a clown with a sad down-turned mouth made of chocolate. I damp-ened some kitchen towel and was wiping his face and hands when his father arrived back.

'Off you go, Eoin. Granny wants to see you.'

Eoin galloped out the door, and Richard and I were left alone. The subject we had been able to avoid the night before was heading for us like an express train and we had nowhere left to run.

'Like some coffee?' I asked, trying to eke out another few seconds before impact.

'No, thanks.' He sat on a stool and sifted through the photographs I had left on the counter the night I had brought Finian home. 'Where did these come from?'

I took a stool opposite him. 'I took them at a place called Grange Abbey. There's a Romanesque church there.'

He was looking closely at the figure carvings. 'And these are over the doorway?'

'Yes. Mostly imaginary men and beasts, as you can see.'

'That's mostly *not* what I see.' He had picked up the

magnifying glass. 'Not on the two innermost arches, anyway.'

'What do you see? I'd be really interested to know.'

'Hey, hold on there, sis. Methinks thou art evading the subject.'

Addressing each other in mock Shakespeare was a habit going back to our childhood, and something that our father didn't approve of in theory but secretly enjoyed hearing us do.

Perhaps humour could derail the locomotive. I puffed out my chest and ratcheted up the decibels. 'What studied torments, tyrant, hast for me? What wheels? racks? fires? What flayings?'

Richard placed both hands on his chest and emoted, 'Make that thy question, and go rot!'

We laughed. We were quoting random lines from *The Winter's Tale*. At least they were from the same play, not something about which we were always particular.

'But seriously, Illaun – about Paddy coming home for Christmas … I had a chat with Mum first thing this morning.' Richard called our father 'Paddy', something I had never been able to do. Had he outmanoeuvred me by getting Mum on side first? 'And I really don't think she's up to having him here tomorrow.'

What was this?

'I asked her if it was because you were opposed to it, but she said that had nothing to do with it. She said she'd love to have him with us, but wants to give her undivided attention to Eoin, as it's his first Christmas here. And you know how she loves to spoil him.'

I could have hugged my mother at that moment. But not in front of Richard, of course.

'Never go against a little boy's granny,' I said.

'She was also concerned about you; she said you've had a heavy week of it and could do with a rest.'

'It's true. But I'd still like to go and visit Dad at some stage tomorrow.'

'Yeah, I guess we all would. Maybe we should work out a roster, so we're not all crowding in on him at the same time.'

'Good idea. That'd be much more enjoyable for him.' I was lying, of course. My father no longer had any capacity for enjoyment. But Richard didn't need to hear me saying that. 'Now,' I said, 'what were you saying about the carvings?'

Richard picked up the print he had been examining and tapped it with a ballpoint he had unclipped from his breast pocket. 'Because of my work with premmies, I've seen most of these creatures at one time or another – in reality. The inner arches of this doorway are a showcase for a whole range of congenital syndromes.'

I took the picture from him and looked at it again. 'But the cyclops, the blemmyae, the cynocephali – they were among the races widely believed to live in the lands beyond Europe.'

'OK, but these carvings could just as well be a

recording of monstrous births and congenital deformities.' He held up the print showing the door-jambs and capitals. 'Look at these faces with the foliage growing out of them: the eyes are closed, the lids rather heavy, the mouths turned down – the classic appearance of an infant born without a brain.' He returned to the arches, using the ballpoint to indicate what he was talking about. 'And take these ones here on the frieze. Cyclopia, for example, is a feature of a syndrome –'

'I've seen one, Richard,' I interjected. 'The poor thing had multiple deformities.'

'And look at this fellow here ...' He had the ballpoint aimed at the figure I had taken to be a blemmya. 'It could easily be an example of an iniencephalic child with hydrocephalus. There's great enlargement of the skull, no neck, the chin's attached to the chest – and so the eyes and mouth seem to be in the body and not the head. Then there's the mermaid. Her legs are fused together; it's a condition called sirenomelia. And her hands are webbed –'

'Syndactyly, isn't that what it's called? The little girl I saw had that, too.'

'Syndactyly covers a number of hand deformities, and one of the most severe is what this guy here is suffering from ...' He pointed to the man with pincers instead of hands. 'It's called by various names: cleft hand, split hand, even lobster-claw hand. Animal references crop up in the terminology quite a bit, probably for the same reason that the sculptors of these reliefs tried to find animal comparisons for the conditions they were depicting: in an effort to make sense of them, I guess. Here's a good example – the lion-headed man. I'd say he's suffering from Paget's disease – the bones of the skull grow hugely thick and massive over time. It's very painful for the sufferer. And this thing that looks like an octopus is a set of conjoined twins: their faces are fused together, forming an outsize single skull, on which there's a third face looking outwards; and those aren't eight tentacles, they're the twins' legs and arms.'

If Richard was right, then many of the imaginary races depicted in the books and maps and stone sculptures of the Middle Ages were actually recollections of things witnessed in childbirth, or found skulking in the corners of dark hovels, or seen once in a cage passing through a village.

Richard looked over the top of the photograph at me. 'Hey, sis, I must say I'm fascinated by all of this, and I'm sure my colleagues would love to hear about it too. Maybe you could e-mail me the photographs and some information about this doorway?'

'Sure, sure. I'll do that.'

Richard went back to his examination of the carvings.

Between what Finian and I had worked out and what Richard had revealed, it was plain that the doorway of the abbey church was bristling with moral

lessons and dire warnings related to sex and pro-
creation. The question was: apart from warding off
supernatural forces, what was the purpose of all this
powerful imagery? Who was it aimed at?

The pregnant girls whom the nuns had delivered
over the centuries were not at Grange Abbey in the
first place; and, as they had already succumbed to the
pleasures of the flesh, they were unlikely candidates for
this lesson. The abbey was a retreat house, a place
where the nursing Sisters could enjoy a break and be
spiritually refreshed too ... Was it possible the nuns
themselves were the target? But why? Was someone
concerned that constantly bringing babies into the
world, then sending them for adoption, could trigger
the nuns' own maternal instincts? And then there were
the postulants: perhaps they had to be given an
illustrated guide to the dangers of sinful intercourse
before being allowed into close contact with sexually
active girls.

Richard got down from the stool and handed me
the prints. 'It's interesting how few of these conditions
are treatable, even today. We can certainly do something for syndactyly if it's attended to early enough;
hypertelorism, too.'

'What's hypertelorism?'

He pointed to the cynocephalus. 'It's what that poor
guy is suffering from. The frontal bone of the skull
grows in such a way that it produces very wide-set
eyes, and the nostrils are turned upwards so they're

highly visible. Before we developed corrective surgical techniques these unfortunates had to endure being called "Dog-face" and the like, and it didn't help that defects of the nose and palate mean they have great difficulty breathing.'

That gave me quite a start, but I didn't show it, although Richard probably thought my response a little odd.

'I know,' I said.

I rang Gallagher from the office.

'My brother has just confirmed that I wasn't imagining what I saw in the church on Wednesday night. I'm pretty sure someone at the abbey has a congenital condition that affects the appearance of the face and interferes with breathing. He or she was on the patio that night in the fog, and at the morgue in Drogheda – and, I'm almost certain, outside Newgrange on the night after O'Hagan's body was found. And it was O'Hagan who told me about a figure in white being seen at Monashee around the time Traynor was murdered.'

'How does your brother know this individual is from Grange Abbey?'

'He doesn't. I do – well, I don't know for certain, but it's seeming more and more probable. Sister Gabriel, a former member of the community, told me the sacristan there wore the old habit and veil that earned them their "Beekeepers" nickname. She described the sacristan as a deaf and dumb lay sister, but maybe she was confused, or maybe someone else from the abbey – as in the individual I saw in the church – is using the habit as a disguise.'

'OK. I'll inquire about it.'

'Another thing she told me: workmen digging in the abbey crypt found something that may have to do with why the abbey was built on that site. It seemed to scare Sister Gabriel. It might be worth asking what, exactly, that was. It could explain certain things about the history of the place.'

'All right, I'll check it all out. *After* I talk to the minister.'

I didn't like the sound of this. 'But he won't be in any condition to talk until the New Year, I'm sure.'

'That's what I thought. But his close encounter with that wee brick seems to have made him very sociable. He's agreed to talk to me in the hospital later this afternoon.'

'That's good to hear. And after that you'll be calling to Grange Abbey?'

'Yes, Illaun, I will. Even though it's Christmas Eve and I'd prefer to be with my kids,' he said sharply. 'As well as which, we *do* have our killer, so I'm not exactly under pressure from anyone to go interrogating a bunch of middle-aged nuns about one of their Sisters who may or may not be inclined to wander the countryside. Anyone apart from you, that is.'

'I'm sorry to be so pushy, Matt. It's just that I can see you losing interest now that you've found the killer, as you believe. How *is* Keelan, by the way?' I added before he could protest.

'Still whingeing. Still protesting his innocence.'

'Something I meant to ask – he was out of the hospital between five and six on the evening of Traynor's death. Has he told you where he went?'

'Oh, yeah. Apparently he called around to Traynor's house and spoke to his wife. The story stands up – almost the only one of his that does.'

'Called to Traynor's house? For what?'

'He claims he was still trying to sell him the bone carving.'

'Which would only make sense if he thought Traynor was alive and kicking.'

'Wrong. It makes sense if he was trying to build an alibi. He was counting on the body not being discovered until much later. Time of death would be harder to pinpoint and would probably encompass the time when he was knocking at his victim's front door. So, for several reasons, he would be an unlikely suspect.'

'What else has he told you that turned out to be true?'

'What do you mean?'

'You guys learn to use words very carefully. You said this was "almost" the only story of his that stands up. Tell me another one.'

'Well … the gift he bought for his sister yesterday in Castleboyne. He had a signed credit-card receipt with the date and time on it.'

'So he couldn't have made that attempt on Ward's life.'

'Well, it could have been a buddy of his.'

Gallagher was still stoutly defending his position. I wondered what it was going to take to make him yield.

Chapter Thirty-Two

I escaped from the icy clutch of the breeze into the hall at Brookfield, in the centre of which stood a large Christmas tree, as was traditional at the farm. Finian met me with a hug and led me into the drawing room.

It took my breath away. In every available space – atop tables and desks, behind prints, along picture rails and pelmets, in vases, on the mantelpiece – there was greenery: garlands and sprays, wreaths and bouquets; ferns, leaves, ivy and other creepers, branches of pine, even sprigs of mistletoe – but no holly. Contrasting with the green were gold ribbons and red candles, two of which, on either side of a gilt carriage clock on the mantelpiece, were lit.

'After reading that piece in the *Meath Chronicle*, I thought I'd have a go at recreating how our ancestors decorated their surroundings. I used anything green I could find in the garden.'

'It's lovely. Happy Christmas, by the way.' I handed him his gift, bought in Lucca in October – a bottle of 1997 Brunello di Montalcino, and the best *vin santo* I could find in the walled city.

'How delightful. Merry Christmas to you too.' He kissed me on the cheek.

I was about to sit down; but Finian, setting his wine on the table, asked me to stay standing. 'I want you to do something,' he said. 'See how some of the foliage is tied in bunches with gold ribbon? One of the ties isn't what it seems.'

I wandered slowly around the room until I came to the fireplace.

'You're getting warm – in more ways than one.'

Under the mantelpiece hung a leafy festoon threaded through with gold ribbon. Then I saw it – just under the clock, encircling the garland: the gold torc we had seen in Dublin on the night of the party. I reached out to touch it, just to be sure.

'Why not take it?' said Finian. 'It's yours.'

'When did you – how … ?' It was a complete surprise.

'Try it on,' he said.

'The torc was an adornment of the Goddess; I'm not sure I'm worthy,' I said with fake modesty. It was heavier than I had imagined it would be, yet when I had put it on it not only sat perfectly but seemed lighter somehow.

'Happy Christmas, Goddess,' he said, coming towards me with his arms outstretched.

'It's beautiful,' I said. 'Thank you. And thanks for all of this –' I glanced around the room.

He put his arms around me. 'I love you, Illaun,' he said, kissing me gently on the lips. For a few moments we looked into each other's eyes. Then we kissed again, tenderly at first, then hungrily, with a passion we had long denied ourselves.

When we eventually unclasped I was aching for him, and I knew he was aroused too.

'We'll have to wait just a little longer,' he whispered. 'Come over here; there's something else.' He picked up an envelope from the mantelpiece and handed it to me. 'Open it.'

There was a card inside, not a Christmas card but a gold-edged invitation.

Finian Shaw wishes to invite
Illaun Bowe
to
THE NEW YEAR'S EVE BALL
At Bunraskin House Hotel, Celbridge
Champagne reception · Dinner · Fireworks display
Overnight in the Penthouse Suite

'The suite has a single bed as well,' he said, smiling.

'You can keep your options open until then.'

'And Celbridge, too,' I said, tears gluing my eyelashes together. On another occasion I would tell him that things had not worked out as we had thought between Peter Hunt and Marie Maguire. Right now he would think it a bad omen, and I wasn't going to spoil this moment.

'Oh, Finian, you put so much thought into this. I love you.' The tears were sliding down my cheeks.

He held me again. 'This moment with you – how I've longed for it … But I wasn't sure you felt the same way.'

'Oh, Finian. How could you doubt it?'

'Because … well, I knew we would always have a special relationship, but I thought you wanted to keep it that way – not complicate it.'

'Cautious, as usual.'

'Yes. And to hell with it, I say.' He stepped away from me and spun around the living room. 'Hey, that's going to be my New Year's resolution – "Let's throw caution to the wind!"'

I laughed. 'Good. I'll raise my glass to that on the night. Now, why not look at your present?'

He sat down, unwrapped it and took the wine from the presentation box. 'Hey, these look very promising.' He grinned. 'I'll keep them for a special occasion.' He placed the bottles on the table, where they glinted in the candlelight. 'And you got them to fit in with the decorations – how clever.'

I could see what he meant. The red and gold

trimmings were perfectly matched by the contents of the bottles.

The clock on the mantelpiece chimed six.

'I made more mulled wine earlier. Would you like some?' Finian seemed unperturbed by the time.

I wanted to stay put, but I had promised to help my mother with some of the preparations for Christmas Day before we went to Mass. But I also knew this was a very special occasion.

'I'd love some,' I said, reaching back to remove the torc.

'Here, let me.'

Finian unclasped the ends of the torc, kissing me on the nape of my neck as he did so. It sent a delicious current of sensation all through me.

'Mmm … I could do with some more of that, too.'

But it wasn't to be. We heard the pounding of a walking-stick coming down the stairs, and old Arthur hallooing for his son to join him.

'I'm coming,' Finian called to his father. He began to put out the lights in the room.

'I'm glad you settled your differences with Maeve,' I said.

'And you?'

'Peace on Earth as well, I'm glad to say.'

Finian put his arms around me. 'In a week we'll be together.'

'Yes, we will,' I said. 'We certainly will.'

Chapter Thirty-Three

I was turning into my driveway when Gallagher rang.

'At last we know what Traynor had on Ward. He's told us everything.'

'Hang on a second.' I parked the car, took the phone from its cradle and held it to my ear. 'Go ahead.'

'I know I shouldn't be telling you this stuff. But I also know you'll pester me until I do, and I want a peaceful Christmas as much as the next man. So here goes: twenty-five years back, Ward and Campion became lovers. Traynor took it badly – lots of ugly scenes with him drunk and threatening violence. Campion couldn't take any more, decided to end it with Ward. Then she got religion and joined the Hospitaller Order. She always had an unpredictable streak, according to Ward. She was posted to their place in north County Dublin but kept in touch with him. Time passes. Campion's religious zeal wears a bit thin. Ward arranges to see her one last time. She sneaks out one night, they get drunk and make love, and she becomes pregnant. But she manages to keep the pregnancy undetected and has the baby with Ursula Roche's help … Are you still with me?'

'Just about.'

'OK. Here's the bit that will interest you most. The baby was stillborn. And guess what? They buried it at Monashee.'

'So how did Traynor find out about the baby?'

'Campion wrote to Ward shortly afterwards and told him what had happened. Unfortunately, Ward showed the letter to Traynor during a drinking session a few years later. Ward had just been elected for the first time; Traynor had put some election funding his way, so Ward thought bygones were bygones between them. But Traynor wasn't thinking like that at all. Campion had just been put in charge of Grange Abbey, Ward was about to get married. Traynor told him he would expose both of them if Ward didn't play ball.'

'And he used that threat all these years to extract favours?'

'And dragged others into the loop as well. Like Muriel Blunden. He was getting greedier, too. Ward reckons he had been putting pressure on Campion recently to sell him bits of property below market value. He claims the reason why he supported Traynor's plan for the hotel was that he knew Campion would leave the area as soon as the abbey was sold, so Traynor's hold on them both would be weakened. That could be why Traynor was upping the ante, according to Ward.'

'To make her stay, you mean?'

'Yeah. Even though he had squeezed all he could out of her and the order, he still needed her around to keep Ward in line.'

'Hmm … so he starts to dig up the field – just to show he's serious, not thinking he's going to find the remains. Then, when he hears a baby's body actually *was* unearthed by the digger, he assumes it's hers – because it doesn't occur to him that it might have been a *cillín* and that there might be other bodies there.'

'Isn't it possible it was her child?' Gallagher asked.

'No. The carbon-dating and the evidence of Thali-domide damage place it in the early 60s. Twenty years too early.'

'But Traynor doesn't know this, right?'

'Right. So let's assume he contacts Sister Campion and tells her that the remains of her baby have been found and, if necessary, can be linked to her by DNA.'

'It's obviously very distressing for her, so maybe she's not thinking clearly enough to say, "Hold on, this isn't necessarily mine." So she agrees to his latest terms.'

'But why is she so worried to begin with? I mean, conceiving a baby might have been a sin, but it certainly wasn't a crime.'

Gallagher remained silent at the other end for a few seconds. Both of us were thinking through what I had just said.

'Unless ... unless Sister Campion's child wasn't stillborn at all. Unless it was murdered.' I was glad Gallagher had said it. He had manoeuvred himself into a corner at last.

'That would explain a hell of a lot,' I said.

'I've arranged to interview Sister Campion at seven o'clock.'

'That's in less than an hour.'

'There's some kind of service in the abbey at eight.'

'Yes. Sister Gabriel mentioned a choral service they hold on Christmas Eve, between vespers and midnight Mass. She said men were never present, but I have reason to think that may have changed.'

'Maybe I'll stay on for it.'

'Are you serious?'

'No way. I'm anxious to see my kids before they go to bed.'

'Is Fitzgibbon going with you?'

'Nah. It's Christmas. He needs some time off.'

Now I was worried. 'I don't think you should go there alone.'

'Hey, what's this? It's a convent I'm going to, not a terrorist training camp.'

'I know. But there's something about that place – something not right. Just … be careful, all right?'

'Don't worry. It's just a preliminary visit, to get a feel of the situation. I'll follow it up in a couple of days.'

'Just promise me you'll phone or text as soon as you're out of there.'

'OK. And I won't wish you a Happy Christmas until then. If you don't hear from me, come and get me!'

'That last verse once more. Let's hear the descant – it's far too timid.'

Gillian was taking us through a couple of carols that needed rough patches smoothed out before the vigil Mass began.

We started the third verse of 'Once in Royal David's City', but Gillian wasn't happy and the organ died. 'Tenors and basses, you're adrift of each other. Let's take it from the top one more time … Sopranos and altos, ready?'

People were already taking their seats in the church, even though there was nearly an hour to go. Once billed as *midnight* Mass, over the years the service had receded to a time deemed more appropriate for families to attend and less opportune for drunks pouring out of the pubs and into the church to snore or snigger throughout the proceedings.

But my own thoughts weren't entirely focused on the service either. As if I were opening a gift-wrapped box in private, I revisited the scene with Finian – the greenery, the gold trimmings, the fire in the grate, the torc, the kiss … I was so exhilarated that I hadn't put any lipstick near my mouth since that moment; I wanted it to linger. Every so often I put my fingers to my lips. He was still there, if ever so faintly now, just as the physical desire I felt had receded to a dull but not unpleasant ache. In his quiet way, Finian had wooed me this past week, and it had all been leading to his dazzling little piece of theatre tonight. It had been manipulative, as all romantic gestures are in the end; but if a woman wants her suitor to be demonstrative, then she must go along with it when he makes a superb effort. For now I would bask in the warm glow of knowing that Finian had finally revealed the truth of his feelings towards me.

We had just put a little extra shine on another carol when Father Burke, our silver-haired parish priest, arrived up in the gallery to have a word with Gillian. As they discussed some minor details of the night's liturgy, I wondered if the church at Grange Abbey, stripped as it was of its furniture and sacred vessels, had been deconsecrated. And what kind of service were they having now? I should really have told Gallagher that the men had been singing a song about holly berries, but I would have felt faintly ridiculous doing so. It brought *The Wicker Man* to mind again: the paganism of the islanders, expressed in risibly risqué ballads and embarrassing-to-watch fertility dances. Surely the visiting police sergeant, even if he *is* a Christian, can't be taking this with anything but a large grain of salt? But the point is that he is serious about his beliefs, just as they are about theirs – deadly serious, as it turns out.

Father Burke bid us all a happy and peaceful Christmas and left. Gillian sat back down at the organ, and we began our selection of carols as the congregation swelled to overflowing. Just before Father Burke and his concelebrants entered in procession from the porch inside the west door, I slipped my mobile phone from my handbag and checked the screen. I had received no messages.

I tried to dismiss my growing anxiety and to concentrate on the ceremony – for me, the most joyful and untrammelled of Christian celebrations. In theory the resurrection at Easter is the high point – a glorious victory over death, prefiguring the fate of all; but it follows too close on events that expose to us the dark side of our nature. Christmas doesn't ask us to reflect on our murkier urges. It insists that we share the wonder and optimism of a new birth, that moment in life that seems, no matter what the circumstances, to deeply touch those who witness it.

You're being naïve, Illaun. Not every birth is a cause for celebration. Think of the carvings on the doorway.

I didn't want those images in my head. *Sing –*

'Silent night, holy night,

All is calm, all is bright …'

Think of Herod.

'Round yon Virgin Mother and Child,
Holy infant so tender and mild …'
Think of what you saw in the morgue.
'Sleep in heavenly peace …'
*Think of Traynor and O'Hagan, their lipless
mouths spilling holly berries.*
'Sleep in heavenly peace.'

I left the church as soon as Mass was over, without
chatting to anyone. As soon as I was outside I checked
my phone again. Gallagher hadn't been in touch. I tried
his phone, but he wasn't answering. I rang Drogheda
Garda station, explained who I was and asked for a
home number; the officer I spoke to couldn't find one,
so I asked for Sergeant Fitzgibbon's mobile number.
When I dialled it, chattering voices and loud music in
the background made it difficult for Fitzgibbon to hear
what I was saying. He was in a pub. I suggested he go
outside, which he reluctantly did.

'What's your problem? It's freezing out here.'

I explained that Gallagher had intended to be at
Grange Abbey for no more than an hour and had
promised to phone me when he left there.

'He's probably gone to visit his kids.'

'Visit them?'

'Yeah, he's only recently separated. They're with the
wife.'

'Have you a telephone number for her?'

'No. They're not on good terms. And Matt's just moved into a new apartment – no phone yet. The best thing is to keep trying the mobile.'

This was useless. 'Dammit, Sergeant, are you not worried about him?'

'Worried? Why should I be worried? We've got the fucker who did the murders locked up. And I'd say as soon as Matt's put the kids to bed he'll be helping himself to a well-earned pint. Which reminds me – I've got one waiting inside. Happy Christmas.'

Fitzgibbon didn't want to know. But it was Christmas Eve and I couldn't blame him.

When I got home, Richard and Greta were watching a ballet version of *Snow White* on TV. Eoin had apparently only fallen asleep in the past half-hour. The Christmas tree was aglow beside the bay window, and my mother had drawn back the curtains and lit a red candle on the sill. She was in the kitchen, pressing cloves and pineapple slices into the fat on top of the ham, which had earlier been simmered in beer for three hours and left to cool down. A coating of brown sugar and an hour's baking would complete the process.

I watched the ballet for a while, then wandered into the kitchen. While my mother's back was turned I picked a fragment from the ham and popped it in my mouth; it was as succulent and spicy as always.

'I'm off to bed now,' she said, arranging things in the dishwasher. 'Don't stay up late yourself. You're whacked.'

'I won't,' I said, and kissed her on the cheek as she passed.

I took a carton of milk from the fridge and was just picking up a tumbler when I noticed something out of place among some of Eoin's play figures, which had been put away in an odds-and-ends basket on the work surface. I put down the tumbler and flicked Spiderman aside to reveal the carving Keelan had tried to sell Traynor.

With all that had happened, I had completely forgotten it. My last memory of it was of Gallagher passing it from one hand to the other. I'd assumed he had taken it away as evidence, but it must have slipped down the side of the couch, where Eoin had found it. For all I knew he had been playing with it all day.

I filled the tumbler, sat on a stool and fished out the carving. Richard and Greta stuck their heads around the door and said good night. I checked the time: just coming up to midnight. Finian would have settled in and be enjoying a glass of wine by now. I sent him a text asking him to give me a call and put my mobile on Discreet.

As fertility symbols, women are represented in as many shapes as nature allows, and more: from balloon-hipped, tyre-legged divas with huge stomachs and pendulous breasts to slim arty types with stylised, abstract features. The small carving I held in my hand had the proportions of a short, stocky woman. Her face was a serene mask with hair flat against it on

479

either side, the nose and eyebrows forming a continuous T around blank almond-shaped eyes, the mouth an enigmatic slit. With the exception of a headband and a neck ornament, she was naked. Her hands were cupped under her apple-shaped breasts; below them, her belly curved gently out and then inwards to a triangle etched between her legs, which were modestly joined together.

From the back, her nudity was for some reason more sensual, possibly because her hips and buttocks were so smooth and rounded, and the choker added a coquettish quality to her. If this was the ugly sister, then 'Goldilocks' must indeed be a stunner. I could see, too, that the incised neck ornament was in fact an attempt at rendering a ribbon torc – symbol of the fertility goddess.

I turned the figurine upside down and realised that it was hollow: the cavity of the animal bone from which it was fashioned formed a circular opening in the soles of the feet. But there was something not entirely natural-looking about the opening. I found my magnifying glass and examined the base of the bone. The entrance to the cavity had been deliberately enlarged and rounded, creating a step running around the inside of the rim.

What did it mean? Had the figurine originally been fixed to something? If it was, as I had originally assumed, another pendant that Mona had been wearing around her neck, then why had it no loop or perforation through which it could have been hung from the leather thong?

Then it dawned on me. This object had been suspended from the other carving.

My mobile buzzed. It was Finian.

'How are you? All nice and cosy there?' I said, keeping my voice down.

'Yes, my love. I can tell there's something on your mind; what is it?'

'I'm worried about Inspector Gallagher.' I brought him up to date.

Finian struck a positive note. 'At this stage, if he was meant to call on his family and hasn't turned up, you can bet your life there are Gardaí out in force looking for him.'

That hadn't occurred to me, maybe because of what Fitzgibbon had said about the relationship between Gallagher and his ex-wife. But it set my mind at rest to some extent.

'There's something else I wanted to tell you.' I described the figurine and how I thought it might have functioned as a pendant.

'Well, why don't you put it to the test? You still have the other one there, don't you?'

'Yes. You're right. Hang on a second.'

Phone and carving in one hand, I opened up the office, turned on the lights and unlocked my desk drawers. In the bottom one I had put away the plastic bag containing the ithyphallic pendant. I stuck the phone under my jaw and gave Finian a running commentary as I took it from the bag and inserted it into the hollow figurine, as far as the base.

'If I just …' I applied some extra pressure and wedged it into position, flush against the soles of the feet. 'Hey, guess what – not only does it fit, but you'd never know it was there. It's a very precise piece of work.'

'From what you're saying, it was worn upside down.'

'Yes.'

'Sounds to me like a sort of portable shrine, a sacred object. It was probably worn under clothing, but even if it was inadvertently exposed, it wouldn't be immediately apparent what it was – especially not the more explicit symbol set into it.'

'So it's a fertility symbol representing both male and female principles. It doesn't represent an either/or, God *or* Goddess culture, but one that revered both.'

'And obviously celebrated sex. Which ties in neatly with something I've been chewing on for the past few days. It's a fact of history that the Anglo-Normans got papal sanction for an invasion of Ireland long before they ever set foot here. And they got it by accusing us of all sorts of vices that needed to be cleaned up – sexual ones in particular. So, if you like, they were able to justify their actions by saying they were on a moral crusade. And I guess that meant they had to find some poor offenders and make an example of them. I think

Mona's pendant was discovered, and it raised suspicions that she had an unwholesome interest in carnal matters. She might even have been regarded as a pagan priestess. It's probably what got her killed.'

'A bit extreme, wouldn't you say – even for those times?'

'Unfortunately for the likes of Mona, it was a period when successive Lateran Councils became increasingly obsessed with heresy and wanted the secular rulers to deal harshly with it. Add in the fact that Henry II was trying to curry favour with the pope after having Thomas Becket murdered, and you've got a recipe for something akin to witch-hunting.'

And, as Sister Campion had reminded me, Henry had come to Ireland in 1171.

Chapter Thirty-Four

Long, long ago, in midwinter, when the snow was falling like feathers from the sky, a beautiful queen sat sewing. She accidentally pricked her finger on a holly leaf and three drops of blood fell onto the snow. Then she said, If I could have a daughter with skin as white, with cheeks as rosy ...

Cheeks as red as the berry, skin as black as the coal ...

Mirror, mirror on the wall, who is the fairest of us all? Greta Goldilocks? Sister Campion? Lord Sol?

Ugly Sister Ursula ran down the steps of the abbey as fast as she could ... The clock was pointing to

sunrise. Bring Goldilocks out to Monashee, said
Ursula; stab her to death and bring me back the lips,
ears and eyes …

Cinderella lost her mirror running from the crypt …
There's death in the glass, blood on the snow, evil in
the abbey …

Lully, lullay, thou little tiny child …

If I could have a son … No! Herod and Henry will
spill his blood … then his skin will go white as the
snow, as black as the coal …

Will you ever have a child at all?

'No, never!'

I woke up, startled by my own voice, my heart
pounding. I could feel rawness in my throat from the
force of the scream.

The disjointed nightmare had left me on the verge of
some dire revelation that slithered away as soon as I
tried to haul it into consciousness. My clock read 4.05.
It would soon be Christmas morning in the Bowe
household. Eoin would be up and about in three hours
or less, judging by my own and Richard's childhood. I
checked my phone again – no message from Gallagher.
If you don't hear from me, come and get me.

This was ridiculous. Gallagher was probably fast
asleep in his bed. But I had to be sure. And that meant
going there on my own. Finian was in Galway; Seamus
Crean was unwell and possibly in hospital; and I
wouldn't spoil the magic of Christmas night by rousing
my brother or Fran.

I made a deal with myself. If I drove to the abbey and didn't see his car outside, then I would turn around and drive off satisfied.

I didn't meet a single vehicle on the thirty-kilometre drive. But all along the way there were shapes melting into the grass verge, red eyes glinting in the hedges. There are few times of the year when humans are not about. This was one of them, and the creatures of the night were making the most of it.

As were the Grange Abbey nuns. It had finally come to me that Christmas Day was probably the one day in the year when they were released from their vows. When Sister Campion had been talking about them getting off on a technicality, she had been about to mention the date but had swerved rapidly to avoid doing so. But in the next sentence she had referred to Christmastime and King Henry, and now I realised that had been a giveaway. Not that I believed the nuns needed any sanction for whatever they might be up to; I just sensed it was in Geraldine Campion's nature to want to do it by the book.

I had just started descending towards the valley floor near Newgrange when I hit fog. It stayed with me even as I climbed up away from the river, towards Grange Abbey. I had to crawl along the narrow road, examining each gateway, until I saw 'La Croix du Dragon …'

The fog thickened as I drove down the avenue, and by the time I neared the house it was impossible to see anything. I had to open the window and listen for the crunch of gravel to be sure I was on the forecourt. Switching off the lights, I was plunged into darkness until I opened the glove compartment to find the flashlight. I got out of the car and discovered the beam was of no value if directed straight ahead, so I aimed it at my feet, where it just about reached the gravel.

With visibility down to zero, I wouldn't be able to tell if Gallagher's car was parked outside or not, unless I literally walked into it. After taking a few steps I realised it wasn't even possible to figure out which direction I was taking. I swept the light in a circle around me but couldn't get my bearings – finding my way back to my own car was going to be a problem. Then my toe hit something, and I saw the corner of the first step leading up to the door of the house.

The outside light came on, surrounding the door in a nimbus of fog. When I reached the top step the light switched itself off, and I could make out a dim glow behind the fanlight. Then I noticed the door wasn't fully closed. I pushed it in. It had been left off the latch; someone had recently gone out of the house, with the intention of coming back soon.

The hall immediately inside the door was lit, but the stairs and the rest of the interior lay in darkness. I swept the flashlight up the stairs and saw that the carpet had been lifted. The place seemed deserted. I was faced with a stark choice: find my way back to the Jazz and wait outside until the fog cleared, or stay in here, where at least I could see my way around.

I made my decision and headed for the stairs. Two flights up, I reached a long corridor and started down it. It was lined with rooms on both sides; the doors were all open, and I flicked the light into each one as I passed. Not one of them had any furniture. Nearing the end of the dormitory, I decided to switch on a light in one of the rooms and take a better look. I had to try three of them before I found a bulb that worked.

The wooden floor was missing a floorboard, the plaster on the walls was peeling, the bare window-frame was coated in dust, and the bulb hanging from the ceiling was naked. No one had occupied this room, or any of the others, in a long time.

I switched off the light and continued to the end of the corridor, turned into a high-ceilinged gallery that overlooked the cloister. I was heading in the direction of the church. And I had another clue to help me: I could hear the nuns singing. What hour of the Divine Office was this? I looked at my watch – 5.50. Matins was around midnight, or an hour later at most, and it was followed by – what was it? – Lauds, at daybreak. But dawn was still two hours away.

I went through a door at the end of the gallery and found myself on a landing. Two other doors led off it: the one on the left would lead down to the cloister, the door facing me must be the entrance to the church.

I cracked open the door into the church and looked

through. A set of stone steps led down into the south transept, which was in semi-darkness. But there were lights on in the nave, and as I went down the steps I could see there was lighting along the walls on both sides, revealing the interior of the church to be almost totally empty. To my right, the marble altar was still in position in the chancel, but there was little else. To my left the floor was bare all the way to the west door, which seemed to be closed.

The voices were coming from behind the altar; the nuns were evidently assembled at the far end of the chancel. I listened, trying to make out what they were singing.

'*In hoc anni circulo …*' At this turning of the year…

'*Vita datur saeculo …*' Life is given again …

I crept up the steps to the altar and peered over it. Directly behind it, a rectangular arrangement of wrought-iron rails with a gate at one end surrounded the steps to the crypt. Leaning against the rails and scattered nearby were pickaxes and sledgehammers, a pneumatic drill, buckets, planks and a couple of wheelbarrows.

The nuns reached the end of the carol. I ducked my head down and went around the side of the altar to get a better view of the east end of the church. It was empty, but near the entrance to the crypt was a trestle table, on which sat, incongruously, a CD player and a set of speakers.

Increasingly bewildered, I left the shelter of the altar,

went to the table and picked up some CD cases that had been left in a small pile beside the player. I read the title of the one on top: *Christmas Carols, Sacred and Secular.*

I didn't need to look at the others. Neither the nuns of Grange Abbey nor some visiting folk singers had been performing the carols, now or on my earlier visits. The music had come from these recordings. I felt ridiculous. And I realised that Sister Campion had ensured that I would be in the vicinity of the church at a designated time, on the previous Sunday, so that they could have the tracks arranged to give the impression of a lively community going about its usual business, whereas now it seemed likely that there were very few nuns inhabiting Grange Abbey. But why go to such lengths? They must definitely have something to hide. On the other hand, the night Finian and I had come here together, they hadn't been hiding anything – just playing music while they worked. So much for a midwinter fertility ceremony.

The gate to the crypt was open. It was decorated in holly and bee motifs.

I approached the gate. *Unholy ground.*

The steps beckoned me downwards.

I picked up a lump hammer from among the implements on the floor and put it in the pocket of my parka. Then I descended.

The crypt looked at first like a typical Romanesque structure: several arcades of massive drum piers and low round arches, dividing the space beneath the nave into deep, barrel-vaulted bays. Two passageways were lit, one to my right, the other straight ahead, leading towards the west end. The piers in that direction seemed to increase in height – the ground was sloping downwards.

If the nave above was built on a shelf of rock sloping in the opposite direction, then the first part of the church to be constructed, the east end, was for some reason built at the start of this second slope, achieving an effect equivalent to two escalators in a store travelling in opposite directions but both leading downwards.

The place smelled of damp, with another less pleasant odour underlying it. I took the passageway straight ahead and, walking along stone flags, came to the last bay on the left, which was enclosed by iron bars like a cage in a zoo. The gate was ajar.

The interior was only dimly lit, but what I saw against the far wall made me enter. As I approached I played the flashlight across it, reducing the intensity of the beam to see through the glass that filled the entire back of the bay.

Running the length of the wall was a display cabinet of dark wood, about four metres long and two high. Behind the dusty glass panels were rows of specimen jars of various sizes, lined along shelves; in between the jars were objects fixed on wooden plinths. Going closer, I saw that they were tiny human skeletons, some no bigger than a bird's and all with evident deformities: jawless, bulbous-headed, open-skulled, one cranium in fragments as though it had exploded. It was similar to the one in Sister Campion's office. A few of the skeletons were fused to one another at the chest or head. Most of them were posed in crouched or standing positions, the delicate bones held together by rods and wire.

In the jars and bottles of formaldehyde were the bleached-looking remains of infants with equally severe defects – some just unrecognisable lumps of putty-like flesh, others with their already distorted features moulded into bizarre shapes by being crammed into the glass containers. Some jars held only organs: a brain without any folds, green-tinged viscera that seemed to be inside out. I saw one with just a head floating inside it, the face split open by a wide fissure from mouth to brow. Beside that sat an entire foetus with a parasitic head growing out of its gaping mouth.

This – not a stained-glass window – was the 'glass' that contained the abbey's secret: flesh-and-bone versions of the carvings on the west door.

The wooden base of the cabinet contained two drawers. I pulled out one of them and found some mildewed blank labels; I assumed they were intended for the items on display, not one of which, I realised, had anything to identify it. In the other drawer were some handwritten labels of the same kind, but the ink was either faded or blotched beyond legibility by damp. I quickly rummaged through them until I found one that was almost readable.

> D tto   Gi vann Pergo esi
> stituto An tomia
> Uni   Bologn

There was also a number, which I took to be a date: '1634'. Another label said:

> ndrew MacPherson
> Edinb gh Medic

They looked like address labels. No wonder Monashee had not been bursting at the seams with human remains. It seemed the Beekeepers had at one time – probably over several centuries – harvested not honey but human children, trading in the preserved cadavers and reassembled skeletons of deformed infants. And presumably they had found a ready market for their wares in the medical schools of Europe as well as in the cabinets of private collectors. The items on display in the crypt must have been either used for teaching these skills or, as in the case of the two destined for Bologna and Edinburgh, left on their hands for one reason or another. Probably there had been more cabinets and display cases in the bays of the crypt, but they had been dismantled, their contents dumped or destroyed – ironically, destroying rare evidence of foetal pathology and congenital deformities that would have been of great interest to twenty-first-century biologists.

Apart from the drawers, the base of the cabinet at first seemed to contain no compartments – it was just a single panel of wood without handles or keyholes. I played the flashlight along it and then around the sides of the cabinet, where I discovered a brass hook-and-eye arrangement on each end that seemed to be holding up the panel. I unhooked each in turn and the entire panel fell forward, but only by a few centimetres. It was still being held back by something.

Halfway along its length was a short brass chain hooked into another eye screwed into the back of the panel. I knelt down and released the chain, and the panel came free. There was another panel behind it, this one made of glass, and on the top of the frame surrounding it was a brass plate engraved with red and black lettering. It looked like an extended version of the 'Please pray for the repose of the soul of ...' plaques found on the pews of many Irish churches. I was about to read it when I heard a sound.

I switched off the flashlight and hid behind a pier. Then I heard it again: a woman coughing. Someone had come down the steps into the crypt. Afraid she was coming to lock the gate, I slipped out and ran across the passage to a bay that was in complete darkness. The smell mixed in with earth and damp was stronger here.

A shadow flitted past the piers as the woman

walked parallel to the way I had come, but several passages away. And then I saw Sister Roche going by, about ten metres from me. She was dressed in a heavy fleece jacket and black jeans and was carrying what looked like a bodhrán. Was it she who had been outside the residence when I arrived?

As if sensing something amiss, Roche paused, back-pedalled and stared in my direction. 'Get up!' she barked.

My heart froze.

Roche came closer. I edged back around the outer pier, almost into the passage.

She stood under the arch at the other side of the bay, silhouetted by the light behind her, just a few metres of darkness between us.

'You lazy animal, Henry,' she scolded. 'There's work to be done. No time for sleep.' For a second I was back in old Sister Gabriel's room. Were they all mad?

Something alive reared up between Roche and me, blocking her from view. I edged further behind the pier as the creature bleated its annoyance at being disturbed.

'Get him back here before the others come,' Roche snapped.

Henry made a sucking noise, as though swallowing his own saliva.

Roche's haranguing voice moved away again. I ran back to the steps of the crypt, the hammer clutched in my hand, ready for use if necessary.

On the landing, I paused to put my ear to the door that led back into the residence. I was sure that I had heard other voices. And I had – they were coming in my direction. I tried the door to the cloister, but it was locked. Heart thumping, I ran up two flights of steps to the tower door. It was open. I went through it just as Sister Campion came onto the landing, talking to someone behind her.

I pressed the door closed and leaned against it in case they tried to come up that way. But her voice faded: they had gone into the church.

I was in the dark again. As my eyes adjusted I saw a pinpoint of light above me. I was looking at a star, through a window high up in the wall. The fog seemed to have receded. I switched the flashlight on and found myself in a narrow passageway that led through the wall of the transept into the tower. Picking my way along, I came to a spiral stone staircase, which I imagined snaked all the way up to the roof of the tower. I began to climb the steps, worrying about whether the door to the roof would be open, whether the roof itself would be intact ... I stopped to catch my breath, reminding myself I had far more to be anxious about.

The door at the top of the steps was hanging off its hinges, and I emerged cautiously onto the flagged roof under a sky in which the star – actually Venus – was sparkling on a bed of deepest blue. But below the tower was a cloud stretching as far as I could see; only the battlements behind which I stood were free of the fog.

Then two things happened at once. The sky behind the ridge to the southeast, under Venus, became lighter; and a breeze started up, beginning to sweep away the top layer of mist.

I thought I heard a noise and looked around, but it was just the rustle of dried leaves, whirling about in a corner where they had been trapped since autumn. Then I noticed something about the door to the stairwell. It hadn't fallen from its hinges because it was rotten. It had been splintered in a recent struggle.

At that moment I knew Gallagher was dead.

I slumped down onto the flags and leaned back against one of the merlons, the upward-projecting teeth of the parapet. In time, the sky grew paler behind the ridge, the Madonna blue lifting to reveal an ivory underskirt flushed with rose.

I stood up again and noticed the fog had thinned out all around the abbey. A blue-grey cloud still clung to the banks of the river; and I saw Newgrange, floating like a flying saucer on top of it.

The sky behind me began to glow. Stray clouds like pulled-out pieces of cotton-wool were underlined in electric pink. The sun was about to come up over the ridge and illuminate the valley. On the far side, Newgrange was already taking on a warmer hue as the light changed. Trees along the ridge stood out starkly as the orb of the sun rose up behind them.

As the sun cleared the ridge. I looked across at

Newgrange and saw an extraordinary sight: a bolt of light shot back out of the chamber, dividing the mist like a biblical finger of God and making it glow and smoulder all the way from the mound to the Boyne. The sunlight coming over the skyline behind me was being split into rays of all sizes by the trees and the craggy contours of the ridge; the shafts streamed over my head, fanning out through the thinning mist between the abbey and the river.

In the distance I could hear a noise like theatrical thunder, a metallic rolling and rumbling. Then the light at the entrance to Newgrange began to shimmer, firing off golden beams like a shower of arrows that intercepted the oncoming rays above the surface of the water. Reflections from the river added to the latticework of light being built above the Boyne. And through it all the mist was burning off, in writhing coils that rose upwards like souls on their way to heaven.

And then shapes began to emerge from the tomb. First they were only vague bendings in the air, created by the light at the entrance; then they materialised into the forms of hooded monks; and then, out in the open in front of the mound, walking in a circle, I saw veiled members of the Hospitaller Order.

I felt as if I had been sent back in a time machine. Was this how it had been a thousand years ago? Had the order somehow inherited the rites of the tomb-builders, and were they re-enacting them as they had done over the centuries – not on the day of the solstice, but on an even more pointed and more blasphemous occasion? 'It still works on Christmas Day, doesn't it?' Sam Sakamoto had asked me, and now his words took on a sinister resonance.

Nevertheless, it was an impressive piece of theatre. Then it occurred to me – if the 'nuns' were coming on stage like actors in a play, how had they arrived at the 'theatre' in the first place? Hardly through the front entrance.

They stood still and, facing the sun, raised their arms in a form of greeting. With the glare all around them, it was difficult to see how many there were. The metallic pounding seemed to be reaching a climax. It had the resonating quality of a cymbal or gong. Then it began to recede, but my ear picked up another noise – regular, like the engine of a distant boat heard underwater: drumming. The nuns began to move in time to it. And there was another sound – regular, too. Wheezing. Coming from behind me. I looked around.

There was a man in a white habit standing in the shadows of the doorway. His head was bare and long twists of matted hair fell onto his shoulders. As he emerged into the light I saw that his massive, domed forehead extended down his face like a helmet with a long nosepiece, forcing his eyes sideways. Below the bone helmet his mouth was bifurcated, a salivating wound of mangled lip and gum exposing four bared rows of teeth.

The dog-man bellowed and sprang towards me, his hands raised like claws. I fell back and my head hit one of the merlons. As darkness closed in, my last image was of him bending over me, his extended tongue dripping saliva.

But my last thought was unconnected with that. It was, *Now I know how they crossed the river in winter.*

Chapter Thirty-Five

I was lying with my head against something warm. A human body. Horrified, I snapped into wakefulness and saw Gallagher beside me. I was slumped against his shoulder.

We were on the floor with our backs against the wall of the crypt, in the same bay as the display cabinet. Both of us were tied up in the same way, hands behind our backs, legs stretched out in front, ankles tied with blue nylon rope. The gate into the bay was locked.

'Thanks for dropping in,' said Gallagher with a wan smile. 'Are you OK?'

'Apart from a bump on the head to match the other one, yes. What happened you?'

'Oldest trick in the book, and I fell for it. Sister Campion explained that they had dug up this artefact that Traynor wanted to buy for nothing. She said Roche would show me. Roche brought me through this passage …' He nodded towards where I had seen the bursar earlier. 'She called it a souter– something …'

'A souterrain.'

'Yeah. It led into a cave that narrowed to a natural tunnel through the rock, just enough room to go through with your head down. Leads all the way to Newgrange, beneath the river, apparently.'

'I knew it. It finally came to me up on the tower – there had to be a passageway under the river. They built this church over an ancient religious site – the entrance to a sacred cave, as you've described it. The priests of the people who built Newgrange must have robed up there for the solstice ceremony and then emerged on the far side as though by magic. Did you go all the way across?'

'No. What I got was probably the same routine they put on for O'Hagan. "You go ahead of me," said Roche, and like a fool I did. When I bent down to enter the passage, I noticed a carving knife under my chin and Henry the Harelip blocking my way. As I backed out, Roche hit me on the head with a rock or something. While I was out cold they tied me up and left me in the outer passage. They moved me here a few hours ago, just before some people arrived. Roche had Harelip working through the night preparing for them. I think that's what saved me. Anyway, it went quiet a few hours ago, after they'd gone through into the cave. Then Henry arrived with you across his back. Roche came and took a look at you, too; it seemed to give her some satisfaction, judging by her expression. So what's your story?'

I quickly told him what had happened and described what I had seen from the tower.

'That had something to do with the artefact, whatever it is,' he said. 'Campion told me its existence was only a legend by the time the abbey was built. It had been walled up inside the mound, but when the excavation of Newgrange was taking place the wall collapsed back into the passage, partially exposing the artefact. The excavators never got near it, so it remained there for years, until "a member of the community" – as Campion put it – found it. It was probably that poor guy Henry on his wanderings down here in the bowels of the earth, where I suspect they keep him most of the time.'

'So they obviously employed a gang of foreign workers to dig it out.'

'But they discovered a problem. It wouldn't fit through the underground tunnel. Roche said she was taking me to its "permanent resting-place". But now it's obvious they had planned to take it out the front of Newgrange early on Christmas morning, when I guess there are no visitors about.'

'But for some reason they put on a full-scale show. That doesn't make sense.'

'Forget it. Let's get out of here.'

'Just untie me and I'll be on my way,' I said facetiously.

'If I had something sharp, I could.'

'Maybe I can oblige,' I said, shuffling over to the display cabinet on my backside. The panel beneath the specimen shelves was still lying open.

'What *are* those things, anyway?' Gallagher asked, looking up at the jars.

'A Cabinet of Curiosities. The order used to export these specimens.'

'Jesus wept.'

I swung my legs over the panel and smashed my heels against the front of the case. It was as thin as light-bulb glass and broke with a tinkling sound.

Gallagher shimmied along the flagstone floor to join me. 'Shit! What is *that*?'

Like the remains of a saint on display in a glass casket, a wizened body lay prone in the base of the cabinet. But, unlike any saint I had seen, this body was naked. The skin had split in many places, and parts of the skeleton protruded through it here and there. It was just a bundle of bones in a bag of dried flesh. The skull had not collapsed like Mona's, so there was no mistaking the familiar pattern: the throat had been cut, the lips, eyes and ears removed. Out of its grimacing mouth spilled a brown hank of brittle-looking holly leaves and shrunken berries. I could tell they had only been there a year, at most: this Christmas, whoever had planted them in the corpse's mouth had been too busy with fresh kills to replace the bouquet.

'It's another body from Monashee,' I said. 'One that turned up over a century ago and then mysteriously disappeared. You could say we're looking at the template for what was done to Traynor and –'

Both of us heard the voices at the same time. People were coming into the crypt.

'And to us, too, if we don't get out of here now,' said Gallagher.

'Quickly – reach back and I'll tell you when you're beside a piece.'

I guided Gallagher's fingers to a suitable shard and he picked it up on his first attempt.

Gallagher moved up close until we were back to back. 'I've only ever seen it done in movies,' he said.

'That's not very reassuring.'

'And not strictly true. We did it once on a training course.'

'Once, eh? That's a lot better. Just be careful you don't cut me at the same time.'

As he began to saw at the nylon rope, we heard a cough. Sister Roche had entered the crypt.

'Out of sight, you,' she said sharply. 'We don't want you scaring our visitors.'

Henry bleated plaintively; then we heard him wheezing and sucking as he rummaged about in his cell. Gallagher paused, waiting for him to settle down.

My heart was beating so loudly I thought it must be audible. To distract myself I started reading the brass plaque on the frame of the display case.

By Decree of the Third Lateran Council, 1179

In support of King Henry II, lately reconciled in the Peace of Christ with His Holiness Pope Alexander III, we call on the aid of all secular princes to cast out this pestilence. And we prohibit, under pain of anathema, anyone to keep the heretical idolaters in his house or on his land. Should a temporal lord fail to purge his land of the Concupiscenti, he shall be excommunicated and reported to the Supreme Pontiff, who shall pronounce his vassals absolved from fealty to him ...

Concupiscenti. As I had suspected, not just people guilty of concupiscence in a general way, but an heretical sect. 'The Idolaters of Desire' was nearer the mark.

And we hereby ratify that the Order of St Margaret of Antioch is charged with the reporting of the heretics in that part of the kingdom where they have been most pernicious and where the Sisters have been granted by the

King an estate of land close by the temple of
these slaves to lust and lechery. Those convicted
by the ecclesiastical court shall be handed over
for due punishment to their secular superiors.

As I had surmised that day in the church in Drogheda,
Mona had been a martyr for her faith. Was it possible
that the 'Concupiscenti' had been in existence since
Newgrange was built – and had they been able to
survive until the Middle Ages by outwardly
subscribing to the prevailing religion, be it Celtic or
Christian?

The King has prescribed that the
Conscupiscenti in that country be punished in
this manner: That the breath first be choked from
their bodies. That they be exsanguinated and a
symbol of the Lord's precious blood placed
about their person. That they be prevented from
using their lips, eyes or ears to offend against
God thereafter, even in Hell. And that they be
buried in unhallowed ground. Thus are the
Concupiscenti punished.

There it was: the fate of Mona and who knew how
many others. A fate partly due to the politico-religious
ferment of Europe at the time, as Finian had surmised.
England's King Henry, out of favour with Pope
Alexander over the murder of Thomas Becket, had

made it up to him by persecuting an 'heretical' sect in Ireland – one that had apparently flourished for over four thousand years.

'Hey, let's take a breather while the others catch up. I've got to say, that went really well. Did you see that bolt of light? Wow!'

'But you'll be able to alter the habits in the pictures?'

'With digital technology, we could turn everyone into Native Americans doing a war dance if we wanted to.'

'Good. We'd hate to have to sue you for breaching our confidentiality agreement.'

Gallagher and I had managed to free ourselves. Standing behind a pier but staying close to the bars, we could hear the conversation. Campion and Roche, another woman and a man, both with American accents.

After some laughter at Roche's remark, Campion said, 'Remember, our main concern is for the community. We don't want to be disturbed. That's why we felt it better to draw up a contract.'

'Sure. That's understandable. What about the guys you hired to dig it out?'

'They're foreigners. They could hardly speak English.'

'Were they the same ones who loaded it onto the trailer this morning?'

'No. We thought it better to hire a different crew.'

'And when are you handing it over to the National Museum?'

There was a pregnant pause. Then Roche said, 'First thing in the New Year. They're closed until then.'

'Well, it's quite a scoop to get the first pictures – well worth the money.'

'Yeah. We'll probably hype it as the twenty-first-century equivalent of Tutankhamun's discovery. Maybe *National Geographic* will come on board.'

'I sure hope so. We'll need their help to cover your fee.'

The voices began to fade. More laughter. Then we heard other voices in the distance, another couple joining them.

Gallagher and I exchanged glances. And only then – I was so disoriented – did I recognise the voices.

'Shit – I know those two journalists!' I said. 'They'll help get us out of here.'

Gallagher cupped his hands around his mouth and shouted, 'Listen carefully. I'm a police officer. I want to talk to you people.'

Not a great come-on, Matt, I thought. I gave it a try. 'Hebe! Sam! It's Illaun Bowe. We need your help.'

There was no response. I could hear their voices echoing faintly off the pillars. They were too far away.

A shadow rippled along the bars.

I made one more effort. 'Hel –'

Henry had his hands around my throat before I

could finish the word. The strength in them was astonishing. I couldn't breathe.

Gallagher launched himself at Henry but failed to dislodge him. Dark spots floated in front of my pupils as the blood trapped in my brain lost oxygen, but somehow I reached into the pocket of my parka and found the handle of the lump hammer. I dragged it out and signalled to Gallagher with my eyes. In an instant he grabbed it from my weakening grasp and smashed it into the side of Henry's skull. Henry grunted and swayed but didn't release his grip. Gallagher raised the hammer again and brought it down on the crown of the man's head with tremendous force. Henry staggered against the bars, then collapsed, bringing us both crashing to the floor.

By the time Gallagher had dragged him off me, the crypt was silent.

'I don't know what the fuck's going on here,' said Gallagher, 'but I'm sure as hell going to put a stop to their gallop as soon as we get to a phone.'

'What about Henry?'

'He'll be out cold long enough for us to escape. What's with the guy's face anyway?'

'He's a cynocephalus ... well, that's what they were once called.'

'A sign-of-*what*?'

'A cynocephalus. He's suffering from a congenital condition that affects the bones of the skull and face. It's repairable nowadays. Leaving him untreated was cruel.'

'He's a simpleton, I take it?'

'Well, Roche certainly treats him as one.'

And he does her bidding, I thought. He had obviously been under her command on every occasion I had encountered him, including that night on the patio. On that occasion she must have intended to break in and destroy any records of what we'd found at Monashee; but when Keelan arrived, they had had to clear off. And then there had been the set-up in the church, Roche phoning my mother to lure me into a trap with Henry primed to attack me. He had probably even been able to communicate to her that I had been taking photographs of the west door. But I didn't bear him any malice.

I glanced at the crumpled heap on the flagstone floor. There was blood snaking down the side of his face and soaking into the collar of his filthy habit. Then I noticed his hands.

'You know he's the killer, don't you?' I said.

'I guess he has to be,' Gallagher replied.

I knelt beside Henry and held up one of his arms by the wrist for Gallagher to see. 'Here's the proof.'

Henry had a broad thumb and no fingers – or, to be precise, what fingers he had were imprisoned inside a glove of skin. His hand looked less like a claw than like the lobes of an oversized wrench encased in flesh.

'Fuck me.'

'But he only did what he was told,' I said.

'And it was all about money in the end. How

fucking predictable.' Gallagher sounded like a man disillusioned by too much exposure to human frailty.

The door to the residence was locked.

'Try that one,' I said, pointing to the third door. 'I think Henry came up that way after seeing me on the tower.'

The door was unlocked and the steps led down to the cloister, as I had thought. We found ourselves looking out on a sunlit square of grass.

I led Gallagher to the west end of the church and across the cobblestones. Hearing voices again, we looked about for a place to hide and headed for the entrance to the walled garden. Inside the red-brick wall, already warm from the sun, I glanced into the garden and saw a row of beehives along a nearby path. They had once been painted white, but the paint was flaked and cracked and there was green slime oozing from the joins.

The conversation ceased and we heard a car taking off.

'Let's move,' I said. 'I hope we're not too late.'

As we emerged from under the arch leading to the front of the abbey, we saw the journalists' car disappearing around a bend in the avenue.

The old Land Rover, with a trailer attached, was parked facing the steps, its engine running, exhaust fumes pluming up in the cool air. In the trailer, a blue canvas tarpaulin covered something that stood higher than the cab. Beyond it was my car, which I saw I had parked at an odd angle in the fog the night before. And I realised, after a brief search in my pockets, that – *Damn!* – once again I had left my phone in it.

Gallagher's white Mondeo was between us and the nuns' vehicle. We ran across and hunched down beside it.

Gallagher looked through the window. 'There's no one in the Land Rover. Let's drive it out of here – no – hold on …'

Roche had appeared at the top of the steps, carrying a suitcase. We ducked as she looked about warily.

'Why don't you phone for backup?' I asked Gallagher.

'They took my phone – and my thirty-eight.'

'Your gun, I presume? That's just great. Let's get in your car right now and drive off.'

'They took my keys too.'

We peered through the window again. Roche was lifting the suitcase into the trailer, but it snagged on the edge of the tarpaulin, and as she struggled to release it the blue canvas began to slide away. I saw part of a wooden crossbeam, supported at one end by vertical planks placed close together; the structure looked square and was obviously designed to hold something in place, like a frame for transporting sheets of glass. The tarp hung there tantalisingly, exposing only the corner of the frame. Roche seemed to be oblivious of the fact that it had slipped. With a final heave she freed the suitcase, and the canvas fell away. We were blinded by sharp sunlight reflecting off whatever was in the trailer.

I shaded my eyes and saw what looked like a gold-plated satellite dish, at least a metre and a half in diameter, standing upright in the wooden frame. Then something – a slight advance in the sun's movement, perhaps – reduced the glare of the reflection and revealed a pattern on the surface of the disk.

From the centre a great spiral spun outwards to the rim. It was like a representation of the sound made by the beating of a gong – an infinitely resonating tone emanating from the centre of the instrument. The reverberations of what was part solar disk, part temple gong, must have been responsible for the fusillade of light that had earlier raked the valley from the entrance of the mound to the river. The disk was an all-in-one sound-and-light machine – an inelegant but accurate description of what I could see was also a priceless work of art. That morning I had witnessed a solar *son-et-lumière* display that had not been seen for five thousand years.

Chapter Thirty-Six

Roche had finally realised the tarp was in a heap in the trailer. She was calling to Campion, inside the house, to come and help her, in between muttering darkly about the laziness of the workers who had draped the cover without securing it.

'Let's get there before the cavalry arrives,' said Gallagher. 'She won't be able to take us both on.'

We emerged from behind the car. Roche heard us crunching the gravel as we approached; she swung around, but the sun was in her eyes, and before she could shield them Gallagher had her in an arm-lock.

'Get your hands off me, you bastard!' she screamed, squirming and kicking at him.

But Gallagher's grip was rock-solid. He jerked his head towards the trailer. 'See if there's something in there we can use to tie her up.'

I looked into the trailer – most of the canvas had collapsed onto the floor on the far side of the frame – and ran around to pick up a length of one of the tie-ropes, which I began to fray against a twisted piece of sharp metal on the side of the trailer. As I was doing it I couldn't avoid glancing up at the sun-disk.

This side was different. Incised into the hammered gold surface was Mona's goddess. She was standing atop the fiery circle of the rising sun, legs apart, one of the rays of sunlight penetrating her.

'Guess what, Goldilocks,' I whispered, winking at her. 'You're the fairest of us all.'

I cut off the length of rope and went back around the trailer. Gallagher had Roche flattened against the passenger door of the Land Rover to keep her from struggling.

'Grab her free hand first and tie her wrist.'

'I wouldn't do that if I were you,' said a low voice. Sister Campion was standing at the bottom of the steps, her suitcase on the ground, Gallagher's gun aimed at me. 'Let her go, Inspector.'

Gallagher released his captive. Roche spun around and spat in his face.

Campion stepped onto the gravel. 'You two, move

right away from the Land Rover. Ursula, will you put my case on board?'

Roche grabbed the abbess's suitcase and dumped it in the trailer. Then she ran back up the steps. 'If they move, shoot them,' she said, and disappeared into the residence.

'And all for this?' said Gallagher, pointing to the disk. 'You've already murdered two people for it. Isn't that enough?'

Campion didn't answer. I noticed that, unlike Roche, she was still attired in the grey and white clothes of the order.

'But it wasn't for this you had Frank Traynor killed – not really,' I said.

'Had him killed? Whatever do you mean?' She seemed genuinely surprised at the suggestion.

'It was because your baby was buried at Monashee.'

'Baby? What are you talking about?'

'Derek Ward was the boy's father. It *was* a boy, wasn't it?'

She didn't respond.

'Traynor blackmailed Ward when he found out he was the father of a nun's child,' I said. 'And recently he'd been doing the same to you, forcing you to sell off your property below market value. Then he heard about the artefact here, from the foreign workers you'd hired to dig it out for you – probably the same guys who stripped the church for him. A disk made of solid gold, they said. He even made one of them draw it for him in his diary. Traynor knew it was priceless, and he wanted it badly. But he always worked "above board", as Sergeant O'Hagan said; he wasn't going to break in and steal the disk from you. So he tried the same old threats – sell it for a fraction of its value, or he'd expose your secret – but you'd had enough. You told him to go ahead: you and Ward would both deny it, and anyway, where was the proof? And that's when he remembered that Ward had told him your baby was buried at Monashee. So he started to dig up the field.'

Campion's eyes were slowly filling with tears.

'Next he told you an infant's body had been found. You couldn't endure it any more. You sent Sister Roche to meet him at Monashee to talk about selling the disk. And that's when Henry garrotted him in his car.'

'Henry could never … Someone killed Frank before Ursula got there.'

'Henry does what he's told by Ursula; you know that. She told him to reproduce the injuries he was familiar with from the mummy in the crypt. He killed Traynor at Monashee and Sergeant O'Hagan here at the abbey.'

'That's right,' said Gallagher. 'Then they hauled O'Hagan's body through the underground passage and dumped it in the field behind Newgrange.'

'You're both lying.'

'You can't be that naïve,' I said. 'I suspect you're like Henry II – asking to be rid of the problem, then going into denial when others have done your dirty work.'

'I have very little interest in what you suspect, Miss Bowe.'

'So what will happen to us?' said Gallagher. 'Do you think Sister Roche will just allow us to walk out of here?'

'Eventually. We just need enough time to hand over the solar disk to our buyer and get out of the country.' She looked towards me as if seeking support for her proposal.

'No way will Ursula let us go,' I said. 'Did you know she also made an attempt on Derek Ward's life?'

'That's another lie. This is getting tedious.'

As we were talking, Gallagher had moved closer to the abbess. Suddenly she raised the .38 and aimed it at his head. 'Get back.' She waved him away to the far side of the steps. 'Over here, you,' she gestured to me.

I walked forward.

'Why are you doing this to me? Dredging up all this … muck?'

'I'm interested in the past. It informs us about the present.' I glanced at Gallagher and we both edged a little closer to her. I doubted she had the will to pull the trigger.

Before we could test that theory, Roche came out of the house, stuffing a sheaf of airline tickets into her handbag. 'What's going on here?' She closed the door behind her and started down the steps. 'Give me the gun.'

'No – wait,' said Campion.

Roche hesitated.

'She says you made an attempt on Derek's life. Is that true?'

'That's ridiculous.'

'As ridiculous as having Henry kill Traynor and O'Hagan,' I said, raising my voice.

'What are you talking about?' Roche remained where she was, halfway down the steps.

Gallagher said, 'Because Monashee held evidence that you didn't want coming to light. If Sister Campion's baby was exhumed, it could be discovered that he'd been murdered. By you.'

Campion cried out, 'It's not true – it's simply not true. He was … he was … he couldn't have lived.'

'What she means is,' Roche said contemptuously, 'he was a monstrosity, just like all those specimens in the crypt, like the carvings on the west door. Now are you happy?'

Campion began to weep bitterly. 'I'd looked so often at those horrors … then one of them grew inside me. Only a vengeful God would have allowed that to happen…' She gathered herself, her expression growing darker. 'So I turned away from Him. And now I've had *my* revenge. I've returned this place to its rightful owners. There'll be people fornicating here every night of the week when the hotel is built. That's justice, isn't it?'

At that moment we heard Henry bleating in the distance.

Gallagher moved nearer to Roche.

With a wheezy cough Henry stumbled through the archway, blood running down his face, a carving knife in his cloven hand.

Roche gave a sidelong glance at him as he slouched towards us, and at that moment the truth hit me like the bolt of light that had shot out of Newgrange.

'I was wrong about you, Ursula,' I said. 'Your motive for murdering Traynor and O'Hagan wasn't to cover up a past misdeed at all. It was pure greed.'

Roche swivelled her head in my direction like a predatory animal.

'In fact, you and Traynor had that vice in common – concupiscence of the eyes, I believe it's called. So you certainly weren't going to let him get his hands on the disk. But he was becoming a nuisance – not only trying to ruin your chance of making a fortune, but probably threatening to use his contacts in high places to prevent you leaving the country with it. And then he was bringing up the awkward subject of Geraldine's child. He had got it wrong about the baby, of course, and you knew that. Not because the remains he saw happened to be those of an infant that died in 1961. It didn't matter one way or the other what he dredged up, because you knew Geraldine's baby wasn't in Monashee. It never had been.'

I turned to the abbess. 'Sister Campion, your son didn't die.'

'What?' She blinked away tears. 'What on earth are you saying?'

'Henry is your child.' I turned back to Roche. 'Isn't that so, Ursula?'

Roche's eyes locked onto mine. 'How dare you say such things?'

I held her gaze. 'You needed to be in charge of some part of her, didn't you? Some part of the woman who had power over you, but whose sexual weakness you despised.'

Roche's stare faltered. Henry had halted a couple of metres outside of our tense circle, waiting for a command.

Campion began to tremble. She had to use both hands to hold the gun steady. 'She told me he was left on the steps ... abandoned. It happened all the time – an unmarried girl, or even a married woman, giving birth to a handicapped baby she couldn't afford to look after. It would be left for us to care for. Usually they died, or we'd get them to a hospital, but Ursula said this one ... this one might as well stay with us ... he'd have a better life with us than anywhere else. I just never thought ... It happened all the time!'

'How long was that after you had given birth? Think.'

'About ... I can't recall – a few weeks, a month perhaps ...' Her face was a mix of bewilderment and dawning awareness.

'And who named him after the king who'd accused the Newgrange heretics of being slaves to sexual pleasure?'

'That was …' Campion turned slowly and looked at Roche, who was still on the steps.

'Henry!' Roche's voice was like a whiplash.

Henry raised the knife. I was the nearest to him.

Roche nodded. He made a lunge towards me.

Campion fired.

Henry jerked sideways. The knife fell from his grip. He collapsed onto the gravel and lay still, a red stain spreading across the back of his habit.

Roche made a break for it, running down the remaining steps towards Campion, who had lowered the gun to her side, tears streaming down her cheeks. But Gallagher was faster. He launched himself into the air and brought Roche down with a rugby tackle. We heard her head crack against the bottom step.

I reached out to take the pistol from Campion's hand, knowing I would meet with no resistance.

Gallagher was feeling Roche's pulse. 'Out cold, but alive.' He stood up and took off his jacket to cover her.

Campion swirled around and fired again. Roche's blood began to spray onto the steps.

I froze. But when the abbess turned around, her expression was one of unfathomable sadness. '*Sic Concupiscenti puniuntur*,' she said, and handed me the gun.

The carvings of the west door had not been able to ward off the evil that had entered. They weren't designed to. It was concupiscence of the eyes, not of the flesh, that had overwhelmed Grange Abbey. Sister Campion had succumbed to it too, and her bitterness had made her blind to its corrosive effects. For her original moment of weakness she had paid a terrible price.

'*La croix du dragon*,' I said gently, reaching out to touch her hand as I had Mona's, '*est la dolor de deduit.*'

New Year's Eve

Epilogue

Finian raised his glass of champagne. 'Happy New Year,' he said.

'Not yet,' I said. 'Wait for the countdown.'

Christmas had passed off well in the Bowe household, although Richard had been taken aback by our father's deterioration. 'He'll not see another one,' was his verdict – and I prayed he was right.

Finian and I were sitting at a window table in the dining room of the hotel. Most of the other guests were outside on the patio, awaiting the fireworks display. They huddled together for warmth; the night was so cold that the water of the hotel's fountain had frozen solid, leaving it looking like a giant ice sculpture.

'It's just occurred to me,' said Finian, gazing at the fountain: 'it must have been glacial melt-water that formed the underground passage at Grange Abbey.'

'And did you know Jack Crean gave me a clue to the existence of the passage? He told me the old name for Newgrange was "the Cave of the Sun".'

'See? You should always pay attention to folklore. It even hints at some folk memory of the reflective disk. The question is how Stone Age people could make something like that.'

'It's unlikely to be Neolithic, even though we know that some pre-metal cultures did make gold objects.' I fingered the torc Finian had given me, which I was wearing for the occasion. 'Whoever built Newgrange probably used a highly polished stone to start with, and then later adherents of their religion created the disk – the same way the Christian altar started out as a simple table and ended up smothered in gold and jewels.'

'And you think their religion lasted into the Middle Ages?'

'It could still be in existence, for all we know. Ecstatic sex as a religious experience has had its devotees throughout history.'

'Really?' said Finian with a sly smile.

There was a murmur in the crowd outside. 'It's nearly time,' I said, smiling back.

'Ten …' The crowd began to chant. 'Nine, eight, seven, six …'

We raised our glasses to each other.

'Five, four, three, two, one …'

The crowd cheered. The first of the fireworks burst into the sky.

Further Reading

For the history and landscape archaeology of the area in which the main events of the novel are set, Geraldine Stout's *Newgrange and the Bend of the Boyne* (Cork University Press, 2002) is a well-illustrated account. Michael J. O'Kelly's *Newgrange: Archaeology, Art and Legend* (Thames and Hudson, 1982) is the definitive record of the excavation and restoration of the mound, while Hugh Kearns's *The Mysterious Chequered Lights of Newgrange* (Elo Publications, 1993) offers an intriguing theory about how it could have been the centrepiece of a spectacular sound and light show. For a leisurely and informative journey along the Boyne from source to sea, Peter Harbison's *Treasures of the Boyne Valley* (Gill & Macmillan, 2003) is highly recommended.

Just finished a great book and dying to dive into another?
Don't know where to start looking?

Visit gillmacmillan.ie/readers for

Sneak peeks
Read a chapter from our books before you buy

Reading guides
Download a guide for your book group

Author interviews
Get the chance to ask our authors your burning questions

Competitions
Win books and advance reading copies

Book news
Get the news on the latest launches and events

All this **and** 20% off every order!

www.gillmacmillan.ie/readers

get more from your reading